ALINE TEMPL... the fishing village of
Anstruther, in the East Neuk of Fife. She has worked in
education and ... a ... Justice of the Peace
for ten years. ... ...wn-up children and
three grandch...ildren; she ... lives in a house with a view
of Edinburgh Castle. When not writing she enjoys cooking,
choral singing, and trav... the back roads of France.

Library Learning Information

To renew this item call:

0333 370 4700
(Local rate call)

or visit
www.ideastore.co.uk

TOWER HAMLETS
Created and managed by Tower Hamlets Council

www.alinetempleton.co.uk

By Aline Templeton

Evil for Evil
Bad Blood

BAD BLOOD

ALINE TEMPLETON

Allison & Busby Limited
12 Fitzroy Mews
London W1T 6DW
www.allisonandbusby.com

First published in Great Britain by Allison & Busby in 2013.
This paperback edition published by Allison & Busby in 2014.

A CIP catalogue record for this book is available from
the British Library.

10 9 8 7 6 5 4 3 2 1

ISBN 978-0-7490-1637-1

Typeset in 10.5/15.5 pt Sabon by
Allison & Busby Ltd.

The paper used for this Allison & Busby publication
has been produced from trees that have been legally sourced
from well-managed and credibly certified forests.

Printed and bound by

CPI Group (UK) Ltd, Croydon, CR0 4YY

For Jane with love

PROLOGUE

1986

She sometimes felt as if her writhing thoughts were a nest of snakes inside her head. From time to time one would raise its ugly head and hiss and spit venom.

That was happening now, with the poison of rage flooding her veins and making a mockery of all the anger management classes she'd been forced to undergo. She'd had enough of being told what to do, more than enough, enough to the point where she felt she might explode.

She daren't, though. Her nails dug into the palms of her hands so hard that later she would find neat, bloody crescents right across them.

He'd said no, the bastard. Just flatly, no, this young man with his earnest gaze, sitting awkwardly on the edge of the chair in her living room. It wasn't the way he usually talked. They were trained to be professionally sympathetic.

Feeble, she called it. She despised him and she certainly wasn't going to take this from him. She gave him a sideways look, the one she had perfected long ago, the 'drop dead' look.

It flustered him. 'Sorry, sorry. I shouldn't have said it that way. But really, you mustn't. It's just that for your own sake you can't do it. It would be crazy.'

'So I'm crazy.' Her voice was flat.

He was starting to sound desperate. 'Look, I can't understand why you would want to do it. You'd be signing your own death warrant.'

She shrugged. 'You can't stop me, can you? The condition is that I report, right?' She wasn't as certain as she sounded.

'Well, I suppose that's true, there are no actual injunctions, but—'

She got up. 'That's it, then. I'm going.'

That forced him to get up too. 'I'll have to take this up with my line manager,' he was bleating as she showed him the door.

She shut it behind him. She'd be long gone by the time he came back and without direct legal authority they wouldn't risk removing her against her will. She'd only have to threaten to scream the place down and they'd back off.

She went to the phone. Her daughter was watching some sort of dumb kids' programme in the corner and she said, 'Switch that thing off!'

The girl eyed her thoughtfully, looking for storm signals. Apparently finding them, she stopped. The expression on her face was too old for her years as she watched her mother pick up the phone.

He'd been waiting for the call; he sounded impatient too.

8

'Well?'

'I told him.'

'What did he say?'

'No. But I told him he couldn't actually stop me and he admitted it. So that's it.'

His voice warmed. 'Well done, girl. Start packing.'

She felt the warm glow of his approval, but as she put down the phone, another snake stirred.

She didn't really want to go back to Scotland – certainly not back to Galloway. She was tired of moving around and yes, she was scared. But he wanted her to move back. He needed her. He'd never said that before.

He was her centre, the core of her being. Girlfriends could be counted on the thumb of one hand; motherhood was just something that happened to you. But him . . .

He'd lied to her, cheated on her, abandoned her. And worse, much worse. Without him, her life would have been – well, she'd long ago decided not to go there. She'd vowed before that she was finished with him, but this time he'd promised it would be different and she almost believed him – almost.

The nasty thought, that it was hardly the first time he'd said that, popped into her mind and she had to force it back into the snake pit. It *was* different. He was different. He needed her, wanted her to be with him. It made her feel as if someone had wrapped a warm, fluffy blanket round her thin shoulders.

She went to her bedroom and dragged the suitcases down off the top of the wardrobe.

PART ONE

1993

CHAPTER ONE

A scream. It ripped through the silence of the trees around the cottage as a knife slashes silk.

Then the silence slithered back again as if no sound had ever banished it, as if this was just another October night with a touch of ground mist so that the pine branches appeared ghostly, floating on the thickened air.

The woman knitting by the fire looked up. 'What was that?' she said.

Caught up in the synthetic excitement being blared out from the TV in the corner as the goal attempt failed, her husband only grunted.

She raised her voice, irritably. 'What was that, I said. It sounded like a scream.'

'Oh – vixen, most likely. They're mating just now.' He sat back in his chair. 'That's half-time. How about a cuppa?'

'You know where the kettle is.' She went on knitting, but when he made no move, sighed, 'Oh, all right then. Just let me finish this row.'

Before she put on the light in the kitchen, she peered out of the little window above the sink towards the direction the sound had come from but she couldn't see anything, except a light glimmering faintly through the mist where the cottage stood on the other side of the main road among the trees. As she watched, it went out.

She shrugged, switched on the light and the kettle. If there were foxes around, they'd be after her hens. He could always get off his backside and go out right now with his shotgun – fat chance!

In the cottage, the girl stirred into pain-filled consciousness. Her head hurt, really badly, and she was lying on her face. With a struggle, she turned over and opened her eyes; that hurt too.

There had been something – some noise . . . She tried to sit up, but she felt so sick and dizzy that she had to lie down again. She wanted to put on the light by her bed but it was too far away to reach without lifting her head.

She put up her hand and tentatively explored the sorest part. There was a huge lump and her hair was wet and sticky. She must have hurt herself. She felt strange, sort of fuzzy and muddled inside.

She couldn't remember what had happened, couldn't remember going to bed. That felt weird. She could always remember everything perfectly. Much too perfectly.

She didn't know what time it was either. It was pitch-dark

outside, but that didn't tell her much. At this time of year it could be dark at five in the afternoon.

Out here by the forest it was always like this at night if there wasn't a moon, but now, with her sore head and her mind being all weird, she was scared. 'Mum!' she called. 'Mum!'

There was no answer, no reassuring sound of movement. Sometimes Mum took pills and couldn't hear her so that when she needed her, if she was ill or something, she had to go and shake her awake, but she knew that if she got up now she'd be sick. She called again but there was still no answer or sound of movement.

She began to cry. The sobs hurt her head and she bit on her lip to stifle them, but she couldn't stop the tears running down into her ears.

It was cold, too. It was never very warm in this house, but there seemed to be a worse draught than usual coming through the open door of her bedroom. She'd begun to shiver and then she realised she wasn't under the covers at all, she was sort of lying as if she'd fallen across the bed. She wasn't in her pyjamas either: she was still wearing her black miniskirt and bomber jacket.

At least she could wriggle under the duvet without lifting her head. That was better. And if she got back to sleep it would be morning when she woke up and Mum would be awake. Probably.

When Marnie opened her eyes again it was daylight – a grudging daylight, gloomy and overcast, with rain streaming down the windowpanes and the trees outside making that roaring noise like the sea. Her head was pounding as if someone was beating it like a drum, and when she sat up, she vomited without warning.

'Mum!' she wailed. 'I've been sick!'

The smell was disgusting and now she could see there was blood on her cover too from where she had been lying – a big dark-red stain. She was frightened now. The next 'Mum!' was a scream, but there was still no reassuring reply.

The door of her bedroom was open and there was cold air blowing through it – really blowing, not just the usual draughts through ill-fitting door frames. Her teeth were beginning to chatter and she couldn't huddle under the stinking duvet or the stench would make her sick again.

Dizzy and unsteady, she swung her legs over the edge of the bed. She was swaying on her feet when she heard a man's voice.

'Hello! Anybody in?'

Why should a man be there? But at least it was someone. Marnie staggered across the room and out into the hall.

There was a man standing there, a man holding a shotgun. She gave a cry of terror; her legs buckled and she fell in a heap on the floor.

Douglas Boyd had been stumping along in the pouring rain, his shotgun broken over his arm, muttering under his breath as he walked along the road. Peggy had been on about the foxes she'd heard last night since she opened her eyes this morning – her and her blasted hens!

She insisted their screams had come from this direction, but there wasn't a chance he'd find a sign of them at this hour of the day when they'd been cavorting all night, and weather like this would wash away even the rank smell that hung around the beasts. The only thing to be said for it was that it got him out the house.

He had been passing the old forestry cottage on the other side of the road when he noticed the front door was standing open, and stopped for a moment, uncertainly.

They didn't have anything to do with the people here, even though they were their nearest neighbours. Peggy had gone over there to say hello when they'd moved in a few years ago, but she'd not even been asked over the threshold and the woman had been a bit tarty-looking, Peggy said, with unnaturally jet-black hair. There was a man around occasionally and Douglas had seen the girl out in the garden quite often but she seemed shy and these days trying to get to know a kiddie wasn't a smart thing to do.

He'd seen Bill Fleming's wife there a couple of times too, recently, her that was with the polis now. When he'd told Peggy, she'd sniffed and said that in that case she wasn't their kind of people and they'd just keep themselves to themselves, thank you very much. So they had.

There was no car outside, but with the front door standing open, it looked as if they'd gone off in a hurry and forgotten to shut it. Well, he and Peggy didn't always lock their own door, living out here, but this was just an invitation to any lowlife passing in a car. He'd been planning to do his good deed for the day and just close it for them, if they weren't about, but he had called as he stepped into the hall in case he was poking his nose in where it wasn't wanted.

His shock at the appearance of the bloodstained girl, her cry of alarm and her collapse, set his heart beating at a rate that wasn't healthy for a man of his age. She was looking up at him pitifully from the floor, her blue eyes wide with fear. He could see there was an ugly wound on the back of her head.

It was rather more than he'd bargained for, doing his good neighbour bit, but this was a poor wee soul needing his help and comfort. He pulled himself together and realised she was staring at the shotgun, transfixed. He set it down hastily.

'It's all right, it's all right. I was just out after foxes that were screaming last night. You know me, don't you? Douglas Boyd, from along the road. Dearie me, whatever's happened to you, lassie?'

She didn't say anything, as if she was too traumatised to speak.

He looked round, helplessly. 'Where's your mum?'

The tears came. 'I don't know! I've been calling and calling.'

Douglas's heart sank. An injured child was bad enough, but a mother who didn't answer, in a situation like this . . . And maybe the scream hadn't been the foxes, after all.

'You're needing to lie down and have a wee rest,' he said. 'Can you stand up, do you think, if I help you?'

Still crying, she pushed herself up onto her feet with his supporting arm but when he tried to lead her back to the room she had come from, she resisted.

'No. It's – messy.'

18

A door to his right was open and he could see a sofa. 'You could go in there,' he suggested, then added hastily, 'just let me take a wee look first to see if there's somewhere you could lie down.'

It was a lame excuse but she didn't seem to notice, standing there obediently as he put his head round the door, braced for what he might find.

The room was very untidy, with a brown imitation leather suite and a wood veneer coffee table and a carpet that seemed a stranger to the hoover. The air stank of stale smoke and there was an ashtray overflowing with stubs among the clutter: magazines, circulars, a wine glass, a bottle of white wine, empty. Discarded clothes were draped over the back of one of the chairs and a pair of shoes had been abandoned on the hearth beside the ashes of a dead fire.

At least there was nothing untoward here. Douglas puffed out a little sigh of relief. Turning to tell the girl she could come in, he noticed a plastic witch's mask tossed down on one of the armchairs, along with a black cardboard pointed hat with an orange frill round the bottom.

Halloween. He was not a superstitious man, but at the thought of what had been happening here on that night of dead souls and unquiet spirits he gave an involuntary shiver.

'Come on in, then,' he called. 'You can have a wee lie-down on the sofa and I'll go and see if I can find your mum. She's probably asleep.'

The girl trailed in, shivering. He helped her onto the sofa and found a cushion to tuck under her poor head; she

19

didn't say anything, just watched him silently as he went back out to the hall.

The doors to the kitchen and bathroom were both standing open so he could see they were empty too. The door to the other bedroom, though, was closed. Taking a deep breath, he opened it.

His first thought was that it had been ransacked, but given the state of the sitting room she'd probably been the kind to use the floor as a laundry basket anyway. The bed was unmade and the kidney-shaped dressing table was covered with pots and jars, some with their lids off, and a thin, greasy layer of powder lay on the glass top. There was another ashtray there as well, with a couple of stubs in it.

Douglas couldn't be sure immediately that this room, too, was empty; there could be . . . anything, hidden under the rumpled duvet on the unmade bed or under one of the piles of clothing on the floor or even in the wardrobe.

The bed first. He pulled back the duvet – nothing below. There was nothing under the clothes, either, which left only the wardrobe.

It was a flimsy construction, with the door sagging a little on its hinges and a key holding it shut. With a feeling of dread Douglas turned it and the door swung open under its own weight.

She wasn't there, either, just some clothes hanging up and a lot of shoes tumbled in the bottom.

He'd been steeling himself for horror and now he felt at a loss. Was the woman outside, perhaps, lying injured or even dead? But the car was gone – an attacker couldn't have driven off in two cars. Could she possibly have walked out on her injured daughter? Or even have done the injuring herself, then left her? It was hard to imagine, but you read such terrible things in the papers these days.

He could hear the child giving the occasional frightened sob. So what now? Police and ambulance, obviously.

The phone was in the hall. He shut the sitting-room door, made his call, then went back in again.

'Your mum seems to have gone out, pet, but you've had a nasty knock on the head so they're going to send an ambulance to take you in to get a doctor to take a wee look at it. All right? I expect your mum'll be back shortly.'

His voice sounded too hearty, even to himself. She didn't say anything, just began to cry again.

The children's ward was bright with pictures and posters, with a corner for toys and games at one end where convalescent children were playing. The patients here expected to be discharged within days: it wasn't one of these heart-rending places where wan and listless invalids lay connected up to machines and drips.

The mother of small children herself, PC Marjory Fleming was grateful for that but she didn't like hospitals anyway. They were too hot and felt completely airless when you were used to the open-air life on your husband's farm. She'd joined the police force last year, not, as her father liked to think, because she wanted to follow in his footsteps but because she wanted a job where she wouldn't spend her days shut up in some office.

As she strode down the ward towards another

policewoman who was sitting by one of the beds, she seemed to bring a breath of fresh air in with her: an athletic-looking woman only a little under six feet, bright-faced, with hazel eyes and chestnut hair pulled into a neat ponytail under her police hat.

The other officer got up as she approached, spoke briefly to the patient, then came to meet her, yawning as she put her hat back on.

'At last! I'm really needing my bed.'

'Sorry! Everything's about at a standstill with the roadworks coming in. How is she?' Fleming nodded towards the girl in the bed, lying staring at the ceiling.

The other woman pulled a face. 'Not saying much, apart from asking when her mum will be coming. I've stalled her so far, but she'll have to be told something soon. They're saying she's fine and they need the bed. Any progress?'

'Car's gone and mother's just disappeared. They're going through the house just now and there's details out talking to the neighbours. If she's feeling chatty I can encourage her but I've been warned it's just guard duty. If I question her before the fancy-pants CID get here they'll have my guts for garters.'

The constable laughed, smothered another enormous yawn and left. Fleming turned to watch her go, nerving herself to approach the girl. She hadn't been entirely open with her colleague; there were reasons for that but it made her uncomfortable.

She couldn't put it off any longer. She took off her hat and jacket, laying them on one of the chairs at the bedside, then sat down.

'Hello, Marnie. Do you remember me?'

The girl had a bandage round her head and her red-gold hair was still matted with dried blood. She was lying back against the pillows as if she lacked the energy to sit up but as Fleming spoke she turned to look at her, blue eyes vivid in her white face.

'Yes,' she said. Her voice was thin and shaky. 'You come to see my mum sometimes. The last time you were wearing a raincoat and it had brown buttons and you had an orange and browny-green jersey and jeans and tan boots. You said, "Hello, Karen, just coming for a chat, all right?" And she said yes and then you both went into the sitting room and shut the door.'

Fleming was amused. 'My goodness, you do have a good memory, don't you?'

'Yes,' Marnie said flatly.

'How are you feeling? That's a seriously impressive bandage.' It sounded phoney, even as she said it, the result of her own unease. The girl was too old – ten, eleven, perhaps? – to be jollied along.

Not surprisingly, it was ignored. 'When will my mum be here?'

'Sorry, Marnie, I'm afraid I don't know. She'll probably be along later.' She hated saying something she didn't believe to be true but she had no authority to say anything else.

'You're in the police. Something's happened to my mum, hasn't it?'

'Possibly' was the answer, and if Fleming were to be truthful that wasn't the worst-case scenario. She deflected the question.

'Something happened to your head. That's why I'm here. We're trying to find out what went on last night.' She risked adding, 'Do you know?' hoping that this wouldn't be stepping on CID toes. She didn't want to wreck her chances before she even got round to applying to join them.

'I-I don't know. I just can't remember. I don't understand it – I can't remember!'

Marnie was getting distressed and Fleming hurried to reassure her. 'You've had a head injury. That's what often happens – you find you've got a blank about it. Sometimes it comes back and sometimes it doesn't.'

She saw her assimilate that, then after a moment Marnie turned her head to meet her eyes squarely.

'You're not going to tell me anything, are you?'

'We don't really know anything, just at the moment.' That, at least, was true. She changed the subject. 'What about your dad? Will he be coming to see you?'

Marnie turned her head away. 'Don't know.'

An uncomfortable area, obviously. Would pursuing it be acceptable chatting or the forbidden questioning? Fleming hesitated, but only for a moment. It was her insatiable appetite for answers that made her so keen to join the CID.

'Does he live with you, your dad?'

'No.'

'Where does he live?'

'Don't know.' Marnie still wasn't looking at her, perhaps uncomfortable at having to admit that.

The instinct to probe the sore spot was too strong to resist. 'Would you like us to try to find him – tell him you've been hurt so he could come and see you?'

24

'No!' The response was too vehement and Marnie winced.

There were more questions Fleming itched to ask but she could see that risked going too far. 'Does your head still hurt?' she asked instead.

'A bit. But it's OK. I just want to go home with my mum.'

'The doctor will have to decide. You'll be getting a day or two off school, that's for sure.'

'I like school. Nothing to do at home and Mum doesn't like me having friends coming round.'

Fleming was opening her mouth to ask the follow-up 'Why?' when she saw DS Tam MacNee coming down the ward towards her: short, wiry, walking with his usual jaunty swagger and wearing his unvarying uniform of white T-shirt, jeans, trainers and a black leather jacket.

She gave a guilty start, but her face brightened too. MacNee had only recently joined the CID and before that had been her sergeant and mentor since she joined the force. She got up and moved away from the bed.

'Just having a wee chat, were you?' He raised an eyebrow and she blushed.

'I wasn't interrogating her, I swear. She just started telling me about her mum – didn't like having people round the place, apparently.'

'She wouldn't, would she? Mmm. Anything else the lassie "just started telling you?"'

Fleming ignored his cynical look. 'She doesn't know where her dad is and she's sensitive about it.'

'Oh, you're the wee girl! We'll have you in the CID

before long, no doubt about it. Maybe not right this morning, though. I'll take over now. Anything else?'

'Just wants to know when her mother's coming.'

'You've not said anything about it, have you?'

'Instructed not to.'

He sighed. 'Well, I'm not wanting to do it either. You know what they're thinking?'

'Oh yes, I know,' Fleming said heavily. 'You're not going to tell her that, though, are you?'

'I'll have to tell her there's someone from social services coming to take her into care. But apart from that . . .' he shrugged. 'I'll just say we don't know. And that's God's truth.'

The little man who said he was a detective kept asking her questions. What was the point of them? He was wanting to know where her mother was – like she didn't? – and he seemed to be expecting her to tell him. There was something about the questions, too, that made her uncomfortable.

Had they had a row last night?

That started it, the spool unrolling in her head as if she was watching a film . . .

She puts on a coat before going into the sitting room to cover up what she's wearing. Mum's in one of her moods at the moment, ready to go mental at the least thing and she'll go radge if she sees the skirt. She's sitting smoking and just staring straight ahead, and she's opened a bottle of white wine.

'I'm just off into the town, Mum.'

Her mother looks at her across the cigarette, eyes narrowed against the smoke. 'What for?'

She holds up her witch's hat and mask. 'Just guising. Halloween, you know?'

Weirdly, her mother looks sort of horrified, staring at her and even choking on her cigarette. 'No! I won't—' Then stops and there's a long moment when she doesn't say anything and her eyes are stretched open wide.

'Won't what, Mum?' She feels uneasy.

'It's, it's . . .' Mum's groping for words, then she says, 'It's not safe, hanging around the streets on your own.'

'I'm meeting Gemma.'

She knows it's the wrong thing to say even before she says it. Her mum hates it when she has anything to do with Gemma – something to do with business and her father. Her mum kicks off.

'I've told you before to steer clear of Gemma—'

'You tell me to steer clear of everyone! You'd rather I didn't have any friends at all, in case they want to come out here. What's with you, Mum? What have you got to hide?'

Her mother jumps up, white with anger. 'That's it, Marnie. You're staying here. You're grounded.'

'I'm not, Mum. I'm going and you can't stop me.' She jinks out of the door but not before her low-cut T-shirt and miniskirt has been noticed.

'You're not to go out looking like a slapper,' her mother screams after her, sounding angry, but as she runs out of the house and walks along to the place where the bus will stop she can hear the sound of crying. It makes her feel guilty and she hesitates, but then the lighted bus is coming round the corner and she shrugs her shoulders and lifts her hand to hail it.

The policeman was sitting patiently, watching her as he waited for an answer. As she focused on his face again, he smiled at her, showing the gap between his two front teeth. He'd looked nicer when he wasn't smiling.

'A row?' he prompted her.

'Well, sort of,' Marnie said. 'She didn't want me going into town to meet my friend. Wasn't anything out of the usual.'

'How do you get on with your mum generally?'

'Oh, fine.'

She felt as if his eyes were boring holes in her, but she wasn't going to say anything else about that. None of his business. She volunteered, instead, that she could remember coming home, but nothing after that.

And then it all starts again.

She's going to have to keep well out of her mother's way, just stick her head round the sitting-room door to say she's home. She and Gemma had necked a couple of lagers and with Mum like she was, anyway, and with the row they'd had, she could go mental. Mum's not in the sitting room, though, and so she drops her hat and mask onto a chair. The fire's not quite out so Mum must just have gone to bed. Great – she only needs to shout through the bedroom door and go to bed herself.

She stands in the hall. 'I'm back, Mum,' she calls and goes on into her bedroom and—

Then the reel snapped and Marnie was back looking at the policeman. He asked her some more questions but it was making her head sore and she turned away and shut her eyes.

She heard him say, 'A lady'll be coming soon to take you somewhere you can stay till we find your mum, OK?'

Marnie knew what that meant – taken into care. Her mum had told her long ago that if she said something silly to a teacher about being left alone in the house or anything else, that would happen. Tears formed and trickled out from under her closed eyelids. All she wanted was her mum to come back and take her home. It wasn't great, living with her mum, but it was all she knew. Surely her mum couldn't have walked out on her?

The terrible thing was, she wasn't absolutely sure that she wouldn't. But if she hadn't, where was she? Marnie started to feel sick again.

Superintendent Jakie McNally was under pressure this afternoon. The chief constable, no less, was making waves and McNally was old school. What the CC wanted the CC got and what he wanted was the Marnie Bruce business wrapped up before too many people started asking questions, so he could do without one of the most junior of the PCs doing just that. She was sitting in front of him now, her bright-eyed eagerness both a threat and a reproach.

'PC Fleming, you know the background as well as I do. You were sworn to complete confidentiality when you took over monitoring from MacNee.'

'Yes, sir, but I—'

He talked across her. 'You know that there is absolutely no sign of an intruder or a struggle, and no evidence that there was anyone in the house that evening apart from Marnie and her mother. You know they've combed the woods and there's nothing. You know the missing car was found in the station car park in Dumfries and they've checked it out – nothing.'

'Yes, but—'

Fixing her with a look, he went on, 'You and I both know why the outcome isn't surprising, surely?'

'Of course I do, sir.' Fleming had taken a deep breath to be ready to power through. 'I know it's a possibility, but I think it's only fair to the child—'

That was as far as she got. 'It was, mercifully, just a knock on the head and she's well on the way to a full recovery. We'll be looking for the woman quietly, of course, but if we go public on this, perhaps you could explain to me in what way this would be "fair" to the child?'

Silenced, Fleming bit her lip.

McNally relaxed. 'You see, Marjory – it is Marjory, isn't it? – policing isn't only about exposing the brutal truth. Sometimes it's about tempering justice with mercy.

'All right? That's a good girl. Run along, sweetheart.'

Seething with anger, PC Marjory Fleming went back down the stairs from the inspector's office, wishing she'd had the courage to say that in her view, what justice was being tempered with was not mercy but expediency.

PART TWO

2013

CHAPTER TWO

Marnie Bruce walked slowly up Oxford Street in the autumn dark, late October starting to tip towards bleak November. The air was damp and heavy with the hint of fog splintering the light from the street lamps and cars and buses into brilliant shards. The shops were closed but the shop window displays cast bright patches of light on the pavement, slicked with damp.

Waves of people swept past her so that she felt almost buffeted in their wake, people who had homes to go to or friends to see or plans for theatres or restaurants or parties, people who weren't walking huddled round the misery inside which felt like a great sharp stone, weighing you down and cutting into you at the same time.

She wasn't sure why she'd come here, just that it was somewhere to go, and she glanced aimlessly into the windows of the shops she passed: clothes she couldn't afford, gadgets she didn't want, souvenirs of a London that bore no relation to the city she lived in. And skull masks, plastic skeletons, witches' hats, bats on nylon strings, swooping across under green and orange light.

Halloween next week. October 31st, All Hallows' Eve. Her mother would never let her celebrate it, and after what happened the one time Marnie had, she didn't like it either: the Day of the Dead, when restless souls stirred from their sleep, awakening heedless mortals to their duty of memory.

Marnie needed no reminder. She never forgot anything. That was the problem.

'You're freaking me out!' he cries suddenly. He's putting his hands up to cover his face, groaning. 'I can't take this any more. It's doing my head in.'

She is still high on the satisfaction of being right, sitting across from him in the tiny rented flat above a Chinese takeaway that they've made so nice. They keep it nice too; she hates mess.

'What do you mean?' She is feeling the adrenaline ebbing away. 'Don't be stupid, Gary. It's just an argument, that's all.'

'Oh no,' he says bitterly. 'It's not an argument. It's a demolition job.'

'Gary, it's just that you said you'd told me yesterday that you were going to be late and you didn't, and I—'

'Yes, you played me back the whole evening, every sodding word. You know how people talk about CCTV cameras spying on them in the street? Try living with one.'

She's beginning to feel panicky, as if someone has put a hand round her throat. 'Sorry, Gary, sorry! I won't do it again—'

She has to stop another clip starting to run in her head, the one when they're out in the park and she's saying, 'Sorry, Gary, I won't do it again.' There are others waiting to follow; she talks over them fiercely.

'I know I've said it before—'

He gives a harsh laugh. 'Yes, you would, wouldn't you? I expect you can tell me every single time, with a description of where we were and what I was wearing and what the weather was like. The thing is you can't help it, no matter what you say.'

She's crying now. 'It's a disability, Gary. You wouldn't blame me if I couldn't walk, or if I was blind.'

He looks down at her – he's tall, Gary, and not specially hot or anything, but she thinks he's nice-looking with brown eyes and a kind smile. He isn't smiling now.

'It wouldn't be weird if you were in a wheelchair or you couldn't see. I've tried, but this is getting to me so it's messing with my brain. I'm sorry, girl.'

And then Gary had been lost, like everything else, including the little flat she loved possibly even more than she'd loved Gary. It had been a proper home, a place where she belonged. She'd never felt she belonged, before.

She couldn't afford to stay on, not on her wages, and she felt upset all the time, looking around knowing she'd have to leave. So tonight she had walked out too. Gary could settle up with the landlord. He wanted this; she didn't.

She hadn't cried. It was pointless, crying. If your mother disappeared when you were eleven and you went into something that was unconvincingly called a home, then if when you were sixteen even that support was removed and you were all on your own, you knew that the only thing crying did was give you sore eyes to add to your problems.

Instead you just tried to shut out everything you had the option to forget and took the misery inside you and carried it around like a stone in your heart until its weight began to seem normal. One day, though, as more and more miseries were added, there would be one that brought you to your knees. It could be this one.

Marnie didn't know where she was going to spend the night. In one of the darker doorways she passed there was what looked like a heap of rags, but then she caught the glint of the woman's dark eyes and long, dark, greasy hair; she had a baby shawled up to her and she held out her hand, saying something in a language Marnie didn't understand.

She fumbled for her purse and found a pound coin. It wasn't true charity; it was to make a clear separation between herself and someone like this, to banish the thought that this was the sort of someone Marnie might become now the ground had shifted from under her feet.

There was no reason to get spooked by it. For the moment, at least, she was all right. She had money and money was safety. She had a decent enough job waitressing and sharing with Gary had meant she'd even been able to save a little bit. If she headed across into North London, where she could walk to work, she'd find cheap lodgings, just a room somewhere. Save on bus fares.

If she walked there now, at the end of it she'd be tired so she might sleep instead of having to watch their last argument, like a bad movie, all night. It was the curse she couldn't escape, the curse that even the shrink she'd been referred to couldn't lift. She'd stormed out, feeling like a freak show when he told her eagerly that she was going to be the subject of a paper he was writing.

Marnie walked on, with purpose now, but still glancing at the windows as she passed. A travel agent's display stopped her short.

A VisitScotland poster: she recognised that picture, knew the soaring arches and the intricate trefoil windows. The Chapter House, Glenluce Abbey, it said under the picture. It took her back, and for a few minutes she wrestled pointlessly with the intrusive memory.

They walk in, giggling and pushing. It's a day out of school, so that's cool, but Miss Purdy their class teacher is seriously uncool so they're mucking about. The teaching assistant is taking charge now, though, and Gemma nudges her to shut up.

He's got a squint but she's not going to mention it because her friend fancies him and she doesn't want to argue with Gemma. He's boring on now about how there were monks and stuff and it's mostly a ruin. But then they go into this building, and she's blown away.

He uses the word 'elegant'. She's only heard it about people before, and not very often, but she takes it in. It's like cool, only more. And this place is so elegant it makes her hurt inside when she looks at it: the white walls and the cleanness and the emptiness and the arches that spring

upwards and cross each other and then fall like a sort of
stone fountain.

That's how she wants everything to be and when she
gets home she yells at Mum because somehow she can't
bear that everything is messy, but when Mum yells back
that she could tidy her room, somehow the beautiful
whiteness splinters and disappears and she just sort of
forgets about it.

Until now, when it had been prompted to reappear in
high definition. Enough! Sometimes, if she pinched her
arm really hard . . . Yes, success, this time.

The photograph prompted an odd sort of hunger, a
feeling that her senses had been starved for years living
in the city. Here in the damp murk she remembered clear
fresh air, sparkling water and low green hills under a wide,
wide sky – should she go back there, back to Scotland?

She had left the place as soon as she could. London is
the answer for a million runaway Scots kids, and she'd had
a bit of luck for once. The man who spotted her at Euston
wasn't a pimp, he was a decent man with daughters of his
own. He'd got her a job in a café and she'd never been out
of work since.

After a while there had been Gary, but she couldn't
even hope now that he'd come back because she knew he
wouldn't. The future was a blank sheet and no one could
fill it in but herself.

Maybe it was time to confront the demons whose
presence she had long ago taught herself to ignore. She
could be in Scotland by tomorrow, ask the questions she'd
suppressed all her life, since that night . . .

She's going to have to keep well out of her mother's way, just stick her head round the sitting-room door to say she's home—

No, no, no! She began to run, in the direction of Euston, London's Scottish gateway. Sometimes physical effort helped, but this time it was inexorable, flooding back in its relentless, pointless detail.

. . . She and Gemma had necked a couple of lagers and with Mum like she was, anyway, she could go mental. Mum's not in the sitting room, though, and so she drops her hat and mask onto one of the chairs . . .

The big kitchen, fitted out in the sort of farmhouse style which no genuine farmhouse has ever aspired to, was ringing with excited squeals as a heavily treacled scone swung from the pulley, with dramatic effect on the eager small boy's face, T-shirt and ultimately hands as he made increasingly frantic efforts to snatch a bite.

'No, no! We told you, Mikey – no hands!' his grandfather instructed, holding them behind the child's back and getting covered with the sticky stuff himself as a result. 'Gemma, haven't you taught your child to play by the rules? Look at this!' Laughing, he held out his hands and went over to the Belfast sink to wash them.

'Come on, Dad, he's only three!' his daughter protested, smiling as her mother held the string still so that Mikey, who was showing signs of frustration, could get at the scone.

Michael Morrison turned round drying his hands. 'Looks to me as if dooking for apples should be next on the agenda. Head right down under the water, Mikey, old chap – that's the best way.'

Gemma watched with an affectionate smile. The traditional Scottish Halloween was dying and Mikey would probably never even remember his grandparents' party for him. They'd gone to so much trouble, with the orange and black balloons and a turnip lantern with a carrot for the nose and green counters for eyes and matchstick teeth in the grinning mouth. She'd just have to watch that he didn't swallow any of the foil-wrapped coins in the champit tatties he'd have with his tea. And even though it was such a miserable night, Dad was determined to set off the rather expensive fireworks he'd got in – nothing was too good for his little namesake.

What would she have done without Dad this past year, after Fergus vanished along with most of their bank account? Dad had just scooped them up and made everything all right, just the way he always used to kiss her and make it all better when she was a little girl. And Mikey had never been happier, lapping up the attention from two doting grandparents.

As her mother filled a basin with water and dropped in half a dozen rosy apples, Gemma watched his dance of excitement with just a shade of sadness. He was growing so fast, and it wouldn't be long before he preferred tacky commercialism and a skeleton outfit from Tesco. But at the moment, he was having the time of his life. Oh, she did love Halloween!

The name Marnie Bruce hadn't crossed her mind for years and years.

* * *

There were voices outside the house. It was dark and windy and pouring with rain; in this quiet street on a night like this, why should there be voices outside in her garden? Anita Loudon, alone in the house she had lived in since her parents died, stiffened.

Then she heard the giggles. Children's voices – oh God, Halloween! She'd managed to forget about it until now. She didn't often achieve that.

It was too late now to put out the lights and pretend she wasn't in. They'd ring the doorbell any minute and if she didn't answer it there would be the festering contents of her carefully separated bins – to save the planet for their future – tipped all over her garden path to be cleared up in the morning.

When had the innocent Scottish guising become the nasty American form of blackmail that went under the name of trick-or-treat? And, of course, she had other reasons to hate Halloween, but she desperately tried not to think about those.

That was the doorbell now. Anita didn't like giving them money but she hadn't any of the usual cheap sweets to buy them off with, ready to distribute as she muttered under her breath, 'I hope they rot your teeth.'

She didn't recognise any of them as kids from the village; they'd come out here from Stranraer, probably, in the hope of better pickings. The leader of the little group on the doorstep, a skinny youth in jeans and a hoodie, had made no effort at disguise though Anita could see a ghost and a skeleton among his entourage. He looked too old to be out begging for sweets and his face brightened as she appeared with her purse. It darkened again as she handed him fifty pence and she retreated inside and shut the door before he could say anything. She waited for the sound of bins being kicked around, but they seemed to have been at least minimally satisfied.

Anita returned to the magazine she'd been leafing through, but the 'Age-defying Tricks that Really Work' article didn't hold her attention. She'd tried most of them already, and they didn't.

Now she knew it was Halloween she'd have to spend the evening trying to quell the guilt and the irrational sense of dread. If it overpowered her she'd have one of her panic attacks, when the room closed in round her and she couldn't breathe. Another noise outside almost set her off until she realised it was just the children returning along the road.

She picked up the *Daily Record* she'd brought in, but she'd lost interest and started flipping over the pages with hands that still shook a little. Then she came to the centre spread and gasped as if a punch had taken her breath away.

The face looking up at her from the page, the bright child's face that had dominated the headlines for so long, all those years ago – forty, she realised now, reading the strapline – was in the largest of the photographs. Other old-fashioned, slightly-blurred family snaps like his were spaced round about the article.

Anita always told herself it was all past, all safely forgotten. The heat in the room was suddenly stifling and she stumbled across to the window, flinging it wide even though the wind-borne rain lashed in, soaking her.

The cold air helped and at last she began to breathe more evenly She shut the window again and collapsed onto her chair, her heart still racing.

It was all right, all right, she told herself. No one had contacted her this time; it was just an off-the-cuff piece. Anita tore it in pieces and threw it in the bin.

She'd phone him tomorrow, though. Any excuse.

The sea was troubled tonight, roaring and crashing against the rocks as the storm swept in up Loch Ryan from the Irish Sea. There would be no ferries setting out to Belfast tonight.

The view from Grant Crichton's large modern house on the loch side just between Stranraer and Cairnryan was incomparable in good weather. Tonight, though, the drawbacks to its position were apparent.

He had been sitting in the lounge with a pile of papers on the small piecrust table beside him pretending to work when he suddenly crashed his fist down, making it rock on its pedestal.

'That damned noise! It's driving me mad. I can't concentrate. We're going to have to do something about it, Denise.'

His wife looked up uneasily from the pile of glossy travel brochures she was leafing through, curled up on the deep cushions of the cream velour sofa beside the living gas fire. She was a neat, sharp-faced blonde, twenty years younger than her husband, fighting the inexorable onset of middle age with every weapon available, short of surgery; Grant had spelt out that he wouldn't spring for that.

'Yes, of course,' she said. It was a dreary sound, admittedly: the drama of the waves was muted by double-glazing and interlined curtains to a low moaning but it was hardly obtrusive. What was distracting her husband wasn't the noise. He'd been impossible all day.

Denise's eyes flicked to a silver-framed photo on the mantelpiece showing a curly-haired little boy pulling a cheeky face for the camera. It was fading a bit but she didn't want to suggest having it redone. Mentioning him at all, she'd learnt in her eight-year marriage, was a bad mistake, always putting Grant into one of his moods which could last for days.

Halloween, of course, was the worst. *She* always phoned on Halloween and he would twitch until she had. She couldn't just phone in the morning and get it over with, could she – oh no, she would know how it preyed on her ex-husband's mind and deliberately leave it late. The year she'd only got round to phoning at midnight Grant had needed Valium to get any sleep at all.

Denise had tried suggesting he phone her instead, but only once. He'd refused bluntly, telling her almost in so many words that this unfinished business from his first marriage was nothing to do with her. That was what he said, but she knew it was only an excuse. Despite years of experience he was clinging to the hope that this year just might be the one when Shelley forgot – as if she would, on the fortieth anniversary. That was racheting up the tension tonight.

When the phone rang at eight o'clock Grant jumped as if he had been jabbed with a pin and when it turned out to be a member of her book club handed it over to Denise with a glare.

She took the call quickly, then went back to her browsing. The sound of the sea became audible again in the quiet room and she braced herself for another outburst from Grant. When the phone rang again, they both jumped.

He picked it up, glanced at the caller ID and grimaced towards her. She nodded, then discreetly lowered her eyes to the brochure again in symbolic withdrawal. This was delicate ground for a second wife.

'Yes, Shelley?' he said wearily.

Denise could hear crying at the other end of the line – loud, uninhibited crying – and saw her husband's face contort with grief, mingled with resentment that his ex-wife had managed to provoke it.

His eyes went involuntarily to the photo on the mantelpiece and they filled with tears as he snarled, 'Yes, of course I haven't forgotten it was today he disappeared.' He put up his hand to rub them away. 'You needn't think you have the monopoly on feeling.'

Denise couldn't hear the words being said but she could hear the voice at the other end rising towards what would in the end become a screaming match. It usually did.

She could bear it no longer. Grant was looking tired and old, running his hand through his thinning grey hair, and his jowly face was beginning to turn an unhealthy mottled purple. She slipped out of the room.

He would be angry at the end of this, very angry. Grant was a powerful man, a controlling man, and the annual reminder of his helplessness had side effects which she and everyone in his vicinity would have to suffer for days.

At times like this she seriously wondered why she had married him. It came perhaps into the category of things that had seemed like a good idea at the time. She'd been rather taken with his forcefulness at first and as forty loomed with nothing to look back on but a string of failed relationships with commitment-phobes it had looked like a no-brainer.

She hadn't quite realised then that with his attitudes he could have co-authored *The Surrendered Wife* – a recent hit at the book club – but on the other hand as a hotel receptionist she wasn't exactly pushing at the glass ceiling.

And there were always the holidays. She was still holding her pile of brochures as she went towards the kitchen. A spot of intensive brochure therapy before he and Shelley finished yelling at each other might put her in a more resilient mood when he came out looking for a dog to kick.

In the Glasgow warehouse nightclub, midnight came with a burst of smoke effect, dramatised with orange and black laser lights. The foetid atmosphere was rank with human sweat and the crush of bodies on the dance floor swayed and stamped to a relentless, mind-numbing, pounding beat.

The girl in the witch's outfit, abbreviated in both directions, was standing at the edge to catch her breath. She was humming to the music, smiling a little vaguely, just nicely high. She was tilting back her long, white throat to drink from a bottle of water when the vampire struck.

She gave a shriek, then giggled as the man in Dracula costume, with pale make-up and a deep peak painted into the centre of his forehead, dropped his fake fangs into his hand.

'Sorry – just, you were asking for it.'

He had to raise his voice above the din and as he grinned at her he still looked a bit wolfish, even without the fangs. He was quite buff too, with dark-blue eyes and a cleft chin, though when she looked closer she realised that under the make-up he was a lot older than she'd thought at first. Normally someone that age would never have got through the check at the doors but hey, even if old guys weren't her style, that had been funny. She wasn't on the pull this evening, anyway – Jezz had only gone out for a fag.

'God, I about had a heart attack,' she shouted. 'You're mental!'

'Can't resist—' As she indicated that she couldn't hear, he moved in closer and spoke in her ear. 'Can't resist the lure of young, virginal human flesh.'

'Here – who're you calling virginal?' she protested. 'What's your name, anyway?'

'Just call me Drax.' He held out his hand. 'Care to dance?'

The old-fashioned way he said it was quite cute. She glanced over her shoulder but there was no sign of Jezz yet so she shrugged. 'Why not?'

He swept her close immediately, which she hadn't bargained for. It wasn't pleasant; she felt hot and sweaty and she could smell his sweat too. Even in the dim light she could see the trails on his make-up.

47

She edged a little further apart. 'This place is pure dead brilliant. I love Halloween, don't you?'

'Sometimes.' The way he said it made her feel as if a door had been slammed in her face. But he pulled her back against him, really quite roughly.

She was starting to feel uncomfortable. Jezz's tap on her shoulder was definitely a relief.

'Hey, babe.' He didn't look best pleased.

Nor did Drax. He was a couple of inches taller than Jezz and a lot broader. Scowling, he said, 'Back off! I saw her first.'

Jezz swore at him. 'First? You stupid or something? She's my girl.'

Drax didn't let go. Her heart began to race; she knew what could happen when guys got started and it didn't do to be standing in the middle. With a violent effort she pulled herself free and evaded the grab he made at her arm.

'I'm away home. Coming, Jezz?'

She walked off without waiting to see if he would follow and when she glanced back they were still squaring up to each other like dogs ready to fight, though neither had made the first move. She had just reached the door when Jezz caught up with her.

'Care to tell me about it, then?' he said, and she realised with a sinking heart that not fighting had left him with a lot of aggression going spare. She was tired and coming down from her high and the last thing she needed was one of these arguments that went on all night. Or worse.

* * *

'Tam – good. Come in.' DI Marjory Fleming smiled as she looked up from the particularly tedious report she was attempting to write as DS Tam MacNee appeared in her office on the fourth floor of the Galloway Constabulary headquarters in Kirkluce. It was a welcome relief from a dreary task on a dreary morning.

Though it was almost eleven o'clock the lights were still on, and it looked as if they'd be on all day. The sky was grey and heavy and the plane trees whose tops she could just see outside her window were bare skeletons, black with earlier rain. That it was only to be expected in November didn't make it any better.

She set aside the sheets of stats she was working from and said, 'I just wanted to tell you we've got a problem with one of the trials calling next week. The Fiscal's saying there's been intimidation of one of the witnesses.'

MacNee took the seat opposite her desk. 'Oh aye. That'll be big Kenny Barclay, right? Well, what did they expect? I suppose I'll need to get round there and do a bit of intimidation myself.'

His voice sounded uncharacteristically flat and she looked at him sharply. Usually his face would have brightened at the prospect of a bit of psychological warfare, at which he was a past master; the Glasgow street-fighter might have reformed long ago but the killer instinct was still there.

Fleming noticed with a pang that his hair was more grey than brown these days and his eyes were becoming hooded. Admittedly her own chestnut crop owed more to Nice 'n Easy than to nature and it was a while since she'd chosen to linger before a mirror in a strong light, but even so . . .

'Something wrong, Tam?'

MacNee put on the irritating face that men tend to put on when asked that question. 'Wrong? Naw. Why should there be?'

'I don't know why there *should* be,' Fleming said crisply. 'But if you go around looking as if someone's stolen your scone, it doesn't take exceptional sensitivity to work out that whether or not something *should* be wrong, all is not bluebirds and sunshine in the world of Tam MacNee.'

He favoured her with a black look. 'So what if there is? It's nothing to do with my work.'

'Can I take it that "my work" is code for "you"? But when going out to do over Kenny Barclay doesn't produce that spark of bloodlust, I wonder how effective you're going to be.'

Fleming waited as he thought about it, chewing his lip. She owed MacNee a lot; he had watched his protégée go past him professionally without rancour and smoothed paths for her which lesser men might have seamed with potholes. With his 'hard man' self-image, he was always reluctant to talk about his problems but there had been a disaster before when he'd brooded alone. She'd kept it light; would he open up?

At last he said grudgingly, 'Oh, all right, then. It's my dad.'

'Ah.' MacNee's elderly father had been estranged from his son for many years, ending up alcoholic and homeless in a Glasgow alleyway and lucky to have survived this long, but MacNee had found him secure and comfortable lodgings and she had thought the problem had been taken care of. 'Back on the streets, is he?'

'If it was just that!' MacNee gave a short laugh. 'No – he's getting married.'

'*Married!*' Fleming gaped. Davie MacNee must be pushing eighty and there were other reasons why she wouldn't have described him as a catch herself. 'Oh – is it the woman that took him in last year?'

'Maggie? If it was Maggie I'd be breaking out the champagne. And I'm not saying it couldn't have been, mind – she's aye had a soft spot for the old devil.

'That's part of the problem – she's jealous.'

'Right,' Fleming said carefully. It wouldn't do to show unfeeling amusement about this version of the eternal triangle being played out among the Glasgow geriatric set. 'Who's the lucky lady, then?'

MacNee looked at her sourly. 'It's all right for you to laugh.'

'I didn't!' she protested.

'Oh, not right out loud, maybe, but I could hear you anyway. It's not funny from where I'm sitting.

'Maggie says this Gloria's an old friend from the backstreets, another alkie, and Maggie's beside herself because she's drawing Davie back to his old ways when he'd got on an even keel. And she can't be expected to go on giving him a home with the pair of them coming in roaring drunk and – well, going up to his room.'

This delicate euphemism almost undid Fleming. It was

a triumph of self-control that she managed to say gravely, 'Very difficult. What are you going to do?'

'I'll take suggestions. You're not meant to have to go around breaking up unsuitable relationships when your dad's eighty next birthday. I'm going to have to away up there now and take time off tomorrow to talk some sense into him – and meet the bride.'

That did it. Fleming began to laugh, and after a reluctant moment MacNee joined in.

'At least you've realised there is a funny side,' Fleming said at last. 'Better out than in, you know.'

'I couldn't tell Bunty. She'd be all for coming up with me to help choose the wedding dress. She's no sense, that woman.'

MacNee's adored wife, with a heart as generous as her figure, could never see the downside of any situation. It was a characteristic which, while endearing in itself, was a source of considerable frustration to her more cynical husband.

'She probably would,' Fleming agreed. 'So what are you going to do?'

MacNee groaned. 'God knows. Like Rabbie Burns said, *O wad some Pow'r the giftie gie us, To see oursels as others see us!* He's needing to see he's looking a right tumshie.

'Still, it's my problem.' He glanced at his watch. 'I'd better look in on Kenny before I go off duty. He's been throwing his weight around lately—'

He broke off as the phone on Fleming's desk buzzed. As she took the call he got up, signalled that he would leave and headed towards the door.

'Who?' Fleming said, then, 'Marnie Bruce? Oh – *Marnie Bruce!*'

Shock showed on her face. MacNee stopped dead, then turned round slowly.

'Tell her to wait.' Fleming put the phone down and stared at her sergeant. 'You heard. What are we going to do about *that*?'

CHAPTER THREE

The early shift was almost over and DC Louise Hepburn was finishing off a report when MacNee came back into the CID room. He'd been short with his subordinates all morning – well, him being five foot six (and three-quarters, don't forget the three-quarters and preferably round it up to five foot seven) made that inevitable, but today something was bugging him and he'd been cutting everyone down to his own size so aggressively that you began to feel you were in an oriental court and obliged to keep your head lower than the king's.

'Oh good,' he said. 'You'll do, Louise.'

Mentally kowtowing, Hepburn said, 'Something you want me to do, Sarge? I'm due off shortly but I'm not in a hurry if you want me to stay on for a bit.'

'Shouldn't take long, but thanks for the offer. There's someone called Marnie Bruce just wandered in off the street and asked to speak to DI Fleming. Find out what it is she's after and then write it up. There's no rush on that – the boss is in a meeting all afternoon so tomorrow'll do fine. Report direct to her – I'm off tomorrow. All right? Thanks, Louise.'

'No problem, Sarge. In the waiting room, is she?'

Hepburn headed off along the corridor feeling brighter. MacNee's black mood seemed to have lifted, and after a morning at the computer it was good to have something more interesting to do.

There was only one person in the waiting room, a slight, neat-featured woman. Her hair, feathered round her face, was an unusual reddish-gold and her light-blue eyes had an odd expression, almost as if she were seeing something more than just the room around her.

'Marnie Bruce? I'm DC Hepburn. What's the problem?'

This wasn't the way Marnie had planned it, which threw her. She could remember Fleming vividly – well, of course she could – and she had gone back over the scenes where she had featured in Marnie's life, looking for any questions arising from them. There wasn't much to go on, really, but she sensed a hidden agenda and she'd had time on the long journey north to work up a determination to find out what it was.

She'd been prepared for disappointment. The PC Fleming she remembered was likely to have moved, or even left the police years ago, but the receptionist had recognised the name immediately and Marnie had felt a great surge of optimism.

This girl, slightly foreign-looking with her untidy mass

of dark curly hair, olive skin and dark eyes, was a let-down. She looked to be in her twenties and certainly couldn't have any recollection of what had happened.

She said firmly, 'There isn't any point in explaining it all to someone else. I wanted to speak to PC Fleming. They said she still works here.'

The other woman's lips twitched. 'I'm afraid she hasn't been PC Fleming for a long time. She's Detective Inspector Fleming now, so as you can imagine she's a very busy woman. I'm to hear what you have to say and then I'll report to her if we can't sort it out now.'

Marnie frowned. This girl seemed to think she could just fob her off. But there had been another policeman – DS MacNee.

'Is – is DS MacNee still here?' she asked, and of course the name triggered the image.

He comes down the ward and sits next to her bed. 'How are you feeling, lassie?' he says.

She ignores the question. 'Where's my mum?'

She was having to peer through what was running in her head and it was very distracting. She saw Hepburn looking at her strangely. Reckoning she was just another nutter, probably – and perhaps that wasn't wrong.

'I'm afraid he's off duty.'

'I'll come back when he's on duty again, then.' Marnie made to get up. 'Tomorrow?'

Hepburn shook her head. 'He's away tomorrow. And I couldn't say when you'd get him – we work shifts and we're out on calls a lot.

'Look, why don't I find a cup of coffee for us and you

can give me some idea what this is all about – OK?'

She was out of the room before Marnie had a chance to respond. She sat back on the padded bench and closed her eyes, allowing the interview with DS MacNee play on in her mind. There was, she realised, very little to go on there. He'd just asked her standard questions, giving nothing away, and unlike PC – no, sorry, Detective Inspector – Fleming he'd had no previous connection with her mother. And it didn't look as if she'd get to see Fleming without talking to this girl. She had resigned herself to it, though with a bad grace, by the time Hepburn came back carrying two paper cups.

'It's not great coffee – warm and wet is about the best I can say for it,' she said cheerfully, setting them down on the low table and producing cartons of creamer, packets of sugar and a wooden stirrer from her pocket.

'Just black.' Marnie sipped at the greyish liquid, though she noticed that Hepburn didn't pick up hers. She put down the cup again, deciding to follow her example.

'Is it all right if I call you Marnie?' Hepburn barely waited for her nod. 'Right, Marnie. Talk to me. What do you want to ask DI Fleming about?'

'I want to know why I never heard anything after my mother disappeared and I was taken into care all these years ago. I want to know if she's alive or dead. I want to know whether she chose to disappear or whether somebody killed her.'

She had the satisfaction of seeing Hepburn's eyes widen in sudden interest, then added, 'And why there was never an inquiry.'

* * *

57

Having bashed out her report, Hepburn saved it and left the CID room. She picked up her rain jacket from her locker, pulling up the hood after a glance out of the window. There was a steady drizzle and under the leaden sky it was getting dark already.

She paused on the doorstep of the police headquarters to light a Gitane, an addiction acquired during visits to her French mother's family, cupping her hands round the lighter to shield the flame, then taking a long, luxurious, and yes, faintly desperate draw.

She should give it up. The cost was becoming ridiculous, on her wages, and she was beginning to feel a bit of a sad loser, huddled round the back by the dustbins in her break, with winter ahead. Yes, she should definitely give it up. Just not now.

She was still reeling a bit from the impact of what Marnie Bruce had told her. A kid of eleven, assaulted and abandoned in a remote cottage with her mother gone – and no follow-up? It couldn't be like that, surely. There must be more to it, but she'd had to be careful that her report didn't have a hint of criticism since it was obviously a case that Big Marge had worked on in the dim-and-distant. She'd stressed, too, that there was something odd about the woman – not exactly a nutter, but definitely strange. There had been hesitations that suggested Marnie might be hearing voices that certainly weren't coming through to anyone else.

It was a pity she couldn't have talked it over with Big Marge today, but she'd had her instructions. She'd just have to go back home now. She inhaled a last lingering puff, then crushed her cigarette out against the waste bin.

Hepburn's feet were dragging as she walked towards her car. She had a long drive ahead of her and it wasn't as if she was looking forward to what awaited her at the other end.

Her colleagues assumed she was saving to get on the housing ladder by living at home, on the edge of Stranraer, and she'd let them think that; it sounded so pitiable to be trapped by her family circumstances. Her mother Fleur had declared English an ugly language and flatly refused to learn it and her father, fluent in French himself, had never insisted. Once he died, Fleur had found herself helpless and friendless.

But still intransigent. There was nothing, Louise reflected bitterly, as stubborn as a French mother who declared that at her age it would not be elegant for her to learn English like some little child. Louise could take over her father's place as social facilitator.

In the first devastation of loss, Louise had given up the flat she'd been renting in Kirkluce and come home. Once the formalities of sorting out her father's estate had been completed, it seemed fairly obvious that Fleur would return to France. Naturally, it couldn't be discussed while she was shocked and confused and clinging to her only child, but Louise would be leaving home again once Fleur got back to normal.

Only she hadn't. The confusion showed no signs of clearing and Louise never knew from one day to the next what she would have to confront when she got home.

The house was a villa, white-harled and standing on

the shores of Loch Ryan looking out along the sea loch between the low hills, a pretty house with a pretty view, but Louise didn't even glance at it.

'*Maman*, I'm home,' she called in the French that was the only language spoken at home, and as her mother appeared from the kitchen at the back of the house Louise was struck, as she so often was, by Fleur's beauty and elegance. The bloom was fading now but her face was still a perfect oval, with high cheekbones and delicate olive colouring, and she had pansy-brown eyes which even as she approached sixty remained luminous and unhooded. Her long dark hair, without even a thread of grey, was caught up in a clip at the back, with wisps slipping forward becomingly. But she was wearing a nightgown.

'Darling, you are so late! But I made coq au vin, so it won't have come to much harm.'

Automatically, Louise glanced at her watch, though she knew it wasn't three o'clock yet. She felt faintly sick. '*Maman*, it's not bedtime. It's still the afternoon.'

A cloud came over her mother's face briefly. Then she laughed, pointing through a window to the gathering gloom. 'No, no, it's dark – look! You work too hard. But come now and have your supper. I'll have a glass of wine to keep you company and you can tell me what kept you so late.'

She went to the kitchen. As she opened the door the delicious, winy smell of the casserole floated out but Louise really wasn't hungry – and not just because it was four hours until supper time.

* * *

There the cottage was, exactly as Marnie had remembered it, just a bit shabbier, and it had been pretty run-down even back then. The trees seem to have sidled closer, though of course they couldn't have, really; they were still on the other side of the sagging wire fence. It was just that the great pine boughs had grown longer, as if they were reaching out in kinship to reclaim the wooden house.

It was one of the cottages built for the workforce needed to plant the massive forests of the Galloway National Park, most of them redundant long ago. The bleached shingles that covered it were a dried-out silver-grey now and indeed rotting in places, Marnie noticed.

Her memory of it was entirely accurate, of course; how could she have expected anything different? Yet with all the repetitions that had replayed in her head these last years it had taken on a sort of unreality, and it was somehow a shock to see it there, as if she'd stepped into an old movie she'd watched too many times.

As the service bus pulled away Marnie walked towards it along the side of the main road, the Queen's Way running from Newton Stewart to New Galloway. The rain, at least, had gone off, but it was damp and dreary and the sky was dark with purplish clouds. Pine needles clumped onto the soles of her shoes as she walked, deadening the sound of her footsteps. Across the track on the farther side of the house, a plantation had been felled leaving a massacre site of stumps and dead branches, making the house look curiously naked.

Marnie had told herself that just going to the house

she'd once lived in wasn't going to achieve anything but even so she'd cherished a slender hope that the occupants might know what had happened after they left. It was something to do, anyway, while she waited for the police to get back in touch.

She reached the five-bar gate. They had never bothered to close it and it stood open still, but rotting at the base and with the hinges rusted. The rough grass round about was untended, with clumps of bracken and nettles and brambles round the edges. No change there, then, and the paintwork round the windows was peeling as if it hadn't been renewed since they left.

There was no one around and the cottage had a deserted feel. The curtains at the windows were hanging limp and there was a big crack in one of the panes. Even so, she hesitated before she walked through the gate and when she reached the door knocked once then paused, listening.

A couple of cars passed, their tyres swishing in puddles on the road, but there was no responsive movement inside. She knocked again; the sound seemed to echo in emptiness and she stepped aside to look through the sitting-room window on the right, cupping her hand against the pane to break the reflection.

It was weird, as if she'd opened a time capsule. She hadn't expected the familiar furniture would still be here, yet there was the brown sofa, the wonky standard lamp with the orange shade, the cheap coffee table, now missing a great splinter of the wood veneer. It was the setting her flashback memories always produced – and yet it wasn't. The familiar, grubby disorder had gone and it was almost clinically tidy and bare. The dissonance gave her a sense of confusion that was close to nausea.

Their landlord must still own it. Who was he? Nothing came back to her, so she presumably had never known; her mother would have looked after all that. Certainly, it looked as if it had been empty for a long time. Who would want a run-down place like this, stuck out in the middle of nowhere?

She wandered round the house. The other windows were too high to look into, and on an impulse she tried the back door – locked, of course. The front door no doubt would be too, but she went back and rattled the handle hopefully. It didn't yield, but the lock looked as if it hadn't been changed and a sudden thought struck her.

The stone at the foot of the pine tree nearest the house was embedded in soil and moss but she was determined, scrabbling and tugging at it and eventually seeking out a smaller, pointed stone to use as a lever. As it came up small pale creatures scuttled and squirmed away from the light in panic but there, speckled with rust and earth, was the key they had always kept there.

Marnie brushed it clean then went to the back door and turned the key in the lock. It opened with a squeal of unused hinges and she stepped inside with a stirring of expectation.

The place felt full of ghosts. Images assailed her, one after the other, until she was dizzy and whimpering in dismay, 'No, no!' Shaking, she struggled to displace them with some rational insight, opening the doors one after another.

There was nothing here. How could there be? It was just a shabby, gloomy, soulless place and it certainly wasn't going to tell her anything about what had happened to her or where her mother had gone. She didn't want to be here any more. She gave a shudder as she left, locking the door behind her.

Marnie hefted the key in her hand, preparing to throw it away into the tangle of scrubby growth at the foot of the forest trees. Then, for no real reason that she could think of, she put it back in its place under the stone and pushed the dislodged earth and the torn moss back round about it.

The meeting had finished early for once. It was just after four when Fleming came out and went immediately to the CID room looking for Hepburn, though without much hope. It would have been good to know what exactly Marnie Bruce was expecting.

Hepburn had gone off duty, of course, and Fleming set off up the stairs to her office with the problem still dominating her thoughts. She'd been far too junior to make decisions at the time – had protested about them, indeed – but those more responsible had left the force. Jakie McNally was dead and Donald Bailey, a DI at the time, had retired as superintendent last year – a nice piece of timing there.

Of course, MacNee had been a DS at the time, while Fleming had been a humble PC, but she knew who Bailey's successor would look to for explanation and it wouldn't be him. She quailed at the thought.

Detective Superintendent Christine Rowley had been fast-tracked in Edinburgh to DCI and then had transferred to the Galloway Constabulary to cut her teeth before, as she made all too plain, she returned in glory to the sort of policing that was worthy of her talents. She viewed both the inhabitants of her present patch and her subordinates with a sort of lofty amusement which edged into high-pitched annoyance when things went wrong.

East Coast and West Coast Scotland have never seen things in quite the same light, but Fleming's attempt to explain to her that the old joke, 'Glasgow and Edinburgh aren't speaking' wasn't just a joke fell on deaf ears. To Rowley it was incomprehensible that they weren't grateful for enlightenment when she explained how things were done in the capital. It was putting a severe strain on MacNee's blood pressure.

She wasn't popular with anyone. Her affected Morningside accent grated and Fleming had taken care not to find out which of her colleagues had coined the nickname 'Hyacinth', after Mrs Bucket of TV fame, but she suspected MacNee was involved. It had become quite hard to think of her in any other way.

Rowley would have fifty fits about the Marnie Bruce case. Fleming had frequently moaned about her predecessor, who had elevated busy idleness to a fine art, but she had taken it all back several times since his departure. At least Donald Bailey had let her get on with the job, whereas Rowley liked playing puppet-master till the strings got tangled and then let everything collapse in a heap which would involve hours of patient sorting out for someone. Usually Fleming.

There was no point in giving a preliminary explanation before she knew just what sort of trouble Marnie Bruce was going to cause, but perhaps it would be wise to trawl the files to see precisely the level of constraint they'd been under at the time, given the situation.

It wouldn't have been computerised. With a sigh, Fleming turned round and went back down the stairs again to the dusty store where the archives were kept. It could take hours to find what she was looking for, and she wasn't looking forward to the search.

But it was a visit to Disneyland compared to the conversation she would have to have with Hyacinth tomorrow.

Marnie Bruce glanced at her watch as she went back onto the road. Three-quarters of an hour till the next bus was due – how could she fill the time? She'd freeze if she hung about here, so she'd be better walking briskly towards Newton Stewart in the hope that the exercise would warm her up. She might even manage to hitch a lift from a passing car.

She was about to set off in that direction when her eye was caught by another cottage a couple of hundred yards down the road on the other side, and she stopped. She remembered it but she'd never been inside. They'd had no real contact with their neighbours, except that morning . . .

He's standing over her with a gun in his hand, and she

66

thinks she's going to be sick again, with terror. He's saying something about foxes then he says, 'You know me, don't you? Douglas Boyd, from along the road.'

She latched on to the name while trying to force the memory away. Douglas Boyd. It gave her a fresh purpose and she turned back, towards the other cottage. It was a quaint-looking grey stone building with small windows and a slate roof. There was a little bit of land round about it and a grassy patch in front where there was a child'n swing and a sandpit, muddy and pooled with water at the moment.

Douglas Boyd and his wife would be long gone but perhaps the current owner might know where they were if they were still alive: an old people's home, most likely, but they might still have something to tell her.

The woman who came to the door looked blank at the name 'Boyd'. She wasn't much older than Marnie herself; there was a child screaming in the background and her expression conveyed that a stranger at the door was pretty much the last straw. They'd bought it from some people called McCrae, she said, and shut the door in Marnie's face.

It wasn't the girl's fault that she didn't know, but she didn't need to be rude. Feeling irritable and dispirited, Marnie walked aimlessly back past the cottage. What lay ahead of her was a long walk under dark purple clouds that threatened rain, and all this expedition had done was to prompt random bursts of upsetting memories without giving her anything more to follow up.

A silvery glint caught her eye and she turned her head.

The trees were thinning now and beyond them there was a glimpse of water, Clatteringshaws Loch. There was a little path leading past the back of the cottage and down to the shore – at least there had been, though it might be overgrown by now. On an impulse she went back into the garden and stepped over the loose wires of the boundary fence.

It was still there. It was some sort of laid path, perhaps a shortcut for the foresters, and it wasn't completely overgrown, though the sprawl of shrubs was encroaching and she had to duck under snagging branches. It was about fifty yards long and she could see the loch glimmering beyond.

Its wide expanse was steel-grey today under the heavy sky. On a sunny day it would be charming, with the backdrop of green native woodland and the soft surrounding hills hazy-purple with heather, but at this time of year with the trees bare and the heather black and dead it looked grim, even menacing.

The path came out in a little car park beside a tea room and information centre, closed of course. She walked down from the green bank onto the narrow pebbled shore and out of long habit bent and chose a flat stone to skim out across the surface of the loch. It was half-in, half-out of the water, the dry half dull grey, the other half glowing with soft blues and pinks and greens. She'd noticed that before . . .

She stares at the pebble. How can just water make it look so different? Maybe it's a different colour anyway? But no, it's drying already. It's going back to grey and she loses interest, sending it scliffing across the water – one, two, three, four, then quicker and quicker five, six, seven, nearly eight, and then it sinks, in circles of ripples. She tries another stone or two then she wanders down to—

The Iron Age broch! She hadn't thought of it until now. It had been a curious structure: a circular drystone wall, overgrown with grass and mosses, with a sort of wigwam of wooden struts added on top to show how they would have lived, that unimaginably ancient tribe who had made their home here, probably to fish in the lake. Perhaps their children had scliffed stones too, maybe even wondered at their colours, as she had done, standing just where she was now. It was a weird thought.

Could it still be there? Marnie was just about to take the path towards it when she was suddenly buffeted by a gust of wind. She turned to look out across the loch and saw the squall coming towards her between the hills, battering down silver spears of rain and ruffling the water into choppy little waves.

She was wearing light rainwear well suited to London showers and had a neat little umbrella in her tote bag, but borne on the wind the rain reached her before she could dig it out and she was soaked through before she could get it open. Once she did, the wind took it, contemptuously blowing it inside out and breaking a couple of its ribs.

The broch would give her shelter – if its roof was still there. Gasping under the shock of the downpour, she ran along the path, her sight blurred by the rivulets pouring down her face. But yes, the roof was there, its timbers blackened by age, and she ducked gratefully under the entrance into the dim interior.

It was smarter than it had been when she was a child, with a neat gravelled floor where once there had been only packed earth, and even a bench. She sat down on it to dig out tissues from her bag to mop her face but rose immediately; there were gaps between the struts and now the seat of her jeans was wet too.

The smell was the same, though – damp, earthy, with an edge of rotting vegetation. She felt a sudden churning in her stomach . . .

'Quick, quick,' Gemma hisses. 'He's coming, he's coming!' She gives a little squeal of delighted terror as they dash into the broch. They clutch each other as they cower at the back, listening for the footsteps.

She says, 'They're getting closer!' and Gemma mutters, 'What if he comes in? What'll we do?' They're both covering their heads with their hands, as if that makes them invisible.

Without even a pause, the footsteps go on along the path. 'That was close,' she whispers to Gemma.

'Better wait a minute or two,' Gemma says. 'In case he looks back and sees us.'

They know, of course, that he's just an ordinary man out walking who hasn't even noticed two silly kids who think it's fun to scare themselves. And it's worked; Gemma might be giggling but she's beginning to feel creepy, as if the ghosts of those people wearing skins and holding clubs resented her being alive when they were long, long dead.

She scrambles up, startling Gemma. She's desperate to get out, as if something horrible might happen if she doesn't escape . . .

Marnie felt the same now. She had the odd prickling down the back of her neck that you get when someone's looking at you, and even though she knew there was no one there she turned to check. She told herself she was being stupid, but her heart rate speeded up and her breathing thickened. Rain or no rain, she was getting out of here.

It had been too heavy to last long. It was stopping already and as she walked back along the path, mocking her own stupidity, the wind blew a rift in the clouds and a sunbeam lit up the farther shore with golden splendour.

It was the fourth time today that Anita had tried his number, but she didn't want to leave a message. There was never any guarantee that he would respond.

'All right, Anita, what do you want?' he said as he answered the phone.

Caller ID always threw her and she was upset too by his unwelcoming tone. 'I-I just wanted to warn you about something.'

His voice sharpened. 'Warn me? What do you mean?'

'The anniversary,' she said. 'It was forty years ago yesterday, and there was a big piece in the *Record*. Maybe others too.'

'So?'

Anita hadn't an answer to that question. 'Well—'

He cut across her. 'Just rehashing the old stuff?'

'I suppose so.'

71

'Tomorrow's chip paper, then. That's all.'

He didn't even say goodbye and she knew she had, yet again, made a fool of herself. She hated the way she'd sounded. Needy. Pathetic. Hearing his voice had been the sort of fix for her addiction that did no more than keep it alive. She knew she should go cold turkey, yet she also knew the flimsiest excuse to call him would prompt a craving she couldn't resist, whatever it might cost her.

CHAPTER FOUR

Marjory Fleming set her mobile into the hands-free slot before she set off home to Mains of Craigie. She didn't always remember but today she was anticipating a phone call – had hoped for it sooner, in fact, and she kept glancing at the phone as she drove as if by the power of the human will she could not only force it to ring but make it say what she wanted to hear when it did.

When at last it obliged, she answered it instantly. 'Cammie?'

'They've picked me. I'm to be in the team on Saturday, Mum.' His voice, securely bass for years now, was so high with excitement that he sounded suddenly thirteen again.

'Oh darling, that's fantastic! Well done! What—'

'Can't talk now. Speak later.'

As she drove on, Marjory couldn't stop beaming. The Scotland under-20 team! Playing for his country had been Cameron's dream since he learnt there was a game called rugby and a national side, aged about three; the baby present his father had brought Cammie in the maternity ward had been a miniature rugby ball, not a teddy. Bill would be – she didn't want to say 'over the moon', but somehow it was the only phrase that covered it. He'd been no mean player in his own day and she knew that it had cost him to turn his back on the game for the sake of the farm and the family, but then Bill would never have sacrificed anyone else for his own ambitions. She wished she could say the same for herself – though not so much, she had to admit, that she'd do something about it.

She knew Bill would be putting a bottle of champagne in the fridge even now, but Cammie was staying with friends in Edinburgh tonight so perhaps it had better wait till he got back. There was something faintly sad about a celebration that involved only two people and more than a couple of glasses of champagne always gave Bill indigestion anyway.

No doubt Cammie would be away a lot more now. Hoping for just this, he'd taken a gap year doing farm work before going to agricultural college. Mercifully the veggie phase had passed as the charms of Zoë of the soft brown eyes had faded.

The Darby-and-Joan life lay just ahead of them. Catriona was back in Glasgow studying social work, her planned career as a vet abandoned. Cat seemed very busy with her life up there and with the evening bar job she'd taken on to help pay the bills; they didn't see much of her.

Marjory tried not to see it as an estrangement, though her conversation with Cat about her choice of a new career had given her the sinking feeling that at least part of its attraction was to be able to take the side of criminal clients against the wicked police. Bill with his usual calm good sense had told her she was being paranoid: she might be, but it didn't mean her daughter wasn't gunning for her.

She wasn't going to let thoughts like that cloud her happiness for Cammie today. Her eyes misted a little as she thought how quickly the funny, affectionate little boy had become this six foot five giant, broad with it, who towered over his tall mother and made even Bill, a very respectable six foot one, look puny.

That was Mains of Craigie now. As she went up the drive she could see that Bill had draped the blue-and-white saltire usually pinned to Cammie's wall out of his bedroom window, and as she got out of the car sheep scattered in the near field as 'Flower of Scotland' blasted out at ear-splitting level.

She'd chosen the Glendale bed and breakfast in Kirkluce for its cheapness not its decor but even so the dingy wallpaper and the random vases of dusty plastic flowers had a lowering effect on Marnie Bruce when she returned chilled from sitting in a bus in her damp clothes. Passing cars had proved unsympathetic and she was footsore as well after the long walk until the bus appeared.

The dismal room with its beige tufted bedspread and brown carpet was cold. The two small electric bars set into the blocked-up fireplace weren't promising but she switched them both on and held her hands out to the grudging glow, shivering. She picked up the one thin towel that was provided and vigorously rubbed her hair, then realised that had made it so damp that she'd have to dry it before she went for the bath she craved. She spread it over a chair and set it in front of the fire while she unpacked her bag.

She'd wanted to stay in Kirkluce because she'd thought she would be going to and fro to the Galloway Police headquarters. Now she wasn't so sure. Maybe the policewoman who had talked to her had just been professionally cautious but she had a nasty feeling that she was going to be choked off without any answers at all.

Her trip out to Clatteringshaws had been completely pointless too – in fact this whole thing was starting to seem a really dumb idea. She could have stayed in London where you never had to walk miles in the rain without shelter, and she could have spent the week's holiday she'd taken from her job looking for somewhere cheap to live near her work. That reminded her of her lovely flat and Gary and misery lapped round her again.

Was there any sense in this attempt to find out what had happened to her mother, after all these years? It wasn't as if she had golden memories of her childhood; the scenes that repeated in her head mainly showed rows or neglect, but if the person who had left her for dead had gone on to kill, her mother deserved justice. And even if she wasn't the perfect mum, the word had a sort of glow about it, as if it could warm the cold loneliness in her heart.

Anyway, she couldn't bear *not knowing*. She who remembered everything, even things she would much have preferred to forget, had nothing but an echoing silence when it came to the most significant event of her life. She had to find out what lay on the other side of that silence.

A long-submerged anger was driving her now too. The authorities should be held to account for rubbing out this section of her childhood so ruthlessly that all these years she had obligingly blanked it out of her own mind. The memories were back now, though, crowding everything else out, demanding her attention.

They would no doubt prefer her to give up and go back to London with her questions unanswered, so she wouldn't. She had a stubborn streak and she wasn't going to be pushed around. If she didn't hear back from them in the next couple of days, she would camp on the doorstep until Inspector Fleming would see her.

But what was she going to do meantime? The landlady had already made it clear to Marnie that she couldn't expect to stay in her room all day.

She was still considering it as she lay in her bath. The tub had brownish stains under the hot tap and the water wasn't as deep as she would have liked, since the hot started running out when it was only half-full, but at least it was warming her up.

Her visit to the broch had reminded her of Gemma, her only real school friend. Was she still around? The Morrisons had lived in Newton Stewart so it shouldn't be too difficult to find them. Gemma was unlikely to know what had happened after Marnie disappeared but her parents might remember, and making contact with them would give her something to do tomorrow.

The only other person she remembered was her mother's friend Anita. She had visited quite often; she and Karen would talk for hours in the sitting room with the door shut, drinking and smoking. Interruptions from Marnie weren't welcomed.

She looks at her watch. It's eight o'clock and she's starving. There's sausages in the fridge but if Mum didn't plan to have them tonight she'll be in trouble.

It's not fair. She's got a right to her supper. She's feeling cross now and she flings open the sitting-room door and hears her mother saying, 'And then he just—'

She breaks off. She's been crying but now she turns angry. 'What the hell do you want?'

There's an empty bottle of wine on the table and another one half-full and the air's thick and smoky. Anita has turned to look at her too. She's slim and small and very smart in a cream trouser suit, with long blonde hair and bright-red fingernails and beside her Mum looks sort of faded with her jet-black hair and grey tracky bottoms and black sweatshirt.

She swallows. 'When's supper?'

'For God's sake, you're ten! You're old enough to get something for yourself.'

Anita smiles at her but doesn't speak. Anita often does that but she hasn't worked out whether it means anything.

'Can I have sausages?' she says.

'You can have champagne and caviar, as far as I'm concerned.' Mum gives a sort of nasty laugh. 'If you can find any.'

It's a stupid thing to say. They never have anything like that. Probably it means she can have the sausages, though, and she retreats.

Anita gives her another smile as she goes. Before she closes the door she hears her saying, 'I should be getting back to Dunmore, anyway.'

That was really all she knew about Anita. She didn't know her surname and she'd never been to her house and she didn't know where Dunmore was. Even if she did, she could hardly go to a strange place and wander round asking for Anita.

It wasn't a common name, though. She'd nothing to lose by trying to find her mother's best and indeed only friend as far as Marnie knew.

The bath water was no more than tepid now, and though she turned on the hot tap again hopefully only a trickle of hot came out and then went cold again. She got out of the bath and rubbed herself as dry as the inadequate towel would allow. At least, though, she had a plan for tomorrow and she went back to her room feeling a little more purposeful.

DC Hepburn had only just come on shift when the summons to DI Fleming's office came, and she had barely entered the room before Fleming, waving her to a chair, demanded, 'Well? What does Marnie Bruce want?'

Hepburn sat down with severe misgivings. Fleming was clearly on edge about this and she wasn't going to like what Hepburn had to tell her. It was just her luck that MacNee was off today; normally she would have filtered it through him. Taking the flak direct from Big Marge was definitely above her pay grade.

She began cautiously. 'I have to say first that she seems

a bit flaky. It's hard to put a finger on it but she often seems distracted when she's talking to you and if she's reporting on something that happened it's – well, it just seems too detailed.'

Fleming raised her eyebrows. 'What do you mean?'

'I'm struggling to explain. It's almost as if she's describing something she's looking at – sometimes she even uses the present tense.'

'Mmm.' Fleming considered that. 'Anyway, what's the general drift?'

Hepburn gave a nervous cough. 'What she *says* is that she was taken into care when she was eleven after her mother disappeared and she wants to know what happened to her mother, whether she's alive or dead and whether she chose to vanish or – or somebody killed her. And, er, why she never heard about any inquiry.'

'I see.'

Judging by the grim expression on Fleming's face, what she was seeing didn't please her one little bit.

Hepburn hurried on, 'I'm sure there would have been and it's just that perhaps being a child she wouldn't have heard about it or she doesn't remember, or something.'

That was Fleming's cue to say, 'Oh yes, of course there was.' She didn't say it. There was just an awkward silence, and feeling required to fill it Hepburn blundered on.

'Were you involved in it, ma'am? Marnie had a very clear recollection of you. You had a ponytail at the time, she said.'

Fleming flickered a smile. 'More like a shaving brush, really. That was to go under my hat. I was just a PC at the time, so no, I wasn't really involved.'

Hepburn was sure that was the truth – apart from anything else, it squared with what Marnie had said – but she was equally sure that it wasn't the whole truth, or anything near. She was beginning to feel very uncomfortable.

'Did you get any impression of what she is expecting?' Fleming asked.

'Not really. Just – well, some answers, I suppose.'

'What was her attitude – cooperative or aggressive?'

Hepburn hesitated. 'I'm not sure. Tense, certainly. And she seemed very determined not to be fobbed off.'

'Right.' Fleming thought for a moment. 'OK, Louise. Have you written up your report?'

'Yes. I can forward it to you immediately, if you want.'

'Fine. Is there anything else came out of the interview that you want to tell me?'

Hepburn thought for a moment then shook her head. 'I said I'd get back to her once I'd spoken to you, ma'am.'

'There's no need for that,' Fleming said quickly. 'Have you got a mobile number for her? Good. Leave it with me – I'll contact her myself. Thanks, Louise.'

Hepburn recognised dismissal. As she walked back down the stairs she was feeling – yes, shocked. The words 'cover-up' were beating insistently in her head.

There was no Morrison at the Newton Stewart address Marnie remembered when she leafed through the local telephone directory her landlady grudgingly produced for her. That was a blow; it was the only definite contact she had.

She could go to Newton Stewart, find the house and see if the new owners knew where the Morrisons had gone,

81

but that meant bus journeys and her experience with the unhelpful woman at Clatteringshaws wasn't encouraging.

She ran her eye down the list of Morrisons. What had Gemma's father been called? Obligingly, the scene popped into her head.

'Michael! Where are you?' Gemma's mum is saying as she comes into the sitting room where they're watching TV. 'Oh, hello, Marnie – you again! I didn't know you were here.'

It isn't said nastily – Gemma's mum's lovely, the sort of mum she wishes hers was – but she sort of curls up inside. Gemma never comes out to Clatteringshaws unless Mum isn't there.

Gemma's mum goes out again. 'Michael!' she calls. They go back to watching Grange Hill. Tucker's in trouble again.

Michael, Michael. She pushed the scene away and went back to the directory. There are quite a lot of M. Morrisons but only two Michaels, one in Wigtown and one strangely enough in Dunmore, the place she associated with Anita.

That was a sign. She could find the information centre in town and ask where Dunmore was and how she could get to it.

The landlady was making pointed clattering noises with a hoover outside her door, obviously trying to dislodge her from her room. Marnie grabbed her tote bag and went out. It was chilly with a brisk wind blowing but at least the sun was shining and the air was so clear and fresh she felt an exhilaration that was close to optimism. This could be the day when she started getting answers.

* * *

82

There was no alternative, and she couldn't put it off any longer. Bracing herself, Fleming went downstairs and tapped on Rowley's door, cherishing the childish hope that she wouldn't be in – as if that would solve anything.

When there was, indeed, no answer, she realised how foolish that hope had been. It only gave her longer to agonise over what lay ahead.

Shelley Crichton's eyes were still red this morning and her head was aching, a hangover from two days of immersive grief. She always felt like this after Halloween: drained and depressed as if it had all happened yesterday and not forty years before. Indeed, it seemed to get worse as she got older, not better.

If Grant was more sensitive, she wouldn't make that punishing phone call every year. She didn't hate him or anything, but after he remarried he seemed able just to put it all behind him as if he didn't want his shiny new life with a shiny new wife to be cluttered up with reminders, not just of her, but of Tommy too. It felt as if he wanted to wipe out the memory that was all that was left now of his son.

He swore he didn't, of course. She knew how angry that accusation made him, so she took care to claim that he'd forgotten, that he no longer cared about Tommy being killed – murdered, though even saying the word made her throat close, her eyes fill.

If he cared, she always said, he'd come with her on her pilgrimage today, the pilgrimage she always made on the morning they'd found Tommy after a whole day of agonised searching for him. Grant had resisted right from the start. Morbid, unhealthy, he'd called it, and her unflinching determination had been yet another nail in the coffin for a marriage that had been dead on its feet even before Tommy was killed. By the time Grant moved out, Shelley had long stopped caring.

All she wanted from him now was recognition for the child they had shared. She might not be his wife any more, but she was still his son's mother and Grant's refusal to engage with her remembrance always made her feel vindictive. She knew her Halloween call always upset him, and Shelley relished her power to make him suffer, at least once a year. It was the only time he couldn't make excuses not to speak to her.

Even thinking about it made her headache worse. She swallowed a couple of paracetamols then went downstairs, made herself a cup of strong black coffee and took it to the chair beside the phone.

The voice that answered her call was cheerful, buoyant. 'Hello!'

'Janette? It's Shelley here.'

Janette's voice flattened. 'Oh, hello Shelley. I was wondering if you would phone.'

Shelley bridled a little. 'Of course! You know what day it is, don't you?'

'Yes. Are you going to the park?'

'Naturally.' She was starting to feel annoyed; Janette was her best, her oldest friend. Janette, above all, should remember.

'Do you think you should go on doing this? It doesn't

do you any good, Shelley. You're depressed for weeks afterwards. Why not give it a miss this year, and see how you feel?'

'*This* year? When it was forty years ago today we found him?' Shelley couldn't believe Janette was so insensitive.

There was a silence at the other end of the phone, then, 'Oh. Sorry. I hadn't realised.'

'Yes, forty years. And *I* remember, even if everyone else has forgotten. It's still as real to me as it was the day it happened. But I won't bother you. I'll just make my pilgrimage myself.' The tears were starting again.

'Oh Shelley, don't be silly. If you want to go, I'll come with you, of course I will. I always have. He was my godson too, remember?'

She could tell that Janette was welling up, and softened. She was the friend who had searched all day, the friend who had made the dreadful discovery of Tommy's pathetic, battered little body in the pirate outfit he'd been wearing for Halloween, the friend who had broken the news, then sat with Shelley through the terrible days and even worse nights. All these years later Shelley couldn't expect her, with her own children and grandchildren round about her, to understand that it still felt like yesterday when all you had was memories.

'Thanks, Janette. I'll come to the house then, shall I? I'll be round in half an hour.'

Janette Ritchie put down the phone with a grimace. Shelley Crichton's visit on the anniversary of the day Tommy was found was a fixture in her calendar but someone from her

Pilates class in Stranraer was having a birthday lunch. She wouldn't be able to go now.

Forty years! Could it really be that long? Yes, of course it could. Her own Jennifer wasn't that far short of fifty and kept moaning about getting old. Poor wee Tommy hadn't had the chance to do that. She felt a pang of conscience that she hadn't remembered.

She should really phone round and get a few people together for Shelley's sake. To start with there had been quite a crowd at the site each year, feeling a sort of collective guilt that this could happen here, with their own bairns. As time passed, though, the crowd had dwindled and for years now it had only been Janette and Shelley, with any of the older locals who happened to pass the play park at the time looking uncomfortable and pretending not to notice.

There was even a sort of unspoken irritation about what it had done to the reputation of the village. 'Cradle of Evil', one of the newspapers had called it, and the name had stuck.

Maybe some bad things had gone on, unnoticed or perhaps just ignored, but till the tragedy Dunmore had mostly been a quiet, respectable, inward-looking community, minding its own business – perhaps too much so.

It certainly hadn't been the sort of place that featured in the media, except maybe a photo in the *Galloway Globe* when someone had raised money to present to a charity. What happened had put a strain on everyone, with the film crews fighting for space in the narrow streets and reporters pushing microphones under your nose and the flashes and machine-gun fire of cameras when all you were doing was going out to the shop. It had been horrible, frightening, really, and the resentment grew every time something prompted another media influx.

What if they turned up today, because of the anniversary? It wasn't very likely; the road from Glasgow to Dunmore was fortunately long and slow, but just in case, she'd have to make sure there wouldn't be a 'Cradle of Evil Village Forgets' story in some rag tomorrow.

Janette picked up the phone again. 'Sheila? Can you spare five minutes this morning?'

The address for the Michael Morrison who lived in Dunmore was a very smart-looking farmhouse surrounded by fields. It was on a slope above the village looking out across Loch Ryan towards the Cairnryan ferry terminal.

As Marnie walked up the steep rise towards it, she could see that the farmhouse wasn't attached to a working farm; the only building beside it was a large garage. The small, ugly, modern box a couple of fields over, with a huddle of dilapidated sheds and a barn beside it, was presumably where the farmer lived now.

She was prepared for disappointment and another wasted day, but when she walked up the long drive and rang the bell it was, to her surprise, Gemma herself who appeared. She'd have recognised her anywhere, though her mousy fair hair was blonde now and she'd grown up rather glamorous, with the sort of gleaming look that only a lot of money gives you. She had a toddler clamped to her hip, a rosy-cheeked little boy who gave the stranger a shy smile and then buried his face in his mother's neck.

'Gemma, I don't know if you remember me—' she began, but after a puzzled moment recognition had shown on Gemma's face.

'Oh my God! You're Marnie Bruce! I don't believe it! Goodness, you haven't changed a bit!'

Marnie was struggling with the flashbacks the sight of her friend had prompted. 'Well . . .' was all she managed, but it didn't matter. Gemma was talking enough for both of them.

'Don't just stand there – come on in! It's wonderful to see you. Where have you been all these years? You just disappeared so suddenly, and no one seemed to know where you'd gone. I made Mum drive me out to the house, you know, but it was all shut up. What happened?'

Without giving her time for a reply, she led her across the hall. A small, dark-haired woman – Asian, Marnie thought – appeared on the stairs behind her carrying a vacuum cleaner, but as Marnie looked up she shrank back into the shadows at the top as if she were startled, or even afraid.

Gemma opened a door into a huge farmhouse kitchen, all glossy surfaces and sparkling glass-fronted cupboards, and went to a flashy coffee machine, pressing buttons as she chattered on.

'This is Mikey, by the way – don't ask about his father. Fergus Napier was another one who did your trick of vanishing out of my life so I came back to stay with my parents – they've been wonderful. Mikey's spoilt to bits.'

Gemma ruffled the child's hair and then set him on his

feet. 'You go and play, sweetie, while I chat to Marnie.'

He eyed her fetching down a tin. 'I want a biscuit,' he demanded, in the tones of one setting out a negotiating position.

His mother smiled at Marnie. 'Doesn't take them long to work things out, does it? All right, Mikey, but just one or you'll spoil your lunch.'

Marnie was relieved when Gemma turned her back to fetch coffee mugs. She was afraid that the spasm of envy that was twisting her insides would leave its ugly mark on her face. Here was someone who had everything; she had nothing and just at the moment it felt as if Gemma had taken all the luck she'd never had.

With Mikey placated and settled in a corner of the room with a small mountain of brightly coloured toys, Gemma brought the coffee over and sat down at the table opposite Marnie.

'Well, that's my life story: finished school, worked in Dad's office, got married, screwed it up, came home with Mikey. What about yours? I bet it's a lot more exciting. You were much the most interesting of my mates – it was really dull after you left.

'Oh, can you still do that crazy thing of remembering absolutely everything? It made you sort of a woman of mystery!' Gemma gave an easy laugh.

Marnie echoed her, but with difficulty. 'Yes,' she said, struggling to keep the two scenes straight in her head: Gemma, aged ten, the centre of a group of chattering girls while Marnie watched from the edge; Gemma now, looking at her with hopeful grey eyes, waiting for her life story.

She wasn't ready yet. 'When did you move away from Newton Stewart?' she asked.

Gemma frowned in thought. 'Can't have been long after you went. Dad's business was mainly in Stranraer and I suppose when this came on the market he just thought it would be better to be nearby. The construction business was doing well then, though of course, just now . . .' She shrugged.

'Anyway, what about you? Why did you leave so suddenly? You never said a word to me.'

'I didn't know myself,' Marnie said stiffly, but then, as if the hot coffee and the warmth of the room with the sun making patterns on the flagged floor had melted something, she began to talk.

Gemma listened in silence, only making the occasional sympathetic noise, and when at last Marnie finished said, 'That's awful,' with obvious sincerity. 'You poor thing! Look, my parents might know what happened afterwards. I'll ask them when they get back home and let you know. Where are you staying?'

It would be humiliating to have Gemma turn up at the squalid little bed and breakfast. 'I'll give you my mobile number,' Marnie said hastily.

'Fine. I'll be in touch. And promise you won't vanish again.'

They had reached the front door when Marnie remembered her other quest. 'I don't suppose you know someone called Anita who lives here in Dunmore, do you?'

'Anita Loudon?' Gemma asked. 'She's the only Anita I know.'

Surely it couldn't be as easy as that. 'The Anita who was

my mum's friend was blonde, quite attractive – at least, she was then.'

Gemma nodded. 'That's her. She's local – knows everyone. She works in my mum's dress shop, actually, but I think this is her day off so you might find her at home. The house is a semi-detached on Lennox Street. Can't remember the number but it's got a bright-red door.

'So you just go back along this road till you reach the one you came up on from the shore. You pass the play park and then it's the next road on the right – or is it the one after that? You'll see it, anyway.'

Marnie thanked her and set off. As she walked down the drive, she noticed the cleaning woman ahead of her on the road below, scurrying as if she were late for something. She wasn't heading towards the town; she must live at the farm next door, that was the only other building in sight – unless she was planning on a long walk. Marnie thought idly.

She was still feeling a little dazed that today everything had fallen into place so neatly. It was encouraging, even if she still hadn't heard from the police.

Janette stood in respectful silence along with three other women as Shelley, mopping her eyes, walked round the little play park. She hated coming here like this, though it had been just a small rough field when, in that frantic hunt after Tommy had gone missing, she had caught a glimpse of something pale against the darker grass over at the farther edge. Where his body had lain, a slide stood now along with a climbing frame, swings and a see-saw – Tommy's memorial.

They waited awkwardly by the gate. Shelley's act of remembrance seemed to take longer each year, as if she was making the point that her grief only grew as time passed. At last she got up, kissed the bouquet of white roses she had brought and laid them on a bench that had a discreet memorial plaque.

Shelley came back towards them. She was stooped today like an old woman, and with a foolish sense of shock, Janette realised that was just what she was. They all were, this group of friends, though Janette liked to think she looked younger than her years. She certainly hadn't been aged by sorrow as Shelley had, and superstitiously she touched the wood of the fence as she opened the gate for her friend. They all filed through behind her.

Shelley's sudden scream took her totally by surprise. She spun round.

A slight, fair-haired young woman was walking towards them – no, it wasn't fair hair. It was reddish-gold, and she had vivid light-blue eyes. Janette felt her own flesh crawl.

'Don't come near me!' Shelley was screaming. 'Don't touch me! Vile, vile! Get back to hell where you belong! Get away, get away!'

Shocked, Marnie gaped at the woman who had accosted her, yelling hate. She was old, but tall and strong-looking with rather wild grey hair and her face was blotchy as if she had been crying. As she stood transfixed, the woman lurched threateningly towards her, her hands like claws reaching for Marnie's face.

There was a group of women with her and one of them

grabbed her, restraining her as Marnie dodged back with a scream of fright.

'I'm sorry, I'm sorry,' this woman called. 'Shelley, stop it! It's all right!'

'Shelley' was mad, obviously. 'She shouldn't be allowed out, your friend,' Marnie said fiercely as her terror subsided into anger and her racing heart slowed. 'She could give someone a coronary, doing that.'

'Yes, I know, I'm sorry. She's not usually like that. It's just . . .' The apology trailed away.

Her friend, her arms still imprisoned, burst into hysterical sobs. 'But it's her, it's her!'

'No, it isn't. It can't be, Shelley. Just think – it can't possibly be.'

Marnie felt a cold shiver run down her back. All right, so this was a crazy woman. But it didn't explain why the others were staring too and her friend, who seemed sane enough, was looking at Marnie with eyes that were wide with shock in an ashen face.

And when she found the house where Anita Loudon lived, in the road that looked out over the play park, there it was again: that same look of horror and dismay as Anita opened the door.

CHAPTER FIVE

For the third time, DI Fleming read through the report of the Marnie Bruce interview. As Hepburn had said, the account she had given was very detailed and, at least to Fleming's more imperfect recollection, factually accurate – uncannily so, in reference to her own occasional visits to Marnie's mother. She had completely forgotten that ill-judged orange and olive-green sweater she had apparently been wearing.

Where on earth did you go from here? Fleming turned to the thick buff file on the desk beside her and flipped through the yellowing transcripts. She checked that there was a marker at the relevant injunctions and in one or two other salient places, then closed it again.

It was still dusty. She took out a wipe and cleaned it up; Rowley wouldn't appreciate getting her hands dirty, either physically or metaphorically. Fleming hadn't been able to settle to anything today as she waited for the superintendent's return from a meeting in Stranraer, apparently, and she'd asked to be told when she got back.

This wouldn't do! She'd a load of stuff she needed to shift and she wanted to get away promptly tonight for Cammie's celebration. Cat was coming down from Glasgow specially and she'd said she'd meet her train at Dumfries just after six, so not being there waiting would be another big black mark. With that threat hanging over her, Fleming selected a pile of requests for authorisation that could be done on autopilot and powered her way through them.

When the summons eventually came, she gathered up her papers and hurried downstairs with a sinking feeling in her stomach. Over the top!

'Come . . . come in,' Anita Loudon managed. As she stared at her unwelcome guest she was struggling with a sense of unreality.

She had thought for a crazy moment when she saw her standing on the front doorstep that her visitor really was Kirstie returned – not the woman who called herself Karen, the woman she had known twenty years ago, with dyed black hair and eyes muddied with coloured contact lenses, but the girl with the red-gold hair and bright-blue eyes.

It was Marnie, of course, Marnie – the child whose memory had haunted her dreams and her three o'clock wakings, with 'Guilt! Guilt! Guilt!' tolling in her head like a great bell. Anita had forgotten how unnervingly like her mother as a girl she had always been.

As the young woman followed her into the house she heard herself babbling, 'My, this is a surprise! How nice to see you. Goodness, how long is it? In here – now do sit down. It's so lucky you found me in – I'm usually working, but this is my day off.'

Marnie didn't sit down. As Anita fluttered round her, she turned to face her squarely. She too was looking shocked, and rigid with tension.

'What's wrong with me?' she demanded. 'Why is everyone looking at me as if I'm some sort of monster?'

Dear God, where did you start with that one? And – everyone? Anita drew a deep breath.

'Marnie, I'm sorry – so rude, to have stared at you like that. It just took me a moment to place you and then it was such a surprise to see you after all these years.'

She saw Marnie open her mouth to speak and deliberately turned away, saying, 'Now, I'm sure you need a coffee. It's quite cold out there, but at least it's not raining today. You just sit down. I won't be a moment.'

She whisked out of the room. Don't panic, she told herself, don't panic. The crushing sense of her own sin threatened to overwhelm her and even before she switched on the kettle, she flung open the back door and slowly inhaled the cool, damp air. She needed all her wits about her.

Marnie wasn't just making a nostalgic visit to the place where she had spent a part of her childhood. She'd come looking for answers and Anita had to think up some to give her in the time it took for a kettle to boil.

And 'everyone'? Who was it who had seen her and thought the same as Anita had?

* * *

Marnie was quite glad to do as she was told and sit down. Her legs still felt shaky after her encounter with the coven down the road. She had felt their eyes on her as she hurried away and came along to the house here. What was it with this place?

And Anita – the Anita Marnie remembered had been petite and slim and had seemed glamorous, at least to her as a child, but she wasn't that any more. Her nails were still manicured and her hair was still long and blonde but it was thinning and meagre now and she was just a thin, worn-looking middle-aged woman trying to seem younger by keeping the look she'd had twenty years before.

No matter what Anita said, when she opened the door she hadn't been surprised, she'd been horrified just like the women in the village. She'd wriggled out of it by going to make the coffee but when she came back Marnie was going to force her to tell her why, however reluctant she might be.

Was she sure she really wanted to know, though? The scene flickered into her mind again.

She's just walking past the play park, trying to read the street name on the board at the end of the next road. There's a group of women coming out of the park and then there's this weird one who suddenly tries to attack her and she's yelling, 'Don't come near me! Don't touch me! Vile, vile! Get back to hell where you belong! Get away, get away!'

Feeling sick and frightened, Marnie buried her face in her hands. What nightmare was this that she had stumbled into?

She didn't have to stay. She could get up right now, walk out of the house, before Anita returned. She could – but then she would never know what this was about and it would drive her crazy. The ache of curiosity was part of her reason for coming back in the first place.

So she was stuck here in this dreary little room, the sort of room Marnie hated. It was old-fashioned, with too much fussy furniture with barley-sugar legs and elaborate machine-carving and every surface was cluttered with knick-knacks: little vases, bowls, china ornaments and photographs – lots of photographs. She imagined taking a big black plastic bag and sweeping the surfaces blessedly clear.

The coffee was taking a long time. She got up restlessly and went across to look at the framed photos grouped on the top of a bow-legged bureau. There was one where Anita had obviously posed for the camera, with her dark eyes looking flirtatiously from under long eyelashes, her blonde hair thick and full, just the way Marnie remembered her. Most of the others were just snaps: there was one of an elderly couple but most were of Anita – Anita laughing in a group of friends, Anita raising a glass at a party, Anita in a paper hat pulling a funny face.

Not very interesting. Marnie was just turning away when her eye caught one right at the back. A photograph of a man.

He was striking-looking, rather than handsome, with very dark hair and eyes and flaring eyebrows marking a narrow face. He was giving a quizzical smile and there was something about his expression that drew you in, making you want to share his amusement.

She couldn't move. She stood, stiff and still, as the images began to whirl in her head, crazy clips and sequences – too many, too many! Then one pushed the others aside and started running.

It's a sunny day, the day after her birthday and she's feeling proud of being a big girl of five. It's hot inside and she's out on the walkway that runs past the front doors of all the flats in the block.

Mum's inside with him. They're shouting at each other so it's better being out here even though she doesn't like the sour smell from people peeing on the stairs. She's left her birthday present doll inside because if the boy next door comes out and sees her playing with it he'll have it off her. So she's bored, and she's hanging over the wall to see what's happening in the car park five floors below.

Not a lot, really, just someone shouting at a big dog that's chasing a little one. She's watching to see if it'll catch it when he comes out of the flat behind her. She turns, warily.

If he's in a good mood he's OK but she's always a bit scared of him. She's had the back of his hand a few times and if he's been fighting with Mum he's bound to be in a bad mood. He's scowling, anyway.

Then he sees her, and suddenly he's smiling. 'Hi, Marnie. What are you doing?'

She feels uncomfortable when he smiles like that. It's not his nice smile, the one that means he's happy and everything's going to be fun.

'Nothing,' she mutters.

He joins her. 'Boring, isn't it? What are we going to

do to cheer things up? I know – why not practise wall-walking?'

She's puzzled. 'Where?'

'Here.' He pats the top of the wall she'd been looking over. It's not very wide, just wide enough for your foot, if you were daft enough to put it there.

She says, 'I'm not allowed to.'

'Oh, of course not – if you were by yourself. That would be dangerous, but I'm here to see you're all right. Come on, it'll be fun. I'll lift you up.'

He's coming towards her, holding out his arms. She hangs back. 'I don't want to.'

He stoops over her and his face is dark again. 'Not scared, are you – a big five-year-old like you behaving like a baby?'

It isn't nice to be called a baby. 'I'm not scared,' she says, and then he's smiling again.

'That's my girl.' And he's picked her up and she's suddenly standing on the ledge and there's a drop on the other side all the way down into the car park. She's not scared, she's terrified, and she's shaking and clinging to the upright.

'Come on, now,' he says, and there's that nasty edge to his voice. 'I want to see you're not a coward, Marnie. I wouldn't like that.'

She takes a step, and another wobbly step. She mustn't look down, away, away down to the car park below. She mustn't – but somehow she has to, just a quick glance. She's feeling dizzy, shaky, as if it's sort of pulling her—

There's a sudden scream. She screams herself, and her balance goes. She's falling!

Somehow she manages to throw herself inwards and not down, down. She lands hard on the concrete, though, grazing her knees and her elbows and her hands and she's wailing.

'What the hell do you think you're doing?' Mum is screaming at him. 'She could have been killed!'

He's shrugging, walking back into the flat already. 'Of course she couldn't. She wanted to try and it was safe enough. I was ready to catch her.'

He wasn't, though. She knows he wasn't. And everything hurts. 'Mum!' she sobs.

Mum looks down at her and sighs. 'Oh, for God's sake. What on earth made you do that? Now I suppose I'll have to clean you up – come on.'

The door opening behind her brought Marnie back with a start.

'Sorry to take so long,' Anita said cheerfully. 'I think I need a new electric kettle. Now tell me, how is your mum these days?'

Marnie picked up the photograph, and turned. 'Who is this?' she demanded and saw Anita's face slowly turn a deep, dark crimson.

'I may be called down to London for the security meetings at MI5, of course,' Detective Superintendent Rowley said. Her rather sallow skin was a little flushed with the excitement of it all, and she put up her hand to her dark bob in a grooming movement as if to be ready for the summons if it came at this very moment.

'They're extremely concerned about illegal immigration,

and of course the upsurge in Irish Republican activity too. I hadn't quite realised how much of a front line we had up here, on the border with Ireland – a large and important entry point into the UK. The Cairnryan Special Branch have their work cut out, Marjory. I've assured them that any help they needed would automatically be given top priority.'

'Of course,' Fleming said gravely. The lads down at Cairnryan had obviously played a blinder. She could almost hear Hyacinth purring; it seemed a shame to have to spoil her fun.

But now Rowley was saying, 'Anyway, what was it you wanted to see me about? I hope it's not going to take too long – I'm due to lunch with the chief constable at one.'

She had been so busy talking that she hadn't noticed the bulky file Fleming had brought, and when the inspector put it on her desk, she gaped. 'What on earth is that? Oh really, I can't think there's time just now to discuss something like this.' She looked at her watch impatiently.

Fleming stood firm. 'I'm afraid it can't wait, ma'am.'

Rowley's lips tightened. With a bad grace and another pointed look at her watch, she said, 'Very well. What's the problem this time?'

Controlling her irritation, Fleming said, 'Do you remember the Dunmore murder case?'

'Well, not vividly, I have to say. But of course it comes up every time there's a child-on-child killing anywhere – the 'Cradle of Evil' village.'

'It was forty years ago.'

'That explains it, then. At the age of one I was perhaps

102

not quite as au fait with the big news stories as I should have been.'

The sarcastic, patronising tone grated on Fleming like a knife scraped sideways on a plate. 'I don't remember it either, obviously. But about twenty years ago when I was a rookie Kirstie Burnside, who killed Tommy Crichton, came to live on this patch. She was calling herself Karen Bruce by then.'

'Surely she shouldn't have been allowed to return to the area?'

'It's actually more than an hour away – she was living up by Clatteringshaws Loch. But yes, you would have thought it was a mistake.' Fleming opened the file at one of the marked places. 'Here, though, you can see that it was questioned and they found there wasn't anything forbidding it. And she seems to have been very determined – threatened to create all sorts of mayhem if they tried to remove her. And here, you see,' she flipped to another marker, 'there really is an injunction to say that nothing must be done which could in any way threaten to reveal the new identity she'd been given. So our hands were tied.'

Rowley barely glanced at the papers. 'So? Look, Marjory, this was all a very long time ago. If there's an immediate point—'

Fleming hurried on. 'I was detailed to visit her from time to time, just routine, never any problem. She'd been taught bookkeeping in prison and somehow or other she'd got a job in some office in Newton Stewart. There was a child, Marnie. She was a ward of court but the assessment was that Karen was a "good enough" mother and there was no real reason to take her away. When she was about ten or eleven she was found in their cottage with a head injury and her mother gone.'

'She'd attacked her own *daughter*?'

'No one could ever prove it. Marnie had concussion and didn't know what had happened, but there was no sign at all of a disturbance inside the house, nothing in the immediate area and the car was found later at Dumfries station. She'd just disappeared and the child was taken into care.'

Rowley pursed her lips. 'With her record, you'd have to assume she'd just lost her temper again. So what was the follow-up?'

This was the hard part. 'I was a PC at the time so of course I have no idea of the discussions that went on. But Superintendent McNally told me he was hamstrung by the identity injunction and since the child had recovered after a night in hospital he didn't want to start a witch-hunt.'

The superintendent was looking sceptical.

'Yes, I know,' Fleming said. 'The thought of another rerun of the whole Cradle-of-Evil thing was probably part of it. She was released on lifelong licence, of course, so presumably he informed the appropriate authorities that she'd broken her parole but they'd be reluctant to admit that they'd somehow lost one of the most notorious killers in Britain.'

'I can see that. Realpolitik, Marjory – sometimes it's impossible to do things by the book. So – has she turned up again?'

'That wouldn't be so much of a problem – she wouldn't

want to draw attention to herself. No, I'm afraid it's worse than that. Her daughter Marnie has turned up demanding to know what steps were taken to find her mother and why she was told nothing at all after she was taken into care. I haven't spoken to her myself, but I gather Marnie thinks her mother was murdered.'

Rowley groaned. 'Causing trouble?'

'Certainly wanting answers.'

'So we give them to her – why not? If she doesn't know who her mother really is it may come as a shock but—'

Fleming was shaking her head. She tapped the file in front of them. 'We can't, not until we can get legal permission for an exemption from the injunction.'

'That could take weeks!'

'Yes. And meantime, if we aren't in a position to give Marnie the information she wants, is she just going to go away quietly or is she going to decide we're covering up and contact the press?'

'An immediate injunction to stop her,' Rowley suggested. 'That would be quick enough.'

'A gagging order?' Fleming said doubtfully. 'The press tend to get very interested in those.'

Rowley obviously realised she was right. 'Well, what do you suggest?' she snapped. 'You were in at the start of this – I wasn't.'

Even though she had known perfectly well what the bottom line would be, Fleming still felt aggrieved. If she'd been in charge, instead of being a humble PC, she'd have – well, what would she have done then? She didn't know, and certainly she didn't know now.

'All I can suggest is that I talk to her, give her as many facts as I legitimately can and try to persuade her that we did our best at the time and thought it wasn't in her interests to start a public hunt.'

'I suppose so.' Rowley didn't sound impressed, but she was looking at her watch again. 'I've got to go – I'm late already.

'Do try to keep all this under wraps, Marjory. It's really very tedious.'

As she swept out, Fleming pulled a childish face at her retreating back.

Shelley Crichton was sitting on the sofa in Janette's front room, still hiccuping a little as she sipped at a glass of cooking brandy. Two of the other women had come back with her and were drinking white wine, being less in need of such robust stimulus

Lorna Baxter was well into her second glass. She was a big, bulky woman who always had high colour and now her cheeks were red as poppies with the combination of alcohol and outrage. 'It's disgusting, coming like that to gloat. That Kirstie must have sent her to report back – that's what it would be! She knows there'd be a lynching if she turned up herself.'

Janette frowned her down. Lorna wasn't a friend of hers – 'coarse', was her private opinion, and the family, from the social housing at the bottom of the hill, weren't what up here on the hill you called 'respectable'. She was a good ten years younger than the rest of them but she'd been part of the vigilante group that had driven Kirstie

Burnside's dysfunctional family out of Dunmore after the trial and ended up in court herself. Perhaps it had been a mistake to ask her to join them at the park, but almost everyone was out at work or busy and Janette had wanted Shelley to feel supported.

'I'm sure that's absolute nonsense,' she said repressively, but Shelley ignored her, sitting up eagerly.

'Do you think so? Do you think that's what it was? How could anyone be so cruel, so wicked?'

Janette exchanged an anxious glance with Sheila who was a real friend, a nice, sensible woman, and she stepped in.

'Don't be daft, Lorna. You don't know that's even any relation of Kirstie's. It was just a lassie with reddish hair and blue eyes – there's plenty of them about. You'd have passed her in the street if it hadn't been the coincidence of her coming along just when we were all thinking about poor wee Tommy.'

Lorna bridled. 'Oh, you think so? I tell you, that girl was the very image of her mother as a bairn. She shouldn't be allowed to get away with it, that's what I think.'

Shelley's face was becoming flushed too and Janette was starting to regret that she hadn't been more careful about the amount of brandy she'd tipped into the glass.

'She went into Anita Loudon's house.' Her voice was shrill. 'You can't deny that Anita knew Kirstie at the time it happened—'

'Of course she did,' Janette said, a little desperately. 'Everyone went to that wee school. It doesn't prove anything.'

She knew she was struggling, though. Right enough, it would be quite a coincidence for a complete stranger who was a lookalike for Kirstie Burnside to drop in on one of her best friends, but it would do Shelley no good at all to believe that a malevolent Kirstie was still somewhere in the picture, mocking her grief. What could she do about it anyway, except put herself through another nightmare frenzy of publicity? Oh, she certainly shouldn't have invited Lorna – troublemaking wasn't so much a hobby as her business in life, and now she was demonstrating that she was determined not to be deflected from it.

'That girl's needing to be told what we all think of her for what she's doing, and what everyone thinks of that murdering besom, her mother, as well. We were never given a chance to tell Kirstie that straight – she's been protected all her life, with her fine new identity that no one's allowed to know and all her "rights" – well, this is the result.

'She's needing stopped, and Anita too – what's she doing, getting involved in this? It was probably her told the girl Shelley'd be at the park.'

Shelley was clinging to the now empty glass. 'That's right, Lorna. That's what needs to happen.'

'You don't know that Anita was expecting her, or that she's Kirstie's daughter,' Janette argued, though without much hope. 'There may be cousins—'

'There aren't,' Lorna said triumphantly. 'There was just a brother, and he's gay – lives in Inverness with his partner.'

Shelley stood up. 'I'm not letting her get away with this. I'm going to look her straight in the face and find out what all this is about, if Kirstie put her up to this . . . this disgusting cruelty. And if Anita's been helping her to do it she's just as bad – worse in some ways, because she knows what we went through. When Grant hears about this—"

Grant Crichton's short fuse was legendary. 'Do you need to tell him?' Janette bleated. 'It'll only upset him.'

Shelley rounded on her. 'And why shouldn't he be upset? I'm upset. He ought to be told what that woman's still doing. And the police too . . .'

'That's right, Shelley.' Lorna set down her empty wine glass and came across to link arms with her. 'Don't you worry. I'll come with you and we'll give her laldie, eh?' She was almost smacking her thick lips.

With a glance at Sheila, Janette reluctantly got up. 'If the two of you are determined to go, we'll come with you. You need to be careful nowadays, you know. If you start in on someone it could be you in trouble with the police. You don't want to end up in court.'

She didn't say 'again' but the venomous look Lorna directed at her as she and Shelley went out of the door, still arm in arm, showed that the barb had gone home.

Anita set down the tray on the coffee table with exaggerated care, waiting for her burning cheeks to cool. She handed Marnie a mug saying casually, 'Oh him? Milk, sugar? Help yourself to biscuits.

'That's an old friend of mine. Haven't seen him in ages. Why? Does he look like someone you know?'

'Yes, he stayed with us quite often when I was little.'

'Oh, I don't think so, dear.' Her voice sounded hollow, even to herself. 'You were down in England then and he lives in Glasgow. I expect it's just a chance resemblance. You can't remember very clearly when you're small.'

'I remember everything.' Marnie stated it as a fact.

'Oh, I'm sure you have a very good memory.' Anita achieved a light laugh. 'But nobody actually remembers everything.'

'I do. I mean it. I have something called hyperthymesia.'

She'd never heard of it. Was it a case for 'I'm sorry' or 'Congratulations'? She raised her eyebrows.

'I told you – I remember everything,' Marnie repeated. 'That's what it is. It's a condition that means I have complete recall of everything that's ever happened to me.'

Anita stared at her. *Everything?* Surely that had to be nonsense. Please, that was nonsense. She couldn't possibly – but now she was proving that she could.

'Would you like me to tell you what you were wearing that time you and Mum took me shopping in Dumfries? You had on jeans and a pink mohair sweater. Your stilettos were cream-coloured with peep-toes and the varnish on your toenails was pink but your fingernails were red. You had a glass pendant with a rose sort of drawn on it.'

The etched crystal pendant was lying in a drawer upstairs. Her expression seemed to amuse Marnie; she gave a harsh laugh and said, 'I can view it like a film, you see. Want any more? You said to my mother, "That so-called sale was just cheap rubbish bought in—"'

'No, no, that's enough,' Anita said. She could feel the hairs rising on the back of her neck. If the child had remembered all that, what else might she have remembered?

Marnie wasn't a child any more, though, and the

110

disconcerting woman she had become was studying her with her mother's ice-blue eyes and a cool, measuring look that was all her own.

'So I remember the man in the photograph, right? Drax, my mother called him. I didn't call him anything. What's his name?'

Anita moistened her lips. 'Daniel Lee.' When was the last time she'd said that aloud?

'So why Drax?'

'Oh, it was just a stupid joke among us kids. He was allergic to garlic so we called him Dracula, Drax for short, and it stuck, somehow. Silly, really.' She gave a little, self-conscious laugh. 'He was just this guy your mum and I both knew from when we were at school, that's all. Nothing sinister. I'm sorry if I made some sort of mystery out of it – I just thought it wasn't likely you would have remembered him.'

That was better. She'd managed to sound calmer, more relaxed.

'Was he my father?'

That threw her again. 'H-how would I know?' she stammered. 'What did your mother tell you?' Then, with sudden inspiration, 'Why don't you ask her about it?'

Marnie's eyes widened. 'You mean – she's still alive? Where is she?'

'Don't you know?'

She saw the animation die out of Marnie's face. 'I never saw her again after I was injured that night at the cottage and was taken into care. I was hoping you might know what happened afterwards.'

Anita gave a little shrug. 'I didn't even know you'd had an accident, dear. All I know is that I tried to phone your mother and when I got no answer I went out to the cottage. There were police tapes around it and no one was there so I tried to find out what was going on, but the police wouldn't tell me anything.'

She spread her hands wide. 'I'm so sorry. It must have been very upsetting for you and I just wish I could be of more help.'

'I . . . see.'

Struggling with disappointment, Marnie looked much more vulnerable now, younger than her years and more like the child Anita remembered. Struggling not to wince at a piercing shaft of shame, she said, 'It's all a long time ago now, of course. It must have been very hard on you, but you've obviously made your own life. Where are you living now?'

Again, Marnie refused to be deflected. 'Maybe you can't tell me what happened then. You can tell me what's wrong here now, though. You know – I saw it in your face. Why did that woman try to attack me?'

How could she tell her? A truthful answer wouldn't put a stop to Marnie's questions, it would just open the way to a whole lot more.

'That's her coming up the path!' Marnie's voice was suddenly sharp with alarm as she stared over Anita's shoulder out of the window on the front of the house. 'She's got people with her . . .'

When Anita spun round to look she saw that Shelley Crichton was indeed coming up the path in a little group, preceded by Lorna Baxter, of all people. Even the way the woman was ringing the doorbell was aggressive.

'Oh dear,' Anita said faintly. 'I'd – I'd better go and speak to them.'

As she opened the door, she was swept aside by Lorna's impressive bulk. 'Where is she, then? We're wanting to talk to her. Shelley's got a few wee questions needing answers.'

But when Lorna burst into the sitting room there was no one there. Marnie might not have understood what this was all about, but she could recognise a lynching party when she saw one.

CHAPTER SIX

Marnie could hear violence in the raised voice at the front door as she crept past in the shadows of the hall, stifling a sob of fear. The kitchen door stood open and she went in, pushing it to behind her, then tiptoed across to a glass panel door leading into the garden. She turned the handle as delicately as she could, grimacing at the slight noise it made.

It resisted – locked! She was trapped, no escape – but as she glanced wildly about she saw a key hung up by the sink, a key with a flowered tag saying 'Garden'. She grabbed it and let herself out, closing the door as quietly as she could. To her left there was a path leading round the side of the house to the front, but she couldn't risk taking it. If Anita hadn't let the women into the house they would be standing at the front door where they would see her as she came round the corner of the house, and with her imagination running riot she could see them falling on her like a pack of wild beasts. . .

The back garden was small but there was a high, solid stone wall at the end of it, separating it from the property beyond. Marnie ran across the sodden, muddy square of grass and launched herself at it, thankful that she was wearing jeans and trainers. Stretching her arms she could reach the top and she levered herself up, her feet scrabbling against the stone. She had no idea what was on the other side of it but she threw herself over, landing awkwardly on the soft earth of a flower bed and staggering violently into a bush. Its thorns scratched her and tore at her clothes but she barely noticed.

This garden, and the house it belonged to, was bigger. Marnie glanced nervously at the windows overlooking it; the householder might not be pleased at his property being invaded like this and she didn't think she'd done the shrub any good either. The sooner she got out of here the better. There was a wicket gate which led past the side of the house leading to the front garden, offering an escape route, and she trotted off across the sweeping lawn towards it.

Then she heard a door opening and a second later, savage barking. A dog was racing across the garden, a small burly dog with the distinctive broad, blunt head of a Staffordshire bull terrier, and its muzzle was drawn back to expose pointed teeth.

With a scream of fright, Marnie sprinted towards the gate. She didn't try to open it, just flung herself across the top to land heavily on her hands and knees on the path beyond. The dog, snarling and snapping, was hurling itself at the wood in such a frenzy of excitement that the gate was bending under its onslaught. If it gave way, burst open—

But there was a shout, then a whistle. The dog stopped, turned and ran panting back to the house. Marnie could hear a man's mocking laughter.

Feeling sick with shock, she picked herself up and limped down the front path into the street beyond. What could she do now? Where could she go?

She could go back to the Morrisons – muddy, with a tear in her jeans and bleeding knees and hands. She could picture Gemma's sympathetic horror at what had happened to her as she admitted her to that immaculate kitchen and her immaculate life, cleaning her wounds with kindness and, yes, pity.

Marnie didn't want pity. Once you were pitiable, once you lost your pride, there was nothing left. All she could do was go back to the main road and wait for the next bus back to Kirkluce.

Then she stopped. If she retraced her steps, she'd have to pass the end of Anita Loudon's road and might walk straight into the coven on their way back, angry that she'd escaped them. She'd have to walk along this road in the other direction instead, hoping it would connect with another one that would lead her back down to the main street along the shore.

It was a circuitous walk, made worse by the constant fear of blundering into her persecutors, and the grazes on her knees were stiffening too by the time she reached the bus stop. She had to endure a nervous wait with her eyes constantly scanning the passers-by, terrified that one of them would react to her with another attack. When at last the bus came she almost threw herself into it; the driver gave her a strange look but didn't comment on her dishevelled appearance and Marnie collapsed onto a seat with a little groan.

Then it was pulling away and she was leaving Dunmore, on the way back, she could only hope, to some sort of normality. Along with the fear she still felt and the pain of her grazes, there was utter bewilderment. What kind of a place was it where complete strangers screamed abuse in your face and people set their dogs on you?

Fleming looked up in surprise when DS MacNee appeared in her office. 'Wasn't expecting to see you today. How are the lovebirds?'

He struck an attitude. 'The great romance is over! See Gloria – *Partly wi' love o'ercome sae sair, And partly she was drunk*? Well, turns out it was all the drink talking, no "partly" about it, and now she's changed her mind. She's dumped the old man, and Maggie's comforting him.'

Fleming, who was in no mood for having Burns declaimed at her, said sourly, 'Glad someone's happy. I've had to tell the super about the Marnie Bruce problem.'

MacNee sobered immediately. 'I'd kinna forgotten about that. Did Louise find out what she wanted?'

'Yes, and I really wish you'd been there to do it instead. Marnie Bruce was very blunt – said she wanted to know what happened to her mother and why there had been no real investigation when she disappeared. Louise was obviously shocked when I couldn't say that there had been,

117

naturally, so there's a problem now with her as well as Marnie.'

'We'll just have to tell her.'

Fleming shook her head. She tapped the bulky file still sitting on her desk. 'Injunction. The legend that was created for Kirstie Burnside can't be disclosed to anyone except officially recognised persons – that means us and superintendent level and above. We can't decide to give a random DC the information.'

'What about the daughter?'

'We're assuming that because she's digging it all up again she doesn't know her mother's history, which may not be true, of course. But, if so, the same applies – we can't disclose anything without a court order. We'd get it, of course, but it would take time and if we can't give Marnie good reason to be patient, she could create havoc.'

'And Louise is just the wee girl to help her do it, if she thinks she's being fobbed off. She's still got all these fancy ideas about justice.'

Fleming gave him a wry smile. 'I had the crusading spirit too, once upon a time. You probably did as well but now all we seem to think about is process and practicality.'

MacNee snorted. 'You'll not get many convictions by giving the jury a wee speech about what you believe in. And that's the way convictions get quashed too – when the lads get round to thinking what they're after is justice, not proof.'

'Oh, I know you're right. But even so, it seems sad, somehow. Another sign of advancing age.'

'Maturity,' MacNee corrected. 'Wisdom, you could say – I kinna like the idea of wisdom.'

'Right. Spare me some of it now. I'll have to phone Marnie Bruce and arrange a meeting. What am I going to tell her?'

'Never mind Marnie. What am I going to tell Louise? She'll be at me the minute I put my head in the door of the CID room.'

'I don't know what on earth you're talking about,' Anita Loudon said with a fine air of bewilderment as Lorna Baxter, with Shelley Crichton close behind her, looked round the sitting room with an expression of baffled rage. The other two women, who looked as if they were suffering acute embarrassment, were hanging back in the hall.

'What is all this about, Lorna?' Anita went on. 'Who are you looking for?'

'Kirstie Burnside's daughter, that's what. We saw her coming in the house here. What are the two of you wanting? Did Kirstie put her up to it? That's what Shelley wants to know.'

'She was there at the play park, gloating,' Shelley burst out. 'I was putting down my flowers for poor little Tommy and when I looked up, there she was, watching me. I really thought it was Kirstie, just at first—'

'This is absolutely ridiculous!' Anger, that was good. 'You burst into my house with some bizarre story about Kirstie Burnside's daughter – did she even have a daughter?

'There was a girl came to the door doing a survey for

a company I bought some stuff from, if that's who you're talking about. She was here about ten minutes, maybe, and then she left. Right enough she'd reddish hair and blue eyes, the same as Kirstie, but that's what you call a Celtic complexion – there's a lot of it about here, after all. The rest is just total rubbish.

'Oh, I can forgive you, Shelley – I know this is a really bad time for you and you've got all my sympathy. But what the hell do you think you're doing, Lorna – stirring all this up? You got warned off before and unless you get out of my house and stop all this nonsense, I'm calling the police myself, right now.'

Shelley looked from one to the other uncertainly and Janette Ritchie came forward to take her arm. 'That's exactly what I told you, Shelley. Come away back with me now and have a wee sit-down – you're overwrought, and no wonder. Lorna, you should be ashamed of yourself.'

Entirely unrepentant, Lorna said, 'I know what I saw. And you know what you saw, too. You're a liar, Anita Loudon.'

She walked out of the sitting room in the wake of the other women, then before Anita could stop her went across the back of the hall to the kitchen. 'Probably hiding in here,' she said, throwing the door open.

Anita, at her shoulder, had to suppress a gasp, but the room was empty. 'How dare you, Lorna,' she said furiously. 'I meant it, about the police.'

Unmoved, Lorna was peering out of the window. 'There's footprints, look! Someone's gone across the grass.'

'Yes, me,' Anita said. 'There was a plastic bag caught on that bush over there and I went to remove it, if you must know.' She was awed by her own inventiveness. 'So get out of my house.'

She wondered what she would do if Lorna stood her ground. The woman was a good two stones heavier than she was and her broad, doughy face was flushed and belligerent.

But Lorna said only, 'Oh aye, that'll be right,' and at last went towards the front door. The others had left already, walking away quickly as if trying to dissociate themselves from what was happening.

On the threshold she turned. 'I said from the very start you knew more about Tommy's death than you ever told. Now I know you did. And this isn't the end of it.'

With a well-timed push, Anita got her off balance and shoved her out, locking the door behind her. Staggering, Lorna had to grab at a railing by the front step so as not to fall and she turned to shout at the closed door, eyes blazing malevolence.

'Oh, I'll get you for this! That's assault – could have broken my leg. And making me out to be a liar – we'll see who's the liar around here.' She walked away.

The adrenaline rush that had powered Anita's defiance left her. Shaking, she went back to the sitting room and half-fell into a chair. She could feel her throat constricting, feel the breathlessness starting as if the air had been depleted of oxygen, but she dared not go to open a window. All she could do was cup her hands round her face and force herself to the rhythm of shallow breaths in, long, slow breaths out. It worked at last, though her heart was still racing.

What was going to happen now? She couldn't begin to guess; she only knew that everything that she had tried to believe was in the past, over and forgotten, had sprung to vicious life.

She'd surprised herself with the facility of her lies, but she didn't think anyone, least of all Marnie Bruce, had believed her. The girl might well have been scared by what had happened here today, but Anita feared that it wouldn't stop her asking questions. She had certainly wanted to know all about Drax.

There was a sick feeling in the pit of Anita's stomach at what he would say when she told him what had happened. She didn't want to be the bearer of bad news, but with Lorna Baxter determined to stir it, rumours would be flying round the village already. If he got to hear what had happened by chance, it would be all her fault for not telling him – instead of only partly her fault somehow for letting it happen at all. He'd be incandescently angry in that luminous, silent, terrifying way.

Why had she allowed herself to remain in thrall to him? He was offhand, even brutal on the phone, frequently inaccessible, unfaithful – no, she couldn't call it that. Faithfulness had never had any part in their relationship, except on her side and that had been her choice. There had been no one else for her, ever, even when Anita was sharing him with Karen. When Karen didn't know.

She hated remembering what she had done to Karen,

and to Karen's daughter. She hated it so much that she'd even tried to atone, though in the cowardly way – the way that meant you weren't there to explain or say sorry, or even 'but it wasn't my fault, it was his' . If you could call that atonement.

Anita couldn't count the number of times she had made up her mind to finish with Drax. And yet with some uncanny form of sensitivity he would always appear just then, without warning, in one of his sparkling moods which would feed her addiction like a glass of champagne pushed into the hands of an alcoholic, and sweep her off somewhere – a dogfight in Liverpool, a bizarre nightclub on a Spanish island, somewhere seedy and crazy and exciting.

Without him, she wouldn't have been a woman with a glamorous secret lover. She'd be just a spinster who'd moved back to the place where she grew up twenty years ago, when her parents died. She'd always thought of it as temporary, but Dunmore was as near him as he would allow her to be, now he had his own nightclub in Glasgow.

Anita felt she'd been on the edge of coming apart for years now. You would think that after all this time you could just forget the secrets that you'd never wanted to know in the first place but they had seemed to weigh heavier and heavier the older she got. Now all this had happened she wondered how long she would actually be able to take the pressure.

Drax had to understand – they must do something. She didn't know what, but she knew it couldn't go on like this, not now Karen's daughter had appeared. She couldn't just lie and lie – sooner or later something would slip.

She should be able to count on his support. He'd been comforting and reassuring in the past when it suited him, but even as she thought about phoning him now, the room seemed to be closing in on her again and her heart was pounding so heavily that she could almost hear it. But then, if a heart attack killed her, it might not even be the worst thing that could happen to her.

'What's happening about Marnie Bruce, Sarge?' DC Hepburn asked as DS MacNee joined the queue in the canteen at lunchtime. She had been watching out for him ever since she heard he was back but he hadn't appeared in the CID room where she'd been writing up a statement.

MacNee gave a disparaging look at the plate she was holding, which seemed to have a lot of green stuff on it. 'Can't think where you'll find the energy to get through the afternoon eating that rubbish,' he said provocatively but Hepburn resisted the attempt to divert her into a familiar argument.

She waited until he got his bridie and beans, then took one of two seats side by side at the table. MacNee hesitated but she patted the chair next her saying, 'Here you are, Tam,' so that he really had no alternative.

'Has Big Marge phoned her yet? She was pretty evasive when I reported to her.'

'Was she?' MacNee said vaguely, then leant across the table towards an officer who was reading the sports pages of a red top. 'Here, Hughie, what're they saying there about the Rangers?'

Hughie grunted. 'Not much.'

Without giving MacNee time to think of some way of prolonging that conversation, Hepburn chipped in again.

'She said that both you and the boss knew her mother.'

'Sorry – who said?'

At this blatant attempt to shut down the subject, Hepburn's eyes narrowed. 'What's going on, Tam? Is this some kind of cover-up?'

At least that got a reaction. 'Cover-up? Course not! The boss is going to phone the woman whenever she's got a minute, right? There's no mystery – it was just that her mother walked out on her. Women do that sometimes – you've maybe noticed?'

Hepburn wasn't going to let him off with that. 'Bludgeoning their children unconscious first?'

He hadn't started on his bridie, she noticed. That was unusual: the speed at which MacNee's unhealthy pastry of choice normally disappeared could only be beaten by DC Campbell who had usually begun eating on his way to the table. Now MacNee made a business of picking up his knife and fork, not meeting her eyes.

'It happens. Not very nice, right enough, but not every mum's the cuddly kind.'

'I'll grant you that, if you'll admit it's unusual, to say the least. Anyway, Marnie Bruce told me there hadn't been an investigation.'

'Course there was,' MacNee said flatly. 'She was too young to know anything about it, that's all. The woman

125

just disappeared, right? We looked for her. Her car was abandoned at Dumfries station and there was no trace of her after that. No sign of disturbance, no sign of anyone else at the house. No great mystery.'

'But a kid, hit over the head by her mother – what did the press make of it?'

MacNee's plate was empty now and he got up. 'In those happy days of auld lang syne, my bairn, there weren't stringers for the gutter press inside the force. And no one thought the kid would be better off for appearing in the *News of the World*. That's all. OK?'

He went out. Hepburn went on with her salad, though without enthusiasm. Lettuce and hard-boiled egg stained pink by pickled beetroot were distinctly unappealing and, she reflected with a sigh, she'd probably have to eat supper in a couple of hours anyway after she went off shift and got home.

She'd definitely been warned off. 'Leave it with me,' Fleming had said, and MacNee's message as he hopped around the subject in his hobnailed boots had been the same. It made her more determined than ever to find out what had gone on in those 'happy days' when the police weren't subject to public scrutiny.

Marnie Bruce deserved answers to her questions and Louise Hepburn was going to see to it that she got them.

Lorna Baxter followed the others out along the street. Janette Ritchie, who had been in earnest conversation with Shelley, dropped back, waiting for her.

'Lorna, I hope you're satisfied, winding Shelley up like

that. It's not done her any good – she's really upset now. And you heard what Anita said.'

'Oh, I heard it, all right,' Lorna sneered. 'And I didn't believe a word of it. Did you?'

Janette went slightly pink. 'We've no reason not to believe it, and I've convinced Shelley not to bother Grant about it. And anyway, supposing it was Kirstie Burnside's daughter – and don't think I'm accepting that – what's the point of digging everything up again?'

'Oh, that's great! She's to be allowed to come and have a good laugh at Shelley's grief and take the joke back to her mother to share, but the people who call themselves her friends just want to let her get on with it? Well, Shelley's got some real friends who won't stand for that. I'm one of them, and there'll be others, no doubt.'

Janette looked at her in consternation. 'For goodness' sake, Lorna – what are you planning to do?'

'"For goodness' sake"? Goodness doesn't come into it, as far as I can see. We're talking about sheer wickedness.'

High on her own self-righteousness, Lorna pushed past Janette and set off down the hill towards the social housing on the other side of the main road. She had just reached it when she saw a bus passing, heading inland along the main road, and in one of the windows she caught a glimpse of reddish-gold hair.

With a turn of speed impressive for a woman of her bulk, she puffed across to her own house just opposite, bundled herself into the car that stood outside, backed out with a fine disregard for the oncoming traffic and drove off in pursuit.

* * *

Marnie had only been minutes on the bus when the call she had been waiting for came through.

'Ms Bruce? This is DI Fleming. I understand you requested a meeting with me?'

'Yes. The sooner the better.' Marnie knew she sounded brusque, and she knew from the tiny pause that the person at the other end had recognised that.

'Shall we say ten o'clock tomorrow?'

'Yes, fine.'

She switched off the phone without saying goodbye. She wanted Fleming to know, before she set eyes on her, that Marnie meant business – and anyway, in this place what would you gain by being polite and patient? So far she'd had abuse, lies and violence.

More than anything, Marnie hated being lied to. She had known Anita Loudon was lying; she just didn't know which bits of what she had said were true – if any. It could have been just a pack of lies from start to finish, considering the way she'd tried to bluff about Drax.

Marnie wasn't sure exactly when she had begun to wonder who this person was who cropped up occasionally in their lives, wherever they might be, so it must have happened gradually. The man seemed to be part of the mystery of her mother's past, the past she wouldn't ever talk about; he would make her mother crazily happy and silly, then provoke hysterical rages and physical attacks on him, while he with his superior height held her off and laughed at her. Marnie never saw him hit her, though sometimes when she was in bed she would hear screaming and the next morning there would be bruises under her mother's make-up and she knew not to ask.

Then a scene was unrolling in her head. She must have been about six, when they were still living in the block of flats.

Drax has just left after one of his visits. She's glad he's gone because he scares her. One of her friends asked her if he was her dad and she said no because she doesn't want him to be. But maybe he is?

She's kept out of his way today, playing in her bedroom mostly. Now he's gone and Mum's alone, she could go and ask her. She heard her crying after he went but she's been quiet for a good while now.

She goes into the living room. It's raining and it's getting dark but Mum's just standing staring out of the window as if there was something to look at.

'Mum, is Drax my dad?' she says.

Her mother turns round. 'Wha'?'

'Is Drax my dad? I don't want him to be. He's nasty.' Then she notices the bottle of whisky on the table, the bottle that had been full at lunchtime and isn't now. She's wishing she hadn't said anything as she backs away.

Mum takes two unsteady steps across the room and slaps her across the face. 'You little bitch! How dare you?'

As she crumples into a crying heap, her mother goes back to the window and stands staring out again.

She had never asked after that. She decided she'd wait till she was too big for her mother to hit her, but she thought about it a lot. She'd even considered asking Drax himself on one of his visits to the house at Clatteringshaws, but her courage failed her and Marnie was never sure if it was because she was afraid of a violent response, or of the answer she might get. She hated to think she might have inherited any part of his character.

She was sure Anita knew, and she had a right to know too. If Anita thought that she'd got rid of her, if she thought Marnie had been scared off, she had another think coming. All that the abuse and lies had done was make her more stubbornly determined to get at the truth even if it meant taking her life in her hands and going back to Dunmore.

And then there was the policewoman. If she was planning to stonewall, she'd regret it.

She glanced down at her grazed hands, her torn and muddy jeans. She didn't want to hang around until three, when she was supposed to get back into the B & B. She needed a change of clothes as well as a clean-up, and if her landlady didn't like it, she could do the other thing. Marnie was in a belligerent mood as she got off the bus in Kirkluce and headed along the High Street then took the first on the right.

She didn't notice the elderly blue Honda that had drawn in behind the bus and now pulled out to drive slowly along Bridge Street behind her, then accelerated past as she reached the B & B and rang the bell.

Lorna Baxter pulled out her mobile and dialled directory enquiries. When they gave her the number she wanted and put her through, it was a secretary who answered.

'Could I speak to Mr Grant Crichton?'

'Your name and business, please?'

130

'Mrs Lorna Baxter, and it's personal.'

She wasn't sure if that would get her through, and she wasn't sure, either, if he would recognise the name, but a moment later Grant came on the phone and he knew who she was all right, since he had the rather wary tone people like him tended to use to people like her.

'Yes, Mrs Baxter. What can I do for you?'

'I wasn't really sure whether I should bother you,' she said primly. 'But something rather odd happened today and I thought you'd like to know.'

CHAPTER SEVEN

Without the lighting effects and the music and the swaying crowds, the nightclub looked grubby and depressing. The three bare bulbs which were the only daytime illumination in the blacked-out warehouse cast enough bleak light to show the detritus from the night before but did nothing to break up the shadows in the corners.

The young cleaner, holding a black plastic bag for the rubbish, looked round with a sort of helpless distaste. She hated the job, hated the disgusting things she had to clear up, hated the smell of stale sweat and stale alcohol – wicked, forbidden alcohol – and the empty, silent place scared her, as if the evil things that went on here could contaminate, even at one remove.

The boss scared her too. If he was in a bad mood he'd yell at whoever was in his way, though sometimes he was all cheerful and would say things she couldn't understand, but if he was smiling she would smile too. The best was if he ignored her completely, the worst was when he was obviously giving her an instruction and she had no idea what it was. He had never actually struck her but he often looked as if he might.

She wished she didn't have to work here. She wished she could stay in the cramped room that was all the home she and her husband had, even if it was dark and very cold, and even if when he wasn't there she cried most of the time for her mother and her sisters back home. But he told her that if they were to be safe she must do what Mr Drax wanted, just the way he did.

So she came each afternoon and tried to withdraw into the shadows when Mr Drax was around and now, when she heard the door of the office upstairs open and close and rapid footsteps descending, she did just that, instinctively pulling her headscarf further round her face.

As he went past her he looked grim, his eyes alight with anger. He didn't so much as glance in her direction, just stormed across the dance floor and disappeared into the lobby beyond. A moment later the whole building reverberated with the noise of the front door slamming.

Gemma Napier was sitting on the edge of the huge kitchen table swinging her legs. Vivienne Morrison was listening to her daughter's account of the surprise visitor as she made tea for her impatient grandson. She had been pretty as a girl and now with her fair hair fading gently into grey she was still a sweet-faced woman with a gentle manner.

'Oh dear, that poor little soul – no, bashing your spoon

on the table won't make it come any quicker, Mikey, and watch . . . the sausage is hot,' she said, setting the bowl down in front of the child. 'I remember Marnie, of course. A funny little creature – I was always rather sorry for her. And her mother was definitely strange. You hardly ever saw her at the school and if you spoke to her you always got the impression she wished you hadn't. I suppose it explains why Marnie seemed a bit – well, awkward or something.'

'It wasn't that, she—Oh hi, Dad!'

Michael Morrison came in and beamed around his family, but it was his grandson he went to first, ruffling his hair.

'Hey, big guy! How's my best pal? Have these ladies been looking after you properly?'

Mikey, his face smeared with baked beans, looked up. '*She* wouldn't let me have chocolate.' He pointed an accusing fork at his mother.

'Not immediately before his tea, Dad,' Gemma protested, and Michael winked at her as he said gravely, 'Dear me, can't have that sort of thing. I'll need to have a word with your mum about that.'

'Cup of tea?' Vivienne said. 'Had a busy day?'

'Oh, the usual. What about the two of you?'

'I was just telling Mum,' Gemma said. 'A blast from the past – this girl I used to know in primary turned up, Marnie – do you remember her? Strawberry-blonde hair, blue eyes – she came round here a lot.'

Her father looked blank. 'You had so many friends, darling. Can't say I do.'

134

'Well, it was ages ago. She just left suddenly when I was about ten or eleven. I really missed her – she wasn't like everyone else. Do you know, she can remember absolutely everything that has ever happened to her, just as if it was playing like a film in front of her eyes?'

'Really?' Michael was openly doubtful. 'All right, she might have a good memory, but no one can do that. She probably bigged it up a bit to make herself more interesting.'

'No, it's true. It's some sort of mental condition, she told me. It's rare, but when there was publicity about one case a while ago a whole lot more people came forward.'

'That would be useful,' Vivienne said. 'Imagine, if you got to the shop and had forgotten what you were meant to get, you'd just look back and see.'

'She says it's very difficult to cope with, actually. But what she doesn't know is what happened when her mother disappeared. She woke up in their cottage with a head injury and no sign of her mum, and then she was taken into care. She's come back to see if she can find out what happened and I said I'd ask you if you remembered anything about it.'

'When was it?' Vivienne asked.

Mikey had finished his tea. 'Up!' he said imperiously, holding out his arms to his grandfather.

Michael didn't seem to notice. 'Marnie, did you say? What was her surname?'

'Bruce,' Gemma said. 'She left when we were in Year 6, and I know exactly when it was – it was the day after Halloween, and we'd gone out guising together. I was worried when she wasn't at school the next day because she'd had an epic row with her mum before she left. I got you to take me out to the cottage where they lived, Mum, but there was no one there.'

Vivienne was frowning in an effort at recollection, but Michael shook his head. 'Complete blank, I'm afraid. I can't remember anything about it.' He picked up his mug of tea and went to the door. 'I'll be through in the office – a couple of things to finish off.'

'Granddad!' Mikey, ignored, wailed in indignation. 'I want up!'

But for once his grandfather didn't even seem to hear what he had said.

The slamming door of Grant Crichton's Mercedes E-Class as he parked it outside his house alerted his wife to her husband's return from work, and the vigour with which it had been slammed sent her to the window to look for storm signals. Yes, he was upset about something; his bushy brows were drawn in a straight line and the corners of his mouth were firmly turned down as he came to the front door.

It might be one of those evenings when he sat in simmering silence and bit her head off if she asked any questions, or it might be one where he wanted to expand at large on the stupidity, dishonesty and plain bloody-mindedness of everyone in the entire world, with particular reference to those who had come into contact with him that day. As Denise went to fetch the decanter of Scotch and his favourite crystal tumbler, she decided that she felt an evening out with one of her girlfriends coming on, whether the girlfriend could make it or not.

'Hard day, dear?' she greeted him tentatively.

Grant sat down heavily in his lounger chair and grunted.

Silence it was, then. 'I'm just going to put the supper on. You take your time.' She whisked out of the room.

She took a bottle of Chablis out of the fridge and poured herself a glass, then picked up the phone. 'Sue? Fancy a drink later? Good – half past eight, then?'

Crichton finished his whisky in two mouthfuls then went across to pour himself another, larger one. He'd barely noticed his wife, lost in his own thoughts as he'd been all afternoon. He'd postponed a meeting and refused a couple of important calls, to his secretary's annoyance, but he hadn't been able to think about anything else since that poisonous woman's phone call this morning.

He was a very proud man, a man accustomed to being in control, to getting his own way, and the humiliation of being told that his son's killer might be obtaining secret satisfaction from his agony, might even be laughing at it, was a painful attack not only on his feelings but on his image of himself.

He had been inclined at first to pooh-pooh Lorna Baxter's story, but then she'd been so convincing about the resemblance. The picture of the little girl with the golden curls and the neat pixie face with bright-blue eyes rose before him yet again.

At the trial she had seemed confused: the story she had told was inconsistent, at times contradictory. But there had

been a coldness in those blue eyes and her defiant attitude –
even rudeness, sometimes, to her questioners – had never
suggested a hint of remorse. It looked now as if for her,
and her hell-spawn daughter, what she had done had been
a source of pleasure, not regret.

Of course, part of his rage was directed at Shelley who
had brought this upon them with her pathetic little annual
ceremony, its only purpose to direct attention to herself.
This wasn't an expression of grief; real grief was suffered
internally and silently. Who knew that better than he did
himself?

There was nothing to say that this was the first time
Kirstie Burnside's daughter had done this either – just the
first time she'd been spotted. Perhaps even a disguised
Kirstie herself had come on a previous occasion, taking a
delight in this demonstration of her lasting power to make
them suffer? Crichton writhed at the thought.

He topped up his glass again as he tried to decide what
he should do. Lorna Baxter was clearly high on the drama
of it all, trying to persuade him to get up a mob to go
round and scare the girl.

He couldn't deny that was tempting. Perhaps, at last, he
could find out where her mother was. It offended him that
she could have a whole new life, at the taxpayers' expense,
protected from the consequences of what she'd done. He'd
even employed a private detective once to try to track her
down, but it had been good money for nothing. The man
had claimed the trail was cold but Grant suspected that
he'd been warned off.

What he certainly wasn't going to do was get involved

in any Baxter initiative. Her prying avidity was disgusting and he'd made his distaste plain. She had definitely taken offence – as if he cared!

He could take it to the police – by a distance the most sensible option. He'd been a Justice of the Peace himself at one time, and this girl's behaviour was pretty much a textbook case of conduct likely to provoke a breach of the peace. Crichton was ready to breach it himself, right now.

The other thing he could do was drive over to Dunmore and take Anita Loudon by the throat. According to Lorna Baxter, she was in on this. She had been one of the child witnesses at Burnside's trial and Lorna claimed that she knew more about it than she'd said at the time. If all these years she'd been facilitating Kirstie Burnside's spying – he took an incautious gulp of whisky and choked, painfully.

He dabbed at his streaming eyes. Sort out Anita, that was the first thing. And if what Lorna had said really was true—

Denise opened the sitting-room door and peeped round it tentatively. 'Supper's ready. But I can keep it hot for you, if you want to finish your drink.'

'No, no, I'll bring it with me.' Crichton stood up, lurching a little as he did. He wasn't drunk enough to think it was reasonable to get behind the wheel of a car, so Anita would have to wait.

Anita was sitting watching *Wallander* on TV. At least, the set was switched on and she was facing it, but if someone had offered her a million pounds for a summary of the plot she would have had to pass.

She kept going over and over Drax's response to her account of events over the phone, which despite all her preparation beforehand had been rambling and a bit incoherent, partly because of the unnerving silence at the other end. When at last she abandoned the attempt to generate a reaction and her own voice trailed into silence, she wondered for a moment if he was still on the line. At last he said, 'I – see.' That was all. Then he did ring off.

'I – see.' Anita could picture his face as he said that: pale, taut, his lips a thin line and those dark eyes lit with a flame of anger, more frightening for being unvoiced, and she shivered. When he was like that he was totally unpredictable. Sometimes he would do no more than emanate icy rage; on other occasions he would lash out without warning, like a snake striking.

She had only taken the brunt of it a few times, but she'd seen the after-effects on Karen too. Karen would stand up to him, scream and strike back, but after the first time Anita had the sense to go down and lie still. Once she'd got a kicking, but usually he turned away as if he had achieved what he wanted. He'd never mention it afterwards but once his anger was spent he would exert himself to please her. An occasional bruised face was a small price to pay.

The other tactic, the best one, was not to be there when Drax was displeased. She'd managed it this time, but she wasn't naive enough to think that was the end of it. He'd summon her, or he'd come here, but distance was safety.

By then he would have had time to calm down, at least a little. She hoped.

She heard a key in the lock first, then the imperious double ring on the doorbell. She'd bolted the door when she came in and her first thought was not to open it. Anita knew it was him – her breathing shortened; her hand went to her mouth in the gesture of a terrified child.

The doorbell rang again, a long ring this time, along with a knocking on the door. As she sat there, unable to move, she heard his footsteps on the path outside the window and heard his voice, light, amused.

'Oh, for God's sake, Anita! I know you're in there. Don't be ridiculous! I really don't want to have to break the window.'

Somehow she got to her feet, went to the front door, shot back the bolts and opened it. Drax had come back to the doorstep and outlined against the light from the street lamps he seemed very tall. With his face in shadow the only definition came from the line of his brows, the glint of his eyes and his smiling mouth, contrasted with the white of his teeth.

He stepped inside, sweeping her into an embrace. Stunned, she clung to him as he kissed her and staggered a little as he released her again, laughing at her confusion.

'What the hell did you think I was going to do to you? Don't ever try to shut me out again, though – naughty girl! Got some Scotch? We've a lot to talk about.'

He went on past her into the kitchen and Anita followed more slowly, rubbing at her lips, still bruised from his kiss, still shaken by her own instant response to it. His behaviour was confusing; she had heard what he said but when he stepped into the lighted hallway she saw the steel behind the smile and the marks of anger in the taut lines of his face. She resolved to keep her distance until she was sure he wasn't going to snap.

But as they sat over the whisky Drax seemed to have relaxed. He was sipping it, not downing it with the sort of cold intensity that always meant mayhem. He was lounging in his chair, making encouraging noises as she went through the whole story again, prompting her with questions until he was satisfied that she had told him all there was to tell.

Then he was silent for a moment or two, holding up his hand when she tried to speak. At last he said briskly, 'Right. To sum up: we don't know why she's come, we don't know who she's talked to already, we don't know where she's staying. Lorna Baxter's vigilante brigade is on the march. The girl can't be convinced that anything she remembers is wrong, so she's difficult to lie to.

'Suppose we just tell her who her mother was, and that she'd better leave before someone takes the law into their own hands?'

Anita shook her head. 'She might go away, perhaps. But it won't stop her trying to find out what happened to Karen.'

She stole a glance at him as she said that, but he was looking into the middle distance. He was frowning, but he had been so understanding that she felt emboldened to say, 'The thing is, Drax, I'm getting frightened. I'm not young, the way I was; I get panic attacks and if it's all stirred up

142

again, if they start on the endless questions, I'm afraid I'll break.'

'Break?' He turned his gaze on her and she realised how wrong she had been to think that he was relaxed. 'Oh no, my sweet, you won't break – will you?'

Anita swallowed hard. 'No, Drax, of course I won't. It was just – oh, me being silly, I suppose.'

'Then don't be silly,' he said, his voice silky, and Anita feeling suddenly cold wondered why she had been foolish enough to think that telling Drax her problems was a wise thing to do.

'I've eaten far too much,' Marjory Fleming said ruefully as she and Bill went up to bed after Cammie's celebratory supper. 'With Karolina pulling out all the stops for the first course and Mum going her length on the puddings, I'm going to have to starve for the next three days.'

'I'm just going to find the Rennies,' Bill said. 'They're an absolutely lethal combination, the pair of them.'

Karolina Cisek, whose husband Rafael worked on the farm with Bill, played domestic goddess to the Fleming household, aided and abetted by Marjory's mother Janet Laird, who suffered from a sense of guilt that she had not managed to impart any of the housewifely virtues to her daughter. Their joint feast for Cammie had been a triumph of culinary skill.

Marjory laughed unsympathetically. 'The penalties of greed,' she called after Bill as he headed for the medicine cabinet.

She was still smiling as she sat down at the dressing

table to take off her make-up. It had been such a lovely evening, the happiest as a family that she could remember for a long time.

Cat had been holding her at arm's length ever since last year's disaster but her pleasure at Cammie's success seemed to have softened her tonight, and she was less abrasive, too, when Janet was around. Cat had always been devoted to her grandmother and with her now approaching eighty, that affection had developed into a touching protectiveness which so far Janet, thank goodness, had shown no sign of needing. She had an active social life and was kept busy, too, with charitable good works for elderly ladies rather younger than she was herself.

Cammie, the star of the show, had been alight with happiness. Seeing his shining face, his mother had felt a pang: how rare they were, those golden moments of unadulterated joy, and how quickly they dissipated. Before long Cammie would be worrying about doing well enough to cement his place in the team.

It had been a golden evening for them all, in fact, and Cat had given her mother a spontaneous hug when she said goodnight, the first for a long, long time. It looked almost as though peace was being declared and Marjory found herself wiping away a sentimental tear along with her mascara.

Shelley Crichton found she couldn't settle to anything. She had a headache for a start, and she was finding it very difficult to sort out her feelings about all that had happened today.

Janette had told her what to think. 'You know what Lorna Bruce is like,' she said firmly. 'That woman would cause trouble in an empty house and she's just using you. Anita explained who the girl was, and the only reason you thought she had such a strong resemblance to Kirstie was because she was so much on your mind at that moment. If you saw her now, you'd wonder why on earth you thought that.'

Shelley, still tearful and feeling a little shocked by Lorna's aggressiveness, had allowed herself to be convinced. But now, at home by herself, she wasn't so sure.

If Kirstie Burnside really had sent her daughter to gloat, as Lorna had claimed, it was almost as wicked as what she had done originally. They had said at the trial that she had an ungovernable temper, that she had just lashed out, and she was only a child at the time – a child whose own experience of family life had been horrifying, violent abuse. The counsellor they'd arranged for Shelley afterwards had stressed that, and of course she acknowledged the child had suffered – of course she did. In a way. It hadn't done anything to assuage her grief for Tommy, though, or tempered her hatred or blunted her wish for revenge.

She still had the dreams, dreams where she confronted Kirstie Burnside – sometimes a child, sometimes a woman with a child's face – and screamed her hatred, until Shelley found there was a knife in her hand and plunged it deep, deep in her heart, and woke up screaming and bathed in sweat.

It had been particularly bad when Kirstie was released

after only a few years, and given what the press called 'a new life'. Tommy couldn't have a new life to replace the one Kirstie had taken away and neither could Shelley, but there was nothing she could do about it. She'd had to learn about forced acceptance the hard way.

Now, though . . . The face of the young woman she had seen swam up before her. The light-blue eyes, the goldy-red hair, the neat sharp line of the jaw: no, she hadn't imagined the resemblance. Kirstie had been a child when last Shelley saw her, but she would have grown up to look like this, the child-woman of Shelley's dreams.

The thought of it made her feel sick. How could she just pretend it hadn't happened? Despite what Janette had said, Shelley was becoming more and more convinced that Anita's story hadn't been true. Tomorrow she was going to go round again to make her admit it, and force her to tell where she could find the woman.

The girl, she told herself, was probably no more than a cat's-paw. Anita, though, was someone she'd known for years, almost a friend. They weren't close but they'd have a chat if they met in a shop, say, and to help Kirstie Burnside get fun out of Shelley's tragedy was disgusting – treacherous, really. She had felt fury when she saw the girl but now what she was feeling was a sort of cold rage.

Getting worked up like this wasn't doing her headache any good at all. She needed to calm down, take something for it and go to bed. The violent emotions of the day had left her feeling drained, almost light-headed with the pain and tiredness. If she wasn't to lie awake all night she needed to put it all out of her head, sleep on it and decide what to do in the morning.

Shelley was on her way upstairs when the phone rang. It was unusual for anyone to call this late, and she was frowning as she answered.

A woman's voice said, without preamble, 'Just wanted to tell you you've got friends, Shelley. We'll get rid of her, don't you worry.'

CHAPTER EIGHT

It had taken Marnie Burnside a long time to get to sleep. The events of the day had formed a sort of continuous strip of scenes – the crazy lady, the attacking dog, the woman who had looked her in the eyes and lied, the luxurious farmhouse kitchen – and all that broke the loop was her own speculation about what she could expect from her interview tomorrow.

Exhaustion overcame her at last, but the mattress was thin and the covers inadequate for a cold night so that she was troubled by half-wakings and unpleasant dreams. It was during one of the periods of deeper sleep, though, that the noise erupted outside in the quiet street.

Shocked awake, bewildered, Marnie sat up and tried to make some sense of what she was hearing. It sounded like a dozen metal drums being beaten in a frenzy, with car horns blaring in the background. Then came the sound of angry voices howling some sort of slogan, and bangs and thumping that echoed through the house. Her bedroom looked out onto the street; still not properly awake, Marnie staggered to the window and drew back the curtains.

It was a mistake. The sight of her seemed to inspire the group below to howling frenzy. They were holding pots and pans that they were beating with spoons and there were cars parked across the street, headlights blazing, as the drivers leant on their horns.

Marnie recognised the fat woman who was beating on the front door as one of the witches in Dunmore and shrank back out of sight with her heart pounding in terror. Was she still dreaming? Was this just another nightmare? She could make no sense of it at all.

She could hear now what they were chanting, though: 'Come – out – and – face – us! Come – out – and – face – us!' On and on it went, on and on, as the noise intensified until she cowered into a corner and covered her ears, sobbing.

When the door to her bedroom opened, she almost fainted with terror. But it wasn't one of the mob from outside; it was the familiar figure of her unpleasant landlady wrapped in a tartan dressing gown. Her face, too, was pale with shock in the orange light from the street lamps, but she had unerringly placed the blame on her guest and was spitting venom.

'What's this all about? I never heard such a thing in the whole of my life. It's you, isn't it? What have you been doing?'

'I don't know! Nothing,' Marnie whimpered.

'You needn't think you're going to stay skulking in here

until they start breaking my windows. They're saying they want you to go out and face them so you'd better get on and do it.'

'No! No!'

The woman advanced on her, seizing her by the shoulder to pull her up just as the sound of a siren rose above the pandemonium outside. As suddenly as it had started, it stopped; there was the sound of car doors being slammed, of engines revving and then there was only the siren and the flashing blue light of the police car.

The landlady released her grip. 'Lucky for you,' she said coldly. 'Now you'd better away down and explain to them what this is all about. You're out of here, first thing tomorrow morning. And don't come looking for your full Scottish breakfast.'

Anita Loudon woke around seven. Drax, sprawling diagonally across the bed, had forced her into a cramped corner and she was stiff and unrefreshed.

She lay for a moment looking at him, seeing the signs of middle age in the slackening around the jawline and the greying strands in his hair. She never noticed them when he was awake: his constant, edgy vitality gave him the air of youth which she knew she had lost long ago. She needed her sleep these days.

With infinite caution she slid out of bed. Drax stirred slightly and she froze: he never took kindly to being disturbed, and anyway, she didn't want him to see her the way she must be looking now. He turned over, sighing, and she quickly sorted out clothes for the day then slipped out of the room, closing the door quietly behind her.

The bathroom mirror was relentlessly well lit. She shuddered at what it reflected back at her and ducked into the shower, as if hot water could wash away the bags under her eyes and the crêpey skin of her neck or even the thinning lips.

Sooner or later, though, she would have to come out. At last she gritted her teeth, faced the mirror again and began an extensive repair job.

When she'd finished, or at least done all she could, she listened outside the bedroom door for a moment but there were no sounds of movement, just heavy, regular breathing. She didn't fancy breakfast; she made herself coffee and sat with her thoughts, looking out into the garden through which Marnie had made her escape.

Anita had no idea what the day would hold. She was due at work in the dress shop at half past nine; if Drax got up before that and he'd made plans involving her, she could phone in sick, but since he hadn't mentioned it last night, she'd better carry on as usual.

Would he be here when she got back? There had been so many occasions when she'd come home in hope then spent the evening in tears but now she hoped he'd be gone. He'd been in a strange mood last night and he'd made her feel – alarmed. Yes, that was the word.

She'd been so frightened, anyway, and she'd made the mistake of confiding her fears. She'd realised, too late, how angry it had made him, but he hadn't lashed out. It wasn't like him. That was scaring her even more.

And now that Marnie had made her think of it, what

had happened to Karen? She'd asked Drax once and all he'd said was that she'd left and he'd lost touch with her – but she never knew when Drax was lying to her. She gave a little shiver.

It was all coming apart, just as she had always dreaded it would. They'd said that to her, when they were asking her what she knew, what she'd seen, all those years ago. 'If you don't tell the truth,' one of the policemen had said, 'you'll be punished later, you know.' She'd believed him at the time and she'd never forgotten. But she'd still lied.

Perhaps it was time she told the truth, to someone at least.

DS Andy Macdonald's lips were compressed as he sat in the car outside the Galloway Constabulary headquarters, drumming his fingers on the steering wheel while he waited for DC Hepburn to finish her cigarette.

His usual partner, the taciturn DC Campbell, was on leave this week and the temporary pairing with Hepburn had been unwelcome to both of them. They had fallen out badly during a murder case last year; he had become emotionally involved with one of the suspects and thought Hepburn's questioning of such a vulnerable woman had been brutal. The case, and the involvement, were long over but he had never forgiven her.

For a time Big Marge had, he suspected, discreetly kept them apart as far as possible, but this week's decision looked like a signal that she thought this had gone on long enough.

She was probably right, but the months of heartbreak had changed Macdonald from the laid-back, cheerful lad he had once been to a harder, sterner, colder man. The most he was prepared to do towards rapprochement with Hepburn was to treat her with icy professionalism – as long as she didn't deliberately irritate him, as she was certainly doing now.

She was putting her stub in the bin at last and he started the engine as she got into the car.

'Did you have to have a fag just before you got in? You stink of smoke and I'm going to end up smelling of it too.' Macdonald knew that sounded aggressive. He didn't care.

Hepburn was unmoved. She gave a very Gallic shrug as she fastened her seat belt, saying simply, 'Get over it.'

With a sidelong look of dislike, Macdonald drove off.

'What's the situation, Sarge?' Hepburn asked as if she hadn't noticed his mood. 'I was caught by a query just as I was going to the briefing.'

She always called him 'sarge', he had noticed, rather than Andy. He avoided calling her anything at all.

'Disturbance outside a B & B in Bridge Street. Cars hooting, people yelling, banging on doors and windows. Scarpered when the uniforms turned up, but there were ten complaints from neighbours and a furious landlady. We've to talk to her, and the lodger, who seems to have been the target.'

Hepburn raised her eyebrows. 'A lynch mob in Kirkluce – whatever next? What's she done, then?'

'No information. The names and address are there.' He fished in his pocket and handed her a notebook with an elastic marker at the place as he slowed down and indicated a turn. 'That's Bridge Street now.'

'Oh – Marnie Bruce!'

Macdonald turned his head at her exclamation. 'Know her?'

'Yes. I spoke to her a couple of days ago. It was a really weird thing – quite a story. Big Marge and Tam are stressing about it. Look, that's the house there.'

He pulled into the kerb and there wasn't time to ask her what she was talking about. Anyway, he'd rather ask MacNee than put Hepburn in a position to patronise him with her superior knowledge.

The furious landlady was still furious this morning. She had the door open before they rang the bell, a short squat woman with greasy grey curls and a soiled apron over a grey jersey dress with part of the hem down, and she talked them all the way through to the sitting room at the back.

The house was chilly and smelt of dust and stale fat, overlaid with sickly synthetic lavender from an air freshener. The decor seemed to have shades of mud as its inspiration and with the utter cheerlessness of it all Macdonald could feel depression settling on him even before he and Hepburn sat down on the beige uncut moquette sofa in front of an electric fire that hadn't been switched on.

'I can tell you one thing,' the landlady declaimed, 'the minute you've finished talking to her, she's out the house. I never heard anything like it – a riot in Bridge Street! That's what it was, you know, a riot. Thought they were going to break down the door and smash the windows.'

'Well, Mrs . . . Wallace,' he said with a sidelong glance

at the notebook Hepburn was still holding, 'we can be thankful the patrol car arrived in time to prevent that. I gather they dispersed immediately – is that right?'

While obviously still feeling that the police should have been in position to stop it before it started, she admitted grudgingly that they had and returned to her main grievance. Her eyes were small and unfriendly behind smeary glasses.

'It's that girl,' she said. 'A perfect bother, right from the start. Always wanting something, complaining about the hot water, complaining about the heating, having to have coffee to her breakfast instead of tea from the pot – and there she was yesterday forcing her way in at dinner time when I'd told her rooms are not available to guests until after three. And a right mess she was in too, I can tell you that – torn clothes, bloody knees and hands. Don't know what she'd been doing, but she'd obviously been causing trouble somewhere.'

'Didn't you ask her what had happened?' Hepburn was looking at the woman with some distaste.

Mrs Wallace sniffed. 'That was her business. Didn't want to get involved.'

'Right,' Macdonald said. 'So you have absolutely no idea what this was all about?'

'No, and I'm not wanting to know. I'm just wanting rid of her. They were chanting, "Come out and face us", and I told her last night, I said, "You get out there and face them, if that's what they want, before they start in to breaking my windows," but of course her ladyship wasn't going to do any such thing. I'd have made her, though, if your lot hadn't come along.' She sounded positively regretful that she'd been denied the chance.

'You didn't feel you had a duty to protect Ms Bruce from an angry mob?' Hepburn's tone was unprofessionally hostile, and Mrs Wallace reacted to it.

'Oh, it's my fault now, is it?' Her voice was shrill. 'I'm the victim here, being terrorised in my own home and I can promise you that Councillor Brunton, who's a friend of mine, will take a poor view of the police attitude when I tell him.'

Macdonald winced at the name of a famously troublemaking local politician and shot Hepburn an irritated glance.

'No, no, Mrs Wallace, I assure you we are entirely sympathetic – a most unpleasant and alarming experience for you. We're here so that we can find out what the problem was and make sure that it will never happen again.'

'Oh, it won't – she's not staying.' She seemed slightly mollified, though, and got up saying, 'I'll send her in to you right now, will I, and then I can get her to clear out. Sooner the better.'

Fleming glanced at her watch: ten past nine. She recognised it as a neurotic action, prompted by her anxiety about the ten o'clock interview with Marnie Bruce. She still hadn't worked out what she was going to say to her, and the disturbance last night was worrying too.

She'd detailed Macdonald to go and find out what it was all about, and only afterwards had remembered that Campbell was off and it was Hepburn he'd be taking with him. That had been a mistake; she'd been hoping to sideline Hepburn until she'd managed to persuade Marnie that there was nothing she could find out here. But it sounded as if the ripples were spreading already in a very alarming way.

Superintendent Rowley's phone summons was seriously unwelcome. She didn't say what it was about, she just wanted to see Fleming as soon as possible.

'I've got an appointment at ten,' Fleming said, though not hopefully, and the reply, as she had feared, was that in that case she had better come immediately.

It seemed unlikely that Rowley had heard about Bridge Street. In her lofty position she took little direct interest in problems on the ground, preferring to wait, as she put it, for significant reports to be filtered through to her. But maybe she'd had more thoughts on dealing with the Marnie Bruce situation, in which case Fleming would be grateful for any constructive idea and even more grateful for the implication of shared responsibility.

Rowley was clearly in a high state of tension this morning, anyway. There were red spots in her cheeks and she said, 'Oh Marjory, there you are!' in a tone that suggested that taking the time to come down three flights of stairs instead of dematerialising and rematerialising on the instant in her office had been an unreasonable self-indulgence.

'I've had a very important phone call from . . . someone,' she said. 'I'm not at liberty to disclose the name, but someone extremely important.'

This was definitely nothing to do with Marnie Bruce.

Rowley had said that in what could only be described as Hushed Tones. Should she, Fleming wondered acidly, curtsey just in case she meant the Queen? Perhaps it would be wiser just to say, 'I see,' in a solemn voice.

'I see,' she said solemnly.

That seemed to pass muster. 'Yes,' Rowley said. 'It's . . . it's very unfortunate. The thing is . . .' She hesitated. 'You know that the government has been very concerned about illegal immigration? Well, naturally you do. And here, as I said to you before, we have an important entry point into the United Kingdom. And of course, I'm not saying Special Branch there don't do a splendid job of policing. Of course they do. And they have my fullest support.'

'Absolutely,' Fleming agreed. Any dealings she'd had with the Cairnryan station had been both efficient and cordial.

'But . . . unfortunately,' Rowley swallowed, 'apparently the police in Strathclyde picked up a group of Asians travelling in a minibus – no papers, of course, and none of them admitted to speaking any English at all to answer questions. The thing was, there were plastic bags in the van with the name of local shops in Stranraer printed on them and . . . well, they've concluded that somehow they slipped through the net here – on my patch!'

If there were illegal immigrants entering the country, an important entry point into the UK would naturally have its share. 'Some are bound to get through even the most effective security checks,' Fleming pointed out. 'If they searched every lorry and shipment the place would grind to a standstill.'

'Oh, don't be ridiculous! Of course I know that.' Rowley's colour was getting even higher. 'And in fact, of course, the intelligence operation is centrally funded so it shouldn't be our direct responsibility. But Marjory, the way he talked about it – it sounded as if he was blaming *me*!'

'He' – not the Queen, then. Fleming was finding it hard to take all this seriously. 'Christine, anyone familiar with the problem will understand the difficulties too. I'm sure you're being too sensitive.'

'But I am sensitive,' Rowley cried. 'I'm very sensitive about damage to my reputation. This could be a stain on my unblemished record.'

Struggling to find a response to such naked egotism, Fleming was relieved when Rowley didn't wait for one.

'I want to give you a special brief. Get down to Stranraer, ask a few questions, find out who's got an operation going. Just discreetly, no need to mention it to anyone, you understand? I need to have a success to report.'

Fleming gaped at her. 'Sorry?'

'Oh, I know it's not really within our remit—'

However inadvisable you thought direct confrontation was, sometimes there was no alternative. 'No, it isn't,' Fleming said flatly. 'I hardly know where to begin on this one. In the first place, I have a more than full-time job keeping on top of the remit we do have. In the second place, Cairnryan has a highly competent DCI with two experienced DIs to deal with all this and they might very reasonably take exception to anyone else moving onto their patch, particularly someone with no experience at all of the particular problems.'

'But they're not to know anything about it! I'm not asking you to take over port security, for goodness' sake.' Rowley's voice was becoming shrill. 'It's our job to know what's going on in one of our towns, since it could quite easily spill over into our area of operations. I've got notes here of the evidence found on these people that links them to Stranraer. So it's just a simple case of following up, chatting to people, keeping an ear to the ground. That's all.'

Grudgingly, Fleming admitted that, at least, was possible.

'Of course it is. And then mopping it up, Marjory, to show that in my sector, at least, we have everything under control.'

'Christine, what can I possibly do that the officers at Cairnryan won't be doing already?'

'Inject a sense of urgency, that's what. They simply won't understand what's at stake. I've spelt it out for you, so the important thing is to get on with it. All right? Thanks, Marjory. I'm glad we understand each other.'

Rowley got up, indicating that the interview was over. 'I'm sure you've lots to be getting on with,' she said with marked graciousness. 'You'll want to clear your desk a bit. Get that team of yours working. Delegate, that's the answer.'

Finding herself bereft of words, Fleming went. That, of course, had been a demonstration of the way people aiming for the top got there and she no longer doubted that one day in the not-too-distant future Hyacinth would be accepting a post as chief constable with becoming modesty and not so much as a glance over her shoulder at the trampled bodies left in her wake.

What on earth was she going to do about this one? She was tempted to phone Nick Alexander, DCI at Cairnryan, for a confidential chat but he might well take exception to the implied criticism and decide to go over Rowley's head and complain – and Fleming knew who would get the blame if he did.

It might be best to keep quiet and do – well, something that wouldn't upset Cairnryan but would keep the woman off her back. She glanced down at the file Rowley had thrust into her hand. Perhaps the 'something' would suggest itself once she had read it.

And at least it had taken her mind off her ten o'clock appointment.

When Marnie Bruce came into the sitting room she looked years older than the composed, assertive woman DC Hepburn had seen a couple of days ago. Her face was pinched with dark blue shadows under her reddened eyes and she was visibly shivering with tension, or perhaps it was just the cold of the unheated house.

DS Macdonald identified himself and Hepburn said, 'Hello again, Marnie. I gather you've been having a bad time.'

'You could say.' Her tone was bitter.

Hepburn glanced at Macdonald. He'd taken exception before to her taking the lead in an interview, but his nod recognised her previous contact as a good starting point.

'Perhaps you could begin by telling us what happened,' she said.

'Hasn't that woman told you already? She'd enough to

say about it last night and again this morning when she stood over me while I packed my bag.'

'Yes, but we'd be interested to hear what you saw. Did you recognise anyone, for instance?'

'Yes, I did. Oh yes! There was a woman banging on the door who was a friend of the woman who attacked me in Dunmore yesterday, who came to Anita Loudon's house to attack me again—'

'Hold on,' Macdonald said. 'Can we take this a bit slower? Are you saying you know why all this happened?'

'Oh no, I don't know *why*. I don't understand any of it. I think that everyone in this part of the world must be completely mad, that's all.'

'Telling us about Dunmore yesterday might be a good place to start,' Hepburn suggested. 'Why were you in Dunmore?'

'I found out that an old friend of my mother's lived there – Anita Loudon.'

As Marnie began her account of the day's events, wringing her hands unconsciously together, Hepburn noticed again the strange, disengaged look on her face as if she wasn't really seeing her questioners at all, and again, the account was extraordinarily detailed: 'There's a tag on the key with green leaves and pink flowers, sort of daisies, I suppose, and it says "Garden" so I know it will unlock the door,' for instance. Much of it was reported in the present tense, though she seemed to correct that when she noticed.

It took a long time and they listened in silence until she reached her return to the B & B, shaken and bleeding, and the landlady's hostile reaction.

'I just ignore her and go past to my room, then I wash my hands but I don't have a plaster or anything.' Marnie held out her hands, showing the raw grazes. As she looked at them, her eyes seemed to come back into focus and she said, a little awkwardly, 'So that's what happened.'

'I see,' Macdonald said. 'And you think that one of the women you saw last night was among the women at Dunmore – and you think you could recognise her again?'

'Oh yes, I could recognise her. Fat, with long, straggly black hair.'

'Right,' Macdonald said. 'That's very helpful. We'll make enquiries and we'll call you again if we've a chance of an identification.'

With a glance at Hepburn, he made to stand up but she hadn't moved and he sat back again, leaving her to make the running.

'Was your mother's friend able to tell you anything about your mother?'

Marnie shook her head. 'She asked me how she was as if she thought we were still together. She claimed she didn't know anything had happened back then, just that she couldn't get my mother on the phone one day and when she came out to the house we'd gone.'

'You don't believe her, do you?'

For the first time, Marnie looked Hepburn full in the face. 'No, I don't. She's a liar – I caught her out in one lie, so I know.'

'What was that?'

Marnie's eyes slid away again. 'Doesn't matter. That's something else. But I want to know the truth, and I'm going to find some way of making her tell me. Too many people have kept secrets and told lies.'

'Leave it to us, Marnie. We'll go out today to see her and get to the bottom of all this. There's probably been some sort of misunderstanding – we don't want things to get any worse until we can sort it out.'

Marnie gave her a contemptuous look. 'Sort it out like you lot did before, you mean? Cover everything up and get me to run away, like a good little girl? I'm not eleven years old now. I'm all grown up and I want to know what happened to my mother, and to me, for that matter.'

Macdonald, though still feeling out of his depth, broke in. 'No one's going to try to cover up anything. We want to understand what happened, too, and when we do I can promise that we'll share any relevant information.'

Marnie said nothing but the look she gave him was eloquent and Hepburn, far less sure than he seemed to be about the openness and honesty that could be expected in this case, added, 'You've got every right to stay as long as you want and ask whatever questions you like. Not knowing whether your mother is alive or dead is a dreadful burden for you to carry and I'll certainly help you to find out the truth in any way I can.'

She could feel Macdonald shifting uneasily beside her, and she knew what he was going to say when he got her out to the car – that her response was far too personal, unprofessional. Perhaps it was, but he wasn't one to talk and she wasn't going to compromise her own values for any set of rules.

Marnie didn't look particularly grateful. She glanced at

164

Hepburn briefly, then away again. She looked down at her watch and got up.

'I've got to go,' she said. 'I've an appointment with DI Fleming at ten o'clock, and then I suppose I'll have to find somewhere else to stay.' She walked out.

Macdonald turned to Hepburn. 'What on earth is all this about?' he said blankly.

She was frowning. 'I don't really know, to be honest. But what I do know is that unless the boss tells her the truth about what's going on this one is going to blow. And I think Big Marge knows but doesn't want to tell.'

CHAPTER NINE

She'd have recognised Marnie Bruce anywhere, DI Fleming realised with a sense of foreboding as, unseen, she watched her sitting in the hall waiting to be fetched for the interview.

It wasn't that Fleming remembered what the child Marnie had looked like: she'd talked to her that time in hospital, but on the visits to her mother she'd barely glanced at the child on the way in. It was her striking resemblance to the photograph of a fair-haired, bright-eyed ten-year-old that the tabloids reproduced every time they ran an article on child killers.

It wasn't exact, of course. Kirstie Burnside's pretty, elfin features had been much remarked on, while her daughter's face was heavier and a little rounder. But with the line of the jaw, with that unusual hair colour and the light-blue eyes . . . Anyone who had known Kirstie, or had even studied the photo, could guess her daughter's identity, and from the sound of what had happened last night, someone had.

Fleming wasn't going to go into that, though. If Marnie raised it, she would say firmly that she would have no information about it until the reports came in later in the day. She was determined to confine the discussion to events in 1993 – nothing before and nothing after. If she could.

She went through the security door into the hall. 'Ms Bruce? I'm DI Fleming. Come on through. I gather you have some questions you want to ask me.

'Coffee and biscuits to room 5, please,' she added to the Force Civilian Assistant at reception, then led the way, making an anodyne remark about the heavy rain.

Marnie followed silently and sat down in the chair nearest the door of the bland, impersonal room. It left Fleming, who was attuned to body language, with an awkward alternative: to sit directly opposite in what would look like a confrontational pose or to start shifting chairs into a more relaxed social position, which suggested an attempt at control. She sat down opposite, wondering how conscious Marnie's choice had been.

Leaning forward to lessen the distance between them, she smiled at her. 'Right, what was it you wanted me to tell you, Marnie – if I may call you that? I still remember you as a little girl!'

'If you like.' Marnie didn't return her smile. 'I want to know what happened the night when my mother disappeared. Halloween, 1993.'

Fleming spread her hands wide in the classic gesture of openness. 'To be perfectly honest, we don't know. My personal involvement was limited to coming to see you in hospital, but I've read up all the reports and the only thing

167

we can really say for certain is that a neighbour of yours at Clatteringshaws Loch found you the following morning. Douglas Boyd – you may remember him?'

Marnie shrugged.

'You had a nasty head injury and you were alone in the house. After that, extensive searches were conducted, inside and throughout the whole surrounding area, but there was no sign to suggest any struggle or violence, or even the presence of another person. We couldn't tell whether your mother had taken clothes and personal effects with her but we didn't find a handbag or any official identity documents, and a car registered to your mother was later found abandoned at Dumfries Station.

'Every effort was made to find her but she has never been traced.'

The light-blue eyes had not wavered from Fleming's face since she had begun speaking and she was starting to feel uncomfortable under their scrutiny. The door opening as the FCA brought in coffee was a welcome distraction.

'Ah, thanks, Sue. How do you take it, Marnie?'

'I won't. Thanks.'

'Oh, right. Well, I'll grab a cup – haven't had time for my usual caffeine fix today.' She gave a little half-laugh, and felt foolish.

'Are you telling me that my mother just hit me over the head and then left me – without knowing how badly I'd been hurt, without knowing if she'd actually killed me?'

Fleming took a sip of coffee. Thinking time. Then she looked up and met the other woman's accusing gaze.

'Yes, Marnie. On the evidence available, I'm afraid

I would have to say yes, probably. We can't prove it, of course. We never found the weapon that was used to hit you – perhaps she took it away with her to dispose of later. But there simply isn't a scrap of evidence to indicate that there was anyone in the house that night, except the two of you.' She felt brutal, but those were the facts and at this stage there was no point in trying to soften them.

Marnie's expressionless face gave no clue to her feelings. Was this really a shock, or could it be something she had suspected?

Fleming went on, 'What sort of relationship did you have with your mother? You were asked at the time but you said, I think, that it was "all right" – the sort of thing most children would say. Would you say the same now?'

'Yes.'

She had expected to be pinned down with questions but this lack of reaction was almost harder to handle. By way of diversion, Fleming turned to the large cardboard box she had placed earlier in the corner of the room, still blackened with the grime of years in the storeroom. When she folded back the lid, the smell of old, unwashed clothes rose from it.

'These are the personal belongings that were found in the cottage your mother had rented. They've been kept in storage in case you wanted to reclaim them. The car had to be scrapped.' She picked up a form that lay on the top and held it out. 'No MOT, illegal tyres, worn brake pads—'

'That would figure.' Marnie sounded defeated, almost resigned. She hadn't even glanced at the contents of the box.

Perhaps it wasn't going to be so difficult after all. 'I know this isn't a very satisfactory outcome for you, Marnie, especially after coming all this way,' Fleming said with genuine sympathy. 'What are you going to do now?'

Suddenly, the blue eyes blazed. 'Find out the truth. What do you think? I'm just going to take your word for it that my mother tried to kill me, say, "Oh dear, I'd better just forget about it then"?

'Anyway, why was it that you used to come to see her? You didn't just pop in to say hello in passing, did you?'

Fleming relaxed too soon. This was the hard part, now.

'No, of course not. My visits were official but there's every reason to suppose that your mother is still alive so I'm afraid I'm unable to discuss that with you. I'm sorry.' It was the best she could do and Fleming found she was holding her breath.

'You're stonewalling. It's the same as the last time – it's all just going to be brushed under the carpet. You're not going to do anything to look again at what happened.'

'Marnie, unless we find your mother, there's nothing more we can investigate. The only other source of information we have about that night is you and you told us you didn't know anything. If we had fresh information, something you've remembered—'

'That's the whole problem! I can remember everything – except this!' There were tears of frustration in her eyes. 'And there's something else I don't understand – the way people treat me here.'

They were getting onto even more dangerous ground. 'Oh yes, I gather there was some sort of problem last night

170

and officers are investigating. I'll make a point of reading the report when it reaches my desk.' She glanced at her watch and stood up. 'Now, if there's nothing else—'

Marnie got up too, looking defeated. 'I suppose there isn't,' she said listlessly. With some relief, Fleming went to open the door. It hadn't been nearly as bad as she had feared; even if she hadn't told the whole truth, she hadn't been asked a question that forced her to lie.

Then Marnie said slowly, 'You knew my mother. Do you think she would have tried to kill me?'

Fleming felt colour creeping into her face. 'I-I simply wouldn't know, Marnie. I've never really considered it.'

That most certainly was untrue and she could see that Marnie knew it was. She added hastily, gesturing towards the box that was standing in the centre of the room. 'Oh, do you want to take away the box? It's a bit bulky – you could collect it later, if you preferred.'

Marnie gave her a contemptuous look then turned away. 'No, I'll leave the things with you. You may need them for the investigation if my mother's body turns up.'

'I see.' Michael Morrison's face was grim. 'What more could she know?'

He listened to the response, his lips tightening. Then he said, 'Yes, I think cancelling is the best we can do, in the circumstances. I'll talk to the others later.'

Putting down the phone he stared blankly at his study wall, plastered with photographs of his wife, his daughter and his grandson – particularly his grandson. Gemma was always teasing him that soon there wouldn't be any need for wallpaper. There was Mikey at a day old, Mikey learning to walk, Mikey on his trike, Mikey looking up at his grandfather with total love and trust.

He had been scribbling notes on a sheet of paper as he listened. In a sudden fury of rage he grabbed the paper up, crumpled it into a ball and threw it into the waste-paper basket, swearing. Then having second thoughts, he retrieved it and walked over to the handsome old-fashioned fireplace where he put it onto the hearth, found a match and burnt it before neatly sweeping up the ashes and tipping them over the piled-up logs set in the grate.

He'd have to get in to the office. There was a big building project he was working on so he was going to be busy, anyway. Morrison was frowning as he went out into the hall and almost tripped over his daughter who was hoovering.

She switched off the machine and smiled at him. 'I'm Mrs Mop today,' she said cheerfully. 'Mikey's at nursery, so I hadn't an excuse not to roll up my sleeves.'

'What's happened to Ameena?'

'They phoned from the farm to say she's got flu and won't be in for a couple of days. She told me her husband's away at the moment so I thought I'd do this and then pop across and see that she's all right – take her some grapes or something.'

'Dear me – a bit Lady Bountiful, wouldn't you think?'

Gemma looked crestfallen. 'Do you think so? I didn't mean it like that.'

'To be honest, she'd probably think you were checking up to see if she's really ill or just throwing a sickie and resent it. I'd leave it, if I were you.'

'I never thought of that. Oh dear, I'm sure you're right – I could have walked straight into it and upset her. I'm too naive, that's my problem.'

She was obviously disappointed at not being able to carry through her charitable impulse, and her father laughed. 'You're a sweet girl, darling. Stay just the way you are and I'll do the cynical bit on your behalf.

'Tell your mum I'll be a bit late back, will you? Busy day at the office.'

'Hope you're not too late. Mikey always acts up if you're not around at his bedtime.'

'I'll do my best but I can't promise.'

He left, with Gemma calling after him, 'See you do! Your title of World's Best Granddad is at stake!'

'You're making this too personal,' Macdonald said to Hepburn as he drove off. 'It could cause a lot of trouble if you take it upon yourself to get involved.'

'You would know about that, of course,' she said lightly with a sidelong glance and saw him colour angrily.

They'd fallen out already over whether they should go and check on Anita Loudon before reporting back. Hepburn had pointed out that if Fleming was busy with Marnie Bruce they could end up kicking their heels when they could be discovering useful information about what had really gone on. Macdonald had given way but with a bad grace and the atmosphere in the car as they drove to Dunmore through the rain was thick with tension.

She was determined not to volunteer any information unless he asked for it and they had been on the road for ten silent minutes before he cracked. Concealing a smug little smile, she told him the story as far as she knew it.

'I don't know what Big Marge's agenda is, but there's definitely something she doesn't want Marnie to find out. It screams cover-up to me, and that's crazy. It's not the mistake that causes the big scandals, it's the cover-up, every time.'

'The boss is totally straight,' Macdonald said flatly. 'I've worked with her for years and if there's something she's not telling Marnie Bruce she'll have good reason for it.'

'Good reason? A kid badly injured, her mother nowhere to be seen, the whole thing obviously hushed up – and all Tam MacNee can say is that fortunately the press didn't bother so much in those days! Her mother could be lying dead somewhere and Marnie has a perfect right to know exactly what happened. If Fleming fobs her off—'

'—it's nothing to do with you.' Macdonald finished the sentence for her. 'Anyway, have you considered that perhaps it's your friend Marnie who has an agenda? Her interest may be financial rather than social – there's a lot of money in compensation for police failure.'

It hadn't occurred to her and it brought her up short. 'Well . . . I can see that, of course, but I don't believe it. I think she's a very troubled person, looking to lay some of the ghosts of her past.'

'Oh, very romantic,' he said sardonically. 'I'll give you troubled, though I'd have said weird. Anyway, what's with the Dunmore business? Do you really believe she doesn't know what it's all about?'

'You don't? For goodness' sake, the woman was terrified

this morning. She told you in detail what happened and she's totally confused.'

'It was the detail that bothered me, quite honestly. She could be some sort of fantasist.'

'She didn't fantasise the mob outside her window,' Hepburn said tartly.

'Yes, I'll give you that. But she provoked it somehow – what did she do?'

'I don't know. That's what I hope we're going to find out. But I believe her, and I'm on her side.'

Macdonald groaned. 'For God's sake, we don't *have* sides if we're police officers. Look, you irritate the hell out of me but I don't want to see you screw up totally. The boss is handling this so leave it to her. You need to look at this as just another professional case.'

'You said.'

Hepburn turned her head to look out of the window, her lips set in a stubborn line, and silence fell again. She knew Macdonald was right, in a way, but there was a more important imperative. Marnie Bruce was a victim, being pushed around by authority and terrorised by bullies. She deserved a champion and, though she might not realise it yet, she'd found one.

Anita Loudon smothered a huge yawn and Vivienne Morrison smiled sympathetically. 'Late night?'

'Can't take it the way I used to.' She tried to sound upbeat but she knew her voice was flat.

Vivienne was looking at her in concern. 'You don't look great. Headache?' She was digging in her bag, 'I've got some ibuprofen somewhere – here you are.'

Anita thanked her and went into the dress shop's tiny back room where there was a sink and a kettle. Her head was indeed pounding but the turmoil inside it was worse. She didn't know how she was going to get through the day.

Vivienne was the most considerate employer anyone could hope for. If Anita said she was feeling ill she'd be told to go home, but Drax would still be there, probably. Somehow here, in the cosy little shop with the thick pile carpet and the pretty wallpaper and the clothes hanging in neat colour-coordinated ranks she felt safe, as if in Vivienne's pleasant, cheerful world nothing could ever go wrong.

She was always so kind, so understanding. Anita suspected that Vivienne knew there was a man involved on those occasions when she'd suddenly wanted a day off – Dunmore wasn't a good place for keeping secrets – but it had never been a problem, there had never been awkward questions.

Anita had occasionally thought of telling her about Drax. The need to talk to someone had sometimes been almost overwhelming, but she'd always managed to resist. Now, though . . .

There couldn't be anyone better than Vivienne to confide in: sympathetic, discreet. If she talked to her in confidence, made her promise not to tell a soul – but if she told her everything, would Vivienne keep it secret? How could she?

Not everything, then – just something, a bit of it. She desperately needed the sort of advice someone sensible, someone just ordinary and normal could give her about the bizarre, awful situation she was in.

Anita took a deep, shuddering breath. Perhaps she could—

The bell on the shop door jangled. With a quick look in the mirror, Anita patted her hair, pinned on a smile and came out to greet the customer.

A man and a woman had just come into the shop and even before they introduced themselves and produced ID, she knew they were police.

There were nine bed and breakfasts on the information centre's list and Marnie Bruce had tried eight of them. Demand for accommodation in Kirkluce seemed to be surprisingly high for a wet Wednesday in November, and seven of the eight had no vacancies. The eighth showed her a room, then on hearing her name, said bluntly, 'Oh, you! Sorry, forget it. I'm not looking for trouble.' The vile Mrs Wallace had clearly done an efficient job.

There was still one she hadn't tried but it was at the other end of the town and Marnie had a pretty clear idea of the response she was likely to get there too. Wet, tired and discouraged, she pulled her case along the High Street, holding her battered umbrella over her head. The sullen intensity of the rain suggested it was on for the day; her town coat was too thin and her hands were red and stinging with the cold.

She couldn't just go on walking aimlessly. There were plenty of cafés in the High Street so she chose one, wrapping her hands gratefully round her mug of coffee when it arrived.

This had to be the turning point. This was when Marnie

could choose to do the sensible thing or to do the crazy, stupid thing that was just asking for pain and grief.

She'd been counting on the interview with Fleming to provide at least some of the answers she was looking for, or suggest a way forward at the very least. She'd psyched herself up for it, determined not to be fobbed off, prepared to be as rude as she needed to be when the inspector ducked and dived.

Only she hadn't. Fleming had readily given her a straightforward account that squared with what Marnie knew herself. She believed, too, that what the woman had said was true, partly because it had been so obvious that she was lying when she'd said she hadn't considered whether Marnie's mother would have attacked her. Clearly she had, and clearly she thought the answer was yes.

She'd even been open about concealing information, but the reason she gave left Marnie with nowhere else to go. She hadn't even got anywhere with her question about what had happened at Dunmore.

Perhaps she needed to accept that this was a mystery she'd never solve, forget about it and get on with her life. The aggression and abuse she'd suffered already wasn't going to stop, might well get worse. Was it really worth putting herself through all this?

Her problem was that she'd never been able to understand the comfortable, casual way people would say 'I can't remember what I did.' She couldn't see why it didn't drive them mad; her brain simply wasn't geared to the state of 'not knowing'. So how could she walk away now?

And there was still one way forward – Anita Loudon.

At the very least she must know perfectly well why there had been shock and anger in Dunmore, because she'd shown the same shock herself. Marnie was much too angry about her lies and deceit to let that go. She needed to see her again, to force her to explain – and perhaps tell her some other things too.

Like how to get in touch with Drax. Marnie gave a little involuntary shiver – a goose walking over your grave, someone had told her once. She hated the thought of bringing him back into her life, but she might have to, if she was going on with this.

No, she certainly couldn't leave now. Not yet. Not until she'd seen Anita.

Which left her with the problem of finding somewhere to stay. She could go to Newton Stewart, say, or even Stranraer – surely the landlady network didn't extend that far. It would be a long way to go on public transport, though, only to find out that it did.

Then another thought occurred to her. She'd had an employer who needed someone to drive a van and had got her driving lessons; she kept her licence tucked away in her purse. If she rented a car, she could move about freely and privately: no more standing around at bus stops, afraid that unfriendly eyes might be watching her.

Renting cars cost money, though, and her nest egg was dwindling fast. She'd have to find somewhere really cheap—

Or free. Suddenly, the picture came up before her.

She's locking the door. She's looking at the key, still dirty with rust-specks on it and she's drawing back her hand to throw it away into the bushes when, for no particular reason, she decides to bury it again and she puts it back under the stone where it was always kept . . .

'Know this? I'm getting a bad feeling about this whole thing,' DS MacNee said. 'A very bad feeling.'

'And you don't think I am?' Fleming was staring gloomily at the file on the desk in front of her. 'I'm not sure it's been a good idea to try to keep us at arm's length from it. I sent Andy to deal with the disturbance at the B & B because I didn't want to put you face-to-face with Marnie, but I forgot it would be Louise going with him and when I buzzed down to speak to them after the interview they'd gone to pursue enquiries at Dunmore. I'm not sure why, but it sounds to me like Louise in full cry.'

'That's all we need. She's got—'

He was interrupted by the phone ringing on Fleming's desk. She listened, then said, 'All right, leave it with me.'

MacNee raised his eyebrows and she sighed.

'That was the duty sergeant. Grant Crichton's come in, wanting to talk to "someone in authority" and he thought I might want to know.' When MacNee did not immediately react, she went on, 'Crichton – Tommy Crichton, remember?'

'Oh, for God's sake! What now? Is this to do with the business last night?'

'He hasn't said that, but it certainly could be. I'd better take that myself.' She stood up.

'Overkill,' MacNee said crisply. 'You're not wanting

him to think there's anything going on that's inspector's business. I'll take it.'

'You're probably right.' Fleming sat down again. 'Anyway, I've got to get on with my commission from the super to solve the problem of illegal immigration with a few well-chosen discreet enquiries.'

'Maybe when you've done that you could fix the economy. And get Rangers back into the Premier League.'

He left her smiling wanly. She picked up the file Rowley had given her and leafed through the first few pages, pausing at a list of local firms operating through Cairnryan. A name caught her eye – Grant Crichton.

It was amazing how often coincidences like these happened, usually in threes. She'd probably see the name again in some different context in the next day or two.

'I understand that Marnie Bruce came to see you yesterday,' the detective whose name was Macdonald said.

Anita Loudon's heart was beating so loudly she thought that everyone in the shop must hear it. 'That's right,' she said, then to give herself time to think before she was asked another question, she added, 'I knew her when she was a little girl. Her mother was a friend of mine.'

'Yes, she told us that. Can you tell me what happened?'

Vivienne, who had been looking awkward, said, 'I'll just go through the back and leave you to it, shall I?' But Anita protested, 'No, no, there's no need for that! There's nothing private about it.' She felt safer, somehow, with Vivienne at her side.

'Marnie just turned up at the door,' she said. 'She was

in the area, a sort of holiday, I think. It was very sad, actually – she seemed to have lost touch with her mother and thought I might know where she was, but I haven't seen her for years. Not since they left the area.'

'When was that?' The woman detective, Hepburn, was studying her in a way that made Anita nervous.

'Oh goodness, twenty years ago, I suppose.'

Unexpectedly, Vivienne chimed in. 'That's right. She visited Gemma my daughter yesterday too – they were great friends at school until she and her mother suddenly vanished. She was a funny wee soul, I remember. Gemma says she has perfect recall of everything that's ever happened to her and perhaps that made her – well, a little dreamy.'

The detectives exchanged glances, then Macdonald said, 'I gather she had an unpleasant experience before she arrived at your house, Ms Loudon.'

Keep the voice level, Anita told herself. 'Did she? She never mentioned it to me.'

'Really?' Hepburn's eyebrows were raised. 'She said she had.'

'I'm afraid I don't recall that.'

'And she said that an aggressive group of women came to your door looking for her and she had to escape out of the back.'

Anita gave a puzzled frown. 'An aggressive group? I don't know what she's talking about. I was chatting to her in the sitting room and when the doorbell rang I went to answer it. It was someone doing a marketing survey and I spoke to her for a few moments.' That had worked before. 'Certainly, when I came back Marnie had gone out of the back door, which I did think was a little odd. But that was all.

'As Vivienne said,' she gave the other woman a grateful smile, 'I did think Marnie was – well, a little strange. She certainly seems to have got very confused in what she was telling you.'

The look that Macdonald gave Hepburn looked oddly triumphant. 'I see. Thanks very much for your help, Ms Loudon. And you don't know anything about a disturbance in Kirkluce last night outside where Ms Bruce was staying?'

Anita felt sick. Lorna Baxter, no doubt, and all the fire-fighting she'd been doing could prove to have been pointless. 'No,' she said, but it was hard to keep her voice steady and the policewoman pounced.

'You don't sound very sure. Where were you last night?'

'I was at home all evening. And it wasn't that I was unsure, I was just surprised.'

'I see,' Hepburn said, and Anita was very much afraid she did. However, she only said, with a look at Macdonald, 'I think that's all for now, anyway,' and they went out.

Vivienne turned to look at Anita. 'That was strange! I wonder what on earth's going on?' Then her voice changed. 'My dear, you're shaking! Is there something wrong?'

Anita burst into tears.

CHAPTER TEN

'All I want is a brief word with this young lady,' Grant Crichton said, his obvious irritation giving the lie to his reasonable tone. 'Perhaps my informant was entirely mistaken about who she is and it would take only a little chat to set the record straight. She's moved from where she was staying, so if you could just find out for me where she's gone—'

DS MacNee ignored the question. 'Who was your informant?'

Crichton bridled. 'We're not talking about my informant, Sergeant. We're talking about a young woman who has caused a great deal of upset and disorder.'

'You may be, I'm not.' MacNee had never met Crichton before but he'd recognised him immediately: the type to confuse the terms 'public servant' and 'personal servant' and they always got up his nose. It wouldn't be long before the taxpayer bit came in.

'You seem to have adopted a very strange attitude, Sergeant. As a taxpayer, I expect to find the police more cooperative—' He broke off. 'Is something amusing you?'

'No, no. Sorry.' MacNee composed his expression. 'The thing is, the young lady, whoever she may be, has done nothing wrong. We're not interested in her, we're interested in finding the folk behind last night's disturbance. Your "informant", as it might be.'

Crichton's face turned a dark red. 'You have absolutely no reason for supposing that. And no, I am not prepared to act as a police spy.'

'Now you see, we'd call it being a responsible citizen,' MacNee drawled.

Enraged, Crichton stood up. 'This is entirely unsatisfactory,' he snarled.

The chief constable's a personal friend of mine – would that be next, MacNee wondered, and if so could he keep his face straight this time?

Fortunately, it seemed that the CC's acquaintance did not stretch as far as Grant Crichton. 'I shall make my own enquiries,' was all he said as he went to the door.

'I would strongly counsel against it, sir. Harassing the young lady could put you on the wrong side of the law, if she made a complaint.'

Crichton behaved as if he hadn't heard that, stalking ahead as he was escorted out. But he gave him a dangerous look as he left. 'MacNee,' he said, quite softly. 'I'll remember that name.'

MacNee went back to the CID room with slight misgivings. He could have misread the man, writing him off

185

as the standard bluff, blustering businessman and having a wee bit of quiet fun at his expense, but now he wasn't so sure. The bad feeling he'd had earlier was getting worse.

Once Marnie tracked down a car rental office attached to a small local garage, hiring one proved surprisingly cheap and surprisingly easy. The small green Fiat was a bit elderly but it worked and it was weatherproof too. After two days of standing in the rain waiting for buses, she liked weatherproof.

It was mid afternoon when she drove out to Clatteringshaws Loch revelling in her new freedom. She'd gone to Dumfries first with a carefully planned shopping list that included a camping gas burner and lamp, a sleeping bag, blankets and a hot-water bottle as well as basic supplies.

She'd have to be careful. A car parked outside the abandoned cottage would be a giveaway to anyone passing – possibly even the owner. And she daren't use her lamp in the front room either.

The rain had stopped, and there was even a slight lightening along the hills on the horizon but with the sky still under heavy cloud, the waters of the loch seemed almost black as she drove past. In the shadow of the trees the cottage looked dark and forbidding and the lift of spirit she had felt was seeping away. It was so derelict, so isolated, so remote—

So exactly what she needed, Marnie told herself firmly. No one could find her here. She would be a completely free agent.

She drove through the rotting gate and parked close to the front door. She'd have to risk leaving the car there while she unpacked her stores, but it wouldn't take long and then she could drive along and leave it in the car park by the loch. With the information centre and tea room closed, no one would think anything other than that it belonged to some passing visitor.

In the half-light it took her a few minutes to find the stone, and as cars passed along the road, she had to stop herself looking round guiltily. But there was the key and she let herself in, fighting once more against the onslaught of images.

'You drank too much last night, that's all,' Drax is saying brutally to her mother, who's looking awful, shaky and white and sick.

She hates it when her mother's like that and she hates it when Drax is angry. Today's the worst, with both together. She goes into her bedroom and tries not to hear, but he's shouting now.

'They've arrived, and you've got to deal with it! Doesn't matter how you feel—'

She hears her mother running to the bathroom. She's crying, and being sick at the same time. It's awful—

With a huge effort of will, Marnie dragged herself back to the present. The house smelt of damp and stale air, but if she opened windows the cold moist air coming in from outside might be worse. She unloaded her purchases, dumping everything in the hall, then went back to move the car.

When she reached the car park, the light was going fast

and the sunset was a lurid green streak outlining the hills to the west. She locked up and walked briskly back along the Queen's Way, cringing as the lights of passing cars swept over her.

Inside the cottage it was almost completely dark. She made sure the doors to the front rooms were shut then carried the lamp through to the kitchen at the back, set it up and got it lit, letting the mellow light spill into the hall while she organised what she'd brought, putting the gas burner by the useless electric stove and setting out the pan, plate and mug she had bought next to it, along with the camping set of cutlery.

She'd have preferred not to sleep in her old bedroom. The torrent of images it prompted was almost painful, but her mother's room was at the front so this would have to do. Marnie spread out her sleeping bag and the blankets on top of the dank, sagging mattress, then went back to the kitchen.

She set up the burner and crawled under the sink to turn the stopcock and get the water running. She was wrestling with it when her mobile rang.

'Marnie?' It was Gemma's voice, bright as always. 'How are you doing?'

'Fine,' Marnie said, hoping her own voice didn't sound hollow.

'It was really just to tell you I drew a blank with Mum and Dad about your mother. Mum vaguely recollected it when I prompted her but she didn't know anything about what had happened and it didn't mean anything at all to Dad. Sorry – I'm sure that's disappointing. I'd have loved to be able to help.'

'That's all right. It was just an idea, that's all.' She hadn't expected anything else, really, except in that tiny foolish part of her brain that still hadn't figured out that luck and Marnie were total strangers.

'How did you get on when you went to see Anita? Was she able to tell you anything?'

She'd forgotten that Gemma knew. 'Oh, she didn't know anything about it either. She thought my mum and I would still be together.' There was no way she was going to embark on the whole tangled story with Gemma.

'That's really sad! Are you going to stick around for a bit or just go back to London?'

'Not sure. Maybe stay a day or two more.'

Gemma's voice warmed with enthusiasm. 'That's great! Let's meet up for lunch or something – where are you staying?'

'I'm moving about a bit. Look, I'll get in touch with you, all right? I'm trying to see a few more people and then I'll be clearer about when I'm free.'

'Well, see you do, or I'll keep phoning. I'm not letting you do the disappearing act on me again! Speak soon.'

Marnie went back to the stopcock. When at last it turned she ran the cold tap to clear the system, her eyes blank as she watched the dirty water belching out. Gemma's open-hearted warmth sounded genuine, but Marnie felt as if she was standing in the cold outside the hospitably open door to a room with a blazing fire, unable to cross the threshold. Perhaps it was the ugliness of her childhood that had bred a wariness of intimacy, a lack of trust. God knew she needed a friend, but Gemma's protected existence had given her a sort of childlike innocence that couldn't begin to understand the dirty reality of the life Marnie had always known. However determined Gemma might be to keep in contact, it was pointless.

At least she had no idea where Marnie was now. No one had any idea. She could do what she liked, go where she liked and if she was careful she could be completely unobserved. Invisible, almost.

She filled the pan she had bought and boiled up the water. The kitchen felt quite cosy now, with the warmth from the gas burner and the gentle light. She sat down to drink her tea, feeling almost dizzy with the sense of freedom.

Shelley had slept badly the night before and then brooded all day over the late-night phone call. She'd thought the voice had been Lorna Baxter's, but when she phoned her in the morning and challenged her about it, she'd just laughed and denied it.

'There's lots of folks in Dunmore on your side,' she said. 'It would be one of them, maybe. Still, you might hear some good news today, you never know.'

Shelley had tried to insist on being told what she meant, but Lorna, who seemed to be in high good humour, refused to be drawn. 'I'll call you if I hear anything, but if you ask me, Kirstie Burnside's daughter won't come bothering us again.'

That sounded like good news – sort of. It wasn't enough, though, that the girl should be driven away. She had to be made to tell where her mother was hiding first.

During Shelley's troubled night, the intoxicating

possibility that she might at last be able to confront Tommy's killer had filled her dreams as well as her muzzy early-morning thoughts. For years she had been schooling herself to accept that the meeting would never happen, even though nowadays some people got that chance. Restorative justice, they called it, but not in a case like this. She would never be given the opportunity to make the murderer of her son come face-to-face with her own evilness, to show her hell gaping at her feet. Oh no, Kirstie Burnside had been hidden by a benevolent state that was still protecting her now. If there was the faintest chance of getting past the protective shield, Shelley wasn't going to let it pass.

What would it achieve, Janette had asked her once when Shelley had been expanding on that familiar theme. She'd stammered a bit, mouthed the words like 'closure' and 'apology' – as if any apology could wipe out Tommy's death. Janette would have been shocked if she'd been able to read her friend's mind.

She'd waited in, hoping that Lorna, or someone, would call and tell her what had been going on but the phone remained obstinately silent. After lunch she'd phoned Janette 'just for a chat' but it was obvious that no local gossip had come her way either.

Anita knew what Shelley needed to know. She'd be out at work just now, but if there was no more news by the evening, she'd have to get hold of her. And if she wasn't keen to disclose Kirstie Burnside's whereabouts – well, Shelley might just have to have that face-to-face confrontation with her instead.

* * *

The house was in darkness when Anita got back from work. There was no sign of Drax's car either and Anita gave a great sigh of relief as she let herself in. She had dreaded finding him still here. She didn't want him quizzing her about her day.

She was getting better at lying, though, lying and telling half-truths. Perhaps she only needed a little more practice and even his eyes, that always seemed able to look right through her, would lose their power.

It was just possible that everything might settle down again. The police obviously didn't know who'd been involved in this disturbance, whatever it was; she reckoned she'd convinced them Marnie was flaky, so if nothing else happened they might not bother to pursue it.

And if Marnie Burnside had been scared off, if Shelley had accepted the story Anita had told her, if Drax had just gone back to Glasgow to await events, she might stop feeling she was standing on the edge of a cliff and the headache that Vivienne's ibuprofen and sympathy hadn't been able to shift might subside.

That was a lot of 'ifs'. But when she drew the curtains and switched on the lamps and the fire and the TV and sat down with a mug of tea, the comfortable normality of it all began to soothe her.

Anita hadn't done much to this room since her parents died. Coming back to Dunmore had been meant as a temporary move, before she went to Glasgow to be at least near Drax, if not with him. It had never happened, though, and here she still was twenty years later. In this familiar room where nothing had changed since she was a small child, it felt as if nothing ever would change. With this treacherous reassurance, she put her head back against the cushions and drifted into a doze.

Marjory Fleming drove back home to Mains of Craigie late as usual after a long, unsatisfying day. Her talk with Marnie Bruce had left her feeling very uncomfortable and the investigations into the demonstration in Bridge Street had gone nowhere, with DC Hepburn sure that Anita Loudon was lying about what had happened during Marnie's visit and DS Macdonald ready to believe that the girl was to some degree, at least, fantasising.

They were certainly no closer to finding out who had been involved in the protest. Given that the crowd had dispersed instantly and no real harm had been done, it simply wasn't worth police time to pursue it.

Looking through the file that Rowley had given her hadn't improved her morale either. It was little more than a list of the shops whose carrier bags had been among the illegal immigrants' possessions and another list of firms nearby that had regular dealings with overseas customers through Cairnryan. There were half a dozen local companies and another ten based in Glasgow, including the consortium which had Grant Crichton's name as one of the directors.

Tomorrow, she supposed gloomily, she would have to send uniforms round the shops asking questions, and get FCAs on to digging out what background they could. If ever there was a waste of scarce resources, this was it.

She arrived at the farmhouse in a gloomy mood. She needed Bill to cheer her up, pour her a drink and talk about something that had nothing to do with police work. In fact, why shouldn't they phone the next-door neighbours and see if they'd like to come over? The Raeburns, running a dairy farm themselves, had the same interests and concerns and Hamish was always good for a laugh.

Her spirits had lifted as she went through to the kitchen. Bill was there, sitting in the sagging chair by the Aga, but he was fast asleep with a mug of tea, still full, balanced precariously on the arm. Meg the collie, wakened by Marjory coming in, registered her arrival with a wave of her tail then shut her eyes again.

Smiling, Marjory went to rescue the mug in case Bill knocked it over as he woke. It was cold so he seemed to have been asleep for a good while. It must have been a very tiring day, for him and the dog, and her spirits sank again. Neither of them were as young as they used to be; there was grey around Meg's muzzle now and Bill, when she looked at him more closely, looked positively drawn.

She cleared her throat and her husband opened his eyes.

'Good gracious, did I doze off?' He sat up. 'What time is it?'

'Half past six. What time did you come in?'

He still looked fuddled with sleep. 'Can't remember – half past five, quarter to six?'

Marjory emptied the cold tea into the sink. 'More tea or a drink before supper?' she said, going across to the freezer. 'There's a goulash here but it'll take an hour at least.'

'Oh, a drink, I think. I'll open a bottle of red. Then an early night. It'll be another heavy day tomorrow.' He heaved himself out of the chair.

'What were you doing today?'

'The tupping's over so Meggie and I were taking the ewes back up the hill. Rafael's sprained his ankle.'

Marjory looked at him in dismay. 'Oh no! And of course Cammie's away for training, just when you really need him. Maybe they'd give him time off—'

Bill recoiled. '*What?* When he's still working to consolidate a place in the team?'

She rolled her eyes. 'Oh sorry, that was blasphemy, I suppose. You'd better call Jake and see if he'll come out of retirement for a bit till Rafael's on his feet again.'

'Lassie, I did it myself for years before I ever got Jake in at busy times. And Cammie'll be back in a couple of days.'

'You were in your twenties then. You're not twenty now. And look at you – you're shattered!'

'Och, it's nothing a sit down and a glass of wine won't sort. And a good night's sleep.' He gave a huge yawn as he opened the bottle and put it on a tray.

No point in suggesting the Raeburns, then, and Bill obviously wasn't going to be in sparkling form either. Marjory felt the gloomy mood descend again.

Denise Crichton put the finishing touches to the little watercolour that she'd started at the class this morning. There was still something wrong with her boat; it didn't seem so much to be floating in the water as lying on top of it, but the artist who ran the class had said she was showing signs of improvement. He was always very encouraging to 'his ladies'.

The other thing that was good about taking the class

was being able to annex one of the bedrooms for her studio. She'd had fun setting it up, though she didn't really need the big easel, and the elaborate box of oil paints hadn't even been opened yet. Most of the time she didn't actually paint at all. The main purpose was to give her somewhere to escape from Grant when he was in one of his moods.

They seemed to be getting more frequent. Yesterday he'd been impossible and had barely seemed to notice whether his wife was there or not and tonight, after a supper when she tried to make bright conversation and got only grunts in reply, she'd retreated to her sanctuary and heard him go into his study and close the door. A little later she thought she heard the car driving away, though she hadn't heard the car door slammed in Grant's usual vigorous way.

She was curious enough to glance out of the window and yes, the car was gone. He hadn't told her he was going out – back to the office, she guessed. She did hope that there wasn't anything wrong on the business side. Being married to Grant without the perks of success would be a bleak prospect.

It was quite a bit later that Denise heard a car's engine and what sounded like tyres on the gravel. She glanced out of the window again, but it wasn't there at the front so perhaps she'd been mistaken. She went back to her boat, but after dabbing at it a bit longer decided with a sigh that she was making it worse, not better. She washed out her brushes and packed away her paints, planning a nice long bath then bed. She wasn't going to wait up for Grant.

But when she went downstairs to finish up in the kitchen she noticed light showing under the door of Grant's study, so it must have been the car after all. She knocked, then put her head round.

'Oh, you're back! I wasn't sure. I'm just going off for a bath – do you want a cup of tea or anything?'

Grant swung round in his chair. 'What do you mean, back? I haven't been out – I've been here all evening.'

Surprise made her incautious. 'But I heard you, going out earlier—'

His face was mottled red with temper. 'Then there's something wrong with your ears! Anyway, how would you know, up there in your so-called studio? I've been here all evening. Is that clear?'

She realised he was actually shaking with his emotion and she knew enough not to argue. 'Fine, if that's the way you want it. You were here all evening.'

'Right, right,' he said. There was a little fleck of spittle at the corner of his mouth and he took out a handkerchief to wipe it away. 'You go on up to bed. I'll come up later.'

'Goodnight,' she said, closing the door and going through to the kitchen. What had all that been about? The car, she suddenly noticed through a side window, had been parked round there, not in the front where he usually put it. He must have been trying to come back quietly.

Why did he feel he had to sneak out? It was really crazy – if he was having an affair or something he could easily just say he was going back to the office and it wouldn't occur to her to question it.

Denise toyed with the affair idea. As she wiped down the sink she thought wistfully of alimony – lots of money and no Grant. But she certainly wasn't going to rock the boat by demanding an explanation until she was quite sure she had all the evidence she needed.

It was one of those perfect late autumn days: clear blue sky, a sharp touch of frost in the air, the leaves on the trees thinning out now, but still showing red and gold. As Janette Ritchie set out on her usual walk down the hill to get her morning copy of *The Herald*, the cold air prickled the back of her throat – almost like the bubbles in champagne, she thought. With the deep blue of Loch Ryan below it was such a perfect picture that she felt quite sorry for all those poor, deluded folk who went off to live in Spain and would never know the sheer joy of a sunny November day in Scotland.

Unconsciously prompted by the brilliant display of berries on a mountain ash growing in someone's garden, she was humming 'O Rowan Tree' as she came to the children's play park. Shelley's flowers, still lying on the bench where she had placed them, caught her eye and she stopped, hesitating.

The petals of the roses had browned into decay and the foliage was withered. Though Janette felt her usual revulsion about going into the park, she really ought to remove them. There was nothing more pathetic than memorial flowers left to rot, she always thought.

She opened the gate and went over to pick up the bouquet, then, with a grimace of distaste, gathered up the slimy petals that fell as she moved it and looked round for a bin. There was one over on the far side, just beside the slide, and she bit her lip. The last time she'd been in that area was forty years ago, and the picture was vivid in her mind even now.

There was nowhere else to put them. She dropped the flowers in the bin and turned. She saw, first of all, the shoes: smart nude beige shoes with a medium heel sticking out from behind the slide. One was lying on the ground beside a foot with toenails painted a bright red. There was a dark red and cream skirt rumpled up the legs. There was a cream sweater – no, a partly cream sweater patterned with great rust-coloured patches that clashed with the skirt. There was a head with blonde, rust-streaked hair – but the top was just a great bloody mass of something.

That was when she screamed, screamed and screamed. But no one came, and she had to stop screaming sometime. She could do nothing here, and if she looked again she thought she might faint. On legs that were barely able to support her, Janette staggered out of the park, looking frantically up and down the deserted street. She was in such a state of shock that she wandered up and down for five minutes before it occurred to her to go to the nearest house and ring the bell.

CHAPTER ELEVEN

The photographer had just left. In her white paper protective suit DI Fleming stood grim-faced beside the slide, looking down at the pathologist as he crouched at his work. After a brief, nauseated glance at the victim she was concentrating her gaze on the back of his hooded head.

'Not killed here, I can tell you that for a start,' he said. 'Method – straightforward enough, unless something emerges later.'

'Any indication about the weapon?' Fleming asked, though given the mess it was hard to imagine that there could be.

'Blunt instrument – that's about all I could say for certain. Something long and narrow, applied with force – a crowbar, possibly. Once we've done some measurements I might be able to be a bit more precise.'

'Was it – was it quick?' The thought that it might not have been sent a shiver down her spine.

He thought for a moment. 'With that degree of force, unconscious after the first or second blow, most likely. May even have been knocked out first.' He picked up first one hand then the other to scrutinise the nails. 'Looks as if she didn't get a chance to fight back, anyway. Hang on, we'll have a look at the back of her head.'

Seeing him grasp the matted hair, Fleming turned away to look over her shoulder. DS MacNee had arrived; he was standing by the gate of the play park in conversation with the uniform detailed to record visitors to the site. She made a gesture encouraging him to put on a suit and come in but he just looked blank. MacNee was even more squeamish than she was.

The pathologist put down the head again. 'Blow to the back, there. Can't say it was definitely the first one but it seems likely to have laid her out.'

That was something, at least. 'I suppose I needn't ask about estimated time of death?'

'Not with any degree of accuracy. There's rigor developing but a frost last night would have speeded that up and I'd need an indication of how long she was there and where she'd been beforehand – a warm room, say, would complicate it further.'

'So it's the usual – ETD sometime between when she was last seen and when the body was found?'

The pathologist gave a weary smile. 'Old ones are the best ones, eh? I daresay you wouldn't go far wrong with an assumption of somewhere between seven in the evening and midnight or thereabouts. Know who the lady is, then?'

'The woman who found her thinks she knows her but with the state she's in we'll need fingerprint confirmation, I suppose.

'Anyway, let me know when there's any more you can give me.'

Janette Ritchie was sitting at the kitchen table in the house next door to the park, a blanket draped round her shoulders, too shocked to cry. There was a woman PC – well, a girl really, since she didn't look much more than sixteen – patting her hand in a tentative way while her hostess hovered, ready to offer more tea, though Janette hadn't even touched the mug in front of her because she was afraid she would spill it if she tried to pick it up.

How could it happen *twice*? To her – why to her? It had been so awful the last time; she'd taken weeks to recover, even though in those days she had been young and busy, with Shelley to prop up, her own kids to look after and no time to brood. She didn't like to think of herself as old but she certainly wasn't as resilient, and this – this had been worse than Tommy with his poor bashed head. This looked as if someone vicious had enjoyed doing it.

'I've got to think about something else,' she said aloud, and as if on cue the door opened and two people came in – a tall woman, smartly dressed in a dark trouser suit, and a short man in a black leather jacket and jeans.

'Mrs Ritchie?' she said. 'I'm DI Fleming and this is DS MacNee. Do you feel able to talk to us? I know you've had a dreadful experience.'

She had a low, attractive voice and her eyes were so

sympathetic that suddenly the tears came. 'It was awful – awful!' Janette sobbed. 'And there, of all places, right there!'

As her hostess tutted sympathetically and found a box of tissues, the detectives sat down at the table. 'There?' Fleming prompted.

Janette scrubbed at her eyes and blew her nose. She mustn't go to pieces now.

'Right where I found Tommy – I found him, you know. Oh, it was a field then, of course, but even after they made it into the play park I couldn't forget. I walk past it every day but it's only because Shelley does her remembrance thing that I ever set foot in it.'

She had to explain, then, all that had happened that day, with the sudden appearance of a woman who looked uncannily like Kirstie Burnside, whose child-face was seared on their memories. The officers listened without speaking, but Fleming's hazel eyes never left her face and she could feel the intensity of their interest.

When it came to the events of the morning, the questions started but they were all straightforward and somehow afterwards it felt as if she had somehow been relieved of at least a part of the horror. At the end, though, she felt totally shattered and DI Fleming seemed to pick that up.

'You've been an enormous help, Janette. But I think you've had enough for today and you should go home and have a lie-down. Is there someone who can stay with you?'

'I could go to my daughter's,' Janette said. 'She's got two little ones, you know, so I'd be better round there with something to take my mind off this. They're ever so sweet, a boy and a girl, four and two.' She went on for a moment, then stopped. 'Sorry, I'm blethering. You haven't time for this – I don't know why I'm going on like this.'

'Shock.' The sergeant spoke for the first time. 'You away round there and see the bairns – that's the best thing. You'll be fine.' He gave her a rather alarming smile and she smiled back, a little uncertainly.

'That's the way!' he said encouragingly. 'You're a wee stoater, isn't she, boss?'

Fleming smiled. 'A star, indeed. Thank you very much for your help, Janette. Someone will take a formal statement later but we'll let you get your breath back first. And now we'll get on with finding the person who did this.'

As they left, Janette said slowly, 'You kind of feel someone's taken charge, don't you?'

As the PC smiled, Janette noticed that she had a rather impish face. 'Oh, that's Big Marge. She's in charge, all right. Wouldn't like to have her after me, I can tell you that.'

Kylie put her ear to the door of Daniel Lee's office and listened. He'd been on the phone and she didn't want to burst in and interrupt him when he was in a bad mood, and he'd been in a *really* bad mood this morning. Hung-over, likely.

As his management assistant in Zombies – one of the most successful nightclubs in Glasgow – she had what was a dream job with nightmare episodes. You met really cool people and Drax was exciting to work for: when he was your best friend it gave you a real high, which was why you didn't just walk out when he took a sadistic delight

in suddenly taking you down. And if you screwed up –
OMG! The stationery cupboard on the landing had been
christened 'The Crying Room' by his previous assistant.

She had only lasted six months and Kylie, coming up
four, was living on her nerves, with her partner making
'it's-him-or-me' noises. She wasn't sure she'd last to six.
There was this morning to be got through, for a start.

She hadn't heard anything for a few minutes now so she
tapped on the door.

'Drax – have you finished phoning?'

Drax was sitting pushed back from his pristine desk in
his starkly white office with his cream leather office chair
tipped back, arms clasped behind his head and long legs
stretched out. He turned to look at her, scowling.

'Guess,' he said.

Kylie's heart sank. Sarcastic was dangerous. 'There was
a message from a Mr Crichton to phone him. He said it
was urgent.'

Lee sat up and swung round suddenly. 'And what did
you say?'

'I-I said you were on the phone, but I'd give you the
message.'

'You said I was here?' His eyes were blazing now.

Kylie shrank away. 'Well, yes—'

'And what if I don't want to speak to him now? What if
I want to put him off without spelling it out? You're there
to intercept unwanted calls, for God's sake!'

Unwanted calls, OK, but calls from his business partners
hadn't come into that bracket before. She knew better than
to argue.

'Sorry, Drax – should have thought.'

'Thought? You are getting ideas above your station, aren't you? Leave thinking to those of us with the equipment for it – when plankton gets ambitious it only causes trouble. Try just doing as you're told.'

'Yes, Drax.'

'Now get out. Unless there's anything else?'

'No – no, that's all,' she said, backing out. She'd got off lightly and she wasn't going to put her neck on the block by sticking around, even though there was a problem with the guy who did the lighting that he'd have to deal with and she'd a list of bookings for their special 'band night' series that needed to be confirmed too.

As the door shut behind her, Lee drummed his fingers on the desk for a moment then picked up the phone.

Crichton was agitated – almost hysterical. Lee held the phone away from his ear, his face taut with annoyance, but when Crichton ran down his voice was soothing. 'Chill, Grant! Getting worked up's not going to change anything.'

It didn't seem to have any effect and Lee's face darkened. 'OK, so this is a complication, but we'll deal with it. And there's no point in kicking off now – we talked it through, remember? Just do what we agreed. That's all. OK?'

Crichton hesitated, then agreed, and Lee finished the call, then brought his fist down on the desk and swore violently. He was addicted to risk, but only when he was in control. For the moment at least, he certainly wasn't.

* * *

DC Hepburn was yawning and looking haggard this morning. She'd been wakened at 3 a.m. by her mother, fully clad, insisting that she'd better hurry to get up for school because she'd been late the last two mornings; it had taken another hour to coax her back to bed and then she couldn't get back to sleep herself.

She wasn't in any mood for DS Macdonald's pointed remarks about Marnie Bruce as they drove to Dunmore.

'I'd have her right at the top of the suspect list. That yarn she spun us about the women coming to Loudon's door to lynch her – what would you say all that was about?'

'I would say that it was about Anita telling lies,' Hepburn said. 'If what she said was true, how come the mob was outside Marnie's window?'

'Good question – the mob outside her window. Suddenly they're out there baying for blood, and she doesn't know why, she didn't do anything, she's baffled? Aye, right! Doesn't make sense, which is why she concocted the stuff about having to escape from Anita's house out the back.'

'She did. Anita agreed with that.' Hepburn glanced sideways at Macdonald, whose face was set in mulish lines. 'Are you saying that just so you can disagree with me?' she demanded. 'Because—'

'No, I'm not!' Macdonald raised his voice. 'I am using my judgement, based on considerably more years of police service and expertise than you have. You might care to remember that, Constable.'

'Pulling rank?' she needled. 'Fine, Sergeant, if that's the way you want it.'

There wasn't really anything more to say after that.

Lennox Street was congested with police vehicles and personnel, as well as gawping locals clustered along the line of the blue-and-white 'crime scene do not cross' tape outside Anita Loudon's house.

'Ghouls,' Hepburn muttered as they drove past to find somewhere to park and for once got a grunt of agreement from Macdonald. They had been tasked with interviewing anyone the uniforms had found with useful information and they were pointed in the direction of a harassed-looking police sergeant.

'Oh yes,' he said. 'I've got one here for you to make a start on. Lady next door. Mrs' – he squinted at a list in his hand – 'Gordon. Elderly, not very mobile, but all the strength's gone to her tongue instead. Nearly had to send in a raiding party to spring my lads. Hope you're prepared for a long stint.'

'Oh good,' Macdonald said hollowly as they headed up the path. The front door was open; they tapped on it and got an eager, 'Come away in, come in!'

Ivy Gordon was white-haired, beady-eyed and in a state of high excitement. She was sitting in a chair beside the window from which she had a commanding view of the activities next door, with a Zimmer frame in front of her.

'I think that's the SOCOs going in now,' she informed them as they came in.

His mouth twitching, Macdonald said, 'Do you watch a lot of crime series on TV, Mrs Gordon?'

'Never miss. *CSI*, that's my favourite. Now, sit down and I'll tell you all about Anita Loudon.'

They did as they were told, after they'd shown their

warrant cards and Macdonald had given their names, though Ivy wasn't much interested.

'The thing you have to understand is that Anita's parents were decent, god-fearing folk. Nothing wrong with the way they brought her up, I can tell you that, but all along she'd a taste for the gutter.'

Hepburn blinked. 'The gutter?'

'Oh yes. That laddie, Daniel Lee – no father, of course, that anyone ever knew about, and wild. Impudent, too. I wouldn't soil my lips with telling you what he said when I gave him laldie for coming over the wall to scrump my apples. And, of course, Kirstie Burnside – there was bad blood in that family. Oh, they said she was a victim of child abuse, but how did that happen? I'll tell you – bad blood.

'But of course the Loudons were fair devastated when it all happened – devastated. To see their wee girl, ten, eleven years old, maybe, up there in the court – well, her parents were just never the same again.'

Macdonald and Hepburn exchanged glances. 'Sorry – in court? Was she charged with something?' he asked.

'No, no, of course not – don't be daft. A witness! Surely you mind what happened?'

'I think I might have been too young,' Hepburn said tactfully. 'What was the trial about?'

Ivy sat back in her chair. 'Mercy me, what's the world coming to when the police don't know something like that? Tommy Crichton's murder, of course.'

Twenty minutes later, when useful background information had strayed into interminable anecdote, desperation gave Macdonald the impetus to push in with,

'Can I just ask you about last night? You told the other officers, I think, that you saw something?'

'Not saw, no,' she said regretfully. 'They've started putting me to bed like a wean at some daft time, now I can't manage myself. But there were comings and goings last night, I can tell you that – my bedroom's on the other side of the hall at the front and her front gate creaks. There were car doors slamming a couple of times, and early on I heard her talking to someone.'

'Male? Female?' Macdonald asked.

Ivy shook her head. 'Only heard Anita's voice and I couldn't make out what she was saying. I switched off the TV to see if I could hear it, but she'd stopped by then.'

It wasn't a lot to go on. They'd had high hopes at the start of having found the ideal elderly woman witness – nosy, observant and eager to share anything she knew. They tried to pin her down on times, but she was vague about when, and how often, she had heard the gate creak.

Disappointed, Macdonald said, 'Thanks very much, Mrs Gordon. That's been a great help, giving us the background.'

He made to get up, but, like the Ancient Mariner, she made a grab at him and fixed him with a rheumy stare. 'But I haven't told you about her lover!' Macdonald sat down again.

'Och, she thought she was being quite canny. Often he'd come after it was dark, maybe, or he'd just park his car outside and she'd come running out and jump in. Been going on for years and years. Not even on, you know –

he'd just maybe pop in when he fancied a wee bit of the hochmagandy, you know?'

Hepburn, ready to laugh at the jocular term, realised Ivy was deadly serious as she went on, 'And he was here yesterday.'

'Staying at the house last night?' Macdonald's voice sharpened.

Ivy hesitated, then reluctantly admitted that she didn't know. 'Saw him going away yesterday – oh, around twelve, maybe. But he could have been back in the evening, for all I know. Why a body has to be put to bed at seven o'clock I don't know. If you're old you need less sleep, not more.' She sounded bitter.

It was a pause that neither officer liked to interrupt and after a moment, she went on, 'I'd like you to get him, though, if he did that to Anita. I mind her so well as a wee lassie.' She produced a handkerchief from her sleeve and dabbed her eyes.

Hepburn said gently, 'But you've no idea who he is?'

Ivy's tears vanished in indignation. 'Of course I do! It's Daniel Lee – him that I told you about.' She pursed her mouth in distaste. 'He got called some silly name – Drax, that's right.'

DI Fleming arrived at Anita Loudon's house along with DS MacNee, gave their names to the constable on duty at the inner cordon and were permitted through. As they struggled with their paper protection suits, MacNee muttered a constant litany of words which included daft and overkill, as well as a choice selection of expletives.

'I tell you what we look like – maggots,' he said as they dodged SOCOs coming and going down the front path.

'Something I've learnt of late is to think as little as possible what you look like, and avoid mirrors. It's a life skill I'm acquiring to cope with middle age.'

MacNee snorted. 'I'm jake with mirrors. They don't answer back. If I didn't have to wear one myself I could get quite a riff going about grubs.'

'I can imagine. Why do you think I make sure you do?'

Fleming didn't feel as flippant as she sounded. A woman murdered in a peculiarly brutal way was bad enough, but she was finding it hard to see it in isolation, as a crime that had happened last night and an investigation that would start this morning. In some way she couldn't as yet figure out, this was harking back to the murder of a little boy forty years ago.

Inside there were white-clad figures moving everywhere. In the lounge there was someone swabbing the corner of a coffee table tipped on its side – a woman, Fleming realised, as she looked up. 'Any luck?'

The SOCO shook her head. 'Nothing to the naked eye. Needs testing, obviously, but I doubt it.' She put the swab into a sterile pouch and marked it. 'Knocked over in a struggle, perhaps.'

'Maybe. Maybe just when she fell. Ask Kevin about that.'

There was another white-clad figure kneeling just beyond her. Kevin looked up when he heard his name. 'Fell here, I reckon. Got a bloody nose, probably – look.'

There was a small patch of blood on the beige carpet.

There was also, Fleming noticed, a much larger bloodstain a foot away.

Kevin pointed. 'I'm moving on to that. Looks to be where the main injuries occurred, at a guess. What happened to her?'

'Got her head bashed in,' MacNee said. He had been moving about, checking out the room.

'Ouch,' the woman SOCO said, taking a fresh swab to the next corner.

'Have a look at these,' MacNee said, indicating the photos arranged along the top of an old-fashioned bureau. 'See her?' His pointing finger ran along the photos of Anita Loudon: blonde and glamorous, in a provocative pose; having a good time with friends; playing the fool.

Then he pointed to the photo of two elderly people at the back. 'See them? It's their room, not hers, isn't it?'

Fleming surveyed the room with its old-fashioned brown furniture and beige-toned decor. 'And what does that say? How long has she lived here without them?'

There was a SOCO sitting at a side table, sifting piles of paper with her plastic gloves. She turned round. 'Funny you should ask that. I've just found a lawyer's letter here, saying that the house was now in Anita Loudon's name.'

Fleming looked interested. 'Date?'

'1992.'

'That's more than twenty years,' MacNee said. 'Did she just not care about how the place looked?'

'Maybe she just never got round to it,' Fleming said,

conscious of certain elements of refurbishment that long ago ought to have been put in hand back at Mains of Craigie. 'But from the way she dressed, you'd think she'd want a smart house as well as smart clothes. Maybe she didn't really plan on staying but it just happened. Anyway – she can't tell us now, can she?'

MacNee was frowning. 'Look at this, boss.' He was pointing to the back of the bureau.

Anita's housekeeping clearly hadn't extended to daily polishing and right at the back of the surface there were cleaner marks in the fine film of dust where something had been standing.

'A photo's gone,' Fleming said. 'And it's gone recently – could even have been yesterday. Now who was in that photo and why did it have to be removed?'

'Janette might know,' MacNee suggested. 'She's certainly been in the house.'

'I didn't have the impression they were close, though. We'll have to circulate the question and find if there's anyone around who knows.

'Let's check out the rest of the house.' With another glance around the room, where apart from the overturned coffee table there was no sign of a struggle, Fleming was moving towards the door when the SOCO who had been sorting through papers called to her.

'DI Fleming! There's something here I think you might be interested to see.'

She was holding a couple of sheets of paper, stapled together, in her gloved hands and Fleming and MacNee moved behind her to read over her shoulder. It had the letter heading of a firm of solicitors in Stranraer, and it was headed 'Last Will and Testament of Anita Frances Loudon'.

They read it quickly, Fleming giving a slight gasp as she reached the beneficiary's name. The signature at the bottom, Anita F. Loudon, was firm and clear, with a circle crowning the 'i' and a little flourish below and it had been drawn up two years before.

'Thanks,' Fleming said to the SOCO. 'You're absolutely right – it's very interesting indeed.'

She and MacNee went out into the hall and stared at each other.

'I'm gobsmacked,' MacNee said. 'Where did that come from?'

'I don't know, obviously. But I'm going to find out, right now. I want Marnie Bruce brought in immediately.'

'Small problem. Do we know where she is?'

'Ah. The landlady wanted her out of the place in Bridge Street, didn't she. Do we not know where she went?'

'Not that I've heard. For all we know, she may even have gone back south – it's what we were kind of hoping would happen.'

'If she's gone, we're going to have to find her and bring her back now,' Fleming said grimly. 'And try all the local guest houses too, in case she hasn't. I'm suddenly anxious to know exactly what she was doing last night.'

'You phoned her, didn't you? You'll have the number in call history.'

'Right enough.' Fleming took out the phone frowning as she scrolled back through the list. 'It'll be unnamed, of course, but I called her late morning on Tuesday. Ah – that'll be it.'

She punched in the number, listened, then pulled a face. 'Not answering,' she said to MacNee, then texted 'Please call me back as a matter of urgency. DI Fleming'.

'Still no response.' The way MacNee said it made that sound highly significant.

'There's more than one reason for not answering. But it would have made me a lot happier if she'd picked up and agreed to meet us back at the station in half an hour.'

MacNee shook his head. *'Through weary life this lesson learn, That man was made to mourn,'* he declaimed. 'Thought you'd have worked that out by now.'

CHAPTER TWELVE

'Wow! That was quite a story,' Hepburn said as she and Macdonald at last escaped Ivy Gordon's clutches. 'But what has it all got to do with Marnie?'

'Who said it does? You're obsessed with the woman.' Only one more day after this, Macdonald told himself; he could take it for one more day. Campbell, thank God, would be back on Monday. 'She was talking about Anita's background, that's all.'

'I don't buy that. Marnie comes back here, tracks down Anita to try to find out about her mother and suddenly all hell breaks loose. There's all that back story that Ivy tells us – what does that say to you?'

'It says to me that Marnie Bruce is right up on the list of suspects, like I said. Oh look, there's the boss. We'd better go and have a word.'

They went up to the edge of the cordon and waited while Fleming and MacNee talked to the SOCO on the doorstep, struggling out of their protection suits. MacNee, gathering them up to put in a plastic sack by the door, noticed Macdonald and Hepburn and said, 'Boss,' with a jerk of his head. Fleming glanced round, finished her conversation and came down the path towards them.

'Anything useful?'

'Couple of things,' Macdonald said. He gave the five-minute version of their hour with Ivy Gordon, finishing with what she had said about Daniel Lee, and saw Fleming look at him sharply. 'Know him, boss?'

Fleming hesitated, then said, 'I suppose it could be the Daniel Lee who's in a local consortium. I'll get someone to check.'

If that was why she knew the name, she'd had a remarkably strong reaction to it, Macdonald thought, but she was going on.

'There's another thing. Louise, you had some contact with Marnie Bruce, didn't you?'

Macdonald saw Hepburn stiffen slightly. 'Well, I interviewed her, yes.'

'But you haven't been in touch with her since?'

Fleming and MacNee were both looking at her with a curious intensity and Macdonald wasn't surprised when Hepburn sounded defensive in her reply. He'd have felt defensive himself if they'd looked at him like a couple of vivisectionists working out where to make the first incision.

'Not personally, boss, apart from when we interviewed her after the Bridge Street incident. You said you would phone her.'

'Mmm. So you've no idea where she is at the moment? She didn't say where she would go when she left the B & B in Bridge Street?'

Macdonald and Hepburn both shook their heads.

'That's unfortunate.' Fleming hesitated, as if trying to make up her mind about something, then went on, 'Look, this isn't for general release so keep it to yourselves. There's a copy of a will among Anita Loudon's papers leaving everything to Marnie Bruce.'

Hepburn flinched. To his credit, Macdonald didn't turn for a triumphant look at her. It wasn't easy.

Fleming went on, 'I've tried her phone but she's not picking up. I left a message, but obviously we need to pick her up. Get back to the station and find the tourist board list of B & Bs in the area and grab anyone you can find to work through them. Tell them we need to talk to her because she visited Anita Loudon recently. Just that, OK?'

Macdonald agreed politely, though he thought she'd be lucky if the rest of the lads swallowed that story. Followed by the crestfallen Hepburn, he went back to the car.

As they drove away, she said defiantly, 'I know you think that shows you're right, but there's no proof. Marnie might not even have known about the will. And I still believe Anita Loudon was lying.'

He could afford to be magnanimous now they were heading back and would probably be in the office for a fair bit of the day too. 'I certainly won't argue that there's still a lot we don't know,' he said.

It was only then it struck him: they'd be working

overtime tomorrow, without a doubt. And over the weekend too, quite possibly. Three more days, then. He could bear it. Probably.

Marnie's phone rang then gave a 'ping' as she was driving up the A77 towards Ayr. A text message: she ignored it. There was so much going on in her head that she wasn't sure she could have a coherent conversation with anyone.

'I think he said they'd lost touch,' Anita is saying. She knows Anita's just trying to get rid of her but she's not leaving till she has the address—

Blot it out – concentrate on the road! It was clear now; she edged out, then put her foot down and passed the lorry in front.

'No, I can't go to the parents' night,' Mum says. 'Drax needs me, we're busy just now.'

She feels tears come to her eyes. She knows there's no point in saying that everyone else's mum will be there because her mother won't pay any attention but she says it anyway.

Mum's angry and like always when she's angry she goes into attack mode. 'What're they going to tell me – that you're not working hard enough, that you're useless?'

'Yes, probably,' she says in the hard voice she puts on at times like this, as if she doesn't care.

'What's the point, then? Anyway Drax has a job for me tonight.'

Desperate to stop the flood of unrelated images, Marnie turned on the car radio. Perhaps that would help.

She had the heater on full too, though she still felt as if

the cold had gone right through into her bones. She hadn't slept till the early hours and then had wakened feeling cramped and stiff, with the hot-water bottle she had gone to sleep clutching acting as an ice pack instead.

It was a glorious day, though, and even in her troubled state the scenery as she drove on up the coast made her catch her breath. The strange, volcanic hump that was Ailsa Craig was on the horizon now and the sea around it was dark blue, sparkling in the sun. Low in the sky there was a single pale cloud, like a winged dragon, Marnie thought fancifully. It would have been good just to stop and stare at it, blank her mind out, let the beauty and the peace wash it clean . . .

The voice on the radio, which had been burbling in the background unheard, suddenly penetrated her consciousness. '—*small village of Dunmore in Dumfries and Galloway. The woman's body was found in a children's play park by a passer-by and police are treating the death as suspicious.*

'*There was more bad news on the economy—*'

Marnie didn't hear the rest. She slowed down dramatically, earning a blast on the horn from the driver of the car behind, which swept past as he held up his finger in a rude gesture that she didn't notice. There was a sign for a lay-by half a mile ahead and she drove there and pulled in.

The phone. It was lying on the seat beside her; she shrank back as if it were a snake that might strike. She had to force herself to pick it up, and her fingers were clumsy as she opened the text.

It was from DI Fleming. What was Marnie to do now?

'As a matter of urgency' – the phrase was chilling. She sat back in the seat and shut her eyes.

She wasn't going to call back. She was invisible, remember? She was going to go on and do what she had planned, once she was calm enough to drive safely.

She opened her eyes again. There were gannets diving out there, white arrows entering the water with barely a splash. Round the foot of Ailsa Craig she could see tiny white ripples where the waves were breaking. The dragon cloud looked more like a horse now.

At last her hands stopped shaking, she put the car in gear and drove on up the road to Glasgow.

Vivienne Morrison's shop was shut when DI Fleming and DS MacNee arrived.

'News travels fast,' Fleming said. 'Have we an address for her?'

'Here somewhere.' MacNee leafed through some scribbled notes. 'Yes – it's a farmhouse on the edge of the village.' He gave her directions and they drove off up the hill.

'So do we reckon it's the lover or the beneficiary?'

Fleming gave him an exasperated look. 'For heaven's sake, don't start picking sides! We've got enough of a problem already with Louise and Andy.'

'At least Louise didn't jump the gun and get in touch with her and it doesn't look as if our Marnie's answering the phone.

'But this "Drax"? What sort of a man would have a name like that?'

Fleming glanced at him. 'You don't remember? Oh, I suppose I've had my memory refreshed recently. He was one of the child witnesses at Kirstie Burnside's trial. He was around when Tommy Crichton was killed.'

'Oh,' MacNee said flatly. 'Don't think I wanted to hear that.'

'I saw that a Daniel Lee was one of the directors in that local consortium but I didn't make the connection till Andy said that. Strangely enough, Grant Crichton is one of his co-directors. You'd think it would be an uncomfortable reminder for him, but I suppose business is business.

'And there was a Michael Morrison on the list too. Vivienne's husband, do you reckon?'

'What is their business?'

'Not sure. The super's been on this rant about illegal immigration – I told you I'd got lumbered with it. That was one of the local firms operating through Cairnryan but I haven't had time to check out the details.' Her face brightened. 'That's one good thing – at least I can say that I definitely don't have time for it now.

'Is that the farmhouse up there? Not our sort of farmhouse, evidently.' As Fleming turned off up the metalled drive, she glanced across the neighbouring acres with a knowledgeable eye. 'Looks as if the farmer put his feet up after he sold off the house. Lots of farm buildings over there but he's not working the fields.'

MacNee followed her gesture with an incurious eye. To him they looked like fields always did – green and a bit messy. His lawn at home, now – he'd begun to take quite a pride in it recently, though when he'd mentioned it to

Fleming she'd looked at him as if he'd announced he was getting a Zimmer.

A young woman answered the door. She was blonde and very pretty, but the pleasant social smile she had greeted them with vanished when they introduced themselves and asked to speak to her mother.

'Oh dear, it's this awful news about Anita, isn't it? I'm her daughter, Gemma. You'd better come in.

'I can't believe it, not here! We don't even bother to lock the doors half the time.'

She led them across the hall into a sitting room straight out of *Country Living* – three sofas with cream linen loose covers drawn up to form a square with the fireplace, a sofa table behind one of them with a large but very tasteful arrangement of silk flowers and, yes, a stash of what Fleming always thought of as property-porn magazines in neatly squared piles. She was pleased, though, to notice on one of the sofas what looked very like an unnoticed smear of chocolate at child level.

'I'll go and get Mummy,' Gemma said. 'She's lying down. Please can you be very gentle with her? She's in a terrible state.'

As he always did, given the chance, MacNee prowled round the room checking it out. A tabletop was devoted to happy family snaps, the majority featuring a fair-haired child. 'Fond grandparents,' he said.

Fleming pointed to one of the many scatter cushions on the sofas. '"If we'd known grandchildren were so much fun, we'd have had them first",' she read out.

MacNee surveyed them, snorting at hearts and flowers

224

and the Union Jack – not to his taste – then with a grin picked up one which suggested 'Keep Calm and Carry On'.

'Maybe I could just hold this up,' he was saying as the door opened. He dropped it hastily.

Vivienne Morrison did, indeed, look in a dreadful state. Her eyes were puffy with tears and she was visibly shaky; her daughter had an arm round her waist as she helped her to sit down and took her own place beside her, holding her hand.

She managed a travesty of a smile. 'I'm sorry, do forgive me. It's just been . . . such a shock.'

'Of course,' Fleming said. 'We'll keep this as quick as possible. I know our officers interviewed you and Anita Loudon at the shop yesterday.'

Making an obvious effort to control her voice, Vivienne said, 'Yes, but it started as just a normal day. We've worked together for years and years—'

She stopped, biting her lip. Fleming said gently, 'You're obviously very distressed but I know you'll want to give us any help you can so that we can find out who did this to Anita. Was there anything, anything at all, that she said yesterday to suggest that she was worried, that something had happened?'

Vivienne broke down. 'Poor, poor Anita,' she was saying, when the door opened and a tall man with greying fair hair, good-looking still, if showing signs of comfortable living, appeared saying, 'I thought you were lying down, darling!'

His face darkened at the sight of the officers.

'It's the police, Dad,' Gemma said.

'I imagined it must be.' He came into the room, holding out his hand to MacNee. 'Michael Morrison. This is a sorry business.'

'I'm DS MacNee. This is DI Fleming.'

He covered up his assumption that the man would be the senior officer quite smoothly. 'Yes, of course. I imagine you want to question my wife and I know she'll want to give you every possible help. But as you can see she's really in no fit state to talk to you. I've phoned the doctor to come and I'm sure he will confirm that.'

Fleming couldn't really argue. All she could do was say, 'If she could possibly just tell us whether Anita said anything that could be of help—'

'I'm sure she gave us a very full account when we were talking about it earlier,' Morrison said. 'Isn't that right, darling?'

Vivienne's shoulders were heaving but she managed to nod.

He had got the officers on their feet already – deliberately, Fleming wondered? – and now moved to hold the door open very purposefully.

'Thank you for your help, anyway,' she said, then as he escorted them to the front door she added, 'Perhaps I can just ask you how well you knew Anita Loudon yourself?'

Morrison shrugged. 'Hardly at all, really. Of course, I knew her as someone in the village but the shop is my wife's business, not mine, and we didn't socialise. She seemed a pleasant lady, though, and my wife was very satisfied with her as an employee.

'So – have you any idea who might have done this?'

Was it just her imagination, or was there tension in his attitude as he waited for her reply. She prolonged the pause deliberately before she handed out the usual response about promising lines of enquiry.

No, it wasn't imagination. Food for thought.

'She's disappeared,' Macdonald said, coming into the CID room. 'That's the last on the accommodation list checked out, and she's not in any of them.

'Have you tried her phone again?' he asked Hepburn, who was sitting at a computer terminal.

She didn't look up. 'Three times.'

'How soon do we decide it's deliberate and start looking for her in earnest?'

'Give her a chance! There's lots of reasons why you might not be taking calls besides trying to do a runner. And maybe she just decided to go back to London, after all that had happened.'

She spoke absently, looking at what had come up on the screen in front of her at the same time.

Macdonald's curiosity was piqued. 'What are you doing? Thought you were supposed to be writing up the Ivy Gordon interview?'

'Done that. Now I'm just checking out the press coverage of Tommy Crichton's murder.' Hepburn scrolled on down, then suddenly sat back in her chair, staring at it. 'Oh my God!'

'What have you found?' He came round to look over her shoulder.

Hepburn pointed to the photograph inset into the

newspaper article, a family snap of a girl with strawberry-blonde hair and striking blue eyes. 'Who's that?'

'Marnie Bruce as a child,' he said slowly. 'Only it isn't, is it? That's Kirstie Burnside, child murderer.'

'No wonder Marnie got a reaction when she strolled into Dunmore, looking like that. And,' Hepburn said with triumphant emphasis, 'it shows she was telling the truth that she couldn't understand what happened. She has no idea who her mother was.'

'It's plausible, I suppose. Kirstie would be given a watertight new identity after her release and full legal protection afterwards, so even if a persistent journalist got on her trail there's no way anything could be published.'

'It'll all come out now, though, surely?'

Macdonald considered that. 'Not necessarily. The press won't have a photo of Marnie to compare it with, and even if someone tells them that someone who looked like Kirstie Burnside was in the village – well, so what? We're certainly not going to make them a present of the connection.'

'And,' he said, triumphant in his turn, 'it explains why Big Marge and Tam have been so cagey with you. Not a cover-up – an injunction protecting Kirstie.'

Hepburn conceded the point. 'But anyway, what happens now? If we want to find her, we'll have to put out an alert. And you know what will happen then.'

'I certainly do.' A general alert to find a police suspect was like ringing a bell to summon the press for a feeding frenzy. 'But if they manage to put two and two together, will they be banned from reporting on Kirstie's child too? You did law, didn't you?'

'Only as a subsidiary.' Hepburn gave it some thought. 'I'd guess there might have been an injunction but probably with an age limit – up to 18, maybe. They'd be unlikely to impose a whole life ban like her mother's, so as long as they didn't bring Kirstie's whereabouts into it Marnie could be fair game, legally at least. The only problem might be that it would expose the surname Kirstie had adopted, though of course we don't know whether Kirstie's alive or dead. If she's dead the rules would be different.'

'You're taking me out of my depth there. Anyway – what now?'

'I'm going to tell Big Marge I know – get things out in the open. Do you think she's back yet?'

Macdonald glanced at his watch. 'Probably not. And even if she is back she'll have to report to the super and maybe take a press conference – unless Hyacinth wants to take it.'

'What do you think – that she's going to resist the chance of taking the limelight? And anyway, the boss will have to task us – they said we're all on overtime for today at least.'

'I'm going to grab some lunch while I can. What about you, Louise?'

It was the longest amicable conversation they had ever had. It had been in Hepburn's mind to rub it in that she'd been right about Marnie Bruce, but she thought the better of it.

'Fine, Andy. Just let me close this down.' You couldn't spit on an olive branch, even if you did think it was likely to wilt before very long.

* * *

Fleming's mobile rang as she and MacNee got back into the car outside the Morrisons' house. She glanced at caller ID and pulled a face as she answered it. 'Fleming.'

MacNee studied his nails as the voice at the other end crackled on. He couldn't make out what it said, but the expression on the inspector's face told him all he needed to know.

'Yes, I appreciate that you're keen to have a press conference as soon as possible,' she said, 'but I have some things to tie up here and I can't afford the time to drive to and from Kirkluce again today.'

The voice crackled again, even at second hand sounding aggrieved.

'Yes, I quite understand. I'll be back as soon as I can.'

'Hyacinth not just jumping for joy?' MacNee said sympathetically as Fleming rang off.

'You could say. Leaves me pushed for time. Still, at least she stopped short of ordering me back immediately.

'Right. Marnie's in the frame, and Daniel Lee. And given the symbolic positioning of the body, Tommy's parents. I'd rather see them myself than leave it to a routine interview, but I can't see us fitting in both of them – I've got to prepare for the super's statement and the afternoon briefing as well.'

MacNee cleared his throat. 'I'm not maybe the best one to visit Grant Crichton at the moment. I'd a wee chat with him yesterday after the stramash in Bridge Street and I'm not sure I'm just his favourite wee boy. He seems kinna sensitive, ken?'

'I think this is probably something I don't want to

know about,' Fleming said with resignation. 'All right, I'll leave him. There's no evidence at the moment that he'd any recent contact with Anita so I'm more interested in Shelley right now – she seems to have been at the centre of all this.

'According to Janette, she'd been talked into accepting Anita's story that the girl they saw was nothing to do with Kirstie – if we can believe her. Not sure I do. It's such a strong resemblance and there were certainly people convinced enough to go and make trouble for her that night.

'And Shelley clearly has a streak of violence – she flew at Marnie on the spot when she saw her. If she thought Anita was in league with Kirstie, could it just have got out of hand again? Got her revenge putting the body where Tommy was found?'

'Kind of a giveaway, you'd think.'

'That's why I'd like to see her myself. Would the payback motive be so strong that she didn't even consider the implications?'

MacNee looked sceptical. 'And you think you can tell that just by meeting her? Respect!'

'Sarcastic isn't pretty, Tam. No, I don't think that, especially when we're unlikely to surprise her, given that the drums will have been beating. She probably do about what's happening at the

's always

open and transparently truthful – she'd be unusual, though I daresay it's possible. But if she's a bit more normal, I want to see for myself what she's incapable of covering up.'

The Glasgow traffic, to someone unfamiliar with the area and an inexperienced driver, was terrifying. Marnie lost count of the number of times someone blasted their horn at her as she tried to read road signs and get herself into the appropriate lane. She didn't have a satnav and trying to read the instructions she had printed out from the computer in the Kirkluce library was an added complication.

Sod's Law was operating too: the industrial park where she would find Daniel Lee's nightclub was on the far side of Glasgow. After one particularly alarming near-miss, Marnie took to driving off the city bypass until she could stop, then memorising the next batch of instructions and returning to it. This made it a slow process but at last the traffic started thinning out and the signs she needed to follow became more obvious.

When she drew up at last in the car park, she was sweating. The sun, so bright earlier on, had disappeared; the air was bitter when she stepped out but she lingered, letting it cool her flushed cheeks. She wanted to be calm, poised and in control before she encountered Daniel Lee. Always supposing he was here. And that he woul

A busy road ran alongside th
There was somethi
but it

were industrial units – an ugly setting, though it would look better when the lights were flashing and darkness concealed the litter that gathered at the corners in wind-blown heaps.

Marnie's knees felt shaky as she walked across the car park, trying to avoid the potholes and puddles. It must have been raining here earlier. The only entrance she could see, apart from a fire exit at one side, was a great industrial-style door with a smaller door cut into it.

She turned the handle. It opened onto a sort of lobby, with a huge, dark cavernous space beyond. She took a deep breath, then stepped over the threshold, trying not to hear the voice inside her head that was murmuring, '*Will you walk into my parlour, said the spider to the fly . . .*'

CHAPTER THIRTEEN

Shelley Crichton's house was a little way out of the village to the north, an attractive white cottage in a well-kept garden with a view out over Loch Ryan. In the chilly sunshine it looked positively idyllic.

The woman who opened the door to DI Fleming and DS MacNee didn't look in any mood to enjoy it. She was quite tall and solidly built, with frizzy grey hair and strongly marked brows; the jersey two-piece she was wearing was an unflattering shade of green. She looked heavy-eyed, as if she had slept badly.

With the memories this crime must have rekindled, Fleming had been braced for dealing with another weeping woman, but there was no sign of tears and she greeted them sullenly.

'Yes, I heard you were going round the doors. I suppose you'd better come in, then.'

Fleming raised her eyebrows and MacNee pulled a face

behind her back as they were taken through the lounge to a large conservatory on the other side. The air was heavy with the smell of damp earth and vegetation and it was teeming with plants, small shrubs and bushes with fleshy leaves and exotic blooms. With the sun streaming into the overheated room it felt positively tropical and when Fleming took her seat on one of the wicker peacock chairs a nearby plant with waxy white flowers gave out a scent that made her feel slightly sick.

Shelley went on the attack instantly. 'I suppose you've got me on the suspect list because of where Anita Loudon's body was found. Oh yes, I know all about it. Janette Ritchie phoned me first thing, and I've had ten other phone calls since.'

Right on cue, a phone rang somewhere in the house. 'Ignore it,' she said crisply. 'Shall I tell you why they all phoned? Oh, they said they were concerned about me – "Such a horrible thing to happen, poor Shelley, you must be feeling dreadful – oh, and by the way, did you beat her head in?" Not in so many words, of course, but that was the message.'

'And did you?' Fleming was unmoved by the display of passionate indignation.

Shelley gasped. Her eyes, slightly prominent anyway, positively bulged with temper and she snapped, 'No, of course I didn't. Satisfied?'

'Not entirely,' Fleming said. Perhaps it was the nauseating perfume that was making her tetchy; she had come prepared to take it gently but Shelley Crichton was no distressed old lady.

'Let me explain,' she went on. 'We are at the very beginning of our enquiries. At the moment, we're trying to establish the relationships and recent contact people had with the victim rather than setting up any list of suspects.

'So perhaps we could start again. Was Anita Loudon a friend of yours?'

Pause for calculation, Fleming thought cynically as Shelley hesitated.

'Well, in a way,' she said at last. 'I knew who she was, of course. If I saw her in the street I would say hello but I've had very little to do with her, really.'

'And of course she was a pal of Kirstie Burnside's as well, wasn't she?' MacNee put in. 'Hard to forget that, eh?'

'It was a long time ago. She was just a child.' Shelley's face was impassive but Fleming noticed that her hands were so tightly clasped together that the knuckles were showing white.

'When was the last time you saw her, Mrs Crichton?'

'Oh, I forget. A little while ago, I think.'

'Last Tuesday, maybe?' MacNee suggested innocently. 'When you and Janette and some pals went round there to challenge her about someone you thought was Kirstie Burnside's daughter?'

'Oh, that's right. Of course,' she said, though the set of her mouth suggested that Janette's friend status was likely to be reviewed. 'I'd forgotten that was when it was. It was all a mistake, anyway. It was just a girl with similar colouring who'd been doing a survey. I felt a bit of a fool, actually.' She gave a little, artificial laugh.

'So you haven't had any contact with her since?'

Shelley shrugged. 'Why would I?'

'You tell me, Mrs Crichton,' MacNee said and was rewarded with a glare.

'There's no reason why I would. That's what I meant.'

'Aye, but did you?'

'No – I – did – not! Right – is that all?' She got up.

'Very nearly, for the moment anyway,' Fleming said, without moving. 'Can you tell me what your movements were last night?'

Under the inspector's scrutiny, Shelley's gaze slid off to the left. 'I didn't have any "movements", as you call it. I was at home all day, I had supper, I watched television and I went to bed. Just a typical sort of day for an elderly divorcee who lost her only child.' She gave an acid smile. 'So there's no one can confirm it but that doesn't mean it's not the truth.' She was standing with her arms folded, waiting for them to leave.

'Of course not.' Fleming, with a glance at MacNee, stood up. 'I think that's all for the moment. Thank you for your cooperation, madam.'

As she passed Shelley, she knocked a gardening magazine off a small table with uncharacteristic clumsiness. 'Oh, I'm sorry!' she exclaimed, stooping down to pick it up and handing it back to its owner.

Shelley took it without thanks, walking behind them as they made their way out, like a sheepdog determined to make sure there were no stragglers.

Just at the front door Fleming turned back. 'Just one more thing. When you went round to Ms Loudon's house, if you had found that her visitor really was Kirstie Burnside's daughter, what would you have done?'

It was a standard ploy. Shelley, holding the front door ready to shut it behind them, had relaxed her guard.

For a second her light-brown eyes blazed and she stammered, 'I . . . don't—' Suddenly the magazine she was holding dropped from her hand and when she'd retrieved it and straightened up her expression was bland. 'Like I said, I don't know. I would have been wounded to think the daughter of the woman who killed my son had been spying on what is for me a sacred moment. But what could I do? Ask her nicely not to do it again?' She gave a harsh laugh. 'I'm just a victim. People like you see to it that we have no rights.' The shutting door almost clipped Fleming's heels.

'She's not wrong there,' MacNee said gruffly. 'But anyway, what was all the stooshie with the magazine?'

Fleming smiled. 'Hers or mine?'

'Oh, hers was plain enough. What about yours?'

'It's nothing like conclusive, of course, but there's some evidence that lying involves a kind of visualisation that means your eyes move to the left, if you're right-handed. And hers did when she said she was in all evening, and she is.'

MacNee snorted. 'Needed evidence, did you? I could have tellt you that.'

The incident room had been opened up and already the boards round the walls were filling up with photos and sketches. The room was crowded; teams were working overtime and uniformed officers and detectives were perching on the edges of tables and bunching at the back behind the two rows of chairs.

Fleming was feeling harassed as she came in. She had impressed on Rowley that she must not hint to the press that there was any sort of connection with the Kirstie Burnside case and the superintendent, whose motto had always been 'what the press wants, the press gets', even if it meant dropping her officers right in it, had ended by appearing shifty. The press, needless to say, picked up on it at once and she'd had a bit of a mauling, for which she had naturally blamed Fleming.

'I dread to think what the media will make of that,' she said bitterly. 'You can take the next conference yourself instead of setting me up for a fall.'

When Fleming left the office Rowley was phoning the chief constable, officially to get urgent clarification about the situation but unofficially to make sure that if a head were to roll it wouldn't be hers. There were no prizes for guessing whose would be bouncing along in the gutter.

Fleming had been braced for ructions when she pointed out that the cover-the-back exercise on illegal immigration would have to be suspended, but they didn't happen. Rowley had been surprisingly relaxed, saying that the lads at Cairnryan, clearly flavour-of-the-month, were treating it with appropriate seriousness, so she was at least off the hook on that one.

It was the only small consolation. Yet another failed attempt to contact Marnie Bruce had deepened Fleming's gloom. She'd had to work out, too, what she could and couldn't say to the assembled officers, while giving them enough information to do their jobs. This was a briefing she was determined would be brief indeed.

She spoke from the notes she had on such information as had come in. Anita Loudon had been battered to death in her own home; the body had then been moved to a play park a few hundred yards away. No weapon had been found. The approximate time of death was now estimated to be between 20.00 and 01.00 hours, with an hour's leeway on either side. There were no eyewitnesses. There were unsubstantiated accounts of visitors to the house earlier in the evening, but as yet no names or descriptions.

'Priority on that. We're looking for confirmation and identities. We want to trace vehicle movements near the play park from 20.00 hours on – no CCTV, unfortunately. We'll be interviewing a number of known recent contacts – more on that as information comes in.

'The SOCOs will be finished by tonight so there will be fingertip searches around the crime scenes at first light tomorrow – and not a great forecast either. Sorry, lads, but someone's got to do it. And if you've recently annoyed Sergeant Naismith, you're probably on the list.

'Jock, more specific interviews and background searches – have you got the details for CID?' Sergeant Naismith nodded and she went on, 'I'll meet with my team in my office after this – ten minutes. Now, I'll take questions, but be sure it's one you need to ask. None of us has time to waste.'

That would, she hoped, discourage fishing expeditions by inquisitive officers. There were too many answers she couldn't give them at the moment, but choking off questions wouldn't send the right message.

She had no problem with the first two: Anita Loudon had been small and slight so no exceptional strength would be needed to move the body; she was local to the area, having grown up there and moved back after the death of her parents.

That was fringing on the area she was keen to avoid and in the brief pause that followed Fleming swiftly gathered up her notes and half-turned away.

'Er . . .'

She turned back, her heart sinking when she saw her questioner. It was Brian Todd, one of the awkward squad, who had a grudge because he'd applied to CID and been turned down. Ever since he'd tried to show them what they were missing.

'Yes, Brian?' she said warily.

'Is it right the body was found exactly where Tommy Crichton's body was found forty years ago, with similar injuries?'

There was a surprised reaction from a number of officers, but by no means all. So the story was out there already, and if Todd knew so would the press by now – and guess who would be taking the next conference with them howling for raw meat?

'Yes,' Fleming said then without elaborating made her exit. The decibel level rose as soon as she was out of the door.

'Boss! Could I have a word before the meeting?' Louise Hepburn's voice spoke behind her.

Oh, she could really do without that! Fleming turned, managing to smile. 'Oh, Louise. Yes, of course.'

'I just wanted to say Andy and I know who Marnie Bruce is.'

Fleming looked at her sharply. 'How did you find out?'

'We saw the photo of her mother in the reports about Tommy Crichton. She's the spitting image.'

Simple as that. 'So who else saw it?'

'Only us, I think. You'd have to have seen Marnie to know and we're the only ones who've talked to her, except maybe the uniforms that went round to Bridge Street the other night.'

And, of course, Shelley Crichton and Janette Ritchie and any of the other ladies who'd been around with them. It was presumably all over Dunmore and the media would have the full story by tomorrow, if not tonight. She could only hope that by then they'd have got clearance to be more open with the press.

Hepburn went on, 'I was wondering – does Marnie know about her mother? If she does, it would be quite brave to go back to Dunmore to ask questions.'

'I think I'd say callous, if she did. But my guess would be that she was never told. It's going to be quite a thing for her to cope with when it comes out. For that reason alone I'm keen to find her, apart from the investigation altogether.'

'I don't believe she killed Anita Loudon.' Hepburn's square, stubborn chin was definitely jutting. 'She walked into a difficult situation, that's all, and—'

Fleming interrupted her. 'Louise, I haven't time for a

discussion just at the moment. We have the meeting in ten minutes to explore our ideas. But taking up a position beforehand isn't constructive and I'll be looking to you to keep an open mind. Understood?'

'Yes of course. But—'

'No buts.' Fleming took the stairs to her office two at a time, fired by her irritation. Hepburn was often a trial but she'd earned her place on the team in their last big case with her sharp, enquiring mind. Macdonald, for all his competence, lacked the spark that could fire up a new direction in an investigation, and Campbell – well, admittedly if he said something it was usually incisive. If.

It would be good to have him back from leave, though. She could only hope Andy Mac didn't succumb to a coronary before that.

Marnie had never liked the idea of nightclubs. Loud music always seemed to pump out aggression and a mob of sweating dancers sounded wild and threatening. The time Gary had persuaded her to go with him hadn't been a success – more a disaster, really. Even though this great barn of a place was empty and silent, the memory surged back.

She is screaming, 'I can't breathe, I can't breathe!' She'd been wanting to scream that ever since they came in but now that she's right at the back of this horrible noisy hell with people pressing up against her she can't keep it in any more.

Gary's looking embarrassed and people around her are

staring. He's bellowing, 'Calm down!' in her ear but she can't, she's hysterical, she doesn't know what to do and people are nudging and pointing now.

Blindly she starts to push her way through and a man stands deliberately in her way, grinning. 'In a hurry, sweetheart?' He makes a grab at her but she pushes past and he dodges in front again.

She knees him in the groin and pushes on without a backward glance and there's a space opening up in front of her and the bouncer holds the door open for her and she's outside gasping the fresh cool air.

The air in here wasn't fresh. It felt stale and sickly as she stood wrestling with the images. There was something creepy about the atmosphere, with no windows and minimal lighting and chipped patches showing white against the matt-black walls. The bench seating was ripped in places with stuffing showing, and the wooden floor was scuffed to bare boards and pitted with the prints of countless stiletto heels. Once the lights and lasers were weaving their hypnotic patterns no one would notice but the sleaziness disgusted her.

Marnie looked round uncertainly. Someone must be here, but there were several doors and she had no idea which one to try. The one she tapped on first led into a storeroom; the second to a small empty office. She was just shutting the door again when she realised that she wasn't alone.

In the shadows by the bar there was a slight figure in black, a woman wearing a headscarf. She was staring at Marnie with huge dark eyes, as if she was afraid of her.

There was a pail and a mop at her feet.

Marnie went over to her and saw her shrink away. 'It's all right,' she said, smiling. 'I'm just here to see Daniel Lee. Where would I find him?'

The girl couldn't be more than twenty. She dropped her eyes and muttered something, looking helpless.

A language problem. Marnie repeated the question, more slowly, but the only response was a helpless fluttering of hands.

She turned her own hands outward in a questioning gesture. 'Dan-i-el Lee. Drax?'

It seemed at last that the girl understood. She hesitated, then with a tiny jerk of her head indicated a door at the other end, beside the dais where the DJ's equipment was, then bit her lip as if she was terrified she had done the wrong thing.

It wasn't reassuring. If Drax's cleaner was so scared, did Marnie really want to allow him back into her life? She paused for a long moment, studying the black-painted flat panel door as if it might have the answer.

Last chance, that was what it said to her. This is your last chance to find out if your mother is dead or alive. It's the only trail you have left to follow. It may not lead anywhere but you've gone through so much, got yourself in so deep, that it would be unbearable to leave it unexplored. Last chance. And afterwards you can just walk out, drive away and disappear again.

Marnie took a deep breath and tapped on the door. There was no answer. She tapped again, then opened it. It led to a staircase that spiralled up into darkness at the top. With her heart thumping, she began to climb.

'The way into my parlour is up a winding stair . . .'

'Let's assume for the moment that Marnie Bruce is genuine in her attempt to find out what happened to her mother,' Fleming said. 'Of course it's possible that she may have returned here with the intention of murdering Loudon to get her inheritance but it would be remarkably naive timing, after setting up a sophisticated cover story.'

'Could she just have lost her temper?' Macdonald suggested. 'Suddenly lashed out for some reason, then found herself with an inconvenient body and parked it to try and shift the blame to someone with an interest in Tommy Crichton's murder?'

Hepburn gave him a sharp look but it was MacNee who spoke. 'From what I saw of the corpse—'

'From a distance,' Fleming said pointedly.

'From a few yards away, it didn't look like someone lashing out. Right, boss?'

In all the pressure of an investigation, you somehow pushed the sickening reality to the back of your mind. It came back vividly now. 'Yes. This wasn't someone who lashed out then was appalled at what had happened. It was savage. This was someone who killed in anger, then went on being angry. Shelley Crichton is certainly angry.'

'Or it could be someone who wanted to suggest that,' Hepburn put in. 'Would someone who wanted revenge for Tommy really invite suspicion by putting the body there?'

Fleming nodded. 'I think we have to consider cold-blooded cynicism. But remember, too, there were people in the village who were angry enough about what happened to form a lynch mob for Marnie, and there is such a thing as vigilante justice, though I have to admit it's hard to see why this would be aimed at Anita Loudon rather than at Marnie herself.

'I couldn't send the lads round the doors to find out who organised all that until there was confirmation that Marnie wasn't still protected but the super phoned a few minutes ago to say she can be identified, so that can go ahead.'

'And put out an alert to pick her up, I suppose,' MacNee said.

Hepburn looked horrified. 'Are you going to do that right now? Can't we see if we can get her to answer the phone first?'

'You've been trying all day,' Macdonald pointed out and got a death stare in response.

Fleming said hastily, 'I can get someone on to tracing the phone if necessary, though it may depend whether she's switched it off or just isn't answering. We'll give them a chance to do that before we go in with the bells and whistles. A general alert means circulating a photograph and the media won't be any slower than you two in realising who she is. It's another reason why I'd like to find her – if she doesn't know about her mother it wouldn't be a good way to find out, and if the press get to her first they'll crucify her.

'Anyway, we can't ignore our other lines of enquiry. Grant Crichton – as far as we know, he hasn't any connection with Anita but as Tommy's father he has to be considered. You could do that on your own, Andy.'

She ignored his involuntary grin. 'The other person we need to talk to as a priority is Daniel Lee. We noticed that a photo seemed to be missing from among a group on a table at her house, and now we know he was her lover it's likely it was one of him and he removed it – that could be significant. I can't take the time to go up to Glasgow myself, but you could take Louise, Tam.' She ignored Hepburn's pleased expression too. 'How long will it take you to get there?'

'Couple of hours? Thereabouts.'

'His business address is a nightclub, Zombies. That's all we have. Here it is – they dug that out for me.' She flicked through papers on her desk. 'Here.

'Now – anything else? No? That's fine, then.'

MacNee hung back as the others left. 'How far back are we going to have to go on this one, Marjory?'

Fleming sighed. 'Back to Tommy, certainly. But that was all meticulously gone into at the time so there probably aren't too many surprises.

'Kirstie Burnside's disappearance – that's something else. You and I both know that good old Jakie McNally swept everything under the carpet and then trampled it flat.'

'We certainly can't say anything about her. Unless she's dead.'

'And we don't know whether she is or not. Unless Marnie's managed to find out something.'

'Something that Anita told her? Say she confessed that she'd killed Kirstie . . .'

'Leaving everything to Marnie by way of redress?' Fleming was struck with the idea. 'It's a more possible scenario than anything else we've come up with.

'On the other hand, Shelley Crichton – I wouldn't put anything past her.'

'Oh yes,' MacNee said. 'The plant I was sitting beside was one of thae kind that eats wee flies and stuff. Not nice.

'Well, I'm away. Here – I'm glad Andy didn't have to take Louise with him to Stranraer. We're not needing another murder to investigate and that would be pushing our luck.'

The upper floor of the building seemed to have been created in the roof space of the old warehouse, a corridor running its length under the steel roof beams with doors on either side, dimly lit so that it vanished into shadows at the end. As Marnie reached the top of the spiral staircase she hesitated, looking about her uncertainly. She thought she could hear faint soft sounds, whisperings, perhaps, but perhaps that was imagination working overtime.

A man's voice speaking suddenly quite close to her made her jump. It came from behind the door just opposite the top of the stairs and it sounded as if he was on the phone.

'No problem,' he was saying smoothly. 'Just send someone round and I'll have all the paperwork ready for you. All right?' There was a pause, then, 'Yes, of course. Not a problem, as I said. Just give me a call to make sure I'm here, all right? Wouldn't like you to have a wasted journey if I was out.'

She heard him say goodbye. A moment later there was

a crash as if something had been thrown across the room. Then he started swearing.

Marnie froze. That was Drax – she recognised his voice – and he was in a temper. She knew what his tempers could be like.

'Go into your room and shut the door,' her mother's saying to her. 'Keep out of the way till I tell you to come out.'

She doesn't argue, even though her bedroom at Clatteringshaws hasn't any heating and there's a hard October frost. She hears Drax's car arriving with a squeal of brakes, then her mother's voice in the hall as she opens the door. She hates the way Mum sounds – sort of feeble and pleading and pathetic. She hears Drax yelling at her, hears her mother starting to cry and then she puts her fingers in her ears so she can't hear any more. Except a crash so loud that she hears it anyway and she feels her heart pounding. What if he's killed her?

But then she hears Mum's voice and she's not screaming so she must be all right. It's a long time, though, before the door opens and she can come out. Drax has gone and Mum doesn't even have any bruises that she can see, so that's good. She's looking funny, though, sort of blank and looking through her daughter as if she isn't there.

That had been not long before it all happened, before her mother disappeared and the world went upside down. It struck her with a sudden chill: the man on the other side of that door could be her mother's killer – and she was going to go in and challenge him about it? Challenge Drax, in a bad mood – she'd have to be mad. She turned, ready to tiptoe down the stairs.

Suddenly, the door was flung open and there was Drax, his face black with temper. He almost bumped into her.

'Oh, I'm so sorry, I didn't mean to startle you,' Marnie bleated, sounding feeble and pleading, like her mum.

'Who the hell—' he began, then stopped. A slow smile came over his face. 'Well, well, if it isn't my little friend Marnie, all grown up! I've been expecting you. Looking for a chat, were you? You'd better come in.'

He was always at his most dangerous when he was angry underneath but switched on the charm. What else could she do, though, except follow him in?

CHAPTER FOURTEEN

Revelling in his own company, DS Macdonald drove along to Stranraer. He drove with the windows open for the first few miles; even without Louise in the car, the smell of her French cigarettes somehow lingered.

It was the least of his problems with her but it was somehow symptomatic of her irritating, immature desire to show that she was 'different', not just your standard police officer – as if the rest of them were happy to settle for 'just standard'. They weren't, but they didn't feel the need to take up extreme positions to draw attention to themselves.

No, however hard he tried – and if he was honest he didn't, always – it was simply impossible to get on with Louise Hepburn. The trouble was that she approached cases as if she was agent for the defence for one suspect or another, and what annoyed the hell out of him was that somehow she always managed to draw him into being agent for the prosecution, instead of being magisterially cool and aloof.

This thing with Marnie Burnside, for instance: he'd found himself almost accusing her of Anita Loudon's murder, though that was wholly unprofessional at this stage of the investigation and wasn't a considered position anyway.

That was another problem: he wasn't even sure what he did think. It was only this week that he'd realised how much he depended on his one-sided conversations with Ewan Campbell to clear his head and shape his thinking. Campbell seldom spoke, but if he thought Macdonald was going off at a tangent he'd cut through the verbiage with a single incisive remark.

Being alone in the car was a good opportunity to get his ideas straight. After all, thinking aloud wouldn't be a lot different from talking to a silent partner. When he tried it, though, it made him feel a right berk and he reverted to the old-fashioned method.

The case he had been urging against Marnie Bruce was pretty flimsy, when it came right down to it. Loudon's will provided a strong motive but there was no proof that Marnie even knew about it. If she had been familiar with her mother's story, she'd hardly have come blundering into Dunmore asking questions like that. And if she didn't know about Tommy Crichton's murder, why would she have moved Loudon's body to the play park – and how would she have known, anyway, exactly where the child had been found? Unless her mother had told her, which brought him neatly full circle.

No, Louise, blast her, was almost certainly right. Marnie Bruce had simply been the catalyst, caught up in something she didn't understand. The trouble was, he didn't understand it either.

This was the point where he could have done with Campbell to come in with one of his terse remarks. He tried to imagine what it would be, but that didn't work – and he was nearly at Stranraer.

The headquarters of Crichton's company wasn't hard to find – a sprawling complex of hangars, workshops and offices on the outskirts of the town. A couple of juggernauts sat in the extensive parking area and a smartly painted sign read 'Crichton. Haulage and delivery services'.

It appeared to be a prosperous business, with a good number of cars parked outside what looked like the main office building. Macdonald left the car there and found a door marked 'Reception'.

The room was functional rather than inviting, lined with untidy boards covered in dog-eared lists of what looked like rotas and schedules. Presumably Crichton didn't expect passing trade, and the woman at the desk seemed mildly surprised as she asked Macdonald if she could help him.

'I was wanting a word with Mr Crichton, please.' He showed his warrant card.

'Oh! Oh yes, of course.' She lowered her voice. 'I think he's at home. I'll check with his secretary but his car's not here. He was in earlier but – you know.'

Macdonald nodded as she made the call. 'Poor man,' he heard her saying, then, 'Oh? Right. He didn't need that, did he?'

She turned back to him. 'Yes, he's at home. He came in this morning even though he must have been quite upset with all this, but then there was a phone call that meant he'd something to sort out at home. You'll get him there. All right? Do you need the address?'

'Got it here. Thanks for your help.'

As he went back to the car, Macdonald wondered what the phone call that had sent Crichton home during the working day had been. A case like this always set the antennae bristling, though it was probably nothing to do with it at all.

Crichton's house was a handsome modern building in a superb position, looking out over Loch Ryan. One of the Irish ferries was just coming in, its white paint and red funnels bright in the watery sunshine, though the gathering clouds suggested it wouldn't last for long.

There was a Mercedes parked outside as well as a smart little BMW 1 Series, so it looked as if the owners were at home, but there was no answer when Macdonald rang the bell. After a pause, he rang again just as the front door opened.

The woman was smartly dressed in neat black trousers and a turquoise sweater that murmured cashmere, but her blonded hair was ruffled and her mascara smudged. She looked, Macdonald thought, half-asleep.

'Sorry to disturb you, madam. DS Macdonald – I was hoping for a word with Mr Crichton, if he's at home.'

'Oh – sorry, yes of course. Come in. I'm afraid you caught me having a snooze.' She looked flustered, and catching sight of herself in a mirror in the hall as she led him in, she gave an exclamation of dismay, patting her hair and taking out a tissue to dab at the smudges.

'Mr Crichton?' Macdonald prompted.

'Oh yes, yes of course. Er . . . I suppose you'd better just come through to his office. This way.'

The response to her tentative tap on the door was a surly grunt. When Denise opened it, Macdonald saw that Crichton was sitting at a desk covered with a jumble of papers, with more files piled around his feet. He looked as if he had been running his hands through his hair and he snarled, 'What is it, Denise? I told you I didn't want to be disturbed.'

'It's the police, wanting a word,' she said and her husband's head swivelled. His face had gone pale and he got up, pushing his chair back in a clumsy movement, then standing where he was blocking the view of the desk from the door.

He gave her a killer look and she stammered, 'Sorry, Grant, I didn't think – I was asleep when he came,' as he said to Macdonald, 'What is this about? As you can see, I'm very busy. Can't it wait?'

'I'm afraid not, sir. I'm Detective Sergeant Macdonald. We're investigating the murder of Mrs Anita Loudon.'

Crichton's face changed. Somehow, this wasn't what he had been expecting, but he didn't look any happier. 'Yes, of course,' he muttered. 'You'd better come through to the lounge.'

He almost pushed the others out and, Macdonald noticed with interest, locked the door behind him. Denise, apologising for the disorder, scurried ahead to fold up a furry throw and plump the cushions on the sofa.

'I'll just leave you to it, shall I?' She made for the door, but Crichton said abruptly, 'No, you stay. There's nothing you can't hear.'

'Did you know Mrs Loudon?' Macdonald asked her.

She shook her head. 'I heard today she worked in Vivienne Morrison's dress shop and I go there sometimes, but I never knew her name.' She tucked herself into one corner of the sofa as if she was trying to efface herself completely.

Crichton sat down in one of the armchairs and Macdonald took the other. 'This must have been a very distressing day for you, sir,' he said.

'Yes. Yes, it was.' Crichton's eyes went to a photograph on the mantelpiece, a snapshot of a little boy. 'Whoever put the body there has a macabre and disgusting mind.'

'Indeed. Do you feel that where it was placed suggested that the killer was someone who was looking for revenge?'

'Revenge? I assume you're thinking of my former wife or myself and it sounds to me like a veiled accusation.'

It was said aggressively; there was no doubt that Crichton was getting his confidence back. 'Not at all,' Macdonald said blandly. 'It may be a clumsy attempt to divert suspicion.'

'Perhaps you could explain to me why killing Anita Loudon would constitute revenge? It wasn't she who killed my son.'

'She was one of the witnesses at the time, I understand.'

'And her evidence helped put Kirstie Burnside behind bars.'

'Yes, indeed. So you had no grudge against her. How well did you know her?'

'Know her?' Crichton bridled. 'I didn't *know* her, Sergeant. Knew who she was, yes. But that was all.'

'You were never, for instance, at her house?'

'No, never.' It was a very firm denial.

'When was the last time you saw her?'

That threw him. 'Saw her? I-I don't know. I probably passed her in the street or saw her in a shop, but I wouldn't have spoken to her. How could I possibly remember? It's a ridiculous question.'

'Right. Is there anything you know about Mrs Loudon that might be helpful to us in suggesting a reason for her death?'

Macdonald had hoped that the invitation to point the finger elsewhere might tempt him, but he was disappointed.

'No.'

'I see. Thank you, sir. Just one final question. What were your movements last night?'

'Simple enough. I had supper with my wife, then I worked in my study until late. Then I went to bed. My wife will bear me out.' He looked across at her, his gaze hard.

There was a slight, fluttery movement from Denise. Then she said, 'Yes, that's right,' in a colourless voice.

Macdonald got up. 'Thank you both. There's nothing further, at the moment at least. But if anything else occurs to you, however trivial, you can contact me on this number.' He put down a card on the coffee table. 'I'll let you get back to your paperwork, sir.'

A haunted look came over Crichton's face. 'Yes,' he said

heavily. 'My wife will show you out.' He left.

Macdonald said quietly, 'You didn't sound terribly sure about your husband's movements last night. Would you have known, if he'd gone out?'

Denise looked at him with something like panic. 'Yes, of course I would!' she cried wildly. 'That's an outrageous suggestion. He was here all night.'

'That's fine. I'm glad to have your confirmation. Thank you for your time.'

But, he reflected as he went back to the car, what validity did an alibi have when it was given by a bully's victim?

Daniel Lee's windowless office was minimalist in style with a glass desk, sleek pale leather chairs and a bank of glossy white filing cabinets against high-gloss white walls. Two Perspex tiered trays held papers neatly piled but there was no form of decoration or ornament to soften the chilling impersonality of the room. The mobile telephone lying on the floor was the only sign of disorder.

Light from aluminium downlighters reflected with almost painful effect and Marnie, dazzled as she stepped in from the dark landing, stopped dead.

Ahead of her, Drax spun round with that quickness of movement she remembered so well and putting an arm that felt like a steel bar around her waist he propelled her into the room, closing the door behind them.

'You wanted to see me. And here I am. Sit!' He pointed to one of the chairs in front of his desk.

The image flickered into life.

'Sit!' he says, pointing to the battered sofa in the lounge.

259

She doesn't want to sit. He thinks it's funny, treating her like a dog. But this isn't funny. She realises Mum's told him what she said and now he's going to make her pay for it.

She doesn't know why she even bothered saying it in the first place because she knows there's no way Mum would ever leave him and find somewhere he doesn't know about, just for the two of them, so he would never come.

'You and your mum on your own?' He's laughing at her. She hates being laughed at. 'Using what for money? I'm the one who gives you everything. If it wasn't for me, you know what would happen? Your mum would have to go on the game – you know what that means?'

She's ten, of course she knows. Dry-mouthed, she nods.

'Of course, there's you too – could get a bit more for you, being underage.'

He's leering at her in that way that frightens her and her mum's looking at her as if she blames her not him.

He's going on. 'She's useless, you see, your mum.'

'Why do you want to keep her, then?' The words come out of her mouth before she can stop them and she's feeling sick with fear and waiting for him to hit her.

He doesn't. He laughs. 'Let's just say she has a special characteristic that suits me. She's my slave, aren't you, babe?'

And her mother, horribly, is laughing too. 'Oh yes,' she says. 'I'm your slave.'

'For God's sake, what's wrong with you?' Drax's voice cut across and she came back to the present. His strongly marked brows had shot up and his dark, dark eyes were wide with what looked like alarm. 'That's weird, you're—'

Then he stopped. 'You're doing that thing Anita talked about. You're going back in time, aren't you?'

Marnie said nothing. She didn't know what to say so she went to the chair he had indicated and sat down. Drax didn't go to the other side of the desk; he sat on it, just beside her, and bent forward staring into her eyes as if they might operate like a film screen.

'What are you looking at?' he demanded.

She moved back in her chair, blinked, turned her head. 'Nothing. It's random, that's all. It doesn't mean anything.'

'What can you remember about when you were at Clatteringshaws and your mother worked for me?'

Everything, every last little thing, was the truthful answer, right up to the moment when she came back on Halloween and someone hit her on the back of the head.

'Nothing much,' she said. 'Just scraps of things, pictures—'

'Do you remember the night your mum had a lot of people to take somewhere and it all got a bit difficult?'

Of course she did. She was even now trying to fight down the pictures: a whole load of foreigners, packing into the Clatteringshaws house, men jabbering, her mother shouting at them and her sent to her bedroom in a hurry . . .

Marnie frowned. 'No, I'm afraid not.'

Drax was still staring at her. 'You're lying, aren't you? Anita said you remembered everything. Absolutely everything.'

He got up abruptly and went round to the other side of the desk and sat down. 'She's dead, you know.'

Through stiffened lips Marnie said, 'I was afraid it might be her.'

'There are a lot of bad, nasty people around. I expect you've realised that by now.'

Oh she had, yes, she had. Marnie nodded.

'You wouldn't want to upset them now, would you?' In the harsh light, his dark eyes seemed to glow.

Transfixed, she shook her head this time.

'The question is, are you as good at forgetting as you are at remembering?'

She grasped at that. 'No one's going to ask me anything. Once you've told me what I want to know I'm going to disappear.'

'Smart decision. That's a useful talent, especially when the police have you as a suspect – which they will, of course, since you visited her. Where are you staying at the moment?'

Her stomach had lurched at the mention of the police, but she said only, 'You can't think I'm going to tell you.' Did he imagine she was stupid?

'Just testing.' He sat up abruptly in his chair, his mood changing. 'I've got too much to do to spend any longer with you. *Far* too much.'

There was something he was angry about, something that was nothing to do with her, and she wondered what it was.

'So you've got two minutes to ask whatever it is you want to know.'

'Where's my mother?'

'Karen? That's easy. I don't know. How would I? What

is it – twenty years since I saw her? More? She could be anywhere. All right? Does that answer your question?'

'Did you kill her?'

That amused him. 'Kill her? Why should I? Disposing of a body is quite a hassle, they tell me. So . . .' He shrugged. 'I didn't, no.'

He got up, but Marnie didn't. She'd come this far and got nothing; what had she to lose now if she asked the question she hadn't had the courage to ask all these years ago.

'Are you my father?'

His lip curled in a sneer. 'Your father? Who knows? I shouldn't think your mother knows either. She was such a little tramp you could have been anyone's.'

The casual cruelty of the reply hit her hard. She got up, trying to master her tears, and stumbled to the door. His laughter followed her as she went downstairs.

The Asian woman she had seen before was standing in front of a cleaning cupboard, winding up the cord on the vacuum cleaner. There was a man standing at the DJ bench wearing headphones who glanced up incuriously as she passed.

When she reached the car park there was a young Asian man sitting in a small grey car with a dent in the wheel arch nearby, waiting patiently for his girlfriend, she guessed. She saw him answer his phone; that would be her, probably, saying she was just about ready to leave. It must be wonderful to be someone who had another person who cared enough to come and wait to take you home, instead of driving miles by yourself in the bleak darkness to a half-derelict house where all that waited for you was loneliness. She'd never know now what had happened to her mother. She'd have to live with the deafening silence, and tomorrow she might as well go back to London.

But as she drove out of the car park, she saw the little grey car was driving off too, so her romantic notion that he was waiting to take his girlfriend home was just that. Ah well.

DC Hepburn woke suddenly as the car braked for a traffic light. She had again had a very disturbed night and she'd fallen so deeply asleep that for a moment she couldn't think where she was. She sat up, rubbing the crick in her neck.

DS MacNee was at the wheel. He was looking at her quizzically. 'Dearie me, lassie, you're far too young to be needing a nap in the afternoon. Too many nights out on the razzle, I don't doubt.'

Her eyes prickled with tears at the injustice, but she said only, 'Oh well, you know how it is,' as jauntily as she could.

'I knew once, right enough,' MacNee said, 'but it's so long ago I've almost forgotten. Anyway, you did the smart thing. The traffic was nose-to-tail all the way in – took an hour and a half longer than it should have. We're nearly there, though.'

Yawning, Hepburn looked around. It was an unappealing area of Glasgow, industrial buildings and run-down tower blocks. 'Funny place to have a nightclub,' she said.

'This is a major road with good bus services,' MacNee pointed out. 'And if you're out here you don't get grief because the neighbours complain. Quite a nice little business. That's it there, look.'

He pointed to a display of flickering lights just ahead. It was evening now, very dark with drizzling rain falling and as they turned into the car park and got the full benefit of the sophisticated show of neon, Hepburn thought it looked quite inviting despite its bleak surroundings.

'Very jazzy. And Zombies – it's a good name.'

MacNee snorted. 'If you say so. All I can say is, they've come a long way from the local Palais. Seemed exciting enough at the time.'

There were quite a lot of cars in the car park now and there was a man standing outside the entrance smoking, a bullet-headed young man of impressive physique with a fine collection of visible tattoos.

He looked curiously at MacNee and Hepburn as they came up. 'We're not open till ten, granddad. Anyway, not really your kinna place.'

Hepburn could only hope that the darkness concealed her grin as MacNee bridled.

'Nae brains, just brawn, that's your problem. We're police. Your licence in order, is it?'

Alarm showed on his face. 'Aye. Probably.'

'OK, you can apply what brain you have to telling me where I'd find Daniel Lee.'

The man looked blank. It seemed to be, Hepburn thought, an expression he was comfortable with and used a lot.

'Drax, then?' MacNee said impatiently.

His face cleared. 'Oh, aye. Be in his office, likely.'

'And where's that?'

'Inside.'

'I'd guessed that. Where inside?'

'Up the stair. By the stage, ken?'

Not pausing to point out that if he knew he wouldn't be asking, MacNee went inside, followed by Hepburn.

A number of people were milling around the huge space. None of them looked to be much over twenty, and there was music blaring out from loudspeakers by the DJ's dais. Spotlights illuminated the dance floor and a burst of coloured lasers played briefly across the room then was switched off again as someone shouted comments. There was a lot of chat and laughter, and though one or two heads turned as they walked towards the door by the dais no one spoke to them.

As they reached the top of the spiral staircase a woman came towards them along the dark corridor. She glanced at them incuriously, then with a sudden sharpening of her gaze. She didn't speak, only pursed her lips and disappeared through a nearby door.

MacNee grinned at Hepburn. 'Always revealing, when they recognise CID at ten yards. She'll be warning the boss right now.'

And sure enough, a mobile with a jazzy tune rang behind one of the doors facing them. Immediately MacNee went to it, knocked and opened it without allowing time for a response.

The man sitting at the desk in this aggressively white room, was hunched over the phone, scowling. 'Where are they now, then?' he said, then spun round as MacNee said, 'Here.'

For a moment he looked confused, then as MacNee made the formal introductions and said insincerely, 'I'm sorry to startle you, sir. I did knock,' a remarkable transformation took place.

The hunched figure relaxed and stretched out, the dark anger vanished and Daniel Lee looked up at them from his chair with a gently rueful expression. There was something very engaging about the winged brows and eyes that held a spark of amusement and invited his companions to share the joke. But in an almost panicky movement he gathered together the papers he had spread out on his desk without losing eye contact with them, as if that would stop them noticing. And, Hepburn noticed with keen interest, he turned them face down.

'Do sit down. Yes, I'm afraid you did catch my secretary tipping me off. If you run a nightclub you get very nervous when the police come round, even if your conscience is totally clear. What am I up for today?'

He gave them both a charming smile, lingering a little longer on Hepburn, though her stony expression didn't suggest it was having the desired effect.

'Anita Loudon's murder,' MacNee said with deliberate clumsiness, watching Lee's smile vanish before he said, 'Oh, sorry, sir, I don't mean that, of course. I just meant that's what we're here about.'

Lee had recognised it as deliberate. His dark eyes were hard as he said smoothly, 'Anita's been murdered? I'm sorry to hear that. What a terrible thing – how did it happen? We're old friends, you know, though I haven't seen her in ages.'

'When was the last time you saw her?' Hepburn said.

'I'd have to think hard about that one. Five years, more? I've got a business to run here, as you can see, so I'm afraid old friendships get neglected. You know how it is.' He unwisely tried another rueful smile in Hepburn's direction. This time her lip visibly curled, and he turned hastily back to MacNee.

'I'm not sure there's anything I can tell you, but of course I'm anxious to do anything that might help.'

'When were you last in Dunmore?' MacNee asked.

'Dunmore? Oh, years and years! I couldn't tell you exactly. Now I'm in Glasgow I don't have any call to be back in the area, really.'

'Despite being in a business consortium based at Cairnryan?' Hepburn's voice was cold. 'Which has an AGM at Crichton's offices there every year?'

MacNee looked at her with some respect. She'd done her homework on this and she'd got Lee rattled.

The smooth charm was fraying as he snapped, 'Oh, yes, of course. I don't think of Cairnryan as the same area, that's all.'

'And what is the business in this consortium?' MacNee pressed him.

'We all have different interests. It's only that it suits us to double up on some services we all need – accountancy, business consultants, that sort of thing.'

He had started fiddling with a pen, avoiding direct eye contact. Hepburn was on to something there and MacNee nodded to her encouragingly.

'I understand one of your partners is Grant Crichton,

the father of the boy who was killed by Kirstie Burnside, one of your school friends when you were a child. Doesn't that make for a tricky relationship?'

'Not really. As you say, I was a child and a bystander – he was dead before I arrived on the scene. Grant's a generous-minded man who wouldn't bear a grudge for that all these years. I was very sorry for him and greatly admired the way he had borne his grief.'

'You felt he had been greatly wronged?'

Lee shifted impatiently in his seat. 'Well, yeah, obviously. Look, where are you going with all this?'

MacNee said, 'Anita Loudon's body was found in exactly the same place as Tommy Crichton's was, suggesting that for some reason she had been killed in revenge for his death.'

'And? What's this about?'

'You see,' Hepburn explained kindly, 'if you felt a great wrong had been done and that in some way Anita had been at the bottom of it, you might have felt you could put it right by killing her and putting her body in the same place.'

Lee jumped to his feet. 'What sort of stupid game is this?' he shouted. 'You're suggesting that as some sort of charitable act to Grant Crichton, I murdered an old friend? If it was revenge, you'd better look at him or his wife. How could you come up with the crazy idea that it's something to do with me?'

'Well, you see, sir,' MacNee drawled, 'it's just that when we're investigating a murder, if someone starts by telling us a lie – a great, stonking enormous lie – we kinna reckon it's because he's got something to hide.

'We have a witness who has stated that you regularly visited Ms Loudon and the last time you did was the day before she was murdered.

'I'm not arresting you as yet, but I'm inviting you to help the police with their enquiries by appearing at the Galloway Constabulary headquarters in Kirkluce first thing tomorrow morning. If you don't appear by midday we'll swear out a warrant.'

MacNee had thought him a good-looking man when first he saw him. Now the slim face with the eyes so dark that they were almost black seemed to have taken on a sharp, beady, rat-like cast.

CHAPTER FIFTEEN

When Marnie Bruce parked her car on the shore of Clatteringshaws Loch it was late in the afternoon. Banks of purple-black clouds pierced by a startling streak of pale turquoise above the pewter-coloured waters of the loch gave it an almost unearthly light and she shivered as she left the warmth of the car to walk along to the cottage.

The road was busy at this time of night and the sweeping beams of the headlights gave erratic illumination. After a blast from an alarmed motorist she took to the verge, stumbling over snagging roots and almost twisting her ankle in an unnoticed ditch. She was half-sobbing by the time she reached the safety of the garden. The last time, she vowed, the last time. By tomorrow she'd be in London.

Inside the house, it was pitch-dark. She groped her way to the kitchen, then had a fumbling search to find the matches for the camping light. She'd have to learn to keep them in the same place. If she was staying. Which of course she wasn't.

Even once she got it lit, the pale gleam wasn't comforting tonight. It just showed up the dismal, grubby hopelessness of everything about her, in a sort of reflection of her own life. Her journey of discovery about her past had been an exercise in futility, and worse.

Drax had reminded her that the police would be looking for her. She knew that already – 'as a matter of urgency', Fleming's message had said – but since she hadn't had anything to do with Anita's death, they probably wouldn't look very hard.

Marnie lit the stove and filled the kettle with hands that were numb with cold. She filled a hot-water bottle to warm them while she heated up a tin of soup she'd bought, along with a sandwich and a bar of chocolate. The long night stretched grimly ahead of her but once she'd eaten she'd go to bed where she would be warmer and if she could get to sleep at once she would wake early and get on her way.

There was just one thing. Her phone. She'd switched it off this morning and hadn't looked at it since but she couldn't ignore it for ever. Look on the bright side, she told herself, there could be a message to say they'd arrested someone and didn't need to talk to her after all. As if.

An envelope in the corner told her she had a new message – three, when she checked. The first two she recognised as coming from DI Fleming; the other number was unfamiliar. Marnie hesitated.

Get the worst over first. She opened the top one on

the list, which was simply a repeat of the message she'd accessed this morning. She deleted it and her finger was poised to delete the next one too when it occurred to her that it might be worth checking.

'I urge immediate contact. More info about your mother now available.'

Marnie was totally taken aback. She read it again, with a sense of disbelief. She had begun to feel as if there was a sort of conspiracy of silence to frustrate her at every turn. Was it possible that just when she had given up all hope this, at last, was real progress?

Or was it a trap? She'd read in the papers that criminals were sometimes invited to some attractive event, simply so that they could be rounded up and arrested. Could she trust Fleming?

The only lie she was sure Fleming had told her was the social one about her mother's character, a lie to soften a harsh opinion. But perhaps she had been clever enough to hide others.

The soup hissed up to the top of the pan and she had to grab it to stop it boiling over. She filled the mug and sat with her hands wrapped round it while she struggled with her thoughts.

There was still the other message. That was unexpected too.

It was from DC Hepburn, the young policewoman who'd talked to her first, and then come to take a statement after the Tuesday night horror. She'd seemed sympathetic, Marnie had thought at the time, but in a general, fairly pointless way.

The message read, 'There's something you need to know. Shouldn't tell you but very important. Please – call me!'

She didn't know what to make of that.

DC Hepburn fell asleep again on the way back. When she woke with a start the car was drawing up outside her house in Stranraer and DS MacNee was looking at her sternly.

'I'm dropping you off here. You can get a lift back to Kirkluce tomorrow to fetch your car with one of the patrols but I don't trust you to drive tonight.

'You're overdoing it, Louise. Being a young hell-raiser's all fine and good – I was a wee bit of an expert myself – but you've a job to do and if you're tired like that you're not fit to do it.'

Still fuddled with sleep, Hepburn again had to fight back tears of exhaustion. 'I wasn't partying,' she said defensively. 'I just didn't sleep very well last night, that's all.'

MacNee's expression changed and his voice was gentle as he said, 'Got a problem, hen?'

The longing to tell, to talk, almost overwhelmed her but exposing her poor, confused mother would feel like betrayal. 'Nothing a good night's sleep won't put right,' she lied and saw in his face that he knew she had.

'Louise—' he began, but was interrupted by her phone ringing.

She glanced at it and recognised the number with a little frisson of excitement. She could hardly take this one in front of her sergeant. She switched it off, saying, 'I'll take it later,' as she unbuckled her seat belt.

'Thanks, Tam, it was kind of you to bring me back. I'll get my head down really early, I promise.'

She was out of the car before he could reply, though she saw him give a suspicious look at her abrupt exit.

The house was completely dark. When she went in and started switching on lights, there was no sign of her mother downstairs. There was no sign, either, of the elaborate preparations for dinner she would normally be making at this time of day.

In bed, then? Louise climbed the stairs slowly, as if the burden of care and responsibility were physically bearing down on her, and quietly opened the door of her mother's bedroom.

Graceful even in sleep, Fleur was wearing an eau de Nil silk nightgown, lying on her side with her cheek pillowed in her hand like a child. Wisps of hair that had escaped from the loose rope of hair she knotted at night framed her face.

It was a touching picture but Louise didn't smile. Fleur had, of course, had a disturbed night too, but when she felt tired she had been able simply to put on her nightgown and go to bed – unlike some other people. And how long had she been asleep? Probably hours by now. She'd wake up quite sure it was morning, prepare breakfast and then come and wake Louise yet again in the middle of the night.

Oh, she was so, so tired! Every bit of her ached with exhaustion and if she didn't get the proper night's sleep she'd promised Tam she would, it would be even worse tomorrow.

Louise glanced at her watch. Nine o'clock. She could

grab a quick sandwich and fall into bed to snatch whatever sleep she could before her mother woke up.

Not before she phoned Marnie Bruce though.

After the call from DC Hepburn Marnie took her hot-water bottle, picked up the camping lamp and went through to her bedroom. In a sort of daze she slipped off her outer clothing, put on a thick soft woolly and socks and climbed into her sleeping bag with a blanket over the top. She cuddled down, trying to restore feeling to her icy hands and feet, hoping the warmth might have an effect on her numbed brain too.

DC Hepburn had sounded both excited and nervous. 'Marnie, thank you so much for agreeing to hear what I have to tell you. First of all, I need you to know that I want to help you.'

Marnie wasn't sure if she wanted to be helped by DC Hepburn. 'Oh?'

'I know, I know, it's what the police always say. But I really mean it. I believe in justice and I don't believe you've had that.'

She was right there, but Marnie wasn't interested in the discussion of abstract principles. 'You said you had something to tell me.'

'Yes . . .' There was a pause, as if Hepburn was wondering whether to go on. 'The thing is, if my bosses discovered I'd told you, my job would be on the line. I'm not saying you have to promise not to tell anyone before I give you the information, I'm just explaining so that you know what the result would be if you did.'

'I . . . see.' The woman was a fool, that was her problem.

'I'm taking a big risk to persuade you to come to the police station and talk to us. It will be so, so much worse for you if we have to start looking. Do you see that?'

'I think so.' This was scaring her; Marnie felt like some small creature desperately snuffing at the air to sense the direction danger was coming from.

'You know that Anita Loudon is dead – murdered?'

Marnie said nothing and Hepburn went on, 'The reason they're so anxious to see you is that she made a will leaving everything to you.'

'*What?*' She didn't know why she said that; she'd heard perfectly clearly. It was just she couldn't connect the words up to any sort of meaning.

Hepburn repeated it more slowly. Then she said, 'You see, if you just disappear they'll track you down. Your name and description will be circulated to every police force in the country and it'll be all over the media. Sooner or later they'll find you and until then you'll be afraid all the time, waiting for the knock on the door that will come one day. It's no sort of life, Marnie.

'I don't believe you killed Anita – it just doesn't add up. But because of her will, if you don't give us your version of what happened, it could easily be assumed that you did. So will you please, please come and see DI Fleming tomorrow?'

Marnie wasn't going to be bounced into anything while she was still suffering from shock. 'I'll think about it.' Then she said, 'What is it Inspector Fleming's going to tell me about my mother?'

The line went quiet. Then Hepburn said, 'She's been in

touch about that, has she? I think I'd better leave that to her. But it's another good reason for coming in, Marnie, I promise.'

'I suppose so,' Marnie had said, then switched off the phone without saying goodbye.

Now as she lay in bed huddled down in the sleeping bag with the extra blanket pulled up over her ears, she tried to think through what had happened. Why would Anita have left everything to someone she'd known only briefly as a child? It made no sense.

Unless . . . unless – guilt? Was this a sort of pay-off for some unknown injury? Was Fleming going to tell her tomorrow that Anita had left a confession that she killed Marnie's mother – and if so, how long would it be before she brought out the handcuffs and charged Marnie with a revenge killing?

She'd told herself that no one knew where she was, that she could vanish without a trace – but not once the police really started looking for her. She had nowhere to run to.

The wind was getting up. The trees outside the window were starting to sway with a low, keening sound, casting shifting shadows across the room. Sick with worry, she lay curled in the foetal position willing sleep to come to her. Then it would be tomorrow and she would have the misery of the night behind her. She'd rather deal with the demons of the day than the demons of darkness.

Louise Hepburn woke suddenly. She had no idea how long she had been asleep or what it was that had wakened her but she sat up in bed.

It was a windy night. She could hear the roaring of waves breaking on the shore just across the road and she could feel, too, a powerful draught sweeping in through her open bedroom door. That must have been what roused her.

Alarmed, she jumped out of bed. Had her mother opened a window somewhere? The rain would come pouring in on a night like this. Shoving her feet into slippers she went out onto the landing.

Not a window. The wind was blowing up the stairs from the open front door. Oh God! Fleur must have got up and gone out – on a night like this! In a flimsy nightie she could be hypothermic in minutes. And how long had she been gone? Louise had no way of knowing and she was feeling panicky as she grabbed a dressing gown and sped downstairs.

She ran out into the garden, looking wildly about her. She was soaked through before she reached the front gate and looking up and down the street she couldn't see her mother. Cars were driving past but with the waves breaking right over the farther pavement there was, unsurprisingly, no one out on foot that she could ask.

Could Fleur have wandered across the road onto the shore, been swept away? With a sob in her throat, Louise ran across to look helplessly at the heaving waters of the loch. What was she to do?

She turned back and there coming along the street towards her was her mother, dressed in the yellow oilskin and sou'wester that was her customary wet-weather gear, along with stylish floral Wellingtons. She was carrying an empty shopping basket and as she neared Louise she broke into a trot, exclaiming in horror.

'Louise! My little one, what are you doing? You are soaked to the skin – what are you thinking about? Get inside at once and change out of these wet things while I make you a *tisane* so you don't catch your death of cold.'

Struck dumb, Louise allowed herself to be scolded and chivvied back inside. When at last she got a chance to speak, she said, 'What were you doing out anyway, *Maman*?'

Fleur's face clouded. 'I just went along to the shops, but I think it must be a holiday. They were all shut.'

'Mmm.' As her mother went through to the kitchen, Louise locked the door and put the key in her pocket. 'Don't worry about the *tisane*. I'll just have a hot bath and go back to bed. I don't need to be in early so I'll have a bit of a lie-in, all right? Don't wake me.'

'That's a good idea. You work too hard.'

Fleur went through to the kitchen – to do what? Louise wondered wearily as she ran her bath. Have breakfast? Lunch? This couldn't go on. She'd been trying to pretend it was just temporary confusion, but now she'd have to call in the doctor.

During the day Fleur would be safe enough. She wasn't in the habit of going very far – she'd never learnt to drive so it would just be into the town or along the shore for a walk, perhaps, and if she mixed up morning and afternoon it wouldn't matter.

But the nights were the problem: Louise was terrified now that next time Fleur really would go out in her nightclothes. She could lock the doors, but if her mother was determined to get out she might climb out of a window and hurt herself that way.

It was bad enough being wakened because Fleur was confused about time. Listening all night for any sound of movement was impossible, if she wanted to keep her job.

What she needed was an alarm system that would tell her if her mother was opening a door or a window. She could arrange that tomorrow – that and the doctor's appointment.

She was just too tired to worry any more. After the warmth of the bath, sleep overwhelmed her the moment she shut her eyes.

Michael Morrison, too, was aroused out of a deep sleep in the middle of the night. At his side, Vivienne was twitching and moaning, giving little cries of distress and he touched her gently, murmuring, 'Sssh, sssh, it's all right, darling.'

She woke instantly, looking round her in bewilderment and then began to cry. 'Oh Michael, it was a terrible, terrible dream!'

'Just a nightmare, darling. That's all. Go back to sleep.'

'It was Anita – and her head – she was still alive, but—' She began to shudder violently.

He switched on the light and took her in his arms, patting her soothingly. 'Put it out of your head. I tell you what – I'll go down and make you a cup of hot milk, shall I? And then you can take another of your sleeping pills and get a proper rest.'

Vivienne clung to him. 'I'll come with you. I don't want

to be left alone. It's guilt, Michael – I feel I should have been able to help her, done something that night instead of letting her go back to the house alone.'

'You did all you could. Now you just need to put it out of your mind, like we said. All right?

'Come on, then – quietly, though. We don't want to wake the Monster.'

She smiled at that, tiptoeing along the landing with a glance at her grandson's bedroom door.

As Michael heated up the milk, he said, 'You know, sweetheart, I was just thinking you ought to get away for a day or two. It's going to be quite upsetting for you here with all that's going on and you wouldn't be opening the shop for a bit, anyway. Diana's always asking you to see her in London – why not just take her up on it? It would do you good.'

Vivienne said slowly, 'Yes, I suppose it might. But I hate to leave you when you're working so hard – and of course Gemma would be on her own with Mikey—'

Michael laughed. 'Stop fussing. Gemma's a big girl now and, anyway, I'm here to see she's all right. Get Diana to take you out for some retail therapy and you'll be a new woman.'

Vivienne's relief showed in her face as she allowed herself to be convinced. As they went back to bed, she was talking happily about an exhibition she wanted to see.

Michael stayed awake until he heard his wife's breathing become soft and even. He was feeling a certain sense of relief himself. His responsibilities were weighing on him painfully and at least he wouldn't have to worry about Vivienne, for the moment, anyway – though with so many threatening clouds gathering one fewer worry hardly mattered.

It was a long time before he got back to sleep.

It was not quite nine o'clock when DI Fleming was informed that Daniel Lee was waiting in reception. She was surprised: to arrive at this time, driving through the Glasgow rush hour, would have meant leaving well before seven, an hour she would have thought unknown to nightclub owners unless approached from the other end.

'Think he's anxious about something?' MacNee said innocently when she collected him on the way down to the interview room.

'Let's hope so,' Fleming said. 'Anxiety's useful.'

'Better than nothing, I suppose, now they've put a stop to waterboarding.'

Daniel Lee didn't look as if he was being gnawed by anxiety, though. He greeted them with an urbane smile, saying, 'I thought we'd better get this nonsense cleared up as soon as possible. My time's precious just at the moment.'

'I feel just the same, sir,' Fleming said cordially. 'This way, please.'

She eyed him narrowly as she ushered him ahead of her. She knew he must be in his fifties but he walked with the swagger of a young man in his skinny jeans. He was, she supposed, good-looking; he certainly had a compelling face and his eyes, so dark they were almost black, did have a magnetic quality but there was something about him that repelled her, though she couldn't quite say why.

In the interview room, she explained that while this was merely an initial interview, it would be recorded and he was entitled to have a lawyer present.

He waved away the offer. 'I don't need to pay someone to tell me to keep my mouth shut. I want to get this cleared up.'

When MacNee had completed the formalities, Lee cut in before Fleming could frame a question.

'Look, I want to put on record that I was a total fool yesterday. I suppose I was . . . well, you can imagine what I was, when I heard that Anita had been killed. I'm sorry. Bad boy.'

He caught Fleming's eye for a second and then he smiled. His narrow face came alive and the dark eyes seemed to light up, charmingly inviting her into this delicious little conspiracy of understanding and forgiveness.

Fleming had to control a quiver of revulsion. 'We're ready to hear whatever statement you wish to make, Mr Lee.'

'Thank you.' He held the smile and the tone was almost caressing. She realised that he didn't know what the effect on her had been; interesting. Overconfidence was almost as useful as anxiety.

MacNee was looking sick. Afraid he might start making retching noises, she hurried on, 'For the record, you told DS MacNee yesterday that you hadn't seen Anita Loudon or been in Dunmore for more than five years. I gather you wish to correct this statement.'

'Yes.' He looked down at his hands for a moment and when he looked up his face was set in lines of sorrow. 'This has been a terrible shock. I heard yesterday from one of my business contacts – I'm afraid I led you to believe that I didn't know, Sergeant.'

'Aye, you did that,' MacNee said dryly. 'Among other things.'

'We were lovers, though I had my life in Glasgow and she had hers here.'

'Not an exclusive relationship, then?' Fleming said.

'We were free spirits. We each led our own life, mine in Glasgow, hers in Dunmore.'

MacNee was unimpressed. 'Kept it kinna quiet, though, didn't you?'

'Yes, we didn't flaunt it,' Lee said smoothly. 'That was Anita's choice. A small place, you know – a lot of old pussycats. But it was a strong relationship that went way back.'

'Of course. Right back to Tommy Crichton's murder, in fact,' Fleming said. 'Which brings us to the question of why Anita's body should have been placed there, on the same spot.'

'Oh yes, they said that on the news. Looks like some sort of revenge motive, doesn't it?' His expression was bland.

'That's what you think, is it?' MacNee said. 'So who'd want revenge on Anita?'

'How would I know? We led our own lives so I'd hardly know if she'd got across someone.' Then he frowned. 'Though, hang about – I do remember her mentioning that she'd had a bit of a run-in with Shelley Crichton. Some sort of misunderstanding about a visitor she'd had, and Shelley got the wrong end of the stick.'

'You mean, when Marnie Burnside visited her?'

Fleming's question had thrown him, definitely. Lee's eyes narrowed and his thin mouth became a taut, straight line, but the speed of his recovery was testament to his quick wits.

'Well, well, that's a name from the past! Marnie Burnside – good gracious. Anita didn't tell me that. The last time I saw Marnie she was just a kid. Her mother was another old friend but I lost touch with her years ago.'

'Another "free spirit"?'

MacNee's tone was heavily sarcastic but Lee didn't rise to the bait.

'If you like.'

'Let's move on, then, to your movements around the time of Anita's death. Start with Tuesday of this week.'

As he hesitated, Fleming went on smoothly, 'If you're calculating how much we know already, Mr Lee, I would advise you to assume it's everything.'

He gave her a look of dislike, the charm switch now definitely set to 'Off'. 'I was ordering my thoughts, that's all.

'I left Glasgow on Tuesday, late afternoon, I suppose. I arrived at Anita's house in the evening. I spent the night there. She had gone to work when I woke up and then I left again mid morning and drove back to Glasgow. End of.'

'A very brief visit,' Fleming said.

'I'm a very busy man.'

'Why did you decide to come down that evening?'

Lee shrugged. 'Hadn't seen Anita for a bit. Nothing special going on at the club that night so I fancied a change of scene. It's not illegal, as far as I know – not yet, at least.'

There was an edge to his voice. He was getting defensive and MacNee picked up on it immediately and goaded him.

'So – just bad timing, then? You come down one night and she's dead the next? Just came down to say goodbye, maybe? One last night of love?'

Lee's face went white with rage. He grasped the table as if to stop himself coming round it to assault MacNee and Fleming could see the cords in his neck standing out.

His voice sounded strangulated as he snarled, 'Yes, if I'd known she was going to die, I would have said goodbye. I wish I had. It is a very sad end to a long friendship.

'I think I've been as helpful as I feel like being, given your attitude. You'll have to arrest me to keep me here and since you obviously haven't the evidence to do that, I'm leaving now.'

'Just one question,' Fleming said. 'Your alibi for Wednesday night?'

He was halfway to the door. 'Ask any of my employees. Or rather, since most of them are kids who have trouble knowing whether it's Tuesday or Christmas, ask my secretary. She always knows what I'm doing better than I do myself.'

He left the room. Fleming said, 'Mr Lee has terminated the interview,' for the benefit of the recording and MacNee switched it off.

'Had that one all ready, didn't he?' he said.

'Oh yes. Think you could get one of your Glasgow pals to send a couple of uniforms round to see his "kids" asap? And tell them not to bother with the secretary – we know what she's going to say already.'

MacNee gave her a cynical look. 'And you think the kids won't back her up? What's the going rate for an alibi these days – twenty quid?'

Fleming sighed. 'Right enough. Even so, wouldn't do any harm to keep up the pressure.'

'The sort of pressure I'd like to put on that one would involve his windpipe. Remember the good old days when you could take them round the back, no questions asked?'

'Tam, you shock me!' Fleming said. But she was grinning as MacNee left.

CHAPTER SIXTEEN

It had been a wild night. The wind in the trees roared like a raging sea and with that, and the cold, Marnie kept waking up. In the early morning the storm abated and she fell into a deep sleep at last, waking only with the first signs of light at eight o'clock.

She climbed out of her sleeping bag feeling grubby and disgusting, ready to sell her soul for a decent shower. Instead, she stripped off her clothes and exposed her shrinking, goose-pimpled flesh to a cold sponge-down in the kitchen and dried herself on a blanket. She'd forgotten about towels.

It was a luxury to climb into the car and put the heater on. She listened to the morning news programme as she left the house but there was nothing fresh about Anita's murder, just a statement that the police were pursuing several lines of enquiry. She clicked off the radio. It felt strange and scary hearing that, when you were one of the lines of enquiry being pursued.

Despite having thought of nothing else in her waking moments she still hadn't decided what to do. The picture DC Hepburn had painted of Marnie's future as a fugitive had scared her but she wasn't entirely convinced it would be like that; they'd find the real killer before long and they wouldn't go to all that trouble to find her if she made it difficult for them. She could still hide; casual work in the catering trade wasn't famous for keeping records.

But then there was Anita's will. She didn't know what it would mean – a bit of money, perhaps, and that wouldn't go amiss – her little savings account was nearly empty. But it could mean the police would decide she'd killed Anita for what she might get and really set out to nail her, though it wasn't like Anita was wealthy. Working in a shop, what she would have had to leave couldn't be much. The thoughts chased each other round and round her head till she felt dizzy with them.

When she reached the police station in Kirkluce there were people hanging around outside with cameras and microphones; there was an edge of frost in the air this morning and they were stamping their feet and swinging their arms as their breath rose in steamy clouds.

Marnie couldn't face shouted questions, cameras shoved in her face, at least not yet. She drove on past and out of the town without any real idea of where she was heading – just not there.

'Glenluce Abbey'. The signpost further on down the road triggered her memories.

She's staring and staring at the arches that spring up and fall back like water in a fountain so that she hardly

hears Gemma and the others giggling or the teacher talking
history. She's gone to a quiet, beautiful place in her mind.

She needed to think clearly, and where better? Marnie
turned off the main road, up through the little village of
Glenluce and then on down the narrowing roads until she
saw the cluster of grey buildings that almost seemed to
grow out of the landscape, the walls of roofless buildings
like stone outcrops. She didn't like the windows without
glass, that looked like empty eye sockets in an animal's
weathered skull, but all round the ruined grandeur was
a working farm like any other farm. There was only one
other car in the car park.

Perhaps, Marnie thought as she went to pay her entrance
fee, there had been sheep in those same fields, tended by
the monks, in the days of the abbey's glory. She fended off
the well-meaning, and probably bored, attendant, keen to
tell her more than she wanted to know, and stepped out
onto the springy turf, crisp with frost.

It was very quiet. A sheep bleated and another
answered, but that seemed part of the historic peace of
the place. She ignored the remains of the great church and
went unerringly to the ornate doorway leading into the
chapter house.

The fountains of stone rose and fell just as she
remembered. The white walls, the grey stone, the warm
burnt orange of the tiles, the glazed windows whose shape
made her think of flowers: it was a sort of silent music.

Marnie stood, letting it still the endlessly chattering
voices and clear her mind. And at last, on the other side of
that silence, she understood. For her, this wasn't about a

death or a will. It was all about her mother.

Drax and Anita, the only two friends Marnie had ever known her have, said they had lost touch with her, hadn't seen her for years. She didn't think she believed either of them. And if her mother was still alive, why should they lie?

Her mother hadn't been the sort of mum you read about in cosy children's books but she couldn't just walk away: if DI Fleming had something to tell her, she had to know what it was. Whatever it was. Even if she had a feeling in the pit of her stomach that afterwards she would wish she didn't know.

It didn't help that as she left with a final glance upwards, fighting her forebodings, she noticed the four grotesque, ugly faces carved around the central pillar.

Daniel Lee had spotted the press as he arrived and parked in the street nearby, then strolled past them confidently. There had been one or two glances cast in his direction but no one had accosted him then, so he adopted the same attitude on the way out and reached his car again unchallenged.

His rage had cooled as quickly as it had flared up. It always did, and latterly he'd got better at controlling it. Once he'd have gone for the jumped-up little prick of a sergeant and throttled him.

With the cooling came a deep unease. He'd believed he'd covered his tracks; it had been a shock that they'd got on to him at all, let alone so quickly.

Had Marnie told them something? She was dangerous,

very dangerous, but she'd said she wasn't going to speak to them. She'd better mean that – they all had enough problems without someone inviting her to do show-and-tell with her freaky memory.

No, it was probably just the good old local spy system that had shopped him. Anita, he could be sure, would have been discreet; he'd told her that the first time he heard of gossip would be the last time she saw him. There was the old bag who was her next-door neighbour, of course, she could give lessons to the KGB.

At least he'd managed to give the police a nudge in Shelley's direction since they were probably too dumb to spot it on their own. Or pinpoint their own backsides, come to that.

Lee had just turned the key in the ignition when he noticed something. That wasn't—

Oh yes, it was. That was Marnie Bruce crossing the road just ahead of him, on her way into the police station. She was going to the police after all – lying bitch!

For a crazy moment he thought about gunning the car's engine and taking her out right there, in front of the assembled media.

Wiser councils prevailed. Everything was under control; he had to keep telling himself that. Keep calm. But as he drove off he tore roughly at a snagging edge on his thumbnail, then winced as a bead of blood appeared . . .

Fleming was dreading the interview with Marnie Bruce and wanted to get it over – always supposing that she appeared.

Since she'd been informed the day before that the injunction against revealing Karen Bruce's identity had been amended to permit her daughter to be told, she'd thought long and hard about how to break the news, had lost sleep over it, even. But whatever she said, Marnie would have to hear the ugly truth that not only was her mother a sort of national hate-figure, but she had chosen to build her daughter's life on deceit. How would Marnie feel when she discovered that even her name wasn't her own?

It was only ten minutes later that Marnie arrived. Fleming had arranged to use one of the smaller waiting rooms as being the nearest thing to informal that the station provided and chatted about the cold weather as they took their seats there, but even so Marnie was clearly nervous. She sat on the edge of the chair, twisting her hands together in an unconscious movement. She was pale with dark shadows around her eyes and looked as if she had slept badly.

Fleming leant forward too, smiling. 'Thank you for coming in, Marnie. I felt I owed you an explanation for having been less than frank with you earlier. I've been authorised now to tell you something that I'm afraid will be very difficult for you. Would you like a drink – tea, coffee?'

Marnie shook her head.

'Right, fine. Could I just ask you first of all, where are you staying? I wasn't sure if my messages were getting through and we need to be able to contact you.'

'Do I have to tell you?'

'Not have to, no, at this stage. But I think it would be advisable.'

'I'm moving about a bit.'

Feeling faint irritation, Fleming said, 'Well, where were you last night?'

'I'm not sure of the address. Just an old cottage. But I'll be leaving there soon.'

It wasn't worth having an argument over. Marnie had answered the phone eventually and once she'd been told about Anita's will the lawyer could take care of all that. First things first, though.

Fleming took a deep breath. 'Marnie, when you asked me about your mother, I wasn't in a position to tell you. She has a protected identity and there was an injunction against information about it being given to anyone, which included her daughter, until the injunction was lifted yesterday – only for you, I have to stress, and that only because of the particular circumstances we find ourselves in.'

Marnie stared at her. 'A protected identity – what does that mean? Was she a witness, or something?'

'No, Marnie, I'm afraid not.' Fleming found she was twisting her hands too. 'Have you heard of Kirstie Burnside?'

She shook her head.

'When Kirstie Burnside was ten she was charged with murdering a child of eight, Tommy Crichton. She served out her sentence and when she was released she was given a new, protected identity so that she wouldn't be persecuted. Kirstie Burnside was—'

Marnie was ahead of her. 'My mother. My mother was a murderer. A child killer.'

295

She had turned so pale that Fleming thought she was going to faint. 'Marnie, you need to understand that she had a terrible start in life. It only came to light when this happened that her father—'

She didn't have a chance to finish. Marnie cut in, 'Abused her? Oh, that makes it all right, then. My mother's a murderer and my grandfather was a paedophile! Anything else you want to share with me?'

There was nothing Fleming could say in the face of her bitterness. She waited until Marnie raged on, 'Why did you tell me this? You think it's something I wanted to know?'

She could have said, 'You asked me.' Instead, Fleming had to give her the next bit of bad news. 'The reason I felt you had to be warned is that if the press hasn't already worked out who you are, they will very soon.'

Marnie looked at her in horror. 'You're going to tell the press?'

'I'm not, no. But people in Dunmore know and they're not going to keep quiet about it.'

'They know? So that's why . . .' Her voice trailed off and a curious look came over her face, as if she was looking into the far distance.

It was a bit uncanny. Louise Hepburn, Fleming suddenly remembered, had said she'd noticed something like that too.

'She's coming straight at me – attacking me,' Marnie murmured, and then her eyes seemed to snap back into focus again and she looked at Fleming as if bewildered. 'But how could she have known? Anita knew at once too, only she wouldn't admit it.'

'I'm afraid it's your appearance – red-gold hair, bright-blue eyes. You're very like your mother as a child.'

'Like my mother? I don't know what you mean. She had dark hair – almost black! And her eyes – they were a sort of greyish-brown, I think. Not really a definite colour at all.'

'Yes, I remember,' Fleming said heavily. 'Her colouring as a child was very distinctive so she dyed her hair and I suppose used contact lenses.'

'Yes, I remember she had contacts. But I never saw her without them.' Again that remote look appeared. 'She's having a problem with one of them. She's got her hand over her eye and she's going out to the bathroom . . .'

'Marnie,' Fleming said gently, bending forward to touch the other woman's arm, 'what are you doing?'

Marnie gave a slight start. 'Oh . . . oh sorry, it's just a condition I have.'

Fleming listened in astonishment to her explanation about hyperthymesia. 'You can remember absolutely everything as if it were happening just now?'

'If a memory's triggered, yes.'

'But you don't remember what happened the night your mother left?'

'I never saw who hit me.' She chewed at her lip. 'So . . . so this is why you believe it could have been my mother who did it?'

'That, and the lack of evidence that anyone else was there.'

'I . . . I see.'

There were tears forming in her eyes. Fleming went

297

on hastily, 'There's another thing that I have to tell you. We found a copy of a will that Anita Loudon had made, leaving everything to you.'

Marnie showed no sign of surprise. That was interesting, Fleming thought. 'Did she tell you she had?'

'No. I don't know why she would.'

'I should stress that this isn't official. There may be another will somewhere with different provisions. We won't know until we've finished going through all her papers and had proper confirmation from her lawyers. But as it stands, you will inherit her estate. So—'

'You don't need to tell me,' Marnie said bitterly. 'She's dumped me in it, hasn't she? You think I killed her to get it. I didn't, by the way, though I don't suppose you'll accept that.'

Relieved to be moving on to more familiar terrain, Fleming said coolly, 'No, I won't "accept" it, but I don't jump to conclusions either. You will have to make a formal statement about any contact you had with Anita Loudon, but I'd prefer to talk through it with you first, if you're willing to do that.'

'I told your detectives all about the first time, when I had to escape – I don't want to go over it all again.'

Fleming nodded. 'I've read the report. There were other occasions, though?'

'Just one.' There was a pause, then the odd look came over Marnie's face again. She muttered, 'Sorry.' Then, 'Give me a moment.

'OK. It was on Wednesday evening. She took a long time to come to the door. I thought she'd maybe been

298

asleep or something – she was yawning and she looks – looked a bit blank for a moment. She was wearing a cream and dark red skirt and a cream top and her lipstick was a little bit smeared. She doesn't – didn't look exactly pleased at seeing me and she didn't ask me in, she just says – said, "Oh – Marnie! I thought you'd gone."

'I say, "Why should I? Just because your friends tried to drive me out?"

'She says she doesn't – didn't know what I meant. I told her and she said she didn't know anything about it. I don't think that's true.

'Then she asks what I'd come back to her for, says there isn't anything more she can tell me about my mother. I'm telling her I want to know how to find Drax.'

The mixture of tenses was intriguing, Fleming thought. Marnie seemed to be describing a current experience and having trouble expressing it as a report of a past event. As she had gone on with the story, she had stopped correcting herself.

'She doesn't want to tell me. I say to her if she doesn't, I'll come and tell the police you should talk to him about the night my mother disappeared and she's getting scared about that.'

'He was there?' Fleming put in sharply.

Marnie's eyes seemed to snap back into focus. 'I don't know what happened – I told you that already. Anyway, she said she'd give me the address for the nightclub, Zombies – you know? – provided I didn't tell him that she had. So she went and wrote it down, handed it to me and shut the door. That was all. She didn't say anything about a will.

She didn't seem to like me much – wanted to get rid of me as soon as possible.'

'You weren't surprised when I told you, though, were you?'

Marnie looked down, sideways. 'Yes I was,' she insisted.

It wasn't convincing. Fleming filed that one away and went on, 'So – you had Drax's address. Are you going to see him?'

'I went yesterday. It was a wasted journey. He said he hadn't seen my mother for years. Until I got your message I was going to give up the whole idea, go back to London – just disappear, back into my old life. Now I wish I had.'

Fleming could sympathise with that but she said, 'You're forgetting that Anita Loudon is dead. We couldn't have allowed you to do that. What time was it that you went to the house? You may have been the last person to see Anita alive.'

Marnie showed signs of alarm. 'Around six, sometime. Look, she was alive when I left. I didn't even step inside the house.'

'I take it you saw no one else there? What sort of mood was she in?'

'Apart from hostile, when she saw me? I don't know.' She put a hand to her head. 'Is there much more of this? I'm very tired—'

'Yes, of course you are. I'm sorry – you've been given a lot to cope with. Just finally, what did you do after you saw Anita?'

'Just went back to . . . where I'm staying.' Marnie got up.

'Any witnesses?'

'No. It's not that sort of place.'

Fleming waited hopefully, but she didn't elaborate. 'We have to order you not to leave the immediate area for the next day or two. Since we have your phone number I won't insist on an address but you must undertake to keep in touch. I'll let you know when we've been able to arrange for the lawyer to see you.'

Marnie nodded. She said nothing more as Fleming escorted her to the front door then went back inside. She couldn't imagine how Marnie must be feeling; she felt totally drained herself, but at least it was over and it was only quarter past eleven.

'Right, Sarge,' DC Hepburn said. 'I'll meet Andy in the car park by the harbour in half an hour.'

She rang off. She'd been hoping that MacNee would arrange for her to link up with one of the patrols to get back to the station but of course, if she and Macdonald were tasked to do interviews around Stranraer this made sense. She just hoped that MacNee hadn't told him she'd been wiped out yesterday. Macdonald would love to have evidence of her unfitness for the job.

She was fine today. She hadn't been aware of any more problems during the night and in an attempt to reset her mother's body clock she'd wakened her when she got up for breakfast herself, despite Fleur's protests that it was too early and she was still tired.

The sea was blue and calm today, the only evidence of last night's storm being the sand and stones on the pavement opposite the house and tangles of seaweed heaped up on the shore and the sharp tang of ozone in the air. Hepburn walked briskly, puffing at the first cigarette of the day – always the best one – and hoping that Macdonald would be there when she arrived. The sun might be shining but there was no warmth in it and she didn't fancy standing freezing.

Fortunately he was prompt and MacNee didn't seem to have shopped her, but he went through the usual routine of coughing and wrinkling his nose about the smell of smoke. She'd been seriously considering giving up but just thinking of Macdonald crowing made her start twitching for the next drag.

She achieved a little half-cough, half-sneeze as she put on her seat belt. 'God, what on earth's that aftershave? I think I'm allergic to it – or maybe I just have a more refined taste than the women you knock around with.'

Macdonald ignored that. 'The detail today is that we go to see Vivienne Morrison first. Anita may have confided in her – seemed under quite a lot of strain when we questioned her at the shop – but she was too distraught yesterday to speak to the boss.' He drove off.

'Good. I'd like to know what was really going on. Anita was lying through her teeth, if you ask me.

'Was there anything new at the morning briefing?'

'Of course, you weren't there. What happened – car break down?'

Hepburn shook her head. 'Just we were late back from Glasgow and Tam dropped me off, knowing guys would be here today who could give me a lift back if necessary. Anyway – new stuff?'

302

'Nothing dramatic. Still no weapon, still no witnesses to anything happening that night. With Anita's house being just opposite the play park there isn't much chance there would be. The boss didn't say anything about your friend Drax in the meeting but Tam clued me in. Sounds as if you had an interesting time.'

She could hear the note of envy in his voice. 'My money's on him. Nasty bit of work. Fancies himself – thinks he's only got to smile at a woman and she'll fall at his feet. Repellent.'

Macdonald gave a crack of laughter. 'Did he not realise he might as well try to cosy up to a rattlesnake? Crazy guy!'

For some reason, that stung her: a rattlesnake? 'Well, I'm not a pushover, if that's what you mean. Anyway I think he's got business worries too – don't know what, but he was on edge and I don't believe it was just the usual nightclub owner's reaction to a visit from the police, like he said.'

'Now that's interesting. His colleague Grant Crichton certainly has – was livid with his wife for showing me through to his study where he was snowed under with papers and he was pretty keen I wouldn't get a glimpse of them.'

'And Morrison's the third member of the consortium. I checked it out on the Companies House register.'

The look Macdonald gave her almost suggested respect. She went on, 'It's a curious set of businesses to link up – haulage, construction, a nightclub. Their profits are fairly impressive, given the downturn, so they must be doing something right. Or else doing something wrong, that they've been pretty good at covering up.'

'Can't be exactly happy about all this happening on their patch, can they? Do you suppose Mr Morrison is as twitchy as the others?'

They had reached Dunmore. 'That's the street we need to take now,' Macdonald said, turning off the main road and up a steep hill, then making a left turn onto a smaller country road. 'That must be the house there.'

'Has to be doing all right,' Hepburn said as they drove up between expensively landscaped gardens. 'I could quite fancy a bit of that myself.'

They were just parking the car in the turning circle in front of the house when the front door opened and a pretty blonde girl came out with a toddler on her hip. She glanced across, smiled and then came to meet them.

'Can I help you?'

They showed their warrant cards. 'I understand Mrs Morrison was too distressed to talk yesterday,' Macdonald said. 'We were hoping to have a word with her today, if that's possible.'

She looked rueful. 'Oh, I'm so sorry. I'm Gemma Napier, Mrs Morrison's daughter. She isn't here. You've had a wasted journey.'

'Oh – when will she be back?'

'Not for a few days, I'm afraid. Mum was just in pieces about poor Anita, and she gets high blood pressure when she's stressed so we were worried about her being here with all that's going on. We've packed her off to stay with a friend in London. Total change of scene, a bit of shopping – you know?'

She smiled at Hepburn who didn't smile back. 'That's

very unfortunate. Can you give us the contact number in London, please?'

Gemma clearly wasn't happy with the suggestion of pressure. 'I wouldn't be happy doing that. Sorry.'

Hepburn would have liked to insist but Macdonald stepped in. 'Perhaps you could undertake to get a message to her that we would like her to return immediately? This is a murder investigation, and until we can talk to her we don't know whether she has information that may be important.'

Gemma said stubbornly, 'I don't think she should. It's a question of her health and, anyway, she told Dad everything. There wasn't anything useful.'

'That's for us to judge,' Macdonald said. 'Perhaps we'd better have a word with your father, anyway. Is he here?'

'No. He's taken her to Glasgow to get the fast London train.'

The toddler, who had been regarding them suspiciously, started jiggling in his mother's arms. 'Mummy, Mummy – time to go to playschool.'

'Yes, darling, we're just going. If you've finished . . . ?' She raised her brows at the officer.

'For the moment,' Macdonald said.

As they walked back to the car Gemma went across to the huge garage which must once have been a barn for the farm, clicking a key that made the doors swing open.

In her designer jeans and fur gilet, with cute toddler accessory, she was the epitome of the yummy mummy. Hepburn struggled to keep an edge of bitterness out of her voice as she said, 'Very convenient. Fully paid-up junior member of the rules-don't-apply club, I'd say.'

'Just worried about her mother, like a nice girl should be,' Macdonald said, as he drove off, adding provocatively, 'but you wouldn't know about that.'

It got her on the raw. 'Wouldn't I?' she said lightly, but she had to turn her head so he wouldn't see the tears of self-pity.

Fleming was just finishing up at ten to twelve when the phone rang. She sighed impatiently and picked it up.

'DCI Alexander from Cairnryan would like a word, ma'am. Shall I put him through?'

'Yes, fine,' she said, then, 'Nick! What can I do for you?'

She'd always had a good relationship with him and she was taken aback when he said abruptly, 'Marjory, what the hell are your lot doing trampling all over our patch?'

CHAPTER SEVENTEEN

Marnie blundered past the reporters on her way out of the police station. One of them came towards her calling out a question but she didn't even hear it and the man stepped back with a shrug.

She got into the car and drove away, not going anywhere: just driving, as if physical escape could distance her from mental torment. At the moment her mind felt blank and dead but it was the sort of numbness you felt before the anaesthetic wore off after a tooth extraction. Pain was waiting there on the edge of consciousness, red and raw.

Mother. The word started to spike through the blankness, bringing with it shafts of horror. What sort of woman would kill another child, all but kill her own daughter? What monster had been called up from the deeps by her questioning?

And what was she, herself? Bad blood, that was what they called it, coming down through the generations. At the thought of what had gone into the making of Marnie she was overcome by nausea. Drax, too? Stopping the car with dangerous abruptness she tumbled out and vomited onto the verge, again and again, as if trying to purge herself of the poison of knowledge.

At last, shaking and shivering in the cold, she looked about her. She had no idea where she was; she had presumably been driving on autopilot since she hadn't hit anything, but now she realised she was only a couple of miles from the Clatteringshaws cottage. With the instinct of a stricken animal she had headed for such home as she had. It would be bleak and cold but there was nowhere else she could think of to go.

Marnie got back into the car and when she reached the loch she slowed down and turned into the car park. It was empty and when she got out she felt as if she might be alone in the world.

It was all very beautiful today, glittering and icy, with the steel-blue sky cloudless overhead and the loch still as a mirror. The scrubby trees along its edge were leafless, the bare black branches like skinny arms with clutching skeletal fingers at the end.

There was a hum of traffic from the road behind her but Marnie didn't hear it. The silence of the hills that encircled the loch seduced her with the promise of peace; the rippling water sang quietly at her feet.

She had longed to know what lay on the other side of the silence she had lived with for so long. Perhaps this was the only way to find out.

* * *

Shelley Crichton was in the conservatory using a leaf-shine spray and a soft cloth to clean the stiff, sharp leaves of the snake plant as tenderly as a mother wiping her child's face. It was the most soothing occupation she could think of but today it wasn't working; her nerves were still jangling like fire alarms going off in her head.

Shelley didn't know what to make of last night's phone call. The caller was a man, certainly, but she didn't recognise his voice and he didn't identify himself. He just gave her the information, then hung up.

How did he know she would want to know? And what else did he know about her – and what might he do with that knowledge? She felt sick at the thought.

Could it be a trap of some kind? If she was wise, she'd ignore it, pretend it had never happened, but she was tempted – so tempted! Anita Loudon's death had felt like a sort of revenge but it didn't satisfy her. The hatred, a constant low-burning flame, flared up until she felt consumed by it.

A leaf snapped off in her hand. Horrified, she realised her grip had unconsciously tightened; she bent over the mutilated plant to assess the damage, murmuring, 'Poor baby, poor baby!'

'Nick, I'm sorry,' Fleming said in bewilderment, 'I haven't the faintest idea what you're talking about.'

'Daniel Lee, that's what I'm talking about.' DCI Nick Alexander was definitely annoyed. 'Look, I know your super is anxious about her precious reputation and thinks we're not getting far enough quickly enough, but if she sends in your lot to trample all over this with hobnailed boots it will screw everything up just as we're hoping to move in for the kill.

'I could take this up with a higher authority but I thought a quiet word with you might be the quickest way to choke it off – if the damage hasn't been done already.'

'She did ask me, yes,' Fleming admitted. 'I told her to leave it in your hands but she made it an order. My plan was to drag my feet as best I could, and then Anita Loudon's murder gave me the ideal excuse to put it on hold, indefinitely.

'The reason we were "on your patch" as you put it, is that Daniel Lee was Anita Loudon's lover and his business associates are at least tangentially involved as well.'

There was an appalled silence at the other end of the phone. Then Alexander said slowly, 'Puts us in a spot of bother, then. We've been watching them for some time but they're smart and we've never caught them with the goods.'

'The human goods, I take it,' Fleming said.

'Yes. Asians mainly, some Chinese. We think there may be a Liverpool-Irish connection. We're liaising with Lancashire and the Garda but they haven't had any luck either and we're trying the Al Capone technique. The tax accounts they file are clean as a whistle – and trust me, we've checked. There's no way we'd get warrants for a fishing expedition but our own experts say there must be a paper trail, so we've got HMRC on to calling in each individual company's records to check them out for discrepancies.'

'There's no reason for them to suppose that our enquiries have anything to do with that,' Fleming argued. 'We might even happen on the sort of evidence you're looking for.'

'Might, perhaps.' Alexander didn't sound convinced. 'But—'

'Exactly,' Fleming said, 'but. Where do we go from here?'

There was a pause, then Alexander said, 'I shouldn't tell you this, but we've had a tip-off about a shipment due in one of Crichton's container lorries. I want you to lay off any action until I give the nod.'

'I don't see how I can, Nick. Murder, remember? The situation's complicated and I still don't know if they're even directly involved, but until we can nail whoever did it, there's someone very dangerous out there. How can I ignore legitimate lines of enquiry?'

He didn't back down. 'We're talking lives at stake too. Just a few days, that's all.'

'Sorry,' Fleming said.

'I'm sorry too. I thought we could have done business without involving the big guns. But—'

'You have to do what you think is best,' Fleming said stiffly, 'but so do I.'

Even so, when she had put down the phone she picked it up again. 'Tam? If you've spoken to your friends in Glasgow about going round to check Daniel Lee's alibi, get hold of them and call it off. The big boys are bullying us and that can wait for the moment.

'Where are you, anyway?'

'In Dunmore. I've a wee notion to find out who was outside Marnie Bruce's window that night. Try out the patter on the locals, ken, and see what I can find out.'

'Have you seen Andy and Louise? I'm wondering how they got on with Mrs Morrison.'

'They didn't. She's done a runner to London.'

'Has she, indeed. Done a runner – or been sent away?'

'Like enough. He's taken her to the Glasgow train so they couldn't question him either.'

'Find out when he'll be back. I want him put over a slow flame before we're called off.'

'What's going on, then?'

'Need-to-know basis.' Fleming was amused at the little 'humph!' of annoyance that came down the line. 'If I told you I'd have to kill you afterwards, but you could maybe work it out if you think of our esteemed superintendent's most recent preoccupation.'

'Aah.'

The sound of satisfied curiosity. At least Tam was quick on the uptake. 'Anyway, good luck. I hope the locals are susceptible to your very particular brand of Glasgow charm. Just a word of advice.'

'Oh aye?'

'Don't smile too often. It tends to alarm the natives.'

Grant Crichton put his head down on the desk on top of the mountain of papers and groaned. He should have been more systematic; now he had no idea what he'd checked and what he'd hadn't. His stomach was churning and he felt as if someone had put his brains through a blender.

He'd a good head for figures normally, he kept telling himself. He oversaw everything that came in and went out, so he wouldn't have put anything in the wrong file. Of course he wouldn't.

But what if he had? What if he'd missed some small, insignificant entry – or what if one of the others had? It had run so smoothly for so many years, perhaps they'd got careless. Perhaps he had, even.

Now it was as if a whirlwind had struck. He was being assaulted from all directions at once and his life was spinning out of control. He couldn't believe what he had done, what he had become.

Even if the records were as clean as he believed them to be, it wasn't the worst of his problems. He might have seen off the sergeant who had come asking questions, but he wasn't kidding himself that he would be the last.

It wasn't fair, it just wasn't fair. All right, what he'd done was wrong, but he could justify it. Most of it. He didn't want to think about the rest.

He sat up and went back to his papers, rubbing his eyes as if that would clear his brain. The knock on the door was an unwelcome interruption.

'Your lunch is ready,' Denise said.

'Lunch? Oh, I'm not hungry.'

Instead of retreating, Denise came further into the room. She held out something – one of the endless holiday brochures she was always looking at.

'I really need you to decide about this now. If we're going to do that Caribbean cruise we talked about, we have to book today. There's only one superior cabin left and—'

'Cruise!' he roared. 'You must be mad!' He gestured at

the laden desk. 'If I can't get this straight, there will be no more cruises, ever, or anything else! Get that into your dim little brain.'

Denise didn't reply. She turned and walked out and he turned to the accounts again. It had relieved the tension to have a legitimate reason to explode and his mind seemed clearer. He hadn't noticed the mutinous expression on Denise's face, or the look of loathing she gave him as she went out.

The relief was short-lived. Just as she shut the door, his mobile rang and when he picked it up Drax's name was in the caller ID box. He looked at it with a mixture of fear and loathing and his stomach started to churn again.

The Cottage Bar, Dunmore's only pub, where the detectives had arranged to meet at lunchtime, wasn't enticing. It wasn't a cottage either; it was a seventies single-storey building with metal-framed windows and an interior that suggested its designer's brief had been to eradicate any vestige of character. If so, it was a *succès fou*, Hepburn suggested.

Getting the gist if not a precise translation, MacNee nodded. 'You're not wrong there,' he said gloomily. He'd never enjoyed a pub lunch the same since having a pint with your pie, or even a half, became a mortal sin. And if his nose wasn't deceiving him, there wasn't going to be the pie either.

'Just sandwiches. Ham, cheese, ham and cheese, cheese and pickle.' Hepburn brought over the drinks on a tray and put a glass of a livid orange liquid in front of MacNee, wrinkling her nose. 'Irn-Bru. And a Coke. I don't know how you two can drink that sickly stuff.' She set down her own lime and soda.

'Oh, very French, very sophisticated,' Macdonald sneered.

'I'm meant to apologise?'

MacNee looked at them with some irritation. Sophisticated? The pair of them hadn't got out of the playground. 'Anyway, orders,' he said. 'Would they rise to cheese, ham *and* pickle, do you reckon?'

'A bridge too far, would be my guess. The girl who served me looks as if remembering two ingredients at the same time will stretch her, but I'll try.'

When she returned, Macdonald and MacNee were discussing the sad situation of Rangers FC – at least Macdonald was talking about it while MacNee sat silent in a grief too deep for words.

'It's finished.' Macdonald, a Hearts man himself, spoke with ill-disguised satisfaction. 'By next season – no more Rangers. You'll have to support a decent club after that, Tam.' Then, seeing MacNee's expression added hastily, 'Just a wee joke.'

It was no joking matter. When it came to the Rangers' plight MacNee felt, to quote Bill Shankly, that it wasn't a matter of life and death, it was more important than that, a subject only to be treated with reverence. He greeted Hepburn's return with surprising enthusiasm, given that she was saying cheese, ham and pickle wasn't on the menu.

'Did Marnie Bruce turn up today?' Hepburn asked.

'Couldn't tell you,' MacNee said. 'I came straight down here after the interview with Daniel Lee.'

'Anything useful?'

'What happened?' Macdonald and Hepburn spoke simultaneously.

MacNee pulled a face. 'Claims he's got an alibi for Wednesday night. We'll have to test it sometime – don't trust him an inch.'

'Manipulative,' Hepburn said. The two men looked at her quizzically.

'His schtick is to draw you in, get you to see things with his eyes. He focused on me because I guess women tend to fall for that sort of humorous charm – you know how they always say the most important thing about a man is having a GSOH. Much more important than, say, previous for GBH.'

'Right enough,' MacNee said. 'He tried it on with the boss too but he didn't get very far.'

Macdonald gave a crack of laughter. 'He's a brave man! Did Big Marge tell him she'd have his guts for garters?'

Hepburn looked at him coldly. 'I know you all say that's her catchphrase but I've never heard her use it.'

'Used to,' MacNee said. 'But she's not daft – she found out what you were saying behind her back. She always does.

'Anyway – this afternoon. We've to see Morrison as a priority, and—'

Macdonald's mobile rang. He took the call, raising his eyebrows as he realised who was at the other end. 'There's an incident room at the village hall in Dunmore,' he said, then, 'No, fair enough. Right, I'll be there. Two-thirty.'

He put the phone back in his pocket. 'I have an

assignation with a lady in a tea shop. She doesn't want to see me at home and she feels the village hall would be too public. Denise Crichton has something to tell me and if it's not about the alibi she gave her husband you can get me lime and soda the next time you're in the chair.'

Michael Morrison arrived back in his office just after lunch. Vivienne was safely on the way to London, which was one less thing to worry about and though he was, as instructed, checking the Morrison Construction records for discrepancies they were in good order and he was confident that he wouldn't find any. His major worry was Grant, who might have a good enough business brain but otherwise needed to have everything explained to him very slowly and clearly, preferably with pictures. He had a tendency to panic, too. That worried him. He and Drax were both on edge about Grant.

He'd no worries about Drax. Drax was a genius, in his way; he'd spotted that when the smart, cocky lad had applied for a job all those years ago and had made himself indispensable in record time. The success of the consortium was largely down to him and though he drove a hard bargain he deserved the rewards in money and in status within the group.

In the current mess, it was Drax who was making the running. He'd cancelled the consignment as being too risky, so they'd have a breathing space to get everything sorted out. He trusted him, and his belief that they would come through all this provided they all held firm was contagious. Most of the time.

He'd better phone Gemma, tell her he was back and see how she was getting on. She was a good girl, his Gemma, and she hadn't deserved the little sod who had done his best to ruin her life – though without him, of course, there would have been no Mikey. An intolerable thought!

Gemma was worried. 'The police came this morning, Dad, and they said we were to tell Mum to come back immediately for questioning. I said she wasn't fit for it and that she needed a break, so I certainly wouldn't tell her. They were a bit snarky – will I get into trouble?'

'No, love, of course you won't,' Morrison said soothingly. 'If they come back I'll speak to them. She hasn't anything useful to tell them and it wouldn't look good for them to go hounding her over nothing at all. Just leave it to me and put it out of your mind.

'How's Mikey today?'

'Had a great time at playgroup. He's done a picture for you – says it's of you but I can't say I think you'll be flattered.'

He chuckled. 'I'll look forward to seeing it.' Then a thought struck him. 'Is Ameena in today?'

'No, I think she must still have flu. I'm being your domestic slave instead.'

'That's the way it should be. I like a daughter who knows her place. See you tonight.'

He set down the phone, then, with a sudden thought, picked it up again. 'Morrison here. Gather Ameena has flu. I think she may take a while to recover. We won't be expecting her back for the time being. Clear? Right.'

He had just rung off when his secretary buzzed through to say that the police were there, wanting to speak to him.

Denise Crichton was obviously nervous. Macdonald had arrived first and he saw her checking up and down the street before she came into the little self-service café. She had chosen it, he guessed, as somewhere that neither she – nor, perhaps more importantly, her friends – regularly frequented.

He had a mug of coffee in front of him, though after he got it he had wondered if he should have chosen tea. However, the look of the mug of orange tea that Denise brought when she slid along the red vinyl banquette to join him in the booth didn't look any better.

There was a bowl of sugar packets in the centre of the table. He offered it to her but she shook her head, though as she started talking she took one out and began to fiddle with it.

'I need to ask you something,' she said. 'Will you give me a straight answer?'

'If I can, but I'm not promising.'

'Is my husband's business under investigation for something?'

He remembered Crichton's chaotic desk. 'I'm afraid I genuinely haven't any idea.'

She considered that, took a sip of the orange tea and shuddered. 'The thing is,' she said carefully, 'I'm afraid something's not right. I'm afraid there's going to be real trouble and I don't want to be dragged into it.'

'Are you involved in the business, then?'

'Oh no, not at all. I'm just a housewife. Grant's been

very successful and my job is to make it easy for him to go on being successful.'

The look in her eyes suggested that this was in itself a business agreement; not only that, but it was one that would be terminated with extreme prejudice should the goods not be delivered.

'But you still seem to be worried that you might in some way be drawn into any problems?'

Denise had managed to tear one side of the sugar packet and a little pile of white crystals spilt onto the table. She scooped it automatically into a neat pile and into her hand, then looked at it helplessly.

'Here,' Macdonald said pushing forward his mug, 'tip it in here. I'm not going to drink it, anyway.

'Look, Mrs Crichton, unless you tell me what your problem is, I can't help you.'

'It's a big decision.' She picked up another sugar packet. 'I could just be getting myself in deeper. But . . . if I tell you something, will you keep it confidential?'

Macdonald sighed. 'This is a murder inquiry. If you mean, will I go straight and tell your husband that you've changed your mind about backing up his alibi—'

Denise gasped. 'How . . . how did you know?'

'Because you were very obviously lying when you did.'

Her face crimsoned. 'He insisted,' she cried. 'I didn't want to lie to you! I've never been in trouble with the police in my life before.'

'Given that you've contacted me, and that you're now going to tell me what really happened, you're not in trouble with the police now. And we won't tell your husband unless the situation demands it.'

Macdonald could see calculation in Denise's face: by that stage, would she have nothing to lose?

'My conscience was bothering me,' she said piously. 'I just kept thinking of that poor woman, and where her body had been put. Of course, I'm sure Grant had nothing to do with it really, but I just wanted to do anything I could to help.'

Up to and including tying a slip knot for a noose round his neck, Macdonald thought sardonically, but he only said, 'Of course,' with a grave inclination of the head.

So out it all came. Grant Crichton, she said, had definitely gone out during the evening. 'Then he bullied me into telling you he hadn't. And so I lied to you. I'm sorry – I didn't want to, truly.' She put on a little girl, penitent face.

Revolted, Macdonald had to struggle to sound warm and reassuring. 'That's all right. I'll just make notes now for a brief statement that I'll bring back and ask you to sign once I've written it up. We won't mention your previous evidence, I promise.'

Michael Morrison greeted the officers without enthusiasm and got his retaliation in first. 'I gather you were speaking to my daughter this morning. She phoned me in some distress about being pressured to tell her mother to return for questioning.'

DS MacNee glanced at DC Hepburn, who said calmly, 'Yes, as my colleague said at the time, we need to talk to her as a matter of priority. She spent the day with Anita

Loudon and may have information that could shed some light on what happened later.'

'My wife told me all that Anita had said that day – poured it out, really, in her distress at the news. I can assure you there was nothing beyond the ordering of new stock and discussion of the latest fashion news – oh, and one client's determined effort to get into a size 14 when in the ladies' opinion a 16 would have been on the small side. I am now also fully au fait with the trends for the winter season, should you want to know.'

He smiled, but neither of the officers did. MacNee said, 'We're needing to speak to Mrs Morrison direct. She maybe heard something that didn't seem important so she wouldn't think of passing it on to you. Where is she staying?'

Morrison's lips tightened. 'I'm not going to have you bullying her. This is a question of her health and if you're going to persist I'll get her doctor to spell it out for you. She's not a suspect—'

'You're all suspects, till we've got evidence to the contrary,' MacNee said bluntly.

Morrison bridled. 'In that case, I'm happy to tell you that you can take her name off the list. My daughter and I can both vouch for the fact that my wife was at home all evening. Since I slept beside her I can definitely state that she didn't go anywhere in the middle of the night.'

'If we could speak to your wife for corroboration, maybe we could take you off the list as well,' Hepburn said chippily.

'I'm sure she'll be feeling less stressed in a couple of

days.' Morrison didn't rise to the bait. 'Now, if there's nothing more, I'm a busy man—'

'Did she take sleeping pills?'

He gave Hepburn a look of intense dislike. 'Occasionally. Very mild ones, when she's stressed, and as far as I can recall that wasn't one of the occasions. All right?'

As they got back in the car, MacNee said ruefully, 'Wasn't much of a grilling, was it? He'd stated already he barely knew Anita Loudon and there's nothing to suggest he did. He says he and his wife can alibi each other, which is probably true. Can't see where we can go from here.'

'At the moment,' Hepburn insisted. 'I don't like him – far too smooth.'

'You don't like Daniel Lee either,' MacNee pointed out. 'And I can tell you Shelley Crichton's no bundle of joy. Doesn't prove any of them did it.'

Hepburn conceded the point. 'So where now, Sarge?'

'Just a wee chat with a pal of mine. Won't take long.'

Janette Ritchie welcomed them warmly, beaming when MacNee said he'd just come to see if she was all right, ignoring Hepburn's cynical look as they followed her in.

'That's really nice of you, Sergeant. Och, I'm fine. Just such an awful shock, you know?'

'Of course,' MacNee said sympathetically. 'You'll have been needing to comfort poor Mrs Crichton, too.'

A cloud crossed Janette's face. 'She's been a bit funny,' she said slowly. 'Probably just shock too, of course. But she's not wanted me to go round, and to tell the truth, she's . . . well, she's not been very sympathetic about poor Anita.'

MacNee hoped that she couldn't see his ears pricking up. 'Still upset about the business with the girl?'

'Shelley thought she'd brought Kirstie's daughter to make fun of her, I suppose. Whether she was right or not . . .' Janette sighed. 'I told her it wasn't, but mind you, the lassie was the dead spit of Kirstie.'

'Other people must have thought so too. That nasty business in Kirkluce . . .' He shook his head.

'Oh, that would be that Lorna Baxter, I've no doubt – her and her nasty friends. It's got her mucky fingerprints all over it. She's just a disgrace to Dunmore, that's what she is.' Janette's cheeks flared with annoyance. 'She got in trouble with the law for that kind of thing at the time when it all happened. She won't admit to it, but you just send one of your chaps in uniform round to give her a scare and you'll see, it'll not happen again.'

'We'll maybe do just that,' MacNee said and got up. 'I'm glad to see you're doing all right, anyway.'

'That was real good of you to come in like that,' Janette said as she showed them out. 'It says a lot for the police force.'

As they went down the path, Hepburn said, 'I hope you feel ashamed of yourself, snowing that nice old lady.'

MacNee grinned. 'I'm long past that. *Let them cant about decorum, Who have characters to lose.*'

DI Fleming gave a final glance at her emails then stood up and slung her bag over her shoulder. There wasn't a lot more she could do today.

The endless routine of statements and interviews was

ongoing, but no clear line was as yet emerging and all she had been able to say to the unimpressed media was the standard 'lines of enquiry' guff. She was pinning her hopes on the forensic tests, and the labs certainly wouldn't be working over the weekend.

Now she'd better make the call to MacNee.

'Tam, I just wanted to warn you. You're on duty tomorrow, aren't you? I should be but I'm going AWOL. OK, it's a murder inquiry but it's becalmed at the moment. Cammie's playing his first game in a Scotland jersey and I'm not missing that.'

She smiled at his congratulations. 'Thanks, I'll pass it on. I haven't told the super, so will you cover for me? I won't have my mobile on till after the game's over.'

MacNee reassured her that he had it in hand.

'Oh, just one other thing, while I remember. Anita Loudon's lawyer said he was going to send over her will and some letter that she left for Marnie. I don't suppose lawyers work over the weekend so I guess it will be Monday before we see it. Can you contact Marnie and make sure that she's here then to open it? I'll see her myself. It'll need a light touch – it may be a very emotional situation again.

'All right, Tam? Thanks very much.'

It was the darkness and the cold that drove Marnie back to the cottage in the late afternoon. Perhaps the cold had done her a favour; when it came to the point of walking into the loch the icy water looked so forbidding that her courage had failed her. Perhaps. She wasn't sure.

Instead, she had walked, walked and walked, stumbling

sometimes on the stony paths, blind to everything except her own thoughts and the endless images of her childhood that bludgeoned her. She cried at some of them: tears of anger that her mother seemed to have been so unloving, tears of pity for the sad child she had been. And eventually, tears of pity for her mother too. She had suffered more in her childhood than Marnie ever had and perhaps it had warped her into being unable to love her daughter.

There was nothing more she could do to find out whether her mother was alive or dead. As she got back to the cottage by the loch, her teeth chattering now and her breath a frozen cloud in front of her face, Marnie admitted defeat.

Tomorrow she would try to strike a deal with the police that would allow her to go back to London and put all this behind her. Just one more night to get through, that was all.

She didn't know what had wakened her. For once Marnie had fallen asleep quickly and slept soundly. Then suddenly, she was wide awake.

She sat up with a formless anxiety, looking and listening. Had she heard a car stopping outside the cottage – and was that a car door being shut, very, very quietly? With her heart racing she got out of bed, thrust her feet into her shoes and shrugged on her discarded jacket against the cold.

She opened the door to the hall. The front of the house was lit up, by the headlights, presumably. Who—?

Marnie wasn't going to wait to find out. She tiptoed

through to the kitchen, leaving the door open so that she could see to find her handbag and the key. It grated in the lock as she turned it, wincing at the sound. As she opened the door, she could smell a heavy, sickly stench on the bitter air. Petrol!

She flung herself out of the house, her clenched knuckle in her mouth to stifle a scream of terror. There was a path down to the loch here at the back – where was it? Where was it?

In the light from the headlights she spotted the gap in the trees. The sagging wire of the boundary fence tripped her and sent her sprawling; she scrambled up, knees bruised and her breath rasping in her throat.

The path was overgrown and brambles snatched at her clothes as she fled, unnoticing, down it. She could see the shimmer of the water ahead but it was all she could see; behind her it was so dark, so dark – someone might already have heard her escape and be following stealthily behind.

Marnie had just reached the shore path when the whole world blew up. She couldn't stifle the scream this time, but it was covered by the noise of the explosion and the roar of a fire.

Staring back through the trees, Marnie could see that where the cottage had stood with its old, dried-out wooden structure, there was nothing except a fireball of red, orange and yellow flames.

CHAPTER EIGHTEEN

There was a wind blowing now, heralding a weather-change. As Marnie stood, still transfixed, she saw a tree take fire, and then another, the resinous pine prime for burning. The path she had only just left was engulfed a moment later.

She would be safe by the shore, protected by the concrete area where her car was parked. She could get into it, drive away – but what if he was waiting for her there?

Someone had meant to kill her. If he had realised she'd escaped, he'd be looking for her, hunting down his prey. She had to hide, away from the pines and the spreading flames, down by the loch side where there was only wet grass.

The broch! She could see its roof in the lurid light and in blind panic she scurried to it like some small, threatened forest creature going to ground. Feeling her legs give way, she slumped down onto the wooden bench that ran round the stone walls.

The smoke was billowing across now, but inside the familiar smell of damp earth triggered the memory.

'Quick, quick,' Gemma hisses. 'He's coming, he's coming!' She gives a little squeal of delighted terror as they dash into the broch. They clutch each other as they cower at the back, listening for the footsteps.

She says, 'They're getting closer!' and Gemma mutters, 'What if he comes in? What'll we do?' They're both covering their heads with their hands, as if that makes them invisible.

She found she was covering her head now, putting it down on her knees and wrapping her arms round herself as if huddling into a smaller space would make her safer. She was listening for the footsteps on the path but now all she could hear was the roar and crackle of the flames. The pungent smoke was getting heavier now, tainting the air; she had to cough, she had to, no matter how she tried to stifle the sound. Her eyes were starting to stream too. Soon she would be forced to leave her refuge or suffocate; he was smoking her out.

Air became more important than concealment. Choking, wheezing, she emerged, looking fearfully about her.

There was no one to be seen on the path, but the rising wind was whipping sparks and small burning branches from the trees onto it. Before long one of the trees would fall. Marnie had to take the risk, now.

The melting frost sizzled and spat as the flames licked at the frozen grass by the side of the path. She tried to dodge the sparks, but the smell of frizzling hair told her she had failed and she beat at it frantically as she ran towards the car park, coughing till she retched.

But there it was – and as she reached the edge there was the sound of sirens and a moment later the glorious sight of flashing blue lights.

Marjory Fleming waited until first light to go out to feed the hens. Even for the sake of making sure they would be in plenty of time for the Scotland Under-20 international against a touring Samoan team, she wasn't going to risk giving the fox that lurked around at dusk and dawn a free feast. The hens, though, were slow to rouse on this cold, wet, windy morning and she muttered at them impatiently. They muttered back.

At least the weather should give the Scottish team an advantage over lads used to tropical warmth. Level playing field – pah! All she wanted was for Scotland to win – though, to be honest, if Scotland lost but Cammie played brilliantly and scored a try, she'd settle for that.

Bill was presiding over the fry-up when she got back and Cat, back for the weekend, was putting the coffee mugs down on the table as she padded in on her stocking soles. She gave her mother a cynical glance.

'Well, what do you suppose the odds are against you actually making it to see your son play and not being called back to do something massively, frighteningly important that only you can do?'

Her father made an exasperated sound, but Marjory said calmly, 'Very low, in fact.' Her mobile was lying on the dresser; she picked it up and demonstrated that it was switched off.

'See?' She pulled a face at her daughter. 'I've told Tam that I can't be reached today.'

'That's something,' Cat admitted. 'You mean, it might be like being a real, normal family when we can look forward to us all going together to do something?'

'Absolutely.' Her daughter might be a pain in the neck but in the barbed remark Marjory could hear the echo of past disappointments and hurt. And at least it showed that whatever she might say, having her mother there still mattered.

They left the house just after eight for a twelve-thirty kick-off at Murrayfield.

Without hold-ups, it should leave them enough time to get the car parked, find their seats and savour the atmosphere before it started.

Bill was fussing. 'I hope we've left enough time. You know what parking's like in Edinburgh and the official car park's just extortionate.'

'It'll be fine,' Marjory said. 'You don't get a huge turnout for a junior international.'

'If we get held up you can always put on your flashing blue light,' Cat said.

'You think?' Marjory said dryly. 'We'll be in plenty of time.'

As they reached the motorway, the car fell silent. Glancing in the mirror Marjory saw that Cat had plugged herself into her iPod and Bill, bless his heart, was sound asleep. He was absolutely exhausted these days; thank goodness Rafael's ankle was better and Cammie too would be home much of the time. She'd have to see to it that Bill didn't overdo it for the next bit.

She quite welcomed the thought of a long, silent drive. It was ideal for thinking, when there would be no distractions and she felt at the moment that she still hadn't got a proper handle on the case. Perhaps the forensic evidence would clear the fog that surrounded it at the moment, but it would do her good to review what she had already and see if that led her to something she hadn't thought of so far.

There was no doubt in her mind that Marnie's arrival had been the catalyst for Anita's murder. Perhaps it really was as straightforward as it looked on the face of it: one of Tommy Crichton's grieving parents couldn't forgive her for allowing Kirstie's daughter to come back to spy on the fortieth anniversary and with Kirstie unreachable had taken vengeance on Anita instead. Putting the body in that telltale position might have been something psychologically necessary – or it could have been some sort of double bluff.

Grant Crichton had an alibi that looked shaky; Shelley had none at all. Fleming had no difficulty in believing that both could have found enough hatred in their hearts to justify what they had done, separately – or even together?

But then there was Daniel Lee. She thought back to her interview with him: his manipulative charm, his sudden white-hot rage, only just controlled. Certainly a dangerous man, even an evil man. It wasn't a word she often used; most people who killed were uncontrolled, damaged or frightened. Where Lee was concerned, she could believe he would act with cold-blooded enjoyment.

What was his background, she wondered suddenly? He had been at primary school in Dunmore; Marnie had known him as a friend of her mother's. Then suddenly, here he was with a lucrative business – where had the money for a prosperous nightclub in Glasgow come from? That could be the key to the whole thing.

Morrison was in the mix somewhere. There was a lot going on there too, obviously; if she knew how the consortium had come about the picture might become clearer but approaching them right at this moment would risk jeopardising Nick Alexander's operation.

She could only hope that the swoop he had talked about would come sooner rather than later. Rowley was getting extremely restive, even though Fleming had patiently spelt out that unless you had direct witness evidence you had nowhere to go until the lab reports came through – always supposing there was anything conclusive after that.

It was intensely frustrating. She would have to wait to try to find out what she wanted to know about Drax's background . . .

Oh no, she wouldn't. Marnie Bruce had known Lee as a friend of her mother's and with her perfect recall she could repeat every conversation she had ever heard between her mother and Drax, as she called him.

The interviews with Marnie had all been about the present, even though the questions Marnie was asking had all been about what had happened to her mother in the past, questions that Fleming now realised she herself had dismissed as being unanswerable. Marnie could be a treasure trove of information about Drax's past.

And with the thought, she felt a cold shiver down her spine. If she knew that, Daniel Lee – and others – knew that too. If information locked in Marnie's brain was dangerous, she was only safe as long as no one knew where she was.

Marnie Bruce was asleep in a corner of one of the waiting rooms when DS MacNee came on duty in the morning. She looked very vulnerable, still clutching a silver survival blanket round her though the room was warm, and there were smears of dirt and soot on her pale face. A frizzled patch of her red-gold hair showed what a narrow escape she'd had.

The woman PC who had been sitting with her got up and tiptoed to the door. 'She's only just dropped off, poor thing,' she whispered. 'Do you have to wake her?'

MacNee beckoned her outside. 'What's she been able to tell us?'

The constable shook her head. 'Nothing much, Sarge. She was too shocked to make a lot of sense at first, and when we got her calmed down she could only tell us that she'd wakened and seen a car outside. The cottage has been abandoned for years and as far as we could make out she's been squatting – said she'd lived there once – so maybe she was just scared it was the owner. Anyway it was lucky she got out.'

MacNee nodded. 'Right enough. Molotov cocktail?'

'Not official yet, but they think so. The noise woke the people in the nearby cottage and they got the emergency services but they didn't see anything, like a suspicious car leaving the scene.'

'There's always occasional cars along the Queen's Way

even at three in the morning,' MacNee said gloomily. He glanced back through the doorway. 'Stay with her, let me know when she wakens up, OK?'

He went back to the CID room, glancing at his watch. Someone had tried to kill Marnie Bruce, and damn nearly succeeded. The boss needed to know about this but she'd told him she'd be incommunicado until after Cammie's game was over. He couldn't blame her: she deserved to share in her boy's moment of glory If he'd had a son representing his country—

The old grief took him unexpectedly by the throat. His wife Bunty had cared more that there were no children, certainly, but he'd had his dreams too: a MacNee striker in the Rangers team. There would never be one, and now it didn't even look as if there'd be a Rangers team either.

Louise Hepburn got up on Saturday morning feeling ever so slightly smug. The new regime was working: she'd insisted her mother went to bed when she did, and provided they got up at the same time, the natural need for sleep ought to do the rest. She'd brought what was, very probably, professionally inappropriate pressure to bear on Jimmy, the proprietor of a local security installation firm that got quite a lot of police business, and he'd installed a makeshift alarm on windows and doors so she'd been able to have a sound night's sleep. If Fleur was seized with an ambition to go on a midnight ramble she'd know all about it.

She wasn't due in at work today after all. With budgets tight, they weren't going to draft in extra manpower if things had stalled, as they seemed to have for the moment. She was in her dressing gown, warming up croissants and roasting coffee beans – the smell was a sure-fire way of seeing to it that Fleur didn't sneak back to bed – when the doorbell rang.

Louise frowned. Who would it be at ten o'clock on a Saturday? If it was work, they'd phone or text.

It wasn't. It was Lintie, a kindly middle-aged neighbour whom Louise had known all her life. She was wearing an anxious frown which cleared when she saw Louise.

'I'm sorry to disturb you this early, pet, but I know you work on Saturday sometimes and I was afraid you'd maybe be gone if I left it any later. Can I have a wee word?'

'Yes, of course, come in. I'm through in the kitchen and I'm just going to put the coffee on. Mum'll be down in a minute.'

Lintie hesitated. 'It was just you, really,' she said awkwardly.

Louise's heart suddenly sank. 'What's wrong, Lintie?'

'It's Fleur, dear. When you're out at work, she's stravaiging all over the place, just wandering around. She doesn't seem to know where she is, if you speak to her. Is there a problem?'

Louise felt sick. 'She's . . . she's just a bit confused. She never quite seemed to get over Dad's death, you know? I'm hoping with me living here now and able to keep an eye, you know, she'll get back to normal, given time.'

'You're a good lassie, Louise. But I wonder if you should maybe make some more arrangements before she comes to harm? Just till she gets better, you know?'

She shrank from the kindly pity in the woman's face. 'That's . . . that's a good idea,' she said. 'I'll see what I can do. Could you possibly keep an eye out for her meantime?'

336

'Of course I will, pet. There's a few of us been worried and we'll all do what we can, but it's difficult when she can't speak the language.'

Louise managed not to cry until Lintie had left but back in the kitchen, with the coffee making the friendly, familiar sound as it percolated, the tears came. Carers were hard to find anyway, and where could she find one who could speak French? Someone who didn't might stand in temporarily but her mother would find it even more confusing and it couldn't go on for ever.

She knew what that meant: she knew the duty of an unmarried only daughter and love came into it as well as duty. But give up the job she adored, abandon the dream career with all its interest and challenge to spend her life cooped up in the house here with a mother whose decline was inevitable but – and she hated herself for even thinking of it – whose general health was excellent.

She heard Fleur's footsteps in the hall. She came in, immaculate as always in a camel skirt and a cream silk shirt with a few gold chains round her neck and a camel cashmere cardigan round her shoulders.

'Coffee! Wonderful, my darling!' She came over, as always, to say good morning with a kiss on each cheek and another for good measure, then looked around.

'Where is your papa? You'd better go and fetch him or his coffee will be getting cold.'

He'd give Marnie Bruce another half-hour, MacNee decided, then he'd really have to wake her and talk through what had happened last night.

Meantime, he went to a computer in the CID room and looked through the reports but no blinding flash of insight struck him. He hadn't expected that it would; it was fairly clear that until they got in the forensic results, there was only more legwork and knocking on doors with a diminishing likelihood of useful returns. There were lads out in the rain doing that now.

He had a gut feeling, too, that if they could get hold of Vivienne Morrison they'd be able to drag something useful out of her. He didn't think for a moment that she was concealing anything; she'd seemed a nice, gentle lady and, being reluctantly fair to her husband, had clearly been utterly distraught at what had happened. Morrison couldn't stall for ever; they'd start getting heavy next week.

He'd just glanced at his watch again impatiently when one of the FCAs came in with a small package. 'This has just been handed in,' he said.

MacNee took it, glancing at it incuriously. It was only when he saw the label – Curtis and Fairlie, Solicitors – that his gaze sharpened. Someone must be keen, working on a Saturday.

He opened it. Inside there was a formal covering letter and two envelopes. One was typewritten, addressed to Miss M. Bruce, and the other was handwritten in a light-blue ink, a loopy scrawl with a little circle above the 'i'.

MacNee turned it over, even held it up to the light in a pointless attempt to see what was inside. He tapped it on his hand: from the feel of it, at least a couple of pages. Just as well there wasn't a kettle in the CID room or he'd have been sorely tempted to steam it open.

338

So what did he do now? Fleming had said yesterday that she wanted to be there when Marnie opened it, afraid it might be something that would distress the girl even more – and she'd had enough over the past few days, even without the hair-breadth escape from death last night, to need very sympathetic treatment.

It was time he spoke to her about the fire, at least, but if there was evidence that might be useful in a murder inquiry you didn't just sit on it. He'd made a vow not to bother Fleming today; he knew she'd had family problems because the job always came first, but reluctantly he decided he had to. She wouldn't need to come back, just to decide whether it could wait. He picked up his mobile.

It went to voicemail. Of course, she'd said it would be off during the match. He didn't know when it would start, but it would be over by early afternoon. The decision could afford to wait until then.

Marjory Fleming felt her throat close with emotion as the wavering strains of 'Flower of Scotland' swelled from the pipe band – a bit of a dirge, certainly, and she sometimes thought the Scottish team would do better if it began the game with something more than nostalgia to stir the blood, but that was her own lad standing on the hallowed turf of the national stadium with a number 8 on his back, singing along with the Scottish team.

She stole a glance at Bill, rigidly at attention for the anthem, and she could see a tear glistening. Pride – or even envy, perhaps, that he in his heyday had never had that chance? She squeezed his hand and he grinned at her and winked.

It was so lucky that Cammie had been picked for this game, the only one of the Under 20s fixtures to be played here this year. The crowd was thin but Murrayfield had an atmosphere and glamour all of its own, despite the downpour and chilly wind. It would be a mudbath out there but any rugby-playing Scot was well used to that.

She joined in the roar as they took the kick-off then settled back to enjoy the game, inasmuch as any mother could enjoy watching her son putting himself constantly at risk of severe physical injury.

'Marnie?'

The voice was gentle but at the sound of her name Marnie's eyes flipped open immediately. She was confused: where was she? There was a terrible crick in her neck and her mouth was painfully dry. She struggled up in the chair.

The small man bending over her was smiling, sort of. 'DS MacNee, remember?' he said and she nodded.

Of course, she'd been brought here after the fire last night.

What was that noise? Was it a car outside – does someone know she's here? She's out of bed and her heart's beating a mile a minute and she's shoving her feet into shoes and it's cold, very cold. She grabs the jacket by the side of the bed, she opens her bedroom door – car headlights—

'Marnie, you all right?' MacNee was tugging at her arm, pulling her out of the flashback.

She licked dry lips and croaked, 'Yes, sorry. Is there any water?'

MacNee looked round; there was a carafe and a glass on

a side table and he poured out the water and gave it to her.

Marnie drank it thirstily. 'Sorry,' she said again. 'I was a bit confused.'

'I'm just wanting to talk through what happened last night. I know they've taken a statement but maybe if we had a wee chat there might be something you'd forgotten.'

Could she think back without going through the whole thing with pictures and action? Probably not, but she'd obviously have to try.

'There wasn't much to tell, really. I think the noise of the car woke me – I shouldn't have been there, after all, and I just wanted to get away before they found me. It was only when I smelt the petrol—'

The fear struck her in overwhelming waves. Someone wants to kill me! I'm going to die!

Then she's running, falling, getting up again, being pulled back by things clutching at her clothes and her face is sore from a scratch and she puts her hand up – she's bleeding and she starts to sob in sheer fright and it's hot, too hot.

The water! The water was too cold before for . . . something . . . but it needs to be cold now and she needs to hide, hide—'

Her shoulder was being shaken and she gasped as she came back to the overheated, stuffy room.

MacNee was looking alarmed. 'I think I should get someone—'

'No,' she said. 'Don't worry. I just get these sort of flashbacks when it's all happening over again in my mind and I'm back there. It's standard. I can't stop them but they pass.'

He was looking at her with sudden interest. 'I've heard about this,' he said. 'You mean you can go back, remember what happened?'

She took a long drink of water. 'Yes. But there isn't anything helpful. I went round it several times last night. Didn't hear a noise, didn't see a number plate – just ran.'

Marnie could see the disappointment in his face. She'd seen that look before, on DI Fleming's face when she'd asked about the night Marnie had been hit on the head, as if they thought she'd some sort of mystical ability.

'I can only remember things I actually saw,' she told him flatly.

'Aye, of course – that would be right,' he said. 'OK, let's leave that. Who knew where you were staying?'

She could answer that. 'DI Fleming. Not precisely, I just told her it was an old cottage – which wouldn't be much help to anyone who might want to kill me, and I doubt if she would pass it on anyway.'

Her tone was sarcastic and the sergeant smiled. 'Likely not. Are you sure? No one?'

She took time to think. Then suddenly, out of nowhere, it came: her romantic interpretation of the young Asian waiting in the car park in the little grey car with the dented wing. The car had pulled out behind her as she left. She'd driven through Glasgow after that, concentrating desperately on her route home, and by the time she got down to any smaller road the winter dusk had set in and all she would have seen in her rear-view mirror was headlights.

'There was this car . . .' she said.

* * *

342

The crowd was roaring, baying him on. The Samoan defenders were huge, roadblocks each one of them, as the Scotland winger streaked up the pitch. There were too many – he couldn't make it – ten yards, five yards, three, two—

He jinked as the crunching tackle came. He went down, but not before he had flipped the ball back over his shoulder. And Cameron Fleming, her Cammie, was there to take it and in a blind charge for the line took it across and downed it.

She was screaming, crying tears of pride, but luckily no one would notice because everyone round about her was yelling too. Bill had flung up his arms with a full-throated roar of triumph and Cat was shrieking at the top of her voice, dancing about. She turned to Marjory.

'That's my wee brother there!' she shouted in her ear and grabbed her in an embrace.

It was only as Marjory disengaged herself that she saw the look on Cat's face. She was looking over her shoulder.

'Oh God, Mum,' she said. 'Dad!'

CHAPTER NINETEEN

They were all over the container lorry the moment it drove off the boat at Cairnryan. Watching the activity from his office window DCI Nick Alexander saw the driver escorted away between port authority officials, looking bewildered – whether genuinely or otherwise. One of his detectives climbed into the cab then jumped down again, clutching a file of documents as he nodded to an official to drive the lorry off into a hangar.

Alexander was unconsciously rubbing his hands as he turned away from the window and waited for the evidence to start arriving.

DS MacNee sat at a desk in the CID room, feeling intense frustration as he eyed the envelopes still lying there, unopened.

He looked at his watch impatiently. He didn't know anything about rugby, but surely a game couldn't go on for more than three hours? It was half past two now, and he'd tried Fleming's phone twice in the last half-hour without success.

Marnie Bruce was getting restless. She'd been asking when she would be free to go and of course they'd no right to keep her if she decided to walk out. He'd gone down himself to apologise for the delay and say it wouldn't be long now, if she could just bear with him, but he was beginning to feel irritated. Family pride was all very well but surely Fleming could take a minute to check her phone?

He tried it again, heard the impersonal voice at the other end and switched it off, swearing.

They sat in silence in the hospital waiting room. The cheerful curtains and pictures and the upholstered chairs were obviously a well-meant attempt at cosiness but somehow the effect was of an unconvincing sitting-room stage set ready for some cheesy drama to be played out, Fleming thought. Blank walls and hard surfaces would have felt more appropriate to tragedy.

Cat, white-faced and shocked, was dry-eyed but every few minutes she would give a convulsive sob. Marjory herself felt strangely detached: her head seemed too light, as if it might float away from her body. They were sitting side by side, but after the first clinging together as Bill – so still, so grey – was removed with impressive efficiency they had withdrawn as if locking themselves into their own misery was the only way they could cope.

As Marjory was driving out to the Edinburgh Royal

Infirmary, forcing herself to concentrate on the road ahead, which seemed more like a film projected in front of her than reality, Cat had said, her teeth chattering, 'At least it happened there, with paramedics on hand, not somewhere up on the sheep walks.'

'Getting to him right away – that's the important thing. He'll be fine.' Marjory managed to form the words but she couldn't manage conviction. After that there was nothing more to say.

Now they were waiting for Cammie. The game, of course, had gone on but by now they would have told him and the joy of his triumphant try would be for ever extinguished.

He would take it badly. Cat and Marjory were alike, self-possessed and contained, but Cammie didn't bottle up his emotions the same way. This would devastate him and Marjory was already summoning up her reserves to produce the comforting he would need. She would have to be very strong for him – and that was hurried footsteps in the corridor outside now. She stood up, ready.

Cammie appeared in the doorway. He seemed to take up most of it; a towering figure in a tracksuit hastily thrown on over his filthy rugby strip. His face and hands were still caked with mud and there was a huge reddening bruise under his cheekbone.

'Oh, Cammie,' Marjory faltered, and felt tears start to her eyes for the first time.

He looked down at her from his superior height, then swept her into an embrace. 'Come on, Mum!' he said. 'Can't have this – he's going to be fine! Of course he is.' He looked over her head at his sister, holding out one arm and Cat too, crying now, came and clung to him.

After a moment he shifted. 'Right, girls, that's enough. There are tissues over there. You've got mud all over your face, Mum.'

Shakily, Marjory laughed and did as she was told. It could have been Bill himself talking.

'I'd a word with one of the paramedics at the stadium,' Cammie said, 'and he said he'd seen a lot worse and the crucial thing was prompt treatment – Dad certainly got that. No one's giving out guarantees, but you can take this two ways. You can be upbeat or you can look on the black side – it won't make any difference either way, but you'll feel better on the way through.'

Cat had recovered her composure. 'My wee brother – the philosopher!' she mocked him. 'Played not a bad game of rugby as well, from the bit I saw.'

Cammie grinned. 'We won, too. I'm just telling you so that if we get called in to see Dad, you'll be able to tell him because it's the first thing he'll ask.'

For just a moment, his voice shook and Marjory looked at him anxiously. But then he sat down and started telling them about coming off the pitch and being told what had happened.

She'd been still thinking of him as a boy, but Cammie was all grown-up, ready to step in as the man of the family – temporarily, please God, but remembering what he had said she firmly suppressed the chilling thought that it might not be.

There was a clock on the wall and suddenly Marjory

noticed the time. She'd said to Tam she would check in later – she'd better call and tell him what had happened. She picked up her handbag, then felt Cat's eyes upon her, cold and hard.

'You're going to phone the station,' Cat said. 'Right now, when we don't know if Dad's going to pull through, you're thinking about the bloody *job*?'

'Cat, I have to let Tam know what's happened.' She knew she was sounding defensive.

'I'll do that. If you do it, you'll get involved in whatever's going on. Give me the phone.' She held out her hand.

Marjory took the phone out of her bag slowly. 'I won't,' she said, but she knew that if she spoke to Tam she wouldn't be able to cut him off. 'It would just be better if I explain—'

'Choose,' Cat said. 'If you don't give it to me, I'll never forgive you, ever.'

Cammie was sitting with his head bent. He didn't look at her.

Wordlessly, she held the phone out to her daughter.

MacNee put the phone down and groaned. His first thought, of course, was for Bill, *the hardy son of rustic toil,* as he'd always called him – not so hardy, perhaps. These big men, reaching middle age carrying a bit of excess weight: not good. He looked down at his own spare, wiry frame for reassurance.

Fleming must really be taking it hard. Cat had said she wasn't even able to speak to him – though from her hostile tone he wouldn't put it past her just to have confiscated her mother's phone. He'd never had much time for Cat Fleming – a skelped bottom at an early age might have done her a lot of good.

Whatever the rights and wrongs of it, this left him in a right mess. Cat had given no indication at all when her mother would be able to speak to him and investigations couldn't just grind to a standstill meantime. There were the envelopes on his desk, just for a start.

Running to the super about this would feel like telling tales and MacNee was no clype. But it didn't sound as if Fleming would be leaping back into the job any time soon and Rowley would have to step in. The thought of answering directly to Hyacinth, without Fleming to act as a buffer, made his blood run cold but it had to be done. He picked up the phone.

'Oh – MacNee! Well, what is it? This had better be important. I'm very busy.'

It wasn't a promising beginning. 'Sorry, ma'am, I'm afraid it is,' he said and explained the situation, without mentioning that Fleming had been unofficially in Edinburgh at the time.

There was a silence at the other end of the phone, then Rowley said, 'Oh, really! That's *too* bad.'

MacNee had a nasty feeling that she wasn't talking about Bill's heart attack.

'Of course I'm sorry this should have happened, but it couldn't have come at a more inconvenient time. I'm just packing to go to an important meeting in London – with *MI5*, you know.' She dropped the name with an almost audible clang. 'They want a report from me about our progress up here so I can't possibly cancel now.

'You'll just have to cope as best you can. No doubt Fleming will be back tomorrow – it's her husband that's ill, not her, and she's responsible for a murder investigation, after all.'

The easiest thing would be to agree, but MacNee was far from certain that she would – and if the worst happened, she certainly wouldn't. 'There's another SIO, isn't there? Perhaps we could draft him in meantime,' he suggested.

'No we can't,' Rowley snapped. 'He's up to his eyes in a case of racially aggravated assault – you can't take someone off a racist investigation. Surely you can manage?'

'Managing' was one thing. Taking over an investigation, making the decisions that would be subject to scrutiny, risking disaster if they were the wrong ones – that was different. MacNee had opted to stay in the sergeant's job because he had never fancied the responsibilities that ran Fleming ragged.

He had another try. 'Maybe the Dumfries force has someone they could spare for a few days—'

'Dumfries?' Rowley screeched. 'Are you mad? What would that say about me – that I couldn't manage to staff my own murder investigation? Are you saying that you're incompetent, MacNee?'

What could he say but no? Her voice was triumphant as she said, 'That's settled, then. You're in charge until Fleming returns. I'll be at the end of the phone if necessary, but only if necessary – I'll be very busy.

'Thank you very much, Tam. It will be good experience for you – professional development, you know?'

MacNee didn't actually slam the phone down on her immediately but his response before he did was brief. Disgusted by her lack of professionalism and feeling faintly sick, he reviewed the situation.

Hyacinth's behaviour broke every rule in the book. He could go over her head and cause trouble but any investigation would throw up Fleming's absence from duty. Anyway, whistle-blowers seldom prospered.

So he'd have to take it on, hoping that it would, indeed, only be for a day or so. He needed to plan for the worst, though.

The lab results would come through soon and any evidence would have to be analysed, acted on and followed up. Grant Crichton would have to be interviewed in the light of his wife's change of story but the budget decision had been not to bring officers in on overtime today, so that would have to wait until Monday. He'd been planning himself to go and turn the screws a wee bit on Shelley Crichton; he'd been struck by her friend's unease about her response to Anita's murder – and he mustn't forget to arrange for uniforms to go and do a scare job on Lorna Baxter. It was possible that something might come of that.

And then there were the letters. He looked down at them, lying on the desk in front of him. He had every right now to satisfy his curiosity; all he had to do was take them along to Marnie Bruce and ask her to open them.

Then what? Fleming had flagged up the problem of her likely reaction and MacNee was well aware that his record for putting the frighteners on people was better than his record for comforting the distressed.

351

Perhaps it needed a woman's touch. If Louise wasn't out partying again maybe she could come in. And if that meant blowing the budget without authorisation he'd be happy to discuss it with Hyacinth when she got back from her own preferred kind of partying.

The young registrar who came at last to talk to the Flemings was almost as tall as Cammie, with dark hair and a cheerful expression. Marjory tried to still her thumping heart; surely he would look more sombre if the news was bad?

He introduced himself, then said, 'I'm pleased to say he's doing very well.'

Such beautiful words! She was struggling with tears again, of relief this time, and she heard Cammie give a sort of long sigh and his shoulders sagged, as if he had been squaring them rigid to hold himself together.

Cat, still tense as a drawn bowstring, said sharply, 'What exactly does that mean?'

The young man turned to her. 'He had a heart attack caused by a clot blocking one of the coronary arteries. The good news is there was no further damage since he got such immediate treatment. He was at Murrayfield when it happened, I gather.'

He turned to Cammie. 'I guess you were on the pitch? It was the Scotland Under 20s today, wasn't it?'

Cammie nodded. 'My first game for them.'

'I turn out for Edinburgh Accies Thirds when I can. How did it go?'

'We won, 7–3.'

'Great! Who scored?'

'Well . . . I did.' Cammie tried to sound modest and failed.

Sensing that an explosion was building in Cat, Marjory stepped in hastily. 'So what happens now, Doctor?'

'We'll be doing an angioplasty – fitting a stent to keep the artery open. It's not a major op, just a local anaesthetic and then if all goes well we might keep him in just for a night.'

Marjory only realised that her own shoulders had been hunched up around her ears as she felt them relax. 'And after that?'

'That should fix it. He'll have some medication, at least to start with, and his GP will advise about statins but after that it's mainly a question of diet and exercise, losing a bit of weight, maybe. Has he been in the habit of eating healthily?'

Conscious of the fry-up only that morning, Marjory made a non-committal noise. 'We'll certainly see to it that he does now – and that he doesn't overdo it. His farmworker's been laid up and he was absolutely exhausted this last bit. He put it down to old age but he'll have to take it easier now.'

She wished she hadn't said it when she saw a cloud pass over Cammie's face. 'Not that it's a problem,' she added hastily.

'He'll probably feel fitter than he has for years,' the doctor said. 'Worst thing he could do is start sitting around thinking of himself as an invalid. He's been lucky enough to get this as a warning and if he makes the sensible changes we outline he'll be absolutely fine.

'You can look in to see him now, but then I suggest you go back home. We'll want him to have a good rest before the operation tomorrow.'

It was a shock to see Bill lying there, linked up to machines and drips and somehow looking smaller. Marjory heard Cat give a sharp little gasp of dismay and she found it hard herself to look suitably cheerful.

Bill, though he looked very strained and shaken, was smiling bravely. 'Sorry about that. Must have given you a hell of a fright,' he said, then, 'What happened?' He wasn't talking about his own dramatic collapse.

'7–3 to us,' Cammie's voice sounded a little flat. 'I scored.'

His father beamed. 'That's my boy! All set for your full Scotland jersey in another year!'

'Oh, we'll see,' was all that Cammie said and Bill looked across at Marjory with a raised eyebrow.

Cat was at her father's side, holding his hand. 'Don't do that again, Dad.' Her voice was shaking. 'It really wasn't a clever idea.'

'Stupid, that's me. But don't worry, lassie. I've learnt my lesson. Maybe I should go veggie from now on, eh Cammie?'

His son managed a weak smile at the reference to his ex-girlfriend and Marjory said, 'That might be too much of a shock to the system. But take it from me, fry-ups are out – the doctor sounded like prosecuting counsel when he asked me about your diet.'

The nurse was hovering, ready to show them out.

Marjory hung back to kiss him. 'Hope it all goes smoothly tomorrow,' she said. 'No more frights, OK?'

'Piece of cake,' Bill said sturdily. 'The doc seems quite relaxed about it.'

'Of course he is,' Marjory said. Agonising wouldn't help and with Bill determined to keep it all low-key, the last thing he needed was her screaming hysterically, 'It's still an operation! I'm still scared!' Instead, she said, 'I love you, Bill.'

He smiled up at her. 'Oh dear – bad as that, is it? I'll be fine, I promise. Oh, and I love you too.'

Just as she left, he said, 'I do feel upset about spoiling Cammie's triumph. He seems very down – tell him we'll celebrate once I'm home.'

'I will,' Marjory assured him but she had a nasty feeling that there was more to Cammie's low spirits than just the anxiety about his father.

'Yes, of course I can,' DC Hepburn said when the phone call came from DS MacNee. 'That's awful about the boss's husband. Do you think he'll be all right?'

'Can't tell you. I only spoke to the daughter – she said Marjory couldn't come to the phone.'

'I'll be with you in half an hour.'

She felt the fizz of excitement that made her job such a rewarding one. A last letter from the dead woman, and she was going to see it before anyone, apart from Marnie herself. She could find that she was holding the key to the whole case.

And she would have to leave her mother to do it. The

fizz dispersed, leaving her with the flat feeling of misery she had been struggling with all day. The neighbourly warning had perhaps made her more alert to the signs of confusion but Fleur seemed to have deteriorated rapidly.

It was making her unhappy too, for the first time. She had fretted all day about her husband's absence and Louise was reduced to lying that he was away on business. Perhaps she should tell her again that he was dead, but would it mean her mother reliving the shock and horror? She needed to talk to a doctor before she did that.

If she left her, might Fleur decide to wander out to look for him? She could lock the doors, of course, but what if something happened – what if Fleur managed to set the house on fire and couldn't escape?

Perhaps she should phone Tam MacNee and say she couldn't manage after all, not until she could find a carer to stay with her mother while she wasn't there herself?

Louise looked into the sitting room. The television was on and Fleur was on the couch in front of it. She looked very comfortable and peaceful and quite often she was happy to sit half-watching the screen for hours on end.

It wouldn't take long, just to go in, hear what the letter had to say and mop up Marnie if necessary. To back out now would mean telling Tam her problem and asking for compassionate leave that, given the situation, might turn into resignation. It was a decision she wasn't ready to take just yet.

She slipped out of the house quietly, feeling leaden

with guilt. But as the miles passed and her thoughts went ahead to what Anita Loudon's letter might tell them, the excitement began to build again.

No one seemed to be feeling chatty as Marjory drove back from Edinburgh. In the mirror she could see that Cat had again put in her earphones and had her eyes shut, but Marjory didn't think she was sleeping. She still looked drawn and there was a little furrowed line between her brows.

Cammie had been limping as he walked to the car and the bruise on his cheek was starting to take on lurid colours. He'd got off lightly, then, Marjory reflected wryly.

'You'll need a long hot bath when we get back,' she told him as Cammie winced, getting himself settled in the front seat. 'You'll probably have to chip the mud off – it's set hard.'

'Maybe I'd better just start in the sheep dip,' he said, making an effort at humour.

'Will you have to come back for physio tomorrow? We'll be over to see Dad anyway.'

Cammie shrugged. 'Maybe,' he said, then lapsed into silence.

Marjory had found the journey over quite constructive for thinking about the investigation but now all she could think about was what lay ahead of Bill tomorrow, and even that was better than going back: the terrible moments when she had thought Bill was dead.

He'd always been the strong one, the one she could rely on always to be there for love and support and good common sense. She'd taken all that for granted; she hadn't given his exceptional tiredness a thought, or his constant munching of indigestion tablets. He must have been struggling with that narrowed artery, feeling awful, and she hadn't even noticed the warning signs. Too wrapped up in the absorbing job, of course, the vampire job that Cat – and even Cammie – felt had sucked the blood out of their family life. She felt crushed by guilt.

At last, desperate to escape her own thoughts and the oppressive atmosphere in the car, she turned on the radio. 'Let's get the Scottish news,' she said brightly. 'Maybe they'll have a report on the game.'

Cammie agreed though without much enthusiasm and Cat took out her earpiece. Marjory half-listened to the latest spat in the referendum campaign between the Yeses and the Noes and tuned out another episode in the ongoing disaster that was the Edinburgh trams. It was only the last brief tailpiece that caught her attention.

'In what the Galloway Constabulary are describing as an arson attack, a cottage by Clatteringshaws Loch, near Newton Stewart, was burnt to the ground in the early hours of this morning. There were no casualties but police are appealing for witnesses.

'And now, sport . . .'

Marjory felt the shock ripple through her. She could hear Marnie Bruce's voice: 'just an old cottage' – and it was a cottage beside Clatteringshaws Loch that Karen Bruce had been living in when she'd been visiting her all those years ago.

An arson attack – someone had tried to kill Marnie

Bruce. At least they hadn't succeeded, but would someone see to it that she was allocated some sort of protection?

Her thoughts must have shown on her face. She glanced in the mirror as she pulled out to overtake a slower car and saw Cat's eyes on her.

'Don't even think about it,' she said fiercely. 'Just for once, try concentrating on your own family. Dad's having an operation tomorrow – oh, they make it sound nothing but he's still in danger. If you loved him you wouldn't even be able to think about anything else.'

'Cat, of course I feel that. But someone may be in danger—'

'And no one else will be able to look after them – just you? Either you're delusional or all your colleagues are incompetent. I back delusional. But you're allowed to choose.' She got her mother's mobile out of her bag.

'Here it is. Take it if you like and make your call. But I meant what I said.' Marjory waited for Cammie to say something – anything, but he didn't. He was staring out of the window as if he hadn't even heard.

She bowed her head. 'All right,' she said.

DC Hepburn felt quite shocked when she went into the waiting room with DS MacNee. Marnie Bruce's bright red-gold hair was dull and stringy, with a patch of frizzled ends near the front; her eyelids were heavy with purple, bruised-looking shadows and puffy with tears and lack of sleep. The room was warm but she was shivering visibly.

'Sorry to keep you, Marnie,' MacNee said. 'You know DC Hepburn, don't you? She's brought along a couple of letters from your lawyer that we need you to read. We'll want to read them afterwards, with your agreement.'

Marnie looked at him coolly. 'And if I don't agree?'

'Then we would have to get a court order. Obviously we'd prefer not to.'

Hepburn held out the letters and Marnie looked at them incuriously. 'Who are they from?'

'This one's from the lawyer, I expect.' Hepburn indicated the typewritten one. 'This one – it's addressed to you in what we believe is Anita Loudon's writing.'

Marnie's eyes sharpened. 'But Anita's dead!'

'She left this with her lawyer some time ago.'

Marnie took the letters and examined them with frustrating carefulness. Then she gave a little shrug and opened the typewritten one. She read it, then held it out to Hepburn.

'He's just asking to see me on Monday, that's all. About her "legacy", whatever that may mean.'

Hepburn glanced at it but said nothing. Marnie was examining the second letter now. She made to open it, then stopped.

She's scared of what it's going to say, Hepburn thought. And no wonder, with what had hit her these past few days. 'Do you want me to open it for you?' she said gently, but Marnie shook her head.

At last she slipped her finger under the flap, opened it and took out the letter. There were three sheets, covered on both sides in Anita Loudon's looping writing. She read it slowly.

Hepburn found she was holding her breath. MacNee,

standing beside her, shifted impatiently. Marnie read the last page then put it down in her lap.

MacNee, unable to contain himself any longer, said, 'Well, what does it say, then?'

The woman looked almost dazed. 'I-I don't quite know,' she said. 'There's too much . . .'

'Shall I take it?' Hepburn said softly and with a gentle, unhurried movement held out her hand.

For a moment nothing happened, and then Marnie gave a little shrug. 'Why not?' and handed it over.

CHAPTER TWENTY

As DC Hepburn sorted the pages of Anita Loudon's letter into order she wondered what a graphologist would make of it: written in blue-green ink, florid, with little round circles as dots over the 'i's and floating 't' strokes that only sometimes connected with the upright. She began to read, with DS MacNee peering over her shoulder.

Dear Marnie

Remember me? Haven't seen you since you were a wee girl. If you're reading this, I must be dead – don't want to think about that.

I've left everything to you – nothing in the bank, but there's the house. Why you? There's no one else – and it's to make up for what I did to you.

Did your mum ever tell you the truth? She said she wouldn't but maybe you know by now she killed a child – she was just a kid herself, though. I was there when she did it and I was a witness at the trial. And I lied. I shouldn't have. It was a terrible thing I did, to her and to you.

It was Drax did it really. Oh, Kirstie – that's your mother's real name, Kirstie Burnside – she killed him, right enough, but it was Drax made her do it. Tommy Crichton was a cheeky little sod and he'd tried it on with Drax, slagged him off about his mum being a slut – well, you didn't do that. He had to pay. Drax said that, like it was some sort of law, or something.

Us kids were allowed out after dark late for Halloween, guising round the doors, running about shouting and laughing. We got Tommy to come along with us – he was chuffed because we were the big kids. We took him away, off into the big field for a special game – Hunting, we told him it was called. And we did. He laughed at first. Then we surrounded him, and he couldn't get away – it was horrible, horrible. I'll have nightmares tonight, writing that.

Drax wouldn't do it himself, of course, he just wound up Kirstie to do it instead. He got a real kick out of that. She was his slave, you see. We both were – we had to be if we wanted to be his friend. And we did. I still do.

We were all yelling, chanting, sort of. Kirstie went crazy, frenzied, Drax yelling her on, Tommy screaming. I covered my eyes but couldn't move, somehow, not till he was just lying there and Drax said, 'Come on, run!' And we ran and ran and it was exciting and awful at the same time – and not real, too, in a way – like it really was a game.

Once the police found out, I had to say he hadn't been there, that he'd come along after. Kirstie wouldn't say anything different – knew she'd never see him again if she did.

Don't know how much she saw him once they let her out. He disappeared for a bit but then he came back here and brought Kirstie to work in his business and we all met up again. She was Karen by then – I still think of her as Karen. He was sleeping with her and with me too. Never told her that.

Then something went wrong and they disappeared. Don't know why. Never saw her again. He appeared at my door a couple of years later, said she'd just done a bunk but I'm not sure. If she was causing trouble he could of killed her. He might, easily.

If I'd told the truth maybe they'd have seen she was a victim, needing help. Drax was two years older and she'd an awful life. Her dad was a drunken monster – got put away for it himself, afterwards.

You'd think it would fade all this time later. But it doesn't. Gets worse. Didn't think about it too much back then but now I think about it all the time. Don't know if I believe in Judgement and that but I just get more and more scared. Mustn't tell about that, though – or about all the other things he's done – or

I'll lose Drax. But sometimes I think I'll die of fear.

Are you his daughter? Karen never said and I never asked. Didn't want to know. All I ever wanted was to marry him and have his kids but he was never the marrying kind. And it's way too late now.

Hope the house sells well for you. You deserve whatever you can get – among us, we really screwed up your life. To be honest, it's to make me feel better about what I did and maybe it has, a little. Only a little.

I'm sorry – I couldn't help it. Don't hate me. If your mother's still alive, she'll tell you she understands.

Anita

There was a brief silence as the officers finished reading. Then MacNee said, 'Right. Thanks, Marnie. I'll leave you with DC Hepburn.'

After he had gone, Hepburn said nothing, waiting for Marnie to speak. Reading it must have been a very emotional experience and though the prolonged silence felt uncomfortable she was determined not to break it.

At last, her voice flat, Marnie said, 'The house – that'll be a lot of money, right? I didn't know about the house, I swear. I expect you'll really think it was me that killed her, now.'

'No, I don't. I suppose you might have known – she could have told you she was leaving it to you when you met – but the cottage being petrol-bombed is a good indication that you're another victim.

'What Anita said about your mother, though – does that make you feel any better?'

Marnie grimaced. 'Better? I don't know. I'm not sure I can feel anything any more. She was always sort of his puppet, being jerked around. OK, he was controlling her but she let him, didn't she? I was just . . . nothing.' Her voice faltered. 'Do you know what I wish? I wish to God I'd never started this.

'Maybe my mother's dead, maybe she isn't. But Anita Loudon wouldn't have got killed if I hadn't come asking questions, would she, and I wouldn't be scared to death because Drax is trying to kill me.'

'We don't know that,' Hepburn pointed out. 'There are other angles we're checking out but what's certainly true is that your life's in danger. DS MacNee says you've refused police protection – I really think that's crazy. You ought to take it.'

Marnie shifted restlessly in her seat. 'It'd be like being a criminal myself, being watched – and anyway they can't protect you all the time, can they?'

'So what are you going to do, then?'

'I don't know.' It was a wail, and then she started to cry. 'They've given me a loan because all my belongings were burnt and they told me to stay somewhere nearby. But that woman from the B & B in Bridge Street put me on a blacklist and I don't know who would take me. They'd know who I was, too, and I can't trust anyone, can I? What am I to do? I'm – I'm scared.'

She looked so helpless! Wrung with pity, Hepburn said, 'You could come and stay with me.'

As she said it, the advice 'Engage brain before putting mouth in gear' came forcibly to mind. She must be mad! If anyone got to know she'd find herself out of a job. But she'd said it now.

'Look, perhaps this is crazy,' she went on, not waiting for a response, 'but that way no one would know where you were. And come to think of it, you'd be doing me a favour too. My mother's started getting very confused and I'm worried about leaving her alone all day. Until I get proper care arranged it would be a relief to know someone was around.

'Oh, she's not mad or difficult or anything. She's a really sweet person, though I have to warn you she doesn't speak English – just French. She's very used to people not understanding, though – she gestures and smiles a lot.'

Marnie had stopped crying and was looking bemused, as well she might. Probably reckons I'm off my head, Hepburn thought, and she could be right.

At last Marnie said hesitantly, 'That's – that's kind of you. I hate taking favours, but I don't know what else I can do. If it helps with your mum I'll feel better.'

It was just what Hepburn had suggested and she managed to say, 'Great!' with suitable enthusiasm, despite a chill of foreboding. 'I'll just go and have a word with DS MacNee, then I'll come and fetch you.' Then she added awkwardly, 'I – I won't mention this arrangement to him. It's just between the two of us, OK?'

'This going to get you in trouble, then?'

Hepburn grinned at her. 'Not if they don't find out,' she said cheerfully as she left.

* * *

367

DS MacNee was brooding over Anita Loudon's letter in the empty CID room. From the lawyer's date-of-receipt stamp, she'd written it quite recently, some time after she'd made the will. Maybe she'd been thinking about it, reckoning Marnie deserved to be told – or maybe it had just been a relief to confess after all the years of living a lie.

What it definitely showed was signs she'd been beginning to crack and Marnie Bruce's arrival would just have piled on the pressure. Did Lee know how much it was preying on her mind? Anita could even have been ready to tell Kirstie's daughter the truth, face-to-face. If she had, and she let him get wind of it, she'd probably signed her own death warrant.

What he'd read confirmed everything he'd thought about that slimy bastard and what he most wanted to do was to get straight up there, put his hands round his throat and choke a confession out of him.

How was it that men like that got such a hold over women? There were plenty of examples – Ian Brady and Myra Hindley, just for a start. And as for an alibi – with the circles Lee moved in, that wouldn't be hard to arrange.

But could he go and pay another visit to Zombies? Fleming had been very specific: they'd been warned off by the Cairnryan branch until further notice and he wasn't going to kid himself that he'd win in a face-off with DCI Alexander. The letter, of course, didn't prove anything except that Drax had escaped being charged with conspiracy to murder when he was – what, eleven, twelve? No one was going to revisit that now, especially when the witness admitting to perjury was dead anyway.

No, that was something else that would have to wait until Monday. Before he knocked off, he'd better work out a rough schedule for the team on the assumption that Fleming wouldn't be coming in on Monday.

At least DC Ewan Campbell would be back on duty. He never said much, but when he did say something it was always to the point – and at least MacNee wouldn't have to spend his time refereeing spats between Macdonald and Hepburn.

He was just thinking that when Hepburn herself appeared. 'How did Marnie react?' he asked.

Hepburn pulled a face. 'Punch-drunk, I reckon. She was more worried than pleased to hear she was being left the house – thought we'd arrest her on sus immediately.

'I think she's almost past caring about her mother, anyway. By the time someone's been murdered and you've only just escaped, it's not surprising you'd kind of lose interest in tracing a mother who showed no sign of giving a stuff about you and might even have tried to kill you herself.'

'You could say.' MacNee sighed. 'Has she left?'

'She's waiting till I come back. I wasn't sure if you'd want to speak to her again yourself.'

'Not much point. Where's she going? I wish she'd agreed to protection – I'm not happy about her at all.'

'She doesn't want anyone to know where she is,' Hepburn said with perfect truth. 'Says she feels safer that way.'

'Thought that the last time too, didn't she?' MacNee said darkly. 'Anyway, that's her choice.

'Right, Louise, thanks for coming in. I'll see you at the briefing on Monday. I'll need all the help I can get. It doesn't sound as if the boss'll be there and Hyancinth's off at a meeting in London so I've been dumped right in it.'

The Asian man came out of a fish and chip shop in Kirkluce High Street and walked back to the small grey car with the dent in the wheel arch, eating chips. He was hungry and cold and bored.

He looked over at the police station he'd been watching for hours now. He'd been starting to wonder if somehow she'd left without him seeing her, but just then he saw her coming out, with another woman, heading for the car park. He sprinted the last fifty feet to his car and jumped in, spilling his fish supper onto the seat beside him, and started the engine. His heart was racing. He could have missed her and he dreaded to think what Drax would have done then.

He'd checked before and the exit from the car park was round the back in a quieter street; it would take them a minute to reach a car and get in, so he should be just in time to follow them.

It was starting to get dark. He turned the corner and pulled in at the side. He didn't recognise the first car to come out but the car he'd tailed before came next, still with its courtesy light on, and before it faded he saw the driver's red-gold hair. He smiled, waited for a moment, then eased the car out along the street behind her.

* * *

Shelley Crichton was sitting in front of the wide-screen TV in her sitting room. It was showing a manic popular quiz show but the gales of hysterical laughter didn't bring a flicker to her face.

She was waiting for the news. She had seen it twice today already but there hadn't been any more detail about the cottage at Clatteringshaws and when at last the bulletin came on the item had been dropped completely.

She clicked the remote to turn it off then sat, stony-faced, still staring at the blank screen. Should she just leave it now – let it drop? Or should she . . .

Shelley's eyes went to the big photo that stood in a silver frame on the little table beside her chair where she could always see it just by turning her head – her Tommy, bright-faced, with that cheeky grin of his that had always melted her heart, Tommy alive.

As always, her eyes filled with tears. That girl deserved it. And then maybe her mother might learn what it felt like to lose a child.

The bed felt terribly big and empty when Marjory Fleming climbed in at night. She tried not to look at Bill's pyjamas, folded neatly on his pillow.

She was exhausted so it should be easy enough to get to sleep, but putting her head down on the pillow seemed to be a signal for the show to start: Bill collapsing at her feet, her own horror, the sense of panic till the paramedics arrived after minutes that felt like hours, on and on. And guilt, guilt.

She'd have nagged Bill to go to the doctor if she'd

noticed something wrong, but she hadn't. A good wife would have noticed. She hadn't been a good wife – or mother, according to Cat.

Supposing the operation didn't turn out to be as simple as a junior doctor thought. Supposing the worst happened – what would she have left?

Her career – the kind described in recruitment ads as 'fulfilling'. Compared to 'loving wife and mother' as a job description it sounded about as cold and empty as the bed did without Bill on the other side. She sat up, pummelled her pillows and lay down facing the other way so she couldn't see it.

It was no use. She tried shutting her eyes but they kept flipping open again and at last she gave up, pulled on her dressing gown and went down to make herself a cup of tea.

The light in the kitchen was on and she hesitated, wary. If that was Cat, she'd just make her cuppa as quickly as possible, then take it back upstairs. She didn't feel she and Cat had anything helpful to say to each other just at the moment.

It wasn't Cat, it was Cammie. 'Good gracious,' Marjory said as she came in, 'I didn't expect to find you here. I thought you'd have crashed out long ago.'

'Couldn't sleep.' He was looking awful, hunched over his mug of tea; the bruised cheek had swollen a bit, and with the mud washed off the other bruises and scratches that were all part of the pleasures of the game of rugby stood out starkly against his exhausted pallor.

'I couldn't either.' The kettle was singing on the Aga and Marjory went over to make her tea. Meg the collie got out of her basket to greet her, though normally she would have been too lazy to do more than open one eye at this time of night; after Marjory had petted her she went over to the door to the hall and snuffled under it hopefully.

'She's looking for Dad,' Cammie said and Marjory, with a lump in her throat, could only nod. She sat down beside Cammie at the big wooden table. Meg, her tail drooping, went back to her basket.

'Are you sore?' she asked. 'Do you need paracetamol?'

'No. It's just the usual,' Cammie said, then, 'Mum, I've been thinking. All this happened because the farm's too much for Dad. If I hadn't been off when Rafael was laid up, this wouldn't have happened.'

'Nonsense!' Marjory said briskly. 'If it's a narrowed artery, it's been going on for some time and it would have happened eventually. If I'd only been around a bit more – noticed that he was getting far more tired than he should be for a man in his forties – I'd have made him get checked out. I blame myself, if you want to know.

'If all goes well – please God – I ought to rethink my job. Maybe shift into traffic, go part-time—'

Cammie stared at her. 'Don't be daft! It's not your fault – you said yourself Dad's problem developed gradually, so by the time you could notice he'd probably have needed the operation anyway. In any case, he's old enough to look after his own health.

'You know he's always been all in favour of your job. Said to me once the thought of you putting all that energy into running our lives made his blood run cold.'

'Cheeky sod!' Marjory said, but she was smiling.

'The thing is,' Cammie went on, 'now this has happened he's going to have to be careful. I can't leave him wearing himself out while I swan off playing professional rugby. Oh, I love the game. It's been my life, but I always knew I'd be farming in the end. There are teams I can play for without the level of commitment—'

Marjory reacted with horror. 'Wash your mouth out, Cameron Fleming! For heaven's sake don't say that to your father when you see him tomorrow or you'll give him another heart attack.

'Look, I don't know if you know this, but your dad really was a serious contender for a Scotland jersey – not a shoo-in, but good enough to have had a trial. If he'd dedicated all his time and energy to it he might have made it, but in those days it didn't pay and your grandfather was a lot older and determined to retire . . .

'Dad gave up his dream to put food on the table for his family. You've been his compensation for that and he'd be crushed if you gave it up. Crushed, that is, after he'd seriously bawled you out for being so daft.'

'But this is different. After this he's going to have to take it easy . . .

Marjory was shaking her head. 'Not according to the doctor. He'll have to take proper exercise and watch his diet – and that's probably my fault too, being useless with anything except the frying pan. He said he'd be fitter than he's been for years, remember?

'Anyway, if he needs more help we can hire it in. It's not a problem, Cammie.'

Cammie's hunched shoulders had straightened. 'Do you really think so?'

'I'm sure so,' Fleming said firmly.

'But of course, you wouldn't be able to afford extra help if you'd only a part-time job, would you?' he said slyly. 'And you'd hate it, and you'd be bad-tempered, which would put a strain on Dad and that would be bad for him too.'

'You're painting a pretty picture of your mother,' Marjory said lightly, but she felt as if a burden had been lifted. She went on slowly, 'Cammie, was I a rotten mother?'

'Fishing for compliments, are you? No, of course you weren't.'

'Cat—'

'Oh, Cat!' her brother snorted. 'Cat's got issues at the moment. She hasn't got over making a mess of vet school before she'd even started and there you are making a real success of your life.'

'But she's always resented me not being able to drop everything for family – and you did too, sometimes, I know.'

'Yes, I'm sure I did. But Dad was always there and most kids with working parents don't have both of them around for everything. It's usually the father who can't be there but it shouldn't be any different for the mother.

'Anyway, Cat's hardly at home now and she's not eight years old any more.'

'I know. But I want us to be close again. This really hurts.'

Cammie gave a huge yawn. 'Sorry. That's not a

375

comment. But where Cat's concerned, it's not you, it's her. She's got to work through her problems herself – there's nothing you can do.'

'You sound exactly like your father,' Marjory said and yawned herself. 'I still wish I could just kiss and make it better, like I used to do when you were wee.'

Cammie got up and held out his injured cheek. 'You can try it on that. I'm off.'

Smiling, Marjory kissed the bruise, then watched him go. It was funny seeing him so like Bill: rather less funny, though, to see Cat showing all the bolshiness that had made her own youth a painful experience, not least for her parents.

She hadn't told her mother about Bill. Janet adored her son-in-law and waiting till the operation was over before she phoned her would spare her a night of anxiety; because of course by this time tomorrow he would be *absolutely fine*.

Even so, she decided, almost superstitiously, that tomorrow all she would do was wait by the phone for news. She'd every confidence in Tam MacNee coping. Of course he could.

It was such bliss to be clean and warm. Marnie had soaked in the bath until her fingers and toes were all crinkled up and then she had snuggled down in a comfortable bed. She had eaten the most delicious meal she'd ever tasted, cooked by Louise's mum who seemed all right, except that judging by Louise's face the things she was saying in French weren't as normal as they looked. She'd got up, too, before they'd finished eating and come back wearing her coat, as if she was planning to go out even though it was dark now and quite late. Louise had a real job persuading her to take it off again.

She and Louise had sat after her mum had gone up to bed, finishing off the bottle of red wine that tasted as if it was made of velvet, and kind of watching a not very good film. Louise had said she was determined not to behave like a policeman when she was off duty but they'd talked a bit about Marnie's freak memory and that had seemed to interest her a lot.

'You can remember everything? Absolutely everything?' she'd asked.

'Yes, if it's something I saw, and the memory is triggered.'

Louise had gone very quiet and thoughtful after that and when the film finished they came up to bed.

Marnie had been afraid that once she lay down the memories would start, the memories and the worries about what would happen next, but lulled by warmth and wine she fell instantly into a deep, untroubled sleep.

Untroubled, that is, until half past two when suddenly all hell broke loose, bells screaming in her ears. Marnie was out of bed and onto the landing before she was properly awake.

Louise appeared a second later. 'Sorry, sorry, I should have warned you! Don't worry, it's just an alarm I got fitted to the doors and windows so that *Maman* couldn't wander out at night without waking me. I'll just go and turn it off.'

There was a cry of confusion from behind them and

when they turned, Louise's mother was coming out of a bedroom further along the landing in a floaty silk nightgown, her hands over her ears. She was visibly upset, calling to Louise in French.

Louise went pale. 'Oh God, what's that, then?'

She headed for the stairs and Marnie caught at the sleeve of her pyjamas. 'There could be someone down there. You'd better call the police.'

Louise jerked herself free. 'I *am* the police,' she said from halfway down the stairs.

Marnie heard her shout above the continuing din, 'Police! Stay where you are! You are under arrest.'

Then the alarm, mercifully, stopped, though Marnie's ears were still ringing. Louise's mother was shivering and crying; from downstairs there was no sound and plucking up her courage Marnie pattered down in her bare feet.

The sitting-room door was open. Louise had switched on the light and when Marnie joined her she was looking grimly at a broken window.

'Don't come any closer, Marnie – there's glass all over the floor. Someone tried to break in. I heard a car driving away just as I got downstairs.'

Marnie's stomach lurched. 'This is because of me. I brought this on you.'

'Don't—' Louise said, but the cries from upstairs were becoming hysterical and with an apologetic gesture she hurried away.

Marnie stood cold with fear and shivering in the draught from the broken window. He'd followed her here too. He must be watching her all the time – even now, perhaps. She scurried back into the hall and shut the door.

She couldn't stay, letting her problem spill over to wreck more people's lives. What was she to do? As Louise's mother's cries showed no sign of abating, she put her head in her hands and wept.

CHAPTER TWENTY-ONE

When Louise Hepburn got up, there was no sound from Marnie's room. She was glad to think she was catching up on her sleep; it had taken more than an hour to calm Fleur down and no one could have slept through that.

She was feeling shaky this morning and the painkillers she'd taken for her thumping headache hadn't kicked in yet. She'd looked in on Fleur before she came down and she was sound asleep; she could only hope that a benevolent aspect of her mother's confusion might be that she didn't remember what had happened, or might think it was a dream.

As Louise sipped black coffee and smoked a Gitane, she ran over the problems lying ahead. Someone to come and fix the window – priority. Fortunately she knew an emergency glazier in the town; he did a roaring trade in replacing shop windows if Saturday night in Stranraer got out of hand.

Then, of course, she'd have to deal with Marnie – she

couldn't leave her here alone with her mother now. And she couldn't call in pretending to be ill tomorrow, with Big Marge off and Tam saying he needed all the help he could get. Anyway, after the break-in she'd have to report it and confess what she'd done.

She felt a bit sick at the thought of that, but not as sick as she felt about the situation with her mother. She certainly couldn't be left alone again.

There had been a woman along the road, she remembered suddenly, who had sometimes helped out in the days when Fleur had still held dinner parties for her father's business clients – perhaps by some miracle she might be free and prepared to come.

She was. She was happy to come first thing in the morning, and Louise put the phone down with a sigh of relief. It wouldn't be a long-term solution, but at least she could cross that off today's list.

Then there was Marnie. She wondered if Marnie would mind doing a sort of informal interview with her; she'd been thinking last night anyway that they should try to tap in a bit more to Marnie's extraordinary memory. If she could think of the right questions to ask her it might be incredibly useful.

Useful – and, it struck her now, dangerous. Louise might not be the only person to think of its potential, if something Marnie had been witness to at some time was incriminating to someone for some reason. Suddenly the attacks on Marnie made sense.

Time she was getting dressed. She stubbed out her cigarette and went upstairs for her shower. There was no sound from Fleur's bedroom as she passed but she'd have to be wakened for breakfast or her body clock would go all wrong again.

Marnie could be left to sleep, though. Louise was just going into her own room when she noticed that Marnie's door, further down the landing, was standing ajar. With sudden misgiving, she pushed it open gently.

The bed was empty and there was a note on the pillow: 'Thanks for what you did. I'm really sorry about your mum – hope she's OK in the morning. Marnie.'

That was all. When Louise looked out of the window, Marnie's car had gone.

It was meant to be helpful, no doubt. Marnie had clearly felt that her being there was endangering her hostesses but in going off like this she had really dropped Louise in it. She hadn't said where she was going and even if she would answer her phone – which was far from certain – she probably wouldn't say.

Louise had been counting on keeping secret what she had done but if Marnie had gone missing she'd have to confess tomorrow and take the consequences, which might be very unpleasant indeed.

Hoping against hope, she dialled Marnie's number. The impersonal voice at the other end informed her that the person she was calling was not available and the further calls she made at intervals had the same result. After a long, long day, Louise gave up and went to bed, feeling sick with worry, both about what might happen to her and, more importantly, what might befall Marnie, alone and unprotected.

* * *

Marnie had suffered some bad days recently, but yesterday had been the worst. She had left Stranraer in the dark and driven on aimlessly along roads that were empty in the Sunday calm, but she kept checking her mirror with neurotic frequency. When as the day wore on the occasional car came up behind her she found it hard to control her panic, but as she desperately turned down smaller and smaller roads to shake it off it never followed her.

She stopped occasionally – to refill the car, to have something to eat, or just to sit somewhere watching the sea, trying to blank out her thoughts – but when she stopped moving she would start twitching with the almost superstitious fear that Drax somehow would home in on where she was.

When darkness fell she still had nowhere to go. She had a sleeping bag and blankets, though, and she found a track leading into woodland where she could park up. But tired as she was, sleep didn't come easily and as the night frosts began the car became an ice-box. Pulling her covers right over her head, she managed at last to drop off but she kept waking with a start of fear at the strange little night sounds of the countryside, and the night seemed to go on for ever.

At first light she woke properly, stiff and rigid with cold and hungry. After two broken nights her eyes were burning and she was worn out, too, by the constant onslaught she had suffered over the last twenty-four hours of images that forced their way into her brain: she was back on the landing with Louise's mother, she was talking to Anita, she was running from the fire, on and on. If this continued it could drive her mad. She craved a quiet mind like a traveller in the desert seeking water. A quiet mind . . .

She's walking across to the abbey. It's very grey and quiet and she can hear the sheep bleating outside, can even hear the tearing sound as they snatch at the grass. The turf's sort of springy and she's almost bouncing as she goes to the chapter house. And it's even quieter inside as if no one has spoken there for hundreds of years so the quietness sort of muffles her ears and even gets into her head.

Glenluce Abbey – she needed to head back to it. She'd been able to think there and after a day of such mental confusion she badly needed to clear her mind.

Down that little quiet road she'd see Drax if he was coming after her. She'd have to wait till it opened but she'd maybe find a café somewhere on the way. Warmth and food and then the peace of the white walls and the grey stone arches – that sounded good, comforting.

She might as well live in the moment. Was there any point in trying to plan a tomorrow that might never come?

'I spoke to DI Fleming's daughter this morning,' DS MacNee said at the Monday morning briefing, 'and her husband is being operated on as we speak. I'll give you news when I have it.'

He was feeling nervous, but his audience of officers was concerned and sympathetic. As he went on to outline the tasks for the day, he heard DC Ewan Campbell, sitting at the back beside DS Andy Macdonald, murmur to his companion, 'Where's Hyacinth?'

'Important meeting in London. Much more important than a murder inquiry.'

MacNee swivelled to give them a glare modelled on his old maths master at school. Macdonald tried to look as if he hadn't spoken.

'Thank you,' MacNee said with heavy sarcasm. 'Not often I get the chance to tell Campbell off for idle chatter. You're lined up to see Grant Crichton, right?'

'Right,' Macdonald said.

'Nothing from forensics yet,' MacNee went on, 'though I'll be chasing them up later today. In the meantime . . .'

He gave out details, took questions and suggestions quite effectively, he thought, and finished feeling pleased with himself on the whole. So far so good. He even had a bit of a strut in his step as he left the room.

DC Hepburn was waiting for him. 'Could I have a word, Sarge?'

A look at her face told him that this was something big, the sort of thing that would normally land on the boss's desk. She had black circles under her eyes that looked as if they'd been drawn on with a crayon and as he looked at her she bit her lip.

There would be other detectives in the CID room at the moment. 'Come up to the boss's office,' he said. 'I've got some chasing up to do on the forensic reports.'

Hepburn nodded. As MacNee climbed the stairs he thought of possible angles – professional, personal? Personal, he was inclined to think. There'd been something going on with her the last bit – could it be drink? Drugs – not likely: he'd have seen signs before now. Man trouble?

His heart sank at the thought. Advice to the lovelorn wasn't his style.

It felt strange to go into Fleming's room when she wasn't there and stranger still to sit down in her chair behind the desk. Hepburn sat down opposite, perching on the edge of the seat.

'There's a problem,' she said.

No point in messing about. 'Personal or professional?'

'Well, both.'

'Oh.' He ought to say something encouraging but nothing came to mind. 'Better spit it out, then.'

Hepburn took a deep breath. 'On Saturday, when Marnie Bruce refused police protection and had nowhere else to go, I – well, I took her home with me.'

'Lassie, are you daft?' MacNee was appalled. 'You know perfectly well that she's still a suspect in a murder case. Even if you don't think she did it, and for the record neither do I, for an investigating detective to have a personal relationship like that could bring the impartiality of the whole operation into question.'

'I know. But I was so sorry for her. She'd nowhere to go – that cow in Bridge Street had put her on a blacklist and she didn't think anyone would take her locally. And even if they did it would have been very public, wouldn't it? Anyone could find out.'

'For heaven's sake, she could have used a false name, couldn't she?'

'I – I never thought of that.' Hepburn looked crushed. 'Anyway—'

'There's more, is there?'

'I'm afraid so.'

'Go on,' MacNee said hollowly.

'There was a break-in that night at my house. I'd got someone to rig up an alarm system on the doors and windows – you see, my mother . . .'

She stopped and took a deep breath. 'My mother is – well, losing the place. I know you thought I was tired because I'd been living it up, but she's waking up at all hours and she went out in that storm we had the other night and I was terrified she'd die of exposure or something. I'm at my wit's end.'

Now he felt guilty. 'You should have told me.'

'I I couldn't. Even telling you today feels disloyal.'

'Could happen to anyone. Just an illness, that's all. And you need your pals, eh? OK, I got it wrong but I'd like to think I was still one of them.'

Hepburn smiled wanly. 'You weren't to know. But there's more.'

'Aye, I was afraid there might be.'

'The alarm went off about two in the morning. When I went down to the sitting room the window had been broken but there was no one in the house and I heard a car taking off in a hurry. The alarm's just a makeshift one – there's no box on the outside or anything, so they wouldn't have been expecting a problem.'

'Looking for Marnie.' MacNee's face was grim.

'I guess we must have been followed. She was driving behind me so of course I didn't notice anything. They'd have had to be watching the station, you know. We were only together for a couple of minutes as we walked to the car park.'

'So where is she now?'

Hepburn was studying her fingernails. 'That's the worst part. I don't know. She's disappeared and she's not answering her phone.'

MacNee swore.

'I know, I know, you don't need to tell me,' Hepburn cried. 'I've completely screwed up. The thing is, I reckon I know why someone's trying to kill her. She swears Anita Loudon didn't tell her anything and yes, it could be that Drax thought she had. But if he knows she was here all day, he'll know that we'd have questioned her till she told us all she knew about that, so killing her afterwards wouldn't solve anything.

'If she's still dangerous to him, it could be because of something else she knows, something about the past, something he reckons we won't have thought of yet but that she could remember if the right questions were asked.'

There was a certain logic to it, admittedly. But if there was one thing his years of service had taught MacNee, it was to keep an open mind.

'You've decided it's Lee, haven't you?'

'Well, you read the letter.' Hepburn was defensive now.

'And he's a scumbag and you took against him because he was glaikit enough to think you were just a wee woman he could cajole. The incriminating stuff in that letter goes way back before Marnie was even born, so it can't have anything to do with her memory, right?'

Hepburn accepted the point, reluctantly. 'So what happens now, Sarge? Do you – do you have to tell the boss once she comes back?'

MacNee knew what the answer should be. He also knew what would happen once the official channels were opened.

'She's not here just now. We'll wait and see. If Marnie gets back in touch and nothing more comes of it, we'll maybe be able to keep it quiet. Let that be a lesson to you, though.'

Her thanks were heartfelt. 'I'll keep trying Marnie. I hope she'll maybe feel she owes it to me to let me know she's safe.'

'We'll both hope. Now, I've a couple of things to do here, but then I want you to come down to Stranraer with me. I want to speak to Shelley Crichton again. Maybe she can tell us she has a rock-solid alibi for the past couple of nights and we can write her off, but until then there's no way I'm crossing her off the list. Or her ex, either.'

DCI Nick Alexander came into work still smarting. The searches on Saturday had turned up absolutely nothing and they'd made fools of themselves in front of the port authority. He was a proud man and he had found it hard to take the lavish sympathy that didn't quite hide glee at the elite force falling flat on its face.

The tip-off had come from a highly reliable source, so the shipment must have been called off. They must have got word of it somehow, or perhaps the 'routine' inspection of accounts by HMRC hadn't been so subtle after all. Of course, the plods stamping around on the murder investigation wouldn't have helped either.

Had Fleming ignored his embargo, gone and leant

on Daniel Lee? If she had, he'd go ballistic. He avoided admitting to himself that he was rather hoping she might have since it would be a convenient excuse for failure.

He grabbed the phone but was frustrated by a bland voice telling him she was unable to take his call. He didn't leave a message; he wanted to catch her before she had time to prepare her self-justification.

The report on the abortive action would have to be written sometime and he was turning reluctantly to his computer when his phone rang.

As Alexander listened to what the woman at the other end was saying his expression changed to one of unholy joy. 'My God, you're a star! Did you stay up all weekend working on that?'

She had, it seemed; she'd picked up a thread in the accounts and had been unable to resist following it to its satisfactory conclusion. More than satisfactory; very, very satisfactory.

'Tell your boss to give you the day off. In fact, tell your boss to give you a week off, staying in a five-star hotel,' he said extravagantly. 'Hang the expense.'

He heard her laughing as he rang off, then he picked up the phone. 'Get in here,' he said to his senior inspector. 'Good news, for once.'

It was blessedly smoke-free in DS Macdonald's car as he drove DC Campbell along to Stranraer. And silent: you always felt obliged to ask about other people's holidays even if you knew it would provoke a day-by-day recital telling you more about Torremolinos than you wanted to know, so it was refreshing that Campbell's reply when asked how the holiday went was 'Fine'.

Macdonald was looking forward to the interview with Grant Crichton. He had taken against the man – and his wife too, come to that – and there was always satisfaction in breaking a witness you'd known was lying.

He briefed Campbell on the situation. 'So his wife's changed her story – the alibi she gave him was false and he was out that night.'

'Think he killed her?' Campbell said.

'I think he knows a lot more about it than he's admitting. But I don't think he actually killed her, no.'

'Why not?'

Macdonald paused. Why not, indeed? The man had got his wife to lie for him, he'd clearly been in an agitated state, showing every sign of guilt at the arrival of a policeman. If, like the other members of the community who had gone to Bridge Street, he believed that Marnie had been sent to mock at the anniversary of his son's death and that Anita had been party to it, he had the classic combination of motive, means and opportunity.

He said, 'Well, doesn't seem the type, really.' He didn't need Campbell's cynical sidelong glance to tell him how lame that sounded.

Changing the subject, he told Campbell about the attempt on Marnie Bruce's life, the evidence of Anita Loudon's next-door neighbour and the reluctance of Michael Morrison to have his wife interviewed, but when Macdonald said hopefully, 'Any thoughts?' Campbell shook his head and silence fell again.

Somehow it seemed a long way to Cairnryan today. Whatever he might feel about Louise, quarrelling with her did pass the time.

'Doing all right, then,' Campbell said as they reached the 'Crichton Haulage' sign and turned into the extensive yard.

It was busier than it had been the last time Macdonald came, and when they went into the scruffy site office and asked to speak to Mr Crichton, the receptionist, a tired-looking woman with frizzy hair, seemed harassed.

'He's been very busy today. I'll buzz his secretary and see if he can see you.'

Saying 'Oh, I think you'll find he can', wouldn't really be constructive. Macdonald only nodded and after a brief phone conversation she said, 'He's got someone with him. You'll have to wait.'

She indicated a narrow vinyl-covered bench that ran along one wall and Macdonald and Campbell, both big men, perched on it.

'They don't go in for the comforts here,' Macdonald murmured. 'Truckers don't merit coffee tables and magazines, obviously.'

'*Reader's Digest*,' Campbell said with sudden animation. 'Should have that.'

'Read it for the jokes, I suppose. So you can entertain your colleagues,' Macdonald said, but it was never any use trying to wind Campbell up.

It was ten minutes before the phone on the desk buzzed and the receptionist called over, 'You're to go through now. Out of the building, turn right and it's across the yard.'

The reception area in this building was quite different. A potted palm stood in one corner beside a sofa and chairs with stainless-steel legs, upholstered in beige tweed. There was a low coffee table which did, indeed, display magazines though not the *Reader's Digest*. Campbell looked faintly disappointed.

The secretary at the smart, dark teak desk was clearly a superior being, with blonde hair swept into a knot at the back, full make-up and perfectly manicured nails.

'I'll ask if he can see you now,' she said, looking as if a bad smell was somehow sullying her pristine space. 'Do sit down.'

Neither man obeyed. As she went to the door to the inner office they followed on her heels so that they heard Crichton groan, 'Oh, I suppose you'd better,' as she asked if she could show them in.

She almost bumped into them as she turned and she gave them a dirty look. 'Will you be wanting coffee?' she asked Crichton.

Macdonald said, 'No,' before he could reply and went in. Campbell closed the door behind them.

Crichton half-rose but with a bad grace. 'You'd better sit down, I suppose. I hope this isn't going to take long – I've got a lot on today. I can't think what you want, anyway – you've interviewed me once and I made a formal statement after that.'

This office was furnished in the same expensive style and there were even fresh flowers on the desk, lovingly arranged by Miss Perfect out there, no doubt. As the detectives sat down opposite him, Macdonald said, 'Yes, the statement was what we wanted to see you about. We wondered if you might like to revise it.'

Crichton's face had registered only bad temper. Now, he froze.

Scared, Macdonald thought with satisfaction as Crichton stammered, 'I-I don't know what you mean! Why should I?'

'It just seems not to be wholly accurate.'

'That's an outrageous suggestion!' He was blustering now. 'I told you that I was at home all evening, and my wife bore me out. Oh, if there's some small, trivial detail of timing or something where I've slipped up, then I apologise, but everything else was perfectly straightforward.'

'The trouble is, sir, that a witness has come forward who can state that you were out that evening.'

Crichton looked about him wildly, as if an answer might be written up somewhere just out of his line of sight. 'They're lying!' he said at last. 'Who is it – oh, I suppose "you're not at liberty to say".' He mimicked an official voice.

'That's right, sir.' Macdonald said stolidly.

'So they can say anything they like about me, quite unsubstantiated, but I don't get a chance to refute it directly. Call that justice? Anyway, where am I supposed to have been?'

'Anita Loudon's house,' Campbell said. He spoke with the authority of a man whose statement is backed by incontrovertible fact and Macdonald looked at him with respect.

Crichton winced visibly. 'I wasn't,' he began, but then

his voice faltered. His hands, on top of the desk, were tightly clasped together and he studied them for a long moment before he looked up again.

'I – I think I'd better explain. All right, I did go round to the house, briefly, around half past eight – nine o'clock, perhaps. I was just going to have a word with Anita about the girl who was spying on my ex-wife – just a word, that's all. It wasn't a very nice thing to do and I wanted to know who had put her up to it.

'I didn't go in, though. There was someone there already – I could see her in the sitting room, standing talking to someone – I couldn't see who it was. I didn't want to talk to her in front of a visitor and I didn't want to wait. I'd work to do at home so I decided to leave it and go round to see her the next day instead. It wasn't urgent.

'Then, of course, I heard what had happened and I'll be honest with you – I was scared.' He gave a smile that was no more than a rictus and Macdonald could see that he was sweating. 'There was nothing helpful I could tell you so, yes, I gave false information. I knew it was wrong but . . .' He shrugged. 'I think it's understandable.

'Now I've set the record straight – that's all there is to it.' He gave another hopeful smile.

'Don't believe you,' Campbell said.

Crichton's lips were trembling and he took out a handkerchief to wipe his mouth, and then his forehead. 'What do you mean? Maybe I wasn't wholly frank with you before, but this is the truth, so help me God.'

Macdonald said conversationally, 'Do you know, when

someone says "This is the truth, so help me God", in my experience they're almost always lying?'

The man recoiled as if he'd been slapped in the face. For a moment he struggled to find breath, then he said, 'I refuse to say anything else until I have a lawyer present.'

'That's probably very wise,' Macdonald was saying, when he heard the noise of an altercation outside. Miss Perfect was squealing, 'You can't go in until I've asked Mr Crichton if he can see you. He has people with him—'

The door opened and two uniformed officers appeared. Macdonald recognised one of them, a lad who worked in the station at the Cairnryan port.

They didn't even glance at the detectives. As they came in they split so that they arrived at the desk one on each side beside Crichton.

'I am arresting you on suspicion of fraud,' the sergeant said. 'You are not obliged to say anything but anything you do say will be noted down and may be used in evidence. Do you understand the caution?'

'Yes,' said Crichton. He was shaking. 'Oh yes.'

There were only two cars in the Glenluce Abbey car park when Marnie arrived. She could see an elderly couple walking arm in arm, staring upwards as he pointed to the glories of the ruined nave, and the other would be the attendant's. With another glance over her shoulder at the little road, empty of traffic, she went in.

The attendant was pleased to see her. 'You must have enjoyed your visit. There's a wee book about it, here—'

'No thanks.' Marnie took her entrance ticket and

walked away, leaving him pulling a face at her back.

She started feeling calmer even as she walked into the chapter house: perhaps the silent sanctity of the place where the monks had read and prayed protected her from the demons howling in her mind. She sat down on the stone bench and allowed her eyes to follow the arches and curves in an almost hypnotic movement and the wheels that seemed to turn endlessly in her head slowed down, slowed down.

For the first time she felt able to consider her new situation clearly. Anita's will, the house – that meant quite a lot of money, didn't it? It still scared her. She believed Louise knew she hadn't killed Anita but she was less sure about the inspector. Being innocent didn't necessarily protect you; she'd seen too many kids she'd known in care be stitched up to believe that.

The lawyer wanted to see her this afternoon but she didn't want to go. Drax might easily work out she'd go there just like he'd worked out she was at the police station. Marnie wasn't going to go back there either, even if she did feel bad about what had happened to Louise's mum.

Whatever she might have said last night, she was too scared to vanish again. If she defied the police, she'd have them looking for her as well as Drax. Where was she going to stay? She wasn't going to try dossing down in the car again, that was for sure. Where could she turn?

In this place of prayer, she somehow found herself praying too, a cry from the depth of her despair. Then she opened her eyes and sat on, gazing at the vaulting arches, and gradually the sense of calm stole over her again.

The ringing of her mobile in this hushed room was so shocking that she jumped in alarm, confused for a moment about where the sound was coming from. Then she scrabbled in her bag, looked at the caller number, hesitated, then answered it.

She listened, said, 'Well . . . I don't know,' then listened again. At last she sighed. 'If you really mean it, then I will. It's kind – I don't know what else I can do. Can we meet just in a café somewhere first – Stranraer, maybe?' She gave a little, awkward laugh. 'I'm a bit paranoid, you see. I just want to make sure I'm not being followed.'

She switched off her phone. It wasn't an answer to anything except where she was going to sleep for a night or two, but it was better than nothing.

CHAPTER TWENTY-TWO

'She's as spiky as one of her own nasty plants,' DS MacNee warned DC Hepburn as he rang Shelley Crichton's doorbell just after midday.

'Good afternoon, madam. I wonder if we could have a word?' He took a step forward, ready to walk in.

Shelley didn't move. 'Why?'

They showed their warrant cards. 'I'm DS MacNee, you may remember . . .'

'Oh yes.'

'We are continuing our enquires into the death of Anita Loudon—'

'You haven't had much success so far, have you?' She had folded her arms forbiddingly across her body.

'That's why we need to talk to you,' chipped in Hepburn, earning herself a glacial stare.

'I don't see that I can help you there.'

'Look, do you mind if we come in?' It was cold there on

the doorstep with the wind whipping in from the sea and MacNee was getting impatient.

Shelley still didn't move. 'I told you what I was doing that evening the last time. There will be nothing else to add so it doesn't seem worthwhile.'

'We are not satisfied with the statement you made and I'm afraid we will need to go over it again in much more detail, madam. Let's go right back to the morning there was the problem at the play park. What time did you get up?'

'Eight o'clock. I always do.' She was starting to look cold too, MacNee was pleased to note, and she was only wearing a skirt and a woollen sweater.

'What did you have for breakfast?' Hepburn asked, entering into the spirit of the thing.

'This is just too ridiculous!' Shelley snapped. 'You—'

Behind her in the hall the phone rang. With a triumphant glance she said, 'Excuse me,' and went back inside.

'Chancing your arm with that last one,' MacNee cautioned. Then they both heard Shelley's voice, high and shrill. 'What? No! Don't be silly – he can't have—'

'Seems to be in distress,' MacNee said. 'Might need help.'

'Better go and see she's all right,' Hepburn agreed and they both walked through the open door.

Shelley, still exclaiming, certainly did seem to be both shocked and upset. 'It'll just be a mistake,' she said at last. 'You're always reading about blunders the police make.' She had turned and was looking directly at them as she said that. 'Call me back if you hear anything more.'

'Bad news?' MacNee said sympathetically.

She didn't seem appreciative. 'I wasn't aware I had invited you into my home. There seems to be no end to police impertinence. I have just been informed that your colleagues have arrested my former husband, presumably because you have made the ludicrous assumption that he would place a dead body on the very spot where our child died, a sacred place – obscene! Whatever I may feel about him, he loved his son. And no doubt once you discover that he didn't, I'll be next!' Her voice had risen to a hysterical pitch.

MacNee and Hepburn were staring at each other blankly. Then MacNee said, 'Thank you, Mrs Crichton, that will be all for the moment.'

He was on his mobile, scowling, before they reached the end of the path. 'Macdonald? What the hell's going on? If you've arrested Grant Crichton I should have heard about it from you, not from the local grapevine.'

He listened for a moment, then said in a milder tone, 'Oh, I see. So you've no details? Right, right. I'll be back in half an hour.'

'Arrested for financial fraud,' he explained to Hepburn. 'The Cairnryan lads, according to Andy. Something to do with his business, I suppose.'

MacNee was abstracted on the way back. Grant was still very much a suspect in the murder case but if he'd been arrested on another charge there would be the sort of complications he didn't feel equipped to deal with. If he couldn't get hold of Marjory he'd have to call Hyacinth back from London and he didn't think she, or Marjory either, would be very happy about that.

Whatever Cat Fleming said, he was going to insist he spoke to Marjory once he'd got back and was able to report on the situation.

Daniel Lee switched the phone off and set it down on his desk very, very gently. He could feel pure rage starting to build inside him and if it erupted he would most likely break whatever was in his hands.

That fool! That fool! He'd known all long he was dangerous. He and Morrison had both known, but he was the useful idiot they had to tolerate. If he could get his hands on him he'd—

But he couldn't. Grant would be locked up where no one could reach him and they would squeeze him and squeeze him. The chances were they didn't have evidence of more than irregularities and given a couple of hours they could probably have created a false trail that would tie the whole thing up for months, if not years. Their lawyer had said just now that he'd ordered him to say nothing.

But Grant would panic. He'd think he would see the chance of getting a short sentence at an open prison by telling them everything they wanted to know and a bit more besides. He wouldn't, given what he was involved in – and he'd be dumped right in it, Drax would make sure of that – but he'd be naive enough to think he would.

Cold fear replaced anger. He'd no idea where Marnie had gone, either; that could be a costly mistake. He didn't like mistakes.

He had a firewall surrounding everything that even Morrison didn't know about. If it was a case of saving your own skin, he was in a good position, he told himself. He could get out of this. He just needed to be ruthless, and he'd never had a problem with that.

MacNee hardly spoke on the way back to headquarters. Hepburn glanced at him a couple of times but seeing the heavy frown between his brows didn't interrupt. There was a lot resting on his shoulders; he'd never been someone who'd wanted more than the day-to-day job, down and dirty, and all this was getting to him. She wasn't nearly as experienced as he was but she didn't think she'd have a problem with taking that sort of responsibility when the time came.

If the time came. She remembered her own situation with a nasty little jolt and took out her mobile to call home. Fleur, it seemed, had just got up and was making lunch and the helper seemed to be looking forward to it. Perhaps that would persuade her to carry on for a bit till Louise found a more permanent solution – whatever that might be . . .

When they reached the station MacNee got out with a heavy sigh. 'Ah well,' he said. '*Hope not sunshine every hour, Fear not clouds will always lour.*'

'True,' Hepburn said very solemnly. 'This too will pass.'

'Right enough.' MacNee gave another sigh as they went in.

The FCA at the reception desk looked up. 'Oh, that's good. DI Fleming wanted you to report to her as soon as you got in.'

MacNee's face lit up as if the sun had, indeed, come out. 'She's back!' he exclaimed.

'Yes. Her husband's all right, apparently.'

'That's good. We're on our way.'

Hepburn hung back as they reached the foot of the stairs. 'Do you think she wants me too? She maybe just wants a catch-up with you.'

'You'd better come anyway. She can always send you away if necessary.' MacNee was taking the stairs two at a time, as if he couldn't wait to lay down the cares of office.

Hepburn followed more slowly. Sooner or later the question of Marnie was going to come up and she had a sinking feeling that despite MacNee's sympathetic attitude, covering up what she'd done would be impossible. Maybe she'd have plenty of time to look after her mother anyway.

Big Marge was in a buoyant mood. 'It's been grim,' she said, 'but they operated first thing yesterday and it was very successful. I saw him afterwards and he was fine. We checked with the hospital this morning and they're keeping him under observation but all being well he can come home later on. Cammie's all set to go to Edinburgh when he gets the summons.

'So – fill me in.'

'Hardly know where to start,' MacNee said.

Fleming listened without interrupting as he went through the details of Marnie's narrow escape and Anita Loudon's letter. Then she said awkwardly, 'I'm sorry this was all dumped on you, Tam. With the family issues it really wasn't possible for me to deal with anything else.'

MacNee made supportive noises and she went on, 'I thought the super would have taken over if there was a problem?'

'Yes, well – meeting in London, seemingly. Very important.'

'Ah, I see,' Fleming said. 'The letter – was Marnie distressed?'

MacNee went quiet. Hepburn said, 'I think she's past caring about her mother. Her big fear was that we'd decide she'd killed Anita for the money.'

'I think I may have scared her by pointing out she might have been the last person to see Anita alive and she took that as an accusation. Where is she now?'

Hepburn gave a sidelong glance at MacNee who was sitting like a statue. He wasn't going to tell on her; she could just say that Marnie had refused police protection and then walked out.

No, she couldn't. It might strictly be true but a lie by implication was still a lie. And if morality wasn't persuasive enough, common sense told her that it was usually the cover-up not the misdeed itself that finished you.

'I did something very stupid,' she said and felt MacNee relax beside her.

It wasn't comfortable, making her confession with Fleming's penetrating hazel eyes fixed on her face, but she got through it.

It seemed a long time to her before Fleming spoke. 'Well, Louise, you don't need me to tell you the problems with that. I expect Tam ran through them with you at the time.'

Hepburn nodded.

'I understand that you did this out of sympathy for someone in trouble but what worries me is your tendency to adopt a personal attitude towards suspects, whether for or against. I understand, too, that you have a passion for truth and justice, which I admire and even share, but it's nothing to do with our job.

'I heard someone say once that books are about truth, courts are about justice and cases are about proof. I've often been grateful that it's not my job to decide someone's guilty. If it was I'd have to live with the consequences of getting it wrong.

'This is a disciplinary matter, of course. But I have broad discretion, and unless a defence lawyer raises a question about bias in the investigation, I'm prepared to overlook it. And it would certainly be a good mark if you could persuade Marnie to come in and talk to us – use emotional blackmail, if she'll listen. She ought to feel some sense of obligation and for her own sake I want to arrange proper protection before she gets herself killed.'

'I can try,' Hepburn said. 'I just wonder if she's a target because of her memory – something the killer thinks she knows that she hasn't told us yet.'

'Yes,' Fleming said. 'It had occurred to me. One of the reasons I'm so anxious to speak to her is that I have some ideas for questions I think she might be able to answer.

'All right, Louise. I think we can leave it there for now. Tam, don't go.'

Hepburn scuttled out. At least it was over and the wounds probably weren't fatal. She knew, and Fleming knew that she knew, that it was very unlikely a defence lawyer would even find out what she had done let alone claim there had been bias, so it probably wasn't the end of her career.

What had cut her to the quick was Fleming's analysis of her own shortcomings as an investigator. The criticisms that go deep are always the ones you recognise as being fair.

Michael Morrison was in an irritable mood as he picked his wife up from the train. Apart from anything else, he had wanted her to stay away a bit longer. The police hadn't come back over the weekend and he was hoping that given time the interview might just somehow never happen. He didn't want to have to coach Vivienne in what she had to say; she was such an innocent that if he did she'd look so guilty they'd probably arrest her.

She greeted him with her usual sunny warmth. 'Oh darling, it's lovely to be home! Diana was sweet, of course, but she has such a busy life I felt I was in the way. And if I stayed any longer, you'd go bankrupt!'

He could never stay irritated with her for long. 'I think I can take the hit. That's what I'm here for – paying for my wife to look beautiful.'

Vivienne laughed. 'You're so good. And how's Mikey?'

'Oh, shaping up for delinquency very promisingly. He's been missing you.'

'I've missed him too. But I got him this gorgeous baby penguin in Harrods . . .'

She chattered on, with him half-listening as they drove back down the A77. They were just south of Ayr when his mobile, lying in the tray between the seats, rang. He glanced at the caller ID, then, despite his wife's disapproving look, answered it.

He didn't react to what he heard, he just gripped the steering wheel tighter until the whites of his knuckles showed. 'I'll call you later,' he said, putting his foot down on the accelerator.

'Michael!' Vivienne protested. 'You shouldn't use the mobile when you're driving and you're going to get flashed if you drive like that. You've got six points on the licence already—'

'Do you think you could just shut up?' he said, through clenched teeth.

Vivienne gasped. He never spoke to her like that and tears came to her eyes. 'I'm sorry,' she said in a small voice. 'I didn't mean to upset you.'

'No,' he said, but he didn't apologise and he didn't slow down.

Vivienne sat in miserable silence all the way home. He didn't even come in with her; he dumped her and her cases on the doorstep and drove off – back to the office, he said. He never snapped at her, even though she knew she sometimes fussed. When she'd been fretting away that day after Anita had opened her heart to her, he'd been so patient and reassuring, seeing she took her sleeping pills and making her hot milk so she got proper rest. For him to speak to her like that must mean there was something wrong – very, very wrong.

'What I've been asking myself,' Fleming said to MacNee, 'is how come this consortium got together in the first place. Construction, haulage, a nightclub – what's the missing link?'

'Maybe it's just the area,' MacNee suggested. 'Crichton and Morrison had businesses here, Lee had a business here according to Anita—'

'So what was it? It suddenly went pear-shaped, and Lee and Kirstie disappeared, leaving Marnie behind. There must be something in her records to say where Kirstie Burnside was working – it was some office in Newton Street, but I can't remember the name. I want that checked out. Your job, I guess, Tam. You'll have access to the restricted files.'

MacNee looked less than happy at the suggestion. 'Well, quicker if we could just check out this famous memory, eh? Anyway, is there any word what the score is with Grant Crichton?'

'Nick Alexander phoned me. It's all technical stuff but they think they've got him on money-laundering. That should draw in Morrison and Lee as well and then they'll be able to swear out search warrants.

'Once they've finished with him they'll let us have a go. I told Nick it was urgent but you know what that lot are like – think their business takes precedence over everything else.'

'Trafficking, is it?'

'That's what he believes. Going on over a period of time. And now I think about it, you can see the link: Crichton's lorries bring them in, Morrison gets what is virtually slave labour for his construction business and Lee sees to laundering the money – lots of cash payments to casual workers – bouncers and musicians and so on. And if you have some illegal immigrants who've paid their way in up front, you can bus them up to the out-of-town nightclub, mix them in with the genuine patrons and at the end of the night off they go. Nothing that would attract attention.

'So what does Marnie know that makes it worth killing her, then?'

'Louise reckons the second shot they had at her proves it's not to do with something she could tell us about Anita. They were aware that she was at the station here so they'd know she'd have given us the answers to anything we asked her.'

Fleming sighed. 'She's a bright girl, Louise, but she's got a lot to learn. Anyway, Grant Crichton – his alibi's gone, he's admitted it and we have him placed at the scene. I've never met the man. Once we get a chance at him, can we crack him?'

MacNee considered. 'Andy would have a better idea about that. I only met him the once, and he got right up my nose. He's got the "you're a public servant, I'm the public so grovel" attitude that makes you want to nut him. My guess is he'll bluster.'

'Usually a sign of weakness. His lawyer will tell him to keep his mouth shut and if he killed Anita he'll probably do as he's told. If he didn't, maybe we can make him an offer he can't refuse?'

'You're gunning for Daniel Lee, right?'

'On gut instinct, yes. But then, Morrison – they're both vermin if they're in the trafficking business, just different types.'

'Lee's a weasel, Morrison's a rat?'

Fleming laughed. 'You could say. Anyway, I reckon it's open season on Lee and Morrison now. What—?'

There was a knock on the door and Hepburn came in. 'Sorry to break in, boss, but I've spoken to Marnie. She won't tell me where she is but she says she'll be in the Pier Café in Stranraer in three-quarters of an hour if someone wants to meet her there.'

At the prospect of getting the information direct, MacNee's face brightened. 'She could tell us where her mother worked, couldn't she?'

Fleming wasn't convinced. 'Maybe, but I still want it checked out.' MacNee's face fell.

'Well done, though, Louise. Did you have to twist her arm?'

'I didn't have to. She phoned me. She sounded reluctant but I think she feels last night was her fault, somehow.'

'All to the good. Right, Louise, car park in five minutes. Tam, if you manage to turn anything up before we get there, call me, OK?'

MacNee grunted. Fleming noticed that Louise, tactfully, wasn't grinning but hadn't quite managed not to look pleased.

Michael Morrison's secretary had opened her mouth to ask whether Vivienne had enjoyed her trip to London but after a glance at Morrison's face as he stormed in she bit her tongue. He went straight into his office and she winced as he slammed the door.

He threw himself into his chair and picked up the phone on his desk.

'Drax? Tell me again.'

He was glad he was sitting down as he listened because

he could feel the blood draining from his face.

'But surely he'll have the sense to say nothing? The lawyer's with him, right?'

As Drax outlined his theory that Crichton would be cooperating with the police, he interrupted, 'But he's in it as deep as we are,' though even as he protested he recognised it had the ring of truth. 'We'll just have to stick together against him, then. We need to meet—'

'Deep? Us? Oh come on, we're not responsible for Grant's problems. Am I my co-director's keeper?' Drax said, laughing.

It wasn't like Drax not to understand implications. 'I think you'll find we are,' Morrison insisted. 'Now the police will be involved and—'

'We'll help them in any way we can. At least I will.'

'Well of course, in a sense—' Morrison was frowning.

'Sorry, hang on – yes, Kylie? OK, I'll be with you in a minute. Sorry, Michael – that's my brainless management assistant in another mess. I've got to go.'

It was only after he had rung off that Morrison understood, with cold certainty, what that had been about. The phone was being tapped, almost certainly. And what he had just heard was Drax's attempt to put himself in the clear.

So, every man for himself. But Drax would be a ruthless opponent, how ruthless probably only he and maybe Grant knew – and Anita Loudon. It was that quality, and the man's quick, clever mind, that had made the consortium so successful and he'd been content to let Drax control it. He'd trusted him. Too much. Far, far too much.

412

Now, he would have to be ruthless too. The stakes were high, but he'd learnt a bit about handling himself in the ugly, dirty, sordid world he'd somehow got involved in, much as he hated it, much as it wasn't the way he saw himself.

Morrison's eyes went to the photographs on his desk: this was his world. His pretty wife, smiling at him as if she were there in the room with him. Gemma, his baby, her head thrown back, laughing, bubbly and confident. And Mikey, his chin stuck out in some toddler defiance – a chip off the grandfatherly block. The family who had everything.

He had to win this one, for them. He wasn't going to let Drax stitch him up.

A small café wasn't exactly the place Fleming would have chosen for the meeting with Marnie Bruce. There were only two tables occupied apart from the one Marnie had chosen right at the back and the women there were chatting to the waitress in a way that suggested they were regulars. As Fleming and Hepburn walked in, they were aware of interested scrutiny.

Marnie had a mug and an empty plate in front of her and as they approached she said loudly, 'Thanks for coming to pick me up. If you can just wait till I've finished this we can get going.'

'Fine,' Fleming said and she and Hepburn sat down. Marnie made a show of sipping at her mug but Fleming noticed that her eyes went constantly to the street outside. She was no fool, Marnie; she was checking to see that they hadn't been followed.

After a detailed discussion about the weather which it hardly warranted – a bit dull, mildly damp – Marnie seemed to be satisfied and went to pay, then they left together.

'Where to now?' Fleming asked, scanning the street herself as they paused outside. There was nothing suspicious that she could see.

'My car.' Marnie strode off along the front to the car park and took them right to the far end where a small Fiat two-door hire car was parked in the front row looking out over Loch Ryan, grey and unpromising in the November afternoon.

Hepburn pulled the driver's seat forward and climbed into the back, leaving Fleming the passenger seat. 'Are we going somewhere?' she asked.

Marnie shook her head. 'I'm fine here. There's a good view all round so I can see if anyone was coming.'

Fleming seized the opportunity. 'Marnie, I'm going to give you police protection, whether you want it or not. It's too dangerous for you to go on like this.'

'No, you're not.' Marnie's voice was flat. 'I've made my arrangements and I'm not relying on the police keeping their mouths shut about where I am. I was obviously tailed from the police station – how did Drax know I was even there?'

Various explanations sprang to mind but it was clear that for the moment, at least, arguing was pointless. Fleming wasn't sure either how long Marnie would be prepared to sit talking to them so when she demanded, 'Well, what did you want to speak to me about?' Fleming went straight to the topic that had been at the top of her mind.

'What did your mother do when you lived here, Marnie? Do you remember?'

She got a glance of contempt. 'Of course I do. Drax had a business in Newton Stewart and she worked for him. Accounts mostly but sometimes she had to arrange stuff for clients.'

Fleming pounced on that. 'Clients?' but Marnie only looked blank.

'What sort of stuff?'

'I don't know, really. She'd be away for a night or maybe two sometimes. She never told me what she did.'

'Where did you go when she went away?' Fleming's mind was on Anita: had she perhaps had a closer relationship with Marnie as a child?

Marnie gave a mirthless smile. 'Go? I didn't go anywhere. Just stayed at home – got the school bus and waited till she got back.'

Hepburn burst out, 'But you must have been quite small. That was awful!' Then she stopped abruptly, with an anxious glance at Fleming.

'I quite liked it, actually. There wasn't someone always nagging me about turning off the TV or going to bed early. Oh, I suppose it got a bit spooky at night sometimes but it meant I could have my friend over – my mum didn't approve.'

'Why not?'

'Didn't like them being well off and we weren't, she said. But I guess she didn't want anyone hanging around. Drax didn't like it, she said once.'

Fleming's ears pricked up. 'Why was that?'

'Don't know. Probably something illegal, knowing what he's like.' Her voice was bitter.

'Was there ever anything, anything at all, that you remember your mother saying or doing that could give us a clue to what it was?' Fleming was getting desperate now; Marnie's memory, restricted to what she had experienced herself, of course, was proving disappointing.

Hepburn, leaning forward, said in what Fleming recognised as a carefully unemotional voice, 'I think there must be something, Marnie, because I believe that's what is behind the attempts to kill you. Did you ever hear a discussion between your mother and Drax about what they were doing? Did she ever bring work home?'

And suddenly, something seemed to click. Marnie was staring straight ahead, as if she was seeing something in the grey clouds hanging over the hills across the loch. 'Yes,' she said, 'I was – I am . . .' She was struggling for coherence.

'Don't report. Just describe what you're seeing for us, Marnie.' Fleming's voice was low, insistent.

Marnie hesitated, but then it poured out, a steady stream of consciousness.

She's watching TV. It's Cheggers Plays Pop *and it's really good but she's got to be ready to put it off when she hears Mum's car because Mum doesn't like it and she's in a mega-bad mood and there's some problems and Drax has been yelling at her down the phone.*

And that's the car now and she's annoyed because the show's not even half over. She's getting up to switch off the TV and she looks out of the window and it

416

isn't her mum's car, it's a minibus and there are foreign people peering out of the window. They must be lost or something.

She won't have to switch it off after all but then that's her mum's car coming in behind so she does. That's funny. She doesn't mind so much about losing her programme because something's going to happen and it's not going to be just another boring evening.

They're all climbing out. She's never really seen black people close up before, though they're not black, really, more sort of coffee-coloured. Mum's hustling them to get inside quickly and then she's yelling at Marnie to go to her room.

She doesn't want to but the way Mum's looking at her she knows she has to. They're all men, about twelve of them, and they're wearing very poor, thin clothes and some of them are shivering. Maybe they're cold but she thinks maybe they're frightened too. They're jabbering and Mum's shouting at them. She's going to her room as slowly as she dares, watching them shuffling into the lounge, then she puts her ear to the door.

The phone's in the hall and Mum's talking to Drax. She's trying to talk him down so he must be mad at her. She says the contact wasn't there when she arrived and she doesn't know what to do and he seems to think she should because she's crying and saying it's not fair.

She can't hear anything after that except the lounge door shutting so she goes to the connecting wall with her bedroom instead because it's so thin you can hear through it. Mum's sounding a bit cross with them too and she tells

them to stop panicking because everything's going to be
fine and it's all being arranged now.

She doesn't know why they should be panicking but her
mum certainly is and she's beginning to feel a bit worried
herself. It's a nasty atmosphere and she knows that nasty
atmospheres are usually bad news for her. She's trying to
stop biting her nails but she can't help it. Then the phone
rings so she goes back to listening at the door.

It must be Drax. Mum's saying, "Thank God for that!"
Then, "Yes, yes, of course I will. Right away."

So it sounds as if they can all stop panicking. It's a
relief, even if she still doesn't know what's going on. Then
she hears Mum say, "Well, of course she has. I had to bring
them back here, didn't I? But I'll tell her to keep her mouth
shut, or else."

She gets back to sitting on her bed just before her
mother opens the door. "I've to take these people to where
they're staying," she says. "And you're not to say anything
about them to anyone – anyone at all, understand? If you
say anything to anyone at school I'll find out and I promise
you, you'll wish you'd never been born."

Sometimes she wishes that anyway but she just says,
"All right." She cries a little bit after they've gone and
when she switches on the telly Cheggers is over and it's just
a boring documentary.

'Then it stops,' Marnie said, as if she'd been watching
a film.

Fleming felt as if she too had seen it passing before her
eyes. 'That's incredibly helpful, Marnie. I – I don't suppose
you remember when it was?'

'Fifteenth of October, 1993.'

Fleming gaped. She had thought she was chancing her arm to ask the question. 'You can remember the date too?'

'It was just a couple of weeks before everything – well, stopped.' Marnie sounded weary. 'I really don't want to go back over that.'

'No, of course not,' Fleming said. 'Can I just check a couple more things with you? You didn't see or hear anything suspicious on Friday night before the break-in, right? And the fire-bombing – nothing then, either?'

'No. But I've been – well, going over what happened before. I'd been to see Drax and there was a car pulled out of the car park there right behind me.' She stopped again, with the odd look on her face, but this time after a moment she went on normally. 'The person driving it was an Asian. I'm not good on makes of car but it was quite small, grey and with a big dent in the wheel arch.'

'We'll circulate the description – try to get him picked up.' This was fascinating. Nick Alexander would pay good money for this sort of stuff – or at least trade favours.

But it made her even more anxious about Marnie. 'Look, I can assign officers to look after you that I know well enough to promise their absolute discretion. I don't want to alarm you but what you know puts you in serious danger.'

'Oh, I think even I'd have managed to get the message by now. No, thank you. I'll feel safer looking after myself.

'Is there anything else? If there is, you'd better ask me now. According to you I might not make it through to the morning.' She gave a sarcastic laugh.

Fleming didn't smile. 'I trust that won't happen. Be very, very careful. And thank you for this – it will help, I promise you.'

'Just get him,' Marnie said. 'I want him to pay.'

Fleming had just opened the car door to get out when she remembered a question she hadn't asked. 'This is the last one, I promise. Do you know what Drax's business was?'

'Not exactly, but I know it sold builders' supplies. Mum was always having problems about deliveries.'

'Builders' supplies,' Fleming said slowly. 'Right.'

Marnie got out to let Hepburn climb through. The last they saw of her was as she stood in the dwindling light, scanning the car park for movement and perhaps a small grey car.

CHAPTER TWENTY-THREE

Fleming sent for MacNee as soon as she got back to her office. He appeared so quickly she thought he must have sprinted up the stairs and he gave her no chance to tell him what she had gleaned from Marnie before he burst out triumphantly, 'Oh, we're motoring now!

'See Marnie's mum? She was working for Daniel Lee. He'd set up a business selling supplies for builders – and guess who was one of his big clients? No prizes.

'Then – this is in 1993, right? – the Immigration lads asked us to take a wee look at it – something not right, not sure what. Ten minutes later, business closes, no sign of Lee. They'd obviously nothing solid against him – reckoned they'd scared him off and left it at that, maybe. So then Marnie's mum disappears. And if you ask me, she's in a shallow grave somewhere.'

'Knew too much – and Marnie left for dead. It all works,' Fleming said. 'Marnie told us about the business.

And she also told us that she witnessed the arrival of a contingent of Asians – that fits with Immigration. I tell you, Nick Alexander will be eating out of my hand when I give him this.'

'That's good, because there's more. They fingerprinted Crichton when they took him in, right, and I got them to check against the SOCOs' report on Anita Loudon's house. He claims he didn't know her, claims he didn't go in because there was someone with her already, but there they were in two or three places.'

'Nick said he'd let us talk to him when they'd finished with him but I'm going to insist that's first thing tomorrow. And whatever he says, I'm going after Lee as well. The trafficking is Nick's problem but Anita Loudon's murder is mine and I'm tired of mucking about.

'I've had the first of the forensic reports and it's not that helpful. They've found fibres they think came from a tartan rug of some kind – green and black – that the body was wrapped in before it was dumped—'

'Likely it's ashes by now.'

'Mmm. Anyway, not much we didn't know. They can tell us the position she was in when she was transported, inside a car and not in a van or a boot, apparently – something to do with the lividity pattern – but it doesn't get us a lot further. I'd more or less assumed they wouldn't have carried the body across the street and along to the park.

'So if Crichton keeps his mouth shut we're still in trouble. Marnie's evidence may bolster Nick's case but it doesn't do anything for ours.'

'Did you find out where she's staying?'

Fleming shook her head. 'Refused to tell us. But she's adamant that she's got it sorted and she wouldn't listen. It worries me, though.'

'She's a grown woman,' MacNee pointed out. 'Old enough to know better, even if she doesn't.'

'I suppose so. Right – I'll get on to Nick now. But that was a great job, Tam. Thanks. See how rewarding trawling the records can be?'

MacNee gave her a look that would have curdled milk at a hundred yards and he shut the door in a marked manner as he left.

Smiling, Fleming placed her call. Nick Alexander was, indeed, suitably grateful.

'Even if it doesn't relate to the present investigation it'll be enough to let us swear out a search warrant. I'll put that in hand right away. Thanks, Marjory – that's really helpful.'

He was about to ring off. 'Hey!' she said. 'That wasn't a present, that was the first part of an exchange. Your part is to let us have a go at Grant Crichton first thing tomorrow morning, whether your lot have finished with him or not.'

He wasn't keen. 'Well, soon, I promise.'

'Not good enough. First thing.'

With a heavy sigh he said, 'Oh, I suppose so. We can let you have an hour. The evidence from the girl should mean we can get an extension to twenty-four hours for questioning.'

'Very generous,' Fleming said caustically. 'Is he cooperating at the moment?'

423

'His brief's muzzling him. We're tempting him with the usual "dish your pals and we'll see you right", but he seems scared of the solicitor – or more likely the guys behind him. Doubt if he's got Crichton's interests at heart.'

'We'll stress that too when we see him. Maybe we can get him to sack his brief.'

'You think the next one will be better?' Alexander's opinion of criminal defence solicitors was inevitably low. 'Anyway, you will look after the girl, won't you, if there have been two attempts on her life? She could turn out to be a very useful part of the prosecution's evidence.'

'Oh yes, of course,' Fleming said hollowly.

She wished she was in a position to do just that. Marnie's stubborn conviction that she could look after herself filled her with foreboding.

Now, however, there was nothing to stop her going home. Cammie had reported that Bill was tired but looking amazingly well and Janet Laird would be making up for not having had the chance to worry herself silly about her son-in-law by waiting on him hand and foot, but she needed to be there, to touch him, just to make sure he was real and there at home and not, as she had feared during those terrible hours, gone for ever.

There was a phone message waiting for DS MacNee when he went back to the CID room. He raised his eyebrows as he read it, then called Shelley Crichton's number.

Despite having asked him to contact her, she still sounded frosty. 'Oh – Sergeant MacNee. Yes, well – I have been considering the statement I made to the police earlier and I think it may have been . . . er . . . misleading.'

MacNee scented blood. 'By "misleading" do you maybe mean "untrue"?' he suggested helpfully.

There was an icy silence, then she said, 'If that's the way you want to put it. I stated that I had not been at Anita Loudon's house the evening she died. The reason I didn't—'

'Was that you felt it would mislead us since you didn't actually kill her?'

He heard a little gasp. 'Well, I—'

'Mrs Crichton, I've had that said to me by folk who were innocent and folk who were killers too. Doesn't impress me. Never mind reasons, just give me the facts.'

The temperature dropped another few degrees. 'Very well. I went round to Anita's to ask her to be truthful about the girl who had visited her. She denied flatly that it was Kirstie Burnside's daughter but I knew it was a lie.' There was a wealth of scorn in her tone.

That was pretty rich, coming from her, but MacNee didn't point it out, saying only, 'How did that make you feel?'

'Oh, you want me to say angry, murderous, don't you? But I won't, because it wasn't true. I felt frustrated and depressed. All my life I had wanted to confront Kirstie Burnside with the reality of what she had done, just to show her what it had done to me, tell her about my blighted life – and in all honesty I don't know what I might have done if I had found her. That's different, but the question isn't going to arise.

'But when I left Anita at around half past seven she was certainly alive. That's all I have to say.'

MacNee found himself actually feeling sorry for the woman. He said, in a kinder tone, 'Thank you, Mrs Crichton. It was very wise of you to admit this now. You will have to come in and make another statement and there may well be further questions we would want to ask you at that time.

'Now, is that everything? I can warn you that trying to change your statement again wouldn't be smart.'

There was a long pause. Then she said, 'Not about the statement, no. But I got an anonymous phone call on Thursday – a man's voice. He told me that Kirstie Burnside's daughter was living in an abandoned cottage out by Clatteringshaws Loch.

'I was tempted to go out there, try to get her to tell me where her mother was. But I knew what had happened to Anita – and to tell the truth I wasn't sorry. I believe she deserved all she got – she knew about that woman's mockery of my remembrance of my son.' There was a break in her voice as she said that.

'But it scared me. Putting the body where Tommy lay – that was to fool you into thinking I had done it – or Grant. He has his faults, God knows, but he would never desecrate the place like that.

'So I didn't go, and I was thankful, after what happened then. Someone was trying to put me at the scene and if you had the least evidence against me I knew I would be done for.

'So I'm telling you now.' The voice was hard again.

MacNee was under no illusions about her reason for making contact. She was trying to put herself in the clear, but he was inclined to give her the benefit of the doubt, despite her low opinion of the police. He pressed her about the phone call but she genuinely seemed to have no idea who the caller was and he let her go, with the warning that she should attend at the Kirkluce headquarters in the morning. They could always trace the call later if they needed to know.

He had little doubt himself that Daniel Lee had made that call. And he could only hope that Marnie had been wise in her choice of accommodation.

Marnie's safety was on Louise Hepburn's mind too as she drove home. There was nothing she could do about it and her own attempt at protecting her couldn't exactly be described as a triumph. If it hadn't been for the alarm, she thought with a shudder, she might have gone in and found her dead in the morning.

There was no doubt, though, that Marnie was currently in serious danger. What she knew about Daniel Lee could be vital evidence towards prosecuting him for trafficking and Louise had no doubt that he knew that. If only he could be picked up and brought in for questioning, she suddenly thought, it would solve the problem.

Would Fleming have thought of that? She didn't have the nerve to phone and suggest it; even though being taken along to the interview with Marnie suggested forgiveness of a sort, she'd still be well advised to keep her head below the parapet meantime.

She might get her chance at the briefing tomorrow. And

she tried to quell the thought that tomorrow might well be too late, if Marnie had got it wrong.

As Louise neared Stranraer she began to think about her own immediate problem. She'd spoken again to the helper and she was delighted to keep coming for the time being – 'Never tasted anything like thon beef stew' – but it wasn't any sort of solution. Fleur would need more and more care as time went on.

The miasma of misery started to envelop her again as she parked outside the house. To her surprise, lights were blazing upstairs and downstairs when normally Fleur would either be in the kitchen or the sitting room. The helper shouldn't have left yet so perhaps she hadn't wanted to stop Fleur if putting lights on in empty rooms was her latest whim, but Louise felt a lurch of unease as she let herself in.

There was a suitcase in the hall and even as she stared at it a tall, elegant figure came hurrying down the stairs towards her.

'*Tante* Coralie!' she exclaimed in amazement as her aunt swept her into a scented embrace with a flood of rapid French.

'My dear, you should have told me! Your *maman* phoned me early this morning, so confused, not happy. There is a nice lady living here who is very kind, she told me, but she thinks there is something wrong with her because she doesn't understand anything you say and Fleur is afraid she is responsible for looking after her. So I just grabbed my credit card and headed for Charles de Gaulle – and here I am!'

Louise's heart was wrung. 'Oh poor, poor *Maman*! But I didn't know what to do – I know she needs me all the time but it's difficult at work just now so I can't even take time off, and anyway I can't think what to do except give it up and look after her—'

Her aunt put her arm round her shoulders and led her firmly through to the sitting room.

'Fleur is asleep – she thinks it's bedtime. I let her go and I sent the "nice lady" home so we could talk.'

The fire was lit in the hearth and two glasses and a bottle of red wine, open already to breathe, stood waiting on a small table. As Coralie poured it out, Louise felt the tears coming to her eyes. It was so comforting, so reassuring, to have someone cherish her, ready to help her find some sort of solution.

'But you mustn't cry, my dear!' Coralie exclaimed. 'It's all right now. I told Fleur whenever your dear papa died that she must come back to France, but you know how totally stubborn she is, especially when she is wrong. She would never listen to reason, never!'

Louise blew her nose to stifle a giggle. Fleur and Coralie had demonstrated their genuine affection for each other by constant sisterly bickering, each as determined as the other that her way was the only way.

'It's very sad for me too, you know,' Coralie went on. 'She is my dear big sister and I can see the terrible tragedy that lies ahead. But she would never have wished to ruin your life by burdening you with her care – not our loving, generous Fleur.'

They were both crying a little now. 'I know what you're

thinking, but she wouldn't want to leave me,' Louise said. 'I thought she'd decide to go back to France after Dad died but she said it mattered more to be with me than anything else.'

'I know, and she is a very loving mother. But we must face reality, Louise. The time will come when she doesn't fully understand where she is, but meantime I can take her back with me "for a holiday" and you can visit – it's not hard to get to Paris for the weekend, you know.

'And there won't be a language problem. She'll enjoy having people to talk to and when the time comes the good sisters from the convent will look after her kindly.'

Louise twisted the glass between her hands. 'You – you make it all sound so easy,' she said.

Her aunt gave her a look of exasperation. 'Oh, you Scots! Always the hair shirt! You think there's something wicked about life not being miserable.

'And you know, I want to see the last of my sister too, before . . . before she goes away completely.'

Her composure gave way and Louise went to hug her as they sobbed together. Not for long, though. Coralie produced a lace-trimmed handkerchief, mopped them both up and refilled the wine glasses.

'We've lots of arrangements to make. But there is a casserole in the oven that will be less than right if we don't eat it now and I think for once we may be inelegant and eat off our knees in front of this cosy fire.'

Even though it was a different house, Marnie felt as if she'd gone back to childhood, arriving yet again as the

Morrisons' guest, experiencing the same awkwardness about accepting hospitality that wouldn't be repaid. She had never told her mother that she went there; any suggestion of contact with Gemma always provoked an outburst.

She took the bag holding the bare essentials she had bought out of the car, looking back along the road as she did so, though there had been no traffic at all on the last half-mile to the farmhouse and she could be fairly sure no one had followed her.

Gemma greeted her with her usual cheerful warmth. 'Come in, quickly! It's so cold, isn't it!' As she drew her into the house and shut the door behind her, she turned to scan Marnie's face anxiously.

'You must be absolutely shattered! I couldn't believe it when I heard about that awful fire. Who on earth would do such a thing?'

Marnie gave a rueful shrug and Gemma rattled on, 'I suppose it's vandals. Can't quite get it myself but there's people seem to do that sort of thing for fun. I just can't bear to think what might have happened.

'Now, come upstairs. I've put you in the bedroom next to mine so if you need to borrow anything you can just pop in. The only drawback is that Mikey's on my other side and when he wakes up he likes to have company, the more the merrier. Hope you're a sound sleeper!'

Marnie smiled. 'Where is he?'

'Oh, he's with Mum. She's been away for a couple of days so she's suffering from grandchild deprivation. I've barely been allowed to see him today.'

Gemma opened the door to a large bedroom at the front of the house, looking out towards Loch Ryan, and went over to draw the curtains – thick, interlined, in a turquoise and coral print.

'It's got a lovely view when it's sunny but it's so gloomy today that we might as well shut it out early. Your en suite's here' – she opened the door on a neat shower room – 'and I've put in some stuff I thought you might be short of – shampoo and things.' There was a row of Molton Brown and Jo Malone bottles on a glass shelf.

'Now, do whatever you feel like – have a shower or a rest if you want. Just come down whenever you feel like it.' As she turned to go out she looked again at Marnie, then reached out and put a hand to her cheek. 'You poor love, you've had such a rotten time, haven't you? But we're going to cosset you now. You'll find us in the kitchen when you're ready.'

Marnie felt a tightening in her throat as she thanked Gemma and put her cheap holdall down on the straw-coloured wool carpet. The sleigh bed was piled with cushions in blues and corals, echoing the fabric of the curtains. It was all very pretty, very feminine, like Vivienne Morrison herself. Her hand was evident, too, in the pile of books and magazines on the bedside tables and the tissues and cotton wool balls on the dressing table.

The luxury was almost stifling. It was as if Marnie had been starving and was suddenly being offered an unwisely rich meal; she had never in her life had so much care lavished on her and she found it hard to accept. It wasn't that she didn't believe Gemma's affection was genuine – no one could act that well. It was just that it related to a world Marnie wasn't equipped to understand.

After a long power shower, she felt a little better. They were kind, she was comfortable, and above all she was safe. It was the sort of house where nothing bad ever happened to anyone. Live for today and let tomorrow take care of itself.

When she went downstairs and tapped tentatively on the kitchen door before opening it, Gemma called, 'Oh, come in, Marnie – no need to knock. Mum, you remember Marnie.'

It was something of a shock when Vivienne turned. It was twenty years, of course, since Marnie had last seen her, when she was still a young woman, but even so she looked older than she would have expected – still pretty, but she looked tense and strained, though perhaps it was the contrast with her daughter's healthy bloom that emphasised it.

She was as welcoming as ever, expressing her own concern at what had happened to Marnie, but it was clear that her attention was fully absorbed by the toddler who was ignoring his fish fingers and beans to study Marnie with solemn blue eyes.

'You came before. Did you bring me a present?' he said before being hushed by his mother.

'No, she hasn't. That's rude, Mikey. Why should she?' Gemma smiled apologetically. 'He's an absolute brat, Marnie, and I blame my parents. They think he can do no wrong, don't you, Mum?'

'It's your father, not me,' Vivienne protested. 'He thinks

it's funny when he's cheeky, Marnie, and then this little tyke plays up to it.' Her smile as she looked at the child, though, was very fond.

'Where is Dad?' Gemma asked casually. 'I didn't know he was going to be late tonight.'

'He – he didn't say.'

She sounded not merely uncertain, but unhappy. Marnie gave her a sharp look but at that moment Mikey upset his mug of milk and there was the fuss of mopping it up.

'I don't think we should wait for him, anyway,' Gemma said. 'Come on through to the sitting room and we can have a drink in comfort – if Mum's prepared to see the monster to bed.'

Vivienne smiled. 'Of course, darling. You girls go on. You can have a glass of Chablis waiting for me.' She was saying, 'No, Mikey, bedtime right after this,' in answer to the ritual protests as they left the room.

But what was it, Marnie wondered, that had been upsetting Vivienne about her husband's absence? Gemma seemed not to have noticed anything, so perhaps she had imagined it. Or perhaps, when you lived in this sort of set-up, it never occurred to you that anything could possibly go wrong.

Bill Fleming looked tired, certainly, but propped up in bed with a supper tray of the sort of healthy food he would normally have turned up his nose at, his colour was good and he was remarkably cheerful.

'They kept telling me how lucky I was and I'm sure they're right,' he said. 'I just have to walk instead of jumping on the quad bike, and learn to love lettuce.'

'It's time I got back in shape too,' Marjory said. 'The dreaded middle-aged spread is getting itself well established and I need to take more exercise too. We can do it together.'

Bill looked doubtful. 'I'm not sure your sort of yomping is what the doctor ordered. Steady walking, he said.'

'Excuses, excuses. Now, it's bedtime for you. I'm going to sleep in the spare room. With all that's been going on I'm not convinced I'll get a peaceful night and I don't want you being disturbed.'

'Where's my dram?' Bill demanded. 'The doc said it wouldn't do any harm – might even do me a bit of good.'

'Not tonight,' Marjory said firmly. 'He said you needed lots of rest too and you just yawned. Have you finished that?' She bent to take the tray off his knees and he pulled her into an embrace.

'Nice to be back,' he said.

Marjory's voice shook as she said, 'Don't ever do that to me again, will you? I can't bear to think what I'd do without you.'

Bill laughed. 'Look on the bright side, love – you might go first.'

'You're exasperating, do you know that? Now go to sleep,' Marjory said, but she was smiling happily as she went downstairs.

Having the terrible burden of responsibility taken from her shoulders should have given Louise Hepburn a lift, but the release of tension made her feel like a puppet whose strings had been cut. She was yawning so hugely that her aunt sent her off to bed at nine o'clock and she went thankfully.

But as she lay in bed, warm and relaxed, she thought again about Marnie. Was she safe and warm too – and where was she tonight, anyway?

Where could she be? She had ruled out hotels and B & Bs and she wouldn't be considering a remote secret hideaway after what had happened at Clatteringshaws. She couldn't sleep in the car in this weather, and she didn't have friends locally—

Oh yes, she did. She knew Gemma Morrison. Perhaps she'd asked her for a bed. If that was where Marnie had gone – and the more she thought about it, the more likely she thought it was – she should be safe enough. Drax was hardly going to burst into his partner's house and murder his daughter's friend.

On that comforting thought, she fell asleep.

CHAPTER TWENTY-FOUR

She heard the pounding of boots on the spiral stairs as she sat in her office, the little room that felt to her like the shell to a snail, with a sick sense of inevitability. Even so, she jumped to her feet and dashed out to protect him from intrusion, just as she always did.

One of the officers, invading aliens in their black gear and helmets, peeled off from the squad and came towards her menacingly. 'Daniel Lee. Where?'

It was no use. She nodded towards the door of Drax's office. She hadn't seen him all afternoon; she'd tapped on the door around seven but either he wasn't there or he didn't want to be disturbed and she knew better than to open it.

The police had no such scruples. The burly man in front opened the door, following through with his shoulder as if he expected it to be locked and didn't care if he smashed it. He staggered slightly as the door swung back, shouting, 'Police!'

The others, following through behind him, came up short and one bumped into him. He had stopped on the threshold.

It seemed as if an action movie had gone into freeze-frame and after that everything seemed to move weirdly slowly. The officer in the door frame turned with a gesture. 'Keep her back!' he ordered, and then she knew. It couldn't be – yet she somehow had always known that here was where it would all end.

With a sudden movement she jinked past the officer who came towards her and she was looking through the doorway at Drax, lying across his desk in a pool of blood, already turning rust-red.

Someone was screaming now, agonised, piercing screams like some animal in pain. It was a moment before she realised who it was, and then she couldn't stop.

Marjory Fleming had just come upstairs to bed in the spare room when her phone rang a little after eleven. She answered it feeling glad that she had followed her instinct and Bill's much-needed rest wasn't being disturbed.

The FCA on the night shift was apologetic. 'I'm sorry to disturb you, ma'am, but there is an urgent message from DCI Alexander at Cairnryan. He asked for you to be alerted at once to make sure that Marnie Burnside's protection is properly in place. He said Daniel Lee had been shot dead in Glasgow and it might have implications. That was the message.'

Feeling as if the floor had given way under her feet,

Fleming managed to say, 'OK. Thanks. I'll be coming right in, if anyone else wants me,' and taking time only to scribble a note to leave on the kitchen table she ran out to her car.

Her mind was whirring. Had they been looking in the wrong direction all this time? She had described Lee and Morrison equally as vermin, but she'd let herself be convinced by Marnie's belief that it was Lee who had her followed.

Of course, she told herself, with the company that Lee kept there might well be others with reason to want to put a bullet in him; guns were easy to come by when you had the right contacts. All that would be in the hands of the Strathclyde police, though, and her job was simply to protect Marnie if this was, as she suspected, a case of thieves falling out.

She had no idea where she might be, though. And Marnie had naively placed herself in danger twice already – once in giving Lee the opportunity, at least, to have her tailed, and once by failing to realise that her being taken to the police station after the petrol bomb would be common knowledge – and she feared that Marnie's confidence that she could look after herself was misplaced.

When she arrived at headquarters she was surprised to find MacNee waiting for her.

'Did Alexander contact you too?'

He shook his head. 'Caught the late-night news after the football tonight. Said there'd been a shooting at a nightclub in Glasgow and I called one of my pals up there. Shot our fox, like you'd probably say.'

Fleming made a face. 'If the fox gets shot it means the hens are safe. Not quite the same. Come up to my office. I'm going to call Nick and see what he can tell us.'

'The big question is, where's Marnie?' he said as she picked up the phone.

'The big question is, how am I going to tell Nick we don't know?' Fleming said. 'I'm not looking forward to this.'

Alexander was predictably both annoyed and worried, and able to add very little more detail to what she knew already. She put the phone down feeling profound irritation herself with the stubborn Marnie.

'So – what next?' MacNee said. 'Get someone checking hotels?'

Fleming had a sudden thought. 'No. Play the man instead of the ball. Let's find out where Morrison is first.' She picked up the phone again.

It was Gemma Morrison who answered, sounding sleepy and, when she heard who it was, indignant. 'Is phoning at this time really necessary? You've wakened me and that's my son awake now.'

Fleming could hear the sounds of a child wailing in the background.

'What do you want, anyway?'

'I am anxious to speak to Mr Morrison. Is he there, please?'

Gemma sighed loudly. 'I wouldn't know – it's a big house and he could be in his study. I suppose I can go and check, but I'm not even sure that he's back yet. He's been working late.'

Drumming her fingers on the desk, Fleming waited. When Gemma returned to the phone she sounded worried.

'He isn't back, no. Has something happened to him? Is that why you're phoning?'

'No, no,' Fleming said. 'We just need to speak to him, that's all. Could you please leave a message for him to that effect?'

'If that's all, I think you could have left it until the morning and not upset people at this time of night.' She put the phone down abruptly.

'Not there. I don't like it,' Fleming said. 'Where is he?'

'Killed Lee then done a runner?' MacNee suggested.

'If I thought that I'd be a happy woman – it would mean he wasn't out there gunning for Marnie. Where is the wretched girl?'

'Ask Louise,' MacNee suggested. 'She maybe doesn't know where Marnie is but she's talked to her a lot. She's in a better position than we are to guess.'

'Good thought.' Fleming dialled the number, then found herself engaged in a conversation with someone who spoke only minimal English. 'I – need – to – speak – to – Louise – Hepburn,' she said slowly, making a puzzled face at MacNee.

'Probably her mum,' he murmured. 'French – you're an expert, right?'

She gave him an acid glance, but when she scraped up some schoolgirl French it seemed to work. 'She sounded disapproving but she's gone to wake Louise.'

'Here – fancy you remembering your Highers! Didn't believe you could still speak it.'

'Neither did I,' Fleming said, then, 'Louise? Sorry to disturb you. But we're getting worried about Marnie. Do you have any idea, any idea at all, where she might be?'

Louise, like Gemma, sounded half-asleep, but at least cooperative. 'Oh, I was thinking about that. I suddenly remembered that she was friendly with Gemma Morrison, so it's quite likely she would ask her for a bed. And, of course, she'd be safe enough there because Morrison wouldn't be very pleased if Lee burst into his house and killed one of his daughter's guests, would he? If I'm right, I should think that's the safest place she could be.'

Gemma was just turning away from the phone, calling, 'It's all right, Mikey, I'm just coming,' when the front door opened and her father appeared.

'Oh Dad!' she exclaimed. 'I was wondering—' She caught sight of his face and stopped, looking horrified. 'Is something wrong?'

He looked exhausted, his face pale, almost grey, and his eyes bloodshot. 'No,' he mumbled. 'Just tired – very tired.'

He looked more ill than tired and it was with some alarm that she went over to him. Then she smelt the taint of spirits on his breath and her face cleared.

'Dad!' she scolded him. 'You're far too old to go out on a bender. Get through to the kitchen before Mum sees you like this. Have you had anything to eat?'

'Not since lunch.'

'You're lucky you got home without being breathalysed. Now, on you go, through to the kitchen.' She listened at the foot of the stairs. 'Good – sounds as if Mikey's gone back to sleep. He got wakened by the phone just now – can you believe it, it was the police wanting to speak to you, at this time of night! I told them they could wait till the morning.

'It's just as well he didn't hear you coming back or he'd have demanded to see you and I'm not sure how well you'd focus on the bedtime stories in that state, you wicked old man! Now, come on through. No arguments – I'm going to make you a bacon butty and a pot of black coffee. And take off your coat – you'll be too hot.'

'Louise is going to keep a watch on the house and she's trying to get Marnie on the phone now,' Fleming said as they hurried down the stairs. 'If she's right about where she is, we can just swoop in and pick her up as long as he's not there.'

'That's if Gemma's not in on it as well. Marnie could be dead by now,' MacNee said gloomily.

'Always the positive thinker. You arrange for a patrol car to stand by for support.'

Then they were in the car and Fleming fixed on the blue light as she turned out of the car park and accelerated off towards the Stranraer road.

DC Hepburn was shaking with nerves as she drove along to Dunmore. She'd tried ringing Marnie but the phone was switched off. She was most likely sound asleep, just as she had been herself. At least, she hoped that was why she wasn't answering her phone.

It only took ten minutes. It would be quarter of an hour at least before Fleming could get here and Hepburn had her orders: she was to ring the doorbell, provided there was no sign of Michael Morrison. If his car was there – she'd been given the registration – she was under no circumstances to approach. She was to keep trying Marnie and liaise with the patrol car which would be told to wait somewhere further out along the road past the Morrisons' farmhouse.

Hepburn stopped just short of the turn-off into the drive. She could see the house now; there was one light on upstairs and another downstairs and there was a large car parked below the lamp over the front door. It hadn't been put away in the fancy garage with the electronic doors, but even so it looked like Morrison's Mercedes.

She couldn't see the number from where she was and she really ought to verify it. After all, it could be his wife's, or even a visitor's, and if Marnie really was there, and if she could get her out before he came back . . .

That was certainly what she would say if she was challenged about disobeying orders about approaching. Actually, she didn't doubt it was Morrison's car; she just wouldn't be able to live with herself if the worst happened and she could have managed to save Marnie by being right on hand. Always assuming Marnie wasn't dead already.

The house phone ringing had wakened Marnie too. She had turned over, wondering what time it was and was about to reach for her mobile to look at the time, but then realised

Vivienne had thought of everything; there was a digital clock on the bedside table: 11.57. An anti-social hour for someone to be phoning, but perhaps the Morrisons were late birds.

Then she heard Mikey start to wail. Poor Gemma wouldn't appreciate that, but it was nothing to do with her and Marnie turned over luxuriously in her comfortable bed and pulled the duvet up over her shoulders. She was just drifting off to sleep again when she heard the crunch of tyres on gravel.

She tried to tell herself that she had nothing to fear here, that being nervous was neurotic, but she couldn't stop herself: she got out of bed and went to peer through the curtains.

There was a light on over the front door and a man was getting out of the car parked at an odd angle just beside it, and she noticed that he staggered slightly as he stepped out. She couldn't really see his face but she guessed it must be Gemma's father. He'd obviously had a few; perhaps he had drink problem. That would explain why Gemma's mum looked so strained.

Just before he reached the front door he looked up suddenly, as if he was studying the house. Marnie shrank back behind the curtain – he would hardly appreciate being spied on – but not before she had seen the look of agony on his face. He looked like a man in torment and she could feel the hairs on the nape of her neck bristling.

Gingerly, she lifted a corner of the curtain again. He was still looking up at the house, not towards her window in the corner but at the others: Gemma's room, the child's room and the next, where presumably Gemma's mother was sleeping. He studied each individually and then he put his hand up to cover his eyes. When he took it away, he wiped the back of his hand across as if to wipe away tears.

He went through the front door. Above Mikey's wails, dwindling a little by now, she could hear Gemma talking to him. Marnie crept to her door and holding her breath opened it. Of course it made not a sound; there would be no creaking doors in Vivienne Morrison's house.

The landing was in darkness but Gemma's door was open, spilling light onto the landing, and there was a light on in the hall below, where she had gone to answer the phone. Marnie could hear the conversation quite clearly.

The police! Why would they have been phoning this respectable household at this time of night? Was it something to do with her? After all that had happened, she would be wise to be afraid, but somehow she felt this was something else.

She risked peeping over the banisters. As Gemma disappeared into the kitchen she saw her father wrap his arms round himself as if suffering some dreadful pain. He gave a strangled sob, then went through the kitchen door. He hadn't taken off his coat.

Sick with foreboding, Marnie tiptoed downstairs in her bare feet. Gemma's father hadn't shut the door behind him; as she stood in the hall, poised to flee back upstairs again if necessary, she could hear Gemma chatting away in the kitchen, telling him some little story about what Mikey had done as she clattered pans.

He said nothing until he suddenly burst out, 'Stop it,

stop it! I can't bear it. It's all over, Gemma, it's all over.'

And as Marnie listened outside, a chill of horror ran through her.

DC Hepburn was close enough now to read the number plate. Yes, that was Morrison's. He was there, in the house. Was Marnie there too? She had no way of knowing. After a hopeful glance at her phone to see if by any chance she had missed a message from Marnie, she switched it to vibrate – it wouldn't do to announce her presence with a ringing phone.

It was very, very silent. The sky had cleared, apart from a few ragged clouds, and a thumbnail of moon was rising over in the west. Avoiding the noisy gravel Hepburn worked her way round the edge of the flowerbeds.

All the windows on the ground floor were dark apart from the fanlight above the front door and the outside lamp. She looked about her; there was a path on the far side of the house leading round to the back garden, but she would have to cross gravel to reach it and there would more than likely be security lights.

On the side of the house she was on, there was only a flowerbed planted thickly with shrubs. At least that would be silent enough, but the bushes looked to have more than the usual number of thorns – for burglar deterrence, perhaps. Grimacing, she began to force her way through.

It was slow painful work and round here it was pitch-dark. As branches snatched at her she could hear the fabric of her jacket ripping; blood was trickling down her face from two vicious scratches and a thorn had embedded itself in her hand, but at last she could see dull patches of light being thrown onto the garden at the back a little distance ahead. From the kitchen windows, perhaps – and she could only hope that the blinds weren't drawn. Hepburn battled on.

A trailing branch tripped her just as she reached the edge of the flowerbed and she fell heavily forward, winding herself. Had anyone heard that?

When she scrambled to her feet there was no sign of anyone coming to look out of the window. That was the good news. The bad news was that the windows were completely obscured by thin blinds.

'Dad! What do you mean? You're frightening me!' Gemma dropped the packet of bacon she was holding, her eyes wide with alarm.

'It's all over,' Michael said savagely. 'We're finished, my darling. All of us.'

'All of us? Is it the business?'

He gave a short laugh. 'Oh, the business and everything else. We've had the good times, though, haven't we, sweetheart? I've looked after you – you and Vivienne and little Mikey. My boy.' His voice softened as he said that. 'You never wanted for anything, did you?'

Gemma shook her head dumbly.

'I was here to protect you from everything that could harm you, to give you the perfect life. Now, it's over.'

She sat down abruptly on one of the chairs by the table, feeling that her legs couldn't support her any more. 'What's happened? For God's sake, tell me.'

'Drax betrayed me. After all these years, he turned against me. And like a fool I handed him the power to do it. I did what he told me, I trusted him. I thought I had protected myself against Grant – that his stupidity was the main threat. But I never thought that Drax would—' He choked on a sob.

In her protected life, Gemma's reaction to any problem had been to run to her father. Now he was the problem, her mother was upstairs in a drugged sleep as usual and there was no one to turn to. She was all alone, yet instead of panic all she felt was a sort of icy detachment.

She said, 'Sit down, Dad. We need to talk this through. Explain to me! I'm a grown woman—'

But he was shaking his head. 'You couldn't cope with this. It's too much. But I'll take care of it, trust me. I won't doom any of you to a life of poverty and shame. It's because I love you, I love you all—'

Tears were pouring down his cheeks now. He slumped onto a chair and the coat he was still wearing swung forward. From the inside pocket a dark, dull metal cylinder poked up and from a hundred crime series she recognised it as the silencer of a gun.

She mustn't faint. If she fainted she would die and Mikey – Mikey! – would die too. From somewhere she found a soothing voice. 'I know you do, Dad.' Her mind raced, searching out possibilities. She couldn't get it away from him; even drunk, he was much stronger. Keep them talking – that's what they always said hostages should do, and now, she realised, that shockingly she was a hostage to her own father, her beloved protector.

'Dad, we both need a drink.' She got up and went across to the cupboard in the kitchen where the drinks were kept, the cupboard by the kitchen door. It was ajar and beyond it she caught a glimpse of movement.

Marnie! He wouldn't know she was there. Gemma stole a quick glance at her father but he was leaning on the table, his hands to his head. As she moved to where she was visible through the door Marnie materialised outside, making a 'Shall I come in?' gesture.

Gemma shook her head frantically. 'Is Scotch all right?' she said conversationally over her shoulder, then with a backwards tilt of her head mimed a gun, and then a baby. She saw Marnie nod and then silently disappear.

She could run, of course, race upstairs and snatch Mikey herself, try to make it to the car, but he would be after her a moment later. Marnie surely would be phoning the police, but how long would they take to get there?

No, her only hope was to sit down at the table again, try to talk him down or, failing that, get him drunk enough to pass out. She took the bottle over to the table and all but filled the glasses.

Swearing silently, DC Hepburn made her way back to the front of the house by the path this time, no wiser than she had been before about what was going on behind those blinds and considerably more worried. Since she had nothing to show for her insubordination she had better get back to her car before the boss arrived.

Fortunately the grass verge at the other side met the path so she was able to run down it after a quick glance back at the blank face of the front of the house to make sure no one was watching her. She saw the beam of a car's headlamps appearing at the end of the road just as she slammed her own car door.

Hepburn was still slightly out of breath, though, when MacNee jumped out and came across to her. He was wearing body armour and he frowned when he saw her face.

'What have you been up to?' he demanded.

'Nothing, Sarge.' She was all innocence. 'I just did a wee recce, that's all, to check it was Morrison's car. They've some nasty bushes around there.'

MacNee's 'Hmmph', was sceptical, but he said only, 'So he's back, then?'

'Yes, but I still don't know if she's inside.'

'The boss is sending for armed response. We'll have to wait till they get here – can't go just ringing the doorbell when the man may be armed.'

'That could be hours! Surely we can't just leave it. If Marnie's there she's in danger every moment now he's in the house.'

'Louise, you're not thinking straight. She may not be here. He maybe was just out working late and Lee got himself killed by some toerag in Glasgow. On the other hand, Gemma Morrison may have lied and he was there all along and Marnie's dead already. OK?

'What we do know is that it's possible the man is a murderer and has a gun. I'm not volunteering to get my head blown off for ringing the doorbell and neither are you. Anyway, where's your body armour?'

'Sorry, Sarge, in the boot.'

'Not much use there, is it? For God's sake, Louise, get a grip.' He went back to join Fleming.

Hepburn got out and obediently strapped herself into the bulky armour. She wasn't starring, at the moment. That really had been stupid – she hated wearing it, and she just hadn't thought it through. She was lucky to have come out of it with just a scratched face.

She spat on a tissue and did her best to wipe the blood off her cheeks and was just pulling at the thorn to remove it when the phone in her pocket vibrated.

Marnie was breathless as she whispered into the receiver. 'Gemma's father's here and I think he's going to kill them all. He's got a gun.'

'Where is he?' Hepburn said.

'In the kitchen. Gemma's with him. I'm upstairs. I don't think he knows I'm here but I've got to rescue her kid. I'm going into his room now.'

'Where is that?' It was Fleming's voice this time.

'Front of the house, above the front door. How soon can you get here?'

'Walking up to the house just now. Can you reach him and get down to the door?'

'As long as her dad doesn't come out of the kitchen. The kid might start crying – he's asleep now.'

'Hand over his mouth, grab him and run,' Fleming directed.

Marnie drew a deep breath and bent over the cot.

* * *

'Here you are – drink up. It's not the answer to everything, but sometimes it helps.' Gemma tried for a smile, but it didn't quite work. At least he took the glass and drank half of it in one swallow.

'You and Mikey have had such good times together,' she said. 'Do you remember the Halloween party? You were both covered with treacle.'

'Yes. Oh yes.' Her father was slurring the 's's just faintly. 'The wee man.'

There was a snap that Vivienne particularly liked standing on the kitchen surface, a pose of Mikey on a visit to a play farm, intent on the day-old chick in his cupped hands. As Gemma went to fetch it, the innocent face of her son almost broke her and she knew her voice was unsteady as she said, 'This was a fun day too.'

He didn't seem to notice, though, just took the photo and stared at it hungrily. 'I'd to stop him loving it to death, didn't I? He's always needed me. And I would always have been there for him, looked after him just the way I always did you.'

'You're a wonderful dad.' And it was true; he had been. Then, without thinking, she said, 'I don't know what I'd do without you.'

She realised her fatal mistake as the words left her lips. Michael Morrison's face changed and he got up and pulled an ugly, snub-nosed handgun with a suppressor fitted out of his pocket.

'My sweetheart, I can't do it to you. Or Mikey. Or my poor, darling Vivienne. They won't know a thing, I promise. I wish it had been the same for you, but I know you can be brave. Remember when I took you to hospital with your broken arm? Like that – chin up! Goodnight, my precious!'

He's quite, quite mad, Gemma thought. He levelled the gun at her and fired.

CHAPTER TWENTY-FIVE

From somewhere, a great cry shattered the quiet night. 'What's that?' Fleming said sharply then, 'Marnie, stop! Don't move! Can you hear me?'

She couldn't quite make out what Marnie said but at least she was still at the other end. 'Do you know what's happened?' She strained her ears to hear the whispered response.

'A sort of muffled bang. Came from the kitchen. I can hear someone crying – I think it's him.'

'No screams or anything?'

'No. Do you – do you think he's killed her?'

Marnie's voice had risen. 'Sssh!' Fleming said, alarmed. 'I need you to stay calm. Find a room with a lock – bathroom, say. Keep out of line with the door. Don't wake the boy till you're ready, then keep him quiet – hand over his mouth if necessary – and hold him tight. Keep the line open.'

'I'm going.'

Fleming, Hepburn and MacNee were crouching behind the Mercedes. The patrol car was blocking the end of the drive and the officers were standing by, waiting for the armed response team.

Fleming turned to the other two. 'It is strictly against regulations to enter this house before armed response arrives. Wait here while I check out what's happening.'

MacNee sneered. 'Aye, right. There's a kid in there and I'm going to say he got killed because I was feart?'

'Can't stop you. But Louise, stay here. That's an order.'

'Sorry, ma'am.' Hepburn took off ahead of them. 'It's round this way.'

MacNee didn't follow but Fleming was close on her heels. She spoke into the phone again, whispering now too. 'Marnie? Where are you?'

'There's a bathroom. I'm going to get him now and lock ourselves in.'

'Tell us when you're safe.'

They were approaching the kitchen windows with infinite caution, keeping low, as MacNee joined them, bearing an axe from the standard rescue kit. 'Double glazing,' he breathed and Fleming nodded.

Even up close there wasn't a chink in the blinds but now they could hear a man groaning and sobbing. Nothing else.

Not a good sign, Fleming reflected grimly. She glanced at the phone, willing Marnie to tell her they had reached the bathroom.

It was the cat that undid them, a sleek black cat about its nocturnal business that dropped down from the roof of

456

a small shed without noticing they were crouched there, and gave a startled yowl. A moment later the blind was lifted and a bleared grotesque of a face peered out at them, then with a yell of anguish disappeared.

MacNee was at the back door, swinging the axe. Fleming was at his shoulder, saying urgently into the phone, 'Marnie. Watch out! He's coming.'

Looking through the window, Louise saw with sick horror Gemma Morrison slumped on the floor, her fair hair plastered to her head with bright blood.

'Mikey, wake up!' Marnie murmured. As the sleepy child opened his eyes she went on, 'Remember me – Marnie? We're going to play a lovely game to surprise Mummy, so we have to be very, very quiet. It's a special surprise.'

Mikey frowned. 'It's night-time.'

At least he wasn't crying. 'That's why it's so special. You're not really allowed, are you? So it'll be fun. Now, really quiet.'

He liked the idea of not being allowed, holding his arms up eagerly. 'Mousey quiet,' he said, too loudly.

Marnie gave an agonised glance over her shoulder. 'Sssh! Yes.'

With him in her arms, she tiptoed out along the landing to the main bathroom. Mikey looked back through the open door of Gemma's room. 'Mummy's not there!' he exclaimed. 'Where is she?'

'Sssh!' Marnie said again, desperately. 'She's downstairs. We've got to hide first.'

They were nearing the bathroom door when she heard

Morrison's despairing bellow and ran the last few yards, almost flinging the child inside so that she could bolt the door.

Mikey wasn't pleased. 'Don't like this game. I want Mummy. And what's that?'

That was Morrison rushing up the stairs. 'Don't worry, it's all right. We just have to hide over here, behind the shower.'

She grabbed him, putting her hand over his mouth. Outraged, Mikey bit it, hard.

'Mikey! Where are you? Where have you gone?'

At the sound of his grandfather's voice Mikey gave a frantic wriggle and Marnie, in pain and unused to the surprising strength of small children, didn't manage to hold him. She heard a woman's voice shouting 'Police! Drop your weapon and come down with your hands up!' just as Mikey shouted, 'Granddad! I'm in here, in the bathroom.'

A second later, the door shook under Morrison's weight. As Mikey stood looking hopefully at it, Marnie heard the sound of a gun being cocked.

She owed Gemma, who had tried to give her safe haven. And what did she care, anyway, about her rotten life?

She threw herself at the child, sweeping him aside and as Morrison shot through the lock she felt something in her chest like a heavy punch, then a searing pain, then nothing.

The thudding metallic sound of a silenced gun being fired brought the officers up short, just below the turn of the stairs which gave them cover. The child was crying, 'Granddad! Granddad!' now.

They couldn't just stand by, waiting for armed response while the tragedy unfolded. Just behind Fleming on the stairs, MacNee poked his head round and saw Morrison standing on the darkened landing. He wasn't looking in their direction; he was staring at the door, splintered around the handle, that had his grandson behind it. All he had to do was open it. There had been no sound from Marnie.

MacNee drew back again out of his sight line. He still had the axe. He hefted it in his hand, wondering whether he could throw it so that the blunt edge would hit Morrison and knock him out. Unlikely, he decided, and too open to disastrous error – if the child came out, say. And if it came to a fight it would be useless against a gun.

He set it down reluctantly just as Fleming stepped out into full view. 'Boss!' he said, alarmed, but she was speaking.

'Michael, can you talk to me just for a moment? You're suffering and we can help.' Her voice was steady.

Courage was one thing, charging down the guns was another. Morrison could simply turn and fire on her; he'd killed already and it got easier. MacNee tensed, poising himself on the balls of his feet.

The man swung round. The gun was loose in his hand and he was swinging his head from side to side like a wounded animal at bay, baffled by its pain.

Fleming was going on, having to raise her voice above the frightened wails of the child. 'You need to put your gun down so we can talk, sort everything out. Put it down, Michael.'

He was shaking his head now. 'No, no. Too late.' He was raising the gun.

MacNee erupted past Fleming, almost knocking her down the stair. As he leapt the last flight in two bounds and launched himself into a rugby tackle he heard her footsteps right behind him.

Just as MacNee grabbed his ankles Morrison, with a final roar of agony and despair, shoved the gun in his mouth and pulled the trigger.

Fleming was still feeling shaken the next morning. She had seen the mess of brain and blood from suicides before but had never herself been in intimate contact. Even after standing for twenty minutes under a shower at headquarters the night before, and taking another this morning, the memory still made her flesh crawl with revulsion as she and MacNee went to interview Grant Crichton at the Cairnryan police station.

It would be good if she could wipe out the memory of the aftermath too – of Vivienne Morrison, still in a drugged half-sleep, staggering out to be confronted by something that looked like a scene from the *Grand Guignol*. At least she had simply collapsed into a faint; the greater problem had been the child struggling to open the bathroom door, the child shut in with at best an injured woman, at worst a corpse. Going in to fetch him, given the gruesome state both she and MacNee were in, would only provoke hysteria.

Hepburn, mercifully, had paused downstairs to see if there was anything to be done for Gemma Morrison. At the sound of the shot she had raced up the stairs and taken in the situation with admirable efficiency, stepping over Vivienne to fetch the duvet from her bed to cover her husband's body. Fleming and MacNee removed themselves hastily to let her bring the child out unharmed, though yelling and resisting.

Then there was Marnie, poor Marnie, who seemed to have taken the bullet that was meant to blast open the door. Perhaps the child, hearing his grandfather's voice, had gone towards it and she had stepped in to save him? They might never know if that was what had happened: the medical prognosis was poor.

Gemma, though, was recovering in hospital. Impaired by stress and alcohol, her father's aim had been wild and the angle suggested that she had actually walked into the bullet by ducking away as he fired. It had skimmed the side of her head, it seemed, without penetrating the skull. Despite a nasty concussion and some blood loss she would make a full recovery, physically. Mentally – that was another question. It was a sad and depressing business.

On the other hand, Grant Crichton was making life easy for them. He'd sacked his brief and waived his rights to appoint another one and, told of the deaths of his partners, he was singing like a whole aviary of canaries, his unctuous desire to prove himself helpful making Fleming feel she would need another shower.

'The thing is,' he was explaining, 'I was always the one who was in the dark. They approached me, you know. They had their business set up and Drax spotted that my haulage company was good cover for them. I never had anything to do with the other side, you know – that was all them.'

'We're not concerned with that,' Fleming said. 'We are investigating the murder of Anita Loudon.'

'So cut the cackle,' MacNee put in. He was on a short fuse this morning. 'You've admitted already that you went to her house that night and we've evidence you were inside there. What went on?'

Crichton was twisting his hands in his lap. 'You've – you've got to understand. As God's my judge, this is the truth I'm going to tell you.'

'Never mind God – we do the judging here. Get on with it,' MacNee snarled.

'I wanted to talk to the girl who'd been watching Shelley's little ceremony. I told you that, remember? It wasn't a nice thing to do. We're divorced, but I don't like to see her made a fool of – and my son.' His face darkened. 'That was Kirstie Burnside's daughter, wasn't it?'

'Go on.' Fleming's voice was cold.

Crichton gulped. 'Right. So I wanted Anita to tell me where I could find her, that was all. Not to kill her over it, for God's sake – why should I?

'When I went round there, I saw that Michael's car was parked outside. That looked like good news – I knew Anita worked for his wife and I thought he could maybe put a bit of pressure on her. So I just went in – the front door wasn't locked. I heard Michael swear as I opened it but I couldn't see him. Then he said, '"Thank God it's you!" and stepped out from behind the door. He was holding this iron bar – crowbar, I suppose you'd say – and when I looked round

462

Anita Loudon was lying on the floor beyond the sofa. Her head . . .' He shuddered. 'Can I have a glass of water?'

Fleming pulled over the carafe on the table between them and poured out a glass. She handed it to him without speaking.

'He told me what had happened. His wife had come home and told him Anita was in a terrible state. She hadn't told her exactly what the problem was but there was something she'd done that was bothering her and there were some things she knew about that made her frightened of what Drax might do next. Well, Vivienne's a nice lady – she'd told her to go to talk to you lot.

'If I'd been Michael I'd have said, just let her tell them—'

'Oh really,' MacNee said. 'Just like you did when you had the chance later.'

Crichton coloured. 'They'd got me in too deep by then, that was the thing. You see, it was all Drax. He was the leader in everything, though it was Michael who put up the money. He bought him the nightclub as a pay-off for what he'd done before – before I knew them – but Drax called all the shots. And he'd this genius accountant, too, who could make everything look the way it should – we needed her.

'That night, though – well, Michael said we were all in danger from Anita, that Drax had said if she wasn't eliminated everything would come out, but he couldn't do it himself because he'd be number-one suspect with his DNA and prints all over the house. Michael would need to do it, unless he wanted the whole thing to blow up.'

He'd used Kirstie the same way all those years ago,

Fleming recalled. It all figured. The puppet-master, pulling the strings.

'I shouldn't have known anything about it, that was the thing.' Crichton sounded aggrieved. 'It was just bad luck – I was in the wrong place at the wrong time. I could never have done it. But Michael . . .' He gave a shudder. 'From the way she looked he had just gone at her, as if he was too angry to stop once he started.

'So he told me that if I didn't keep my mouth shut, he and Drax would both swear that I'd confessed to killing her. And he said – I'll never forget it – "You know what Drax is like, if it comes to disloyalty".'

'What is he like, Grant?' Fleming's voice was gentle, but he reacted as if she had jabbed him with a needle.

'Oh – I don't mean – he doesn't like it, that's all, and he – he can be very, well, unpleasant.'

Fleming raised her eyebrows but she was more interested in hearing the end of the story.

'I went home after that. I was in shock, I think. I didn't know what he was going to do with her body and I didn't want to know. When I heard in the morning where he'd put it, right where Tommy lay, I-I – well, I panicked.'

He took out a handkerchief and wiped at his forehead, then his trembling mouth. 'I said it would look as if it was me or Shelley did it, but they said no, no, it was to implicate the vigilantes who'd attacked the girl already – that was the sort of thing they would do.

'I just felt sick. I've felt sick ever since. And scared – I realised then that their plan was to drop me in it all along. But I couldn't come to you, not once all this started.' He

464

gestured round the Cairnryan interview room.

'Chief Inspector Alexander says the more I cooperate the better it will be for me. And you can say I have, can't you?' He leant forward eagerly. 'I'll answer any questions you have – anything you want to know.'

'Just the one,' MacNee said. 'The fire-bombing of the cottage at Clatteringshaws Loch – did you know where the girl was staying?'

Crichton's face went crimson. 'No, I—' he began, then under the cold disbelief of both detectives, he changed his mind. 'I didn't want to know,' he cried. 'Drax phoned and told me. I didn't know why – not until I heard what had happened and then I knew that was all part of their attempt to fit me up for that too. He knew I was angry with the girl and he hoped I'd go out there and his dirty work would be blamed on me. That's if he did it – maybe he just set up Michael to do that for him too.

'Well, they're both dead now, and may they rot in hell for what they did.'

With a glance at MacNee, Fleming got to her feet. 'Terminating the interview, 10.38,' she said for the benefit of the tape and switched it off.

'That's all, Mr Crichton. And yes, you have cooperated but in this case it won't do you much good. You're accessory to a murder and more than that, you have blood on your hands because you said nothing, just to save your own worthless hide. There's a woman fighting for her life in hospital as we speak and it's only chance that Morrison's wife, his daughter and his grandson didn't die too before he blew his brains out.

'Perhaps they may rot in hell, but I wouldn't be at all certain about your own destination.'

She swept out. MacNee gave her a sideways look as he joined her. 'Well, you certainly tellt him.'

'Foul creature!' She gave a shudder of distaste. 'We'd better pop into Nick's office. I want to suggest they might find there were some instances of Lee's "displeasure" that Grant hasn't told them about yet.'

DCI Alexander was in high good humour. 'We've so much stuff coming in now we hardly know where to start,' he said.

'An *embarras de richesses*,' MacNee said. It was a phrase he had adopted from Hepburn, though without adopting her pronunciation, and the look Alexander gave him was faintly puzzled.

'We've discovered that Morrison owned the farm next door and there were almost a dozen illegal immigrants living in a squalid barn, mostly working as virtual slaves in his construction business. The farmer's decided that cooperating fully is in his best interests.'

'It's your charm that does it, Nick,' Fleming said. 'You'd softened Crichton up for us nicely too.'

'Get what you wanted? That's good. Last night sounded a bit messy.'

Fleming winced. 'You could say. There's a victim in a very bad way too. Any idea what's happened in Glasgow?'

'Another good haul up there. They'd a sort of dormitory above the nightclub and it looks as if that was a temporary stopping-off point before they filtered the immigrants into Glasgow. Some, of course, must have gone south, but that was riskier – the busload that was picked up on the M6 was our breakthrough.

'Oh, and there was one quirky little detail. They were running a double set of books, of course, and the accountant working them at the nightclub – top grade, according to our forensic staff – seemed to be in some sort of relationship with Lee. When they fingerprinted her they discovered she was actually Kirstie Burnside – do you remember her? Child murderer, Dunmore's only local celebrity.'

For once, Fleming was lost for words. It was MacNee who said, 'Oh aye, we ken her all right. We'd have dug the place up looking for her body, if we'd had any suggestion where to start.'

'I'm having a dram, anyway,' Bill said firmly as they cleared up after a supper of poached salmon with green beans and boiled new potatoes. 'The medication makes allowance for that – in fact, I shouldn't miss it.'

'So you say. Bed at nine, though,' Marjory said. 'And no farm work at all, not so much as a walk round the hill, until you've had your check-up.'

'He said I wasn't to think of myself as an invalid, so stop fussing.' Bill fetched the bottle of Bladnoch and the heavy crystal tumblers from the cupboard and headed off to the sitting room with Meg the collie importantly leading the way.

Marjory put a match to the fire that Karolina had laid and sank down into her armchair with an exhausted sigh.

'You're needing an early night more than I am,' Bill said

as Meg, looking reproachful at the absence of immediate warmth, settled on the hearthrug.

Marjory took the glass from him. 'Just a bit depressed,' she said, then corrected herself. 'That's not right – how could I be depressed, when I've got you sitting across there looking better than you've any right to look, and Meg there by the fire whinging – just be patient, Meg, it'll get hotter in a minute. And a dram – what more could a girl want? *Sláinte!*'

Bill sat down opposite. 'Still depressed, just the same?'

'My whole world hasn't fallen apart, thank God, but it's hard to feel cheerful about the inquiry into Morrison's death as we tried to arrest him, and the inquiry into defying firearms regulations and not preventing my staff from doing the same hanging over my head.

'And the devastation that solipsistic sod caused! He was too arrogant to accept the humiliation of being exposed for what he was, and conceited enough to believe he was so central to their existence that his family would prefer to die than to live on without him.

'I went to see Gemma today and it was pitiful. She's going to need a lot of help; she's trying to square the loving father she knew all her life with the monster he became and it's not working – she's in pieces. She's a nice girl, Bill, but she'd been kept dependent. He'd never let the wind blow on her and I can't think how she's going to weather the hurricane now.

'He thought he was such a big man but really he was nothing more than Daniel Lee's puppet. I doubt if he'd even have thought of the whole illegal immigration racket if it hadn't been for Lee – he was definitely the brains behind the operation, along with Kirstie Burnside.

'It's so strange, Bill – she seems to be very clever, a brilliant accountant, they said when they'd checked out the way the consortium's books had been falsified. She'd even done a set that clearly the other two partners knew nothing about, which ran all the money-laundering stuff through a separate account in their names.'

'Sophisticated stuff, then. She'll be wasted where she's no doubt headed. There'd be banks queuing up to employ her, with talents like that. They'd probably never have found out about the Libor scandal if she'd been in charge.'

Marjory smiled. 'Bill Fleming, the cynic! But yes, it makes me very sad to think of the life she might have had, if Lee hadn't seized on her. It was all about control with him – a psychopath, with all the characteristic charisma and cunning, getting his satisfaction out of operating at one remove.

'I don't know whether calling his nightclub "Zombies" was deliberately significant, but it certainly wasn't a random choice. Anita Loudon and Kirstie Burnside were little more than that. They both called themselves his slaves, as if that was a badge of honour.

'There may be more to come out about his operations once they've worked Crichton over. The consortium's treatment of the immigrants is going to be a major investigation, apart from anything else. And I'm happy to say that with no one to share the blame, they'll throw the book at Crichton.'

Bill shook his head. 'Hard to take in the scale of the

destruction Lee caused. And to that poor girl Marnie, as well.'

'Between them they inflicted a miserable life on her and now she's still in intensive care, thanks to them. The outlook isn't good, from the medical reports we've had.'

'Don't write her off,' Bill said. 'She must be tough. Maybe if she's used to weathering hurricanes she'll have the strength to fight through.'

'If she wants to try.'

The fire was burning strongly now, with the flames licking at the apple logs and their warm scent filling the room. Meg stretched herself out with a sigh and Marjory leant back in her chair tiredly.

'I've had enough for today. Let's talk about something else. Do you know, Cat actually called me today, wanting to ask me about managing probation orders for a paper she's doing for the course? Maybe it's a sign of a thaw. It's about the first time she's asked for my input since she went to senior school.'

'She was just preparing herself for the hurricanes,' Bill said.

'She wouldn't have to if she didn't whip them up for herself,' Marjory said dryly. 'But look at the time, Bill! Get to bed, right now!'

'Haven't finished my dram,' he grumbled, but he drank what was left in his glass and got up. 'You should come too – you're looking awful.'

'Oh good, that makes me feel so much better. I'll take these through and then I'll lock up.'

At the door, Bill turned. 'You haven't told me all

the gory details but since there's to be an inquiry about firearms regulations I assume you were right in there with the man with the gun. Next time you feel a bout of heroism coming on, just remember you've a husband with a heart condition who might take badly to a shock and wait for armed response, OK?'

'Thought you told me you weren't to think of yourself as an invalid?' she said, but as she set the fireguard in place she thought guiltily of the number of times Bill must have thought he might be left with a broken world. Perhaps she owed it to him to be more sensible in future, though it was easier to decide that in principle than in practice. Somehow she couldn't quite see herself in the heat of the action stopping to think. 'Ah! Mustn't do anything rash.'

Bill's health was still a worry, of course. They were all putting on a brave front, pretending everything had been put right, as if he'd broken his leg and now it had been fixed. Bill himself was in a sort of euphoric haze at the moment, which was natural enough. If you were facing execution and had been given a reprieve, you would feel almost giddy from relief – she was experiencing a touch of that herself right now.

But once that wore off, in the dark days of winter that lay ahead, what would stick with you would be that very graphic reminder that you were mortal. Even more than the wrinkles and the grey hairs, actually believing that one day you would die, whether tomorrow or in thirty years time, marked the end of youth. When you were young, though you knew all about death in theory, you blithely didn't believe it would really happen to you. She and Bill had been young, by that definition, until last Saturday afternoon. They weren't any more.

Bill had suffered from depression once before. She would have to watch out for the signs and make sure it didn't take hold this time.

Meg was waiting for her by the back door, her tail wagging in happy anticipation of the final run around outside before bedtime and Marjory looked at her with a rueful smile. Dogs had it right; live in the moment and enjoy it to the full – a lesson both she and Bill would have to learn.

EPILOGUE

2014

She didn't recognise her mother when she came in.

Somehow DI Fleming had managed to arrange a prison visit out of hours. The visitors' room, with its vending machines and children's toys in one corner, seemed vast and as she sat waiting at a scarred table Marnie had time to consider jumping up, saying it had all been a mistake and leaving.

Then a door at the further end opened and a prison officer ushered in an old woman, very thin, with slumped shoulders and untidy, rusty-white hair. She looked across and without any sign of animation or interest came over to Marnie's table and sat down. She had bright-blue eyes.

Like her own, Marnie realised. It was a shock. She remembered her mother with black hair and eyes that were an indeterminate grey; she couldn't be much more than fifty now but this woman looked twenty years older than that.

'Mum?' she said uncertainly.

The woman gave a thin smile. 'I suppose so. They said my daughter wanted to see me.'

'Did you want to see me?' It was all she could think of to say.

Kirstie shrugged. 'I don't want anything, really, any more. I've had enough.' She leant forward across the table. 'They watch me, you know. They won't let me do it.'

Marnie had imagined her mother cruel, harsh, mocking. In hopeful dreams she'd imagined her at last responding to the ties between them. She'd never thought of this. Struggling with a sense of unreality, she said, 'I wanted to ask you a couple of things.'

'If you like.'

'When you left me at the cottage, when I was struck over the head, was it Drax who hit me?'

A little animation came to her face at the name. 'Drax?' She lingered on it lovingly. 'No. He wasn't there. He was waiting for me, of course.'

Sick bile rose in Marnie's throat. 'You hit your own child? You hit me, then you left me? I could have died.'

'I told you,' Kirstie said, as if she was explaining to a child. 'Drax was waiting for me at the station. It had all gone wrong, the business. We had to go. He wanted you out of the way – you just came back at the wrong time.'

She was disposable, worthless. When she was tense, the scar from her bullet wound hurt; it was hurting now. With her throat stinging from suppressing the tears, Marnie said, 'Was he my father?'

'No!' It was a cry of pain. 'He should have been. But he

would never give me a child. You were just a mistake. He'd left me then, you see.'

Marnie heard the words but if she didn't block their meaning she couldn't go on. Just one more question, then she could leave.

'Who was he, then?'

'One of the screws at the prison. Peter Redford. Never said anything but I knew he fancied me.' She smirked. 'I was pretty then, you know, prettier than you are. When I was discharged I'd nowhere to go so I went to him and he took me in. Didn't care what I did – Drax was gone.

'I said I'd marry him. Then Drax came back, so of course I left.'

'Did he – did he know about me – my father?'

'Never saw you.'

'Did he – did he look for me?'

'I don't know. We'd gone.'

'You didn't want me. Why didn't you leave me with him?' Marnie burst out.

Kirstie gave her an impatient look. 'I was only six months gone. I couldn't have.'

'You could have waited—'

'Drax would have vanished by then. Don't you understand?' Her voice was impatient.

And somehow, all of a sudden, Marnie did. His name had been short for Dracula and he had sucked out the essence of her mother's humanity and left her less than human too.

She had only one more question. 'What was my father like?'

475

'Oh kind, soft – a fool!' There was nothing but contempt in her voice.

Now she could go. Without farewell, without a backward glance, Marnie walked to the exit door and said to the prison officer, 'I want to leave now.'

Outside the prison, the air was very fresh and cool. It had stopped raining for the moment and Marnie walked fast, as if to put distance between herself and the woman she had known as mother.

It would be easier now. It wasn't that Marnie was worthless, it was simply that long before she was born Kirstie Burnside had no love left, as Peter Redford had found.

Peter Redford. It wouldn't be hard to trace him, the 'kind, soft fool' who was the better part of her heredity. By now, the heartbreak he had felt would be long forgotten, though, and he would have his own life.

She wouldn't try to find him. The price she, and others, had paid already in her search for answers was too high. She was simply Marnie Bruce, a name without connections, a name that was hers alone. Tonight she would be back in North London in the tiny flat Anita Loudon's legacy had bought her, beginning on the task of quelling the memories, clearing the ruins of the past and trying to build her new life.

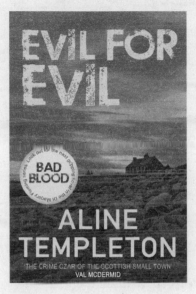

Lovatt Island is one of a group of beautiful, uninhabited islands, near the isolated village of Innellan in south-west Scotland. The skeleton found in one of its sea-caves, shackled to the rock, looks like the relic of some long ago conflict between rival smuggling gangs, but the modern watch clasped around its bony wrist gives the lie to that.

It presents a challenging, if not perhaps an urgent case for DI Marjory Fleming. But in the village there is an atmosphere of fear and tension and seemingly unconnected incidents start to happen: unpleasant vandalism; a house is set on fire. The rank smell of hatred is in the air and Fleming, desperate to prevent more violence senses a pattern she cannot see, a deadly uncompleted design becoming uglier and uglier.